Also by Jayne Ann Krentz

Written under the name Jayne Castle

Published by POCKET BOOKS

JAYNE ANN KRENTZ

DEEP WATERS

POCKET BOOKS
New York London Toronto Sydney Singapore

This book is a work of fiction. Names, characters, places and incidents are products of the author's imagination or are used fictitiously. Any resemblance to actual events or locales or persons, living or dead, is entirely coincidental.

 POCKET BOOKS, a division of Simon & Schuster, Inc.
1230 Avenue of the Americas, New York, NY 10020

ISBN: 0-671-52420-8

First Pocket Books paperback printing December 1997

14 13 12 11 10 9 8 7 6

POCKET and colophon are registered trademarks of
Simon & Schuster, Inc.

For information regarding special discounts for bulk purchases,
please contact Simon & Schuster Special Sales at 1-800-456-6798
or business@simonandschuster.com

Front cover illustration by Gina DiMarco

Printed in the U.S.A.

For my brother,
Stephen Castle,
with love

Prologue: Charity

—⟨∘⟩—

The sea lures the unwary with the promise of freedom,
but it harbors great risk.
—"On the Way of Water," from the journal of Hayden Stone

The panic attack struck as Charity Truitt swept
through the glass-paned French doors of one of the
most exclusive business clubs in Seattle. It hit her with
the force of a stiff jolt of electricity. Her pulse
pounded. She could scarcely breathe. Perspiration suddenly threatened to ruin her outrageously sophisticated red silk dress. Luckily, she hadn't paid retail for
the overpriced scrap of designer whimsy. Her family
owned the store in which it had been on display in
the couture section.

Charity came to a halt in the doorway of the private
lounge that had been reserved for the occasion. She
struggled to take a deep breath. She put up an even
more valiant fight to conceal the fact that she had a
major problem on her hands. It occurred to her that

1

those in the well-dressed crowd who noticed her hovering there on the threshold probably thought she was making an intentionally dramatic entrance. The truth was, she was on the verge of panicked flight.

With the iron-willed discipline of a woman who had been running a corporation since the age of twenty-four, she forced herself to smile while anxiety shredded her insides.

It wasn't the first panic attack she had endured. They had been striking with increasing frequency during the past four months, destroying her sleep, making her edgy and restless, and, worst of all, raising dark questions about her mental health.

The attacks had driven her first to her doctor and then to a therapist. She got some technical explanations but no real answers.

An unprovoked fight-or-flight response, the therapist had said. An evolutionary throwback to the days when we all lived in caves and worried about monsters in the night. Stress was usually a contributing factor.

But now, tonight, Charity suddenly knew the real reason for the attacks. She realized at last what, or, rather, who, triggered the surges of panic. His name was Brett Loftus, owner of Loftus Athletic Gear. He was big, well over six feet tall, and, at thirty, still endowed with the body of the varsity football star he had once been. He was also blond, brown-eyed, and good-looking in an engaging, old-fashioned, western hero sort of way. Just to top it off, he was hugely successful and a really nice man.

Charity liked him, but she did not love him. She was pretty sure that she could never love him. Worse, she had a strong hunch that her stepsister, Meredith, and the easygoing, good-natured Brett were perfect for each other. The recent panic attacks had not diminished all of her near-legendary intuition.

Unfortunately, it was Charity, not Meredith, who was supposed to announce her engagement to the heir to the Loftus empire tonight.

The merger was to be a business move as well as a personal union. In a few weeks, Loftus Athletic Gear would be joining with the family-owned Truitt department store chain to form Truitt-Loftus.

The new company would be one of the largest privately owned retailers in the Northwest. If all went well, it would begin expanding into the exciting Pacific Rim market within two years.

For the sake of the family and business responsibilities that she had shouldered so early, Charity was about to marry a man who gave her anxiety attacks every time he took her into his arms.

It was not Brett's fault that he was so big that she got claustrophobic when he kissed her, she thought wildly. It was her problem. She had to deal with it.

It was her responsibility to solve problems. She was good at that kind of thing. People expected her to take command, to manage whatever crisis happened to present itself.

Charity's hands tingled. She could not get any air into her lungs. She was going to faint, right here in front of some of the most influential and powerful people in the Northwest.

She had a humiliating vision of herself collapsed facedown on the Oriental rug, surrounded by bemused friends, business associates, competitors, rivals, and, worst of all, a few chosen members of the local media.

"Charity?"

The sound of her own name startled her. Charity whirled, red silk skirts whipping around her ankles, and looked up at her stepsister, Meredith.

A long way up.

At twenty-nine, Charity was five years older than

Meredith, but she was only five foot four inches tall on her best days. Even the three-inch red heels she wore tonight did not put her at eye level with five-foot-ten Meredith, who was also wearing heels.

Statuesque and crowned with a glorious mane of strawberry-blond hair, Meredith was always a stunning sight. Never more so, however, than when she was dressed to the teeth, as she was this evening. No one, Charity thought wistfully, could wear clothes the way her stepsister did.

With her strong, classical features and subtle air of sophistication, Meredith could have made her living as a professional model. She had actually done some in-store fashion work for the Truitt chain during her college days, but her savvy talent and her love of the family business had propelled her straight into management.

"Are you all right?" Meredith's light, jade green eyes narrowed in concern.

"I'm fine." Charity glanced around quickly. "Is Davis here?"

"He's at the bar, talking to Brett."

Unable to see over the heads of the people who stood between her and the club bar, Charity peered through cracks in the crowd. She managed to catch a glimpse of her stepbrother.

Davis was a year and a half older and three inches taller than Meredith. A deeply ingrained flare for retailing and boundless enthusiasm for the Truitt chain had defined his career path, also. Charity had recognized his abilities from the start. Six months ago she had decided to ignore whining accusations of nepotism and promote him to a vice presidency in the company. It was a *family* business, after all. And she, herself, had become president at an extraordinarily early age.

Davis's hair was the same arresting shade as his

sister's, and his eyes were a similar pale green. The colors and the height had come from Fletcher Truitt, Charity's stepfather.

Charity had received her own dark auburn hair and hazel eyes from her mother. She had few memories of her biological father. A professional photographer, Samson Lapford had abandoned his family when Charity was three years old to travel the world shooting pictures of volcanoes and rain forests. He had been killed in a fall while trying to get a close-up of a rare fern that only grew on the sides of certain South American mountains.

Fletcher Truitt was the only father Charity had ever known, and he had been a good one. For his sake and the sake of her mother, she had done her best to fill his shoes since their deaths five years before and hold the family inheritance together for her step-siblings.

The crowd shifted slightly, allowing another view of the bar. Charity saw Brett Loftus, sun-bright hair gleaming in the subdued light, broad shoulders looking even more massive than usual in a tux. A good-natured Norse god of a man, he lounged with negligent ease next to Davis.

Charity shuddered. Once again all the oxygen in the room seemed to disappear. Her palms were so damp she dared not dry them on the expensive fabric of her gown.

Davis was big, but Brett was huge. Charity told herself that there were any number of women in the room who would have traded their Truitt credit cards for a chance to be swept off their feet by Brett Loftus. Sadly, she was not one of them.

The reality of what was happening sent a shock wave through her. With searing certainty she suddenly knew that she could not go through with the engagement, not even for the sake of her step-siblings' inheritance, the altar on which she had sacrificed the past five years of her life.

"Maybe you need a glass of champagne, Charity." Meredith took her arm. "Come on, let's go join Brett and Davis. You know, you've been acting a little strange lately. I think you've been working too hard. Maybe trying to combine the merger with your engagement plans was a bit too much. Now there's the wedding to schedule and a honeymoon."

"Too much." The panic was almost intolerable. She would go crazy if she didn't get out of here. She had to escape. "Yes. Too much. I have to leave, Meredith."

"What?" Meredith started to turn, an expression of astonishment on her face.

"Right now."

"Calm down, Charity. What are you saying? You can't just run off. What would Brett think? Not to mention all these people we've invited."

Guilt and the old steely sense of duty swamped Charity. For a few seconds, the combination did battle with the anxiety and managed to gain control.

"You're right," Charity gasped. "I can't run away yet. I have to explain to Brett."

Meredith looked genuinely alarmed now. "Explain what to Brett?"

"That I can't do this. I tried. God knows, I tried. I told myself that it was the right thing to do for everyone. But it's not right. Brett is too nice, he doesn't deserve this."

"Deserve what? Charity, you're not making any sense."

"I've got to tell him. I hope he'll understand."

"Maybe we should go someplace private to discuss this," Meredith said urgently. "How about the ladies' room?"

"I don't think that's necessary." Charity rubbed her

forehead. She could not concentrate. Like a gazelle at the water hole, she kept scanning the bushes, watching for lions. "With any luck, I won't be sick until after I get out of here."

Through sheer force of will, a will that had been tempered in fire when she had assumed the reins of her family's faltering department store chain, Charity fought the panic. She made her way through the crowd toward the bar. It was like walking a gauntlet.

Brett and Davis both turned to her as she emerged from the throng. Davis gave her a brotherly grin of welcome and raised his wineglass in a cheerful toast.

"About time you got here, Charity," he said. "Thought maybe you got held up at the office."

Brett smiled affectionately. "You look terrific, honey. Ready for the big announcement?"

"No," Charity said baldly. She came to a halt in front of him. "Brett, I am very, very sorry, but I can't go through with this."

Brett frowned. "Something wrong?"

"Me. I'm wrong for you. And you're wrong for me. I like you very much. You've been a good friend, and you would have made a fine business partner. But I can't marry you."

Brett blinked. Davis stared at her slack-jawed. Meredith's eyes widened in shock. Charity was dimly aware of the hush that had descended on the nearby guests. Heads turned.

"Oh, lord, this is going to be even worse than I thought," Charity whispered. "I am so sorry. Brett, you're a fine man. You deserve to marry for love and passion, not for friendship or business reasons."

Brett slowly put down his glass. "I don't understand."

"Neither did I until now. Brett, I can't go through with this engagement. It would not be fair to either of us. We don't love each other. We're friends and business associates, but that's not enough. I can't do it. I thought I could, but I can't."

No one said a word. Everyone in the room was now staring at Charity, transfixed. The panic surged through her again.

"Oh, God, I've got to get out of here." She swung around and found Meredith blocking her path. "Get out of the way. Please."

"Charity, this is crazy." Meredith caught hold of her shoulders. "You can't run off like this. How can you not want to marry Brett? He's perfect. Do you hear me? *Perfect.*"

Charity could hardly breathe. She was reeling from the shock of her own actions, but she could not pull back from the brink. A devil's brew of guilt, anger, and fear scalded her insides.

"He's too big." She flung out her hands in a helpless, desperate gesture. "Don't you see? I can't marry him, Meredith. *He's too big.*"

"Are you crazy?" Meredith gave Charity a small shake. "Brett is a wonderful, wonderful man. You're the luckiest woman alive."

"If you think he's so damn wonderful, why don't you marry him yourself?" Horrified at her loss of control, Charity jerked free of her stepsister's grip. She hurtled straight into the crowd.

The stunned onlookers dodged this way and that to clear a path for her. Charity dashed across the Oriental carpet and out through the French doors of the lounge.

She did not pause in the mellow, old-world club lobby. A startled doorman saw her coming and leaped to open the front door for her. She rushed past him and went down the front steps, precariously balanced on her three-inch heels. She was breathless when she reached the sidewalk in front of the club.

It was five minutes after eight on a summer evening. Downtown Seattle was still basking in the late sunlight. She spotted a cab that was just pulling up to the curb.

The rear door of the cab opened. Charity recognized the middle-aged couple who got out. George and Charlotte Trainer. Business acquaintances. Invited guests. Important people.

"Charity?" George Trainer looked at her in surprise. "What's going on?"

"Sorry, I need that cab." Charity pushed past the Trainers and leaped into the backseat. She slammed the door. "Drive."

The cab driver shrugged and pulled away from the curb. "Where to?"

"Anywhere. I don't care. Just drive. Please." From out of nowhere, an image of the open sea flashed through her mind. Freedom. Escape. "No, wait, I know where I want to go. Take me down to the waterfront."

"You got it."

A few minutes later, Charity stood at the end of one of the tourist-oriented piers that jutted out from Seattle's busy waterfront. The breeze off Elliott Bay churned her red silk skirts and filled her lungs. She could breathe freely at last. At least for a while.

She stood there clutching the railing for a long time. When the sun finally sank behind the Olympic Mountains, briefly painting the sky with the color of fire, Charity forced herself to face reality.

She was burned out at the age of twenty-nine.

At a time in life when others were just getting their careers into high gear, she was going down in flames. She had nothing left to give to the family business.

She could not go back to the presidential suite of the Truitt department store chain. She hated the very thought of ever stepping foot into her own office.

Wearily she closed her eyes against the guilt and shame that seized her. It was almost unbearable. For five long years, ever since her mother and stepfather had died in an avalanche while skiing in Switzerland, she had tried to fulfill the demanding responsibilities she had inherited.

She had done her best to salvage her step-siblings' legacy and preserve it for them. But today she had reached the limits of whatever internal resources had brought her this far.

She could not go back to Truitt, the corporation that she had never wanted to run in the first place. She could not go back to Brett Loftus, whose bearlike embrace induced panic.

She had to escape or she would go crazy.

Crazy.

Charity gazed down into the dark waters of the bay and wondered if this was how it felt to be on the edge of what an earlier generation would have called a nervous breakdown.

Prologue: Elias

~~~

Revenge and deep water have much in common. A man may get sucked down into either and drown before he understands the true danger.

    —"On the Way of Water," from the journal of Hayden Stone

Elias Winters looked into the face of the man he intended to destroy and saw the truth at last. With a shock of devastating clarity, he understood that he had wasted several years of his life plotting a vengeance that would bring him no satisfaction.

"Well, Winters?" Garrick Keyworth's heavy features congealed with irritation and impatience. "You demanded this meeting. Said you had something to discuss concerning my company's business operations in the Pacific."

"Yes."

"Let's hear it. You may have all day to sit around and shoot the breeze, but I've got a corporation to run."

"This won't take long." Elias glanced at the deceptively thin envelope he had brought with him.

Inside the slim white packet was the information that could cripple, perhaps even fatally wound, Keyworth International. The contents represented the culmination of three years of careful planning, endless nights spent studying the host of variables involved, countless hours of cautious maneuvering and manipulation.

Everything was at last in place.

In the next few weeks the big freight-forwarding firm known throughout the Pacific Rim as Keyworth International could be brought to its knees because of the information contained in the envelope. The company would likely never recover from the conflagration Elias was ready to ignite.

Elias had studied his opponent with a trained patience and discipline that had been inculcated in him since his sixteenth year. He knew that Keyworth International was the most important thing in Garrick Keyworth's life.

Keyworth's wife had left him years ago. He had never bothered to remarry. He was estranged from his son, Justin, who was struggling to build a rival freight-handling company here in Seattle. What friends Keyworth had were the type who would disappear the moment they heard that he was in financial trouble. He could not even take satisfaction in his renowned collection of Pacific Islands wood carvings. Elias knew that Keyworth had collected them because of the status they afforded, rather than because of any intrinsic interest they held for him.

The company was Keyworth's sole creation. With the monumental arrogance of an ancient pharaoh, he had built his own version of a modern-day pyramid, a storehouse of treasure on which he sat alone.

But Elias had loosened several of the support stones that sustained the massive weight of the Keyworth pyramid. All he had to do now to ensure that the dark waters of vengeance flowed was to keep the contents of the little envelope secret for a few more weeks.

All he had to do was walk out of Keyworth's office right now. It would be so easy.

"You've got five minutes, Winters. Say what you have to say. I've got a meeting at eleven-thirty." Garrick leaned back against his gray leather executive chair. He toyed with the expensive inlaid pen that he held in one beefy hand.

The hand did not go well with the elegant pen, Elias thought. For that matter, Garrick Keyworth did not go very well with his own office. He clashed with the sophisticated ambience the designer had created.

He was in his mid-fifties, a bulky, burly figure in a hand-tailored suit that could not camouflage the thickness of his neck.

Elias met Garrick's shrewd, predatory gaze. It would be such a simple matter to bring him down, now that every piece on the chessboard was in place.

"I don't need five minutes," Elias said. "One or two should do it."

"What the hell is that supposed to mean? Damn it, Winters, stop wasting my time. The only reason I agreed to see you is because of your reputation."

"You know who I am?"

"Hell, yes." Garrick tossed aside the pen. "You're a major player in the Pacific Rim trade. Everyone here in Seattle who is in the international market knows that. You've got contacts, and you've got the inside track in a lot of places out in the Pacific where no one else can get a toehold. I know you've made a killing consulting for off-shore investors." Garrick squinted slightly. "And word has it that you're also a little weird."

"That pretty well sums up my life." Elias got to his feet. He set the envelope carefully down on top of the polished surface of the wide desk. "Take a look inside. I think you'll find the contents—" He paused, savoring the next word with bleak amusement. "Enlightening."

Without waiting for a response, he turned and walked toward the door. The knowledge that Hayden Stone had been right closed around him like the icy waters of a bottomless lake. Years had been wasted. Years that could never be recovered.

"What is this?" Garrick roared just as Elias reached the door. "What game are you playing? You claimed you had something important that you had to tell me about my Pacific business operations."

"It's all in the envelope."

"Goddamn it, people are right when they say you're strange."

Elias heard the sound of tearing paper. He glanced back over his shoulder and watched as Garrick yanked the five-page document out of the envelope. "There's just one thing I'd like to know."

Garrick ignored him. He scowled at the first page of the report. Anger and bewilderment twisted his broad features. "What do you know about my business relationship with Kroy and Ziller?"

"Everything," Elias said. He knew that Keyworth had not yet realized the import of what he held in his hand, but it wouldn't take him long.

"This is confidential information, by God." Garrick raised his head and regarded Elias with the kind of stare a bull gives a matador. "You have no right to possess information about these contract arrangements."

"Do you remember a man named Austin Winters?" Elias asked softly.

"Austin Winters?" Astonishment and then deep wariness appeared in Garrick's eyes. "I knew an Austin Winters once. That was twenty years ago. Out in the Pacific." His eyes hardened with dawning comprehension. "Don't tell me you're related to him. You can't be."

"I'm his son."

"That's impossible. Austin Winters didn't even have a wife."

"My parents were divorced a couple of years before my father moved to Nihili Island."

"But no one ever said anything about a boy."

The knowledge that his father hadn't even talked about him to his friends and acquaintances was a body blow. With the discipline of long practice, Elias concealed the effects of the direct hit Garrick had unwittingly delivered.

"There was a son. I was sixteen years old when you sabotaged my father's plane. I arrived on Nihili the day after they recovered the wreckage. You had already left the island. It took me a long time to learn the truth."

"You can't blame Austin Winters's death on me." Garrick heaved himself to his feet, his florid face working furiously. "I had nothing to do with the crash."

"You cut the fuel lines, knowing it would take months to get replacement parts from the mainland. You knew that Dad only had one plane and that if he couldn't fly, he wouldn't be able to fulfill his freight contracts. You knew his business would collapse if it was put out of action for several weeks."

"A pack of goddamned lies." A dark flush rose in Garrick's jowly cheeks. "You can't prove any of that."

"I don't have to prove it. I know what happened. Dad's old mechanic saw you leaving the hangar the morning that the problem with the fuel lines was discovered. You wanted to take over my father's new freight contracts, and the easiest way to do it was to make it impossible for him to meet his delivery deadlines."

"Austin should never have taken off that day." Garrick's hands clenched into broad fists. "His own mechanic told him the plane wasn't fit to fly."

"Dad patched up the fuel line and took his chances because he had everything riding on those contracts. He knew he stood to lose his entire business if he failed to make the deliveries. But the fuel line cracked open when the Cessna was a hundred miles from land. My father never had a chance."

"It wasn't my fault, Winters. No one held a gun to Austin's head and made him climb into that old beat-up Cessna that day."

"Have you ever studied the nature of water, Keyworth?"

"What's water got to do with any of this?"

"It's a very unusual substance. Sometimes it's incredibly clear, magnifying everything viewed through it. I am looking through that kind of water now. I can see you sitting on a pyramid built on the ruins of my father's Cessna that lie on the floor of the sea."

Garrick's eyes widened. "You're crazy."

"The broken pieces of the plane are beginning to disintegrate, aren't they? The whole structure will eventually crumble beneath you. And when it does, your pyramid will collapse and you will fall into the sea, just as my father did."

"The rumors are right. You're really out there in the ether, aren't you?"

"But I see now that there's no need for me to rush the process. It will all happen in good time. I wonder why it took me this long to understand that."

Garrick looked torn between fury and incredulity. "I don't have any use for this nonsense. Or for you. Get the hell out of my office, Winters."

"When you read those papers you're holding, Keyworth, you'll realize how close you just came to disaster. I've decided not to sabotage your Pacific operations the way you sabotaged my father's plane. It will be interesting to see what you do with your reprieve. Will you tell yourself that I was weak? That I didn't have the guts to carry out my plans? Or will you look down into the water and see the rot on which you've built your empire?"

"Get out of here before I call security."

Elias let himself out of the plush office and closed the door behind him.

He took the elevator down to the lobby, walked outside, and came to a halt on Fourth Avenue. It was the last week of July, and it was raining in Seattle.

He turned and started down the sidewalk. His reflection watched him from the windows of the streetfront shops.

He could see the past clearly through the painfully transparent water that covered it. But the gray seas that hid his own future were murky and opaque. It was possible that there was no longer anything left of value to seek in that uncharted ocean.

But he had to start the search. He no longer had a choice. Today he had finally realized that the alternative was oblivion.

Without conscious thought, he turned at the corner and started walking down Madison Street toward the waterfront. As he gazed out over Elliott Bay, he made a decision.

He would begin his new life by accepting the legacy that Hayden Stone had left to him: a pier known as Crazy Otis Landing and a small curiosity shop called Charms & Virtues, both in the northern part of the state in a little town named Whispering Waters Cove.

1

Only the most discerning observer can sense the deep, hidden places in the seas of another's life. And only the unwary or the truly brave dare to look into those secret depths.

—"On the Way of Water," from the journal of Hayden Stone

He waited deep in the shadows at the back of the poorly lit shop, a patient spider crouched motionless in his web. There was something about the very stillness emanating from him that made Charity believe he would wait as long as necessary for his prey to venture too close.

"Mr. Winters?" Charity hesitated in the open doorway, clipboard in hand, and peered into the gloom-filled interior of Charms & Virtues.

"Ms. Truitt." Elias Winters's voice came out of the darkness behind the cash register counter. "Please come in. I had a feeling you might show up sooner or later."

He had spoken softly from the far end of the cavernous old wharf warehouse, but Charity heard every word. A tiny tingle of combined interest and alarm went through her. His voice was as deep as the sea, and it beckoned her with the same dangerous allure. She took a cautious step through the doorway and tried to shake off the strange mix of wariness and excitement that gripped her. She was here on business, she reminded herself.

"Sorry to bother you," she said briskly.

"It's not a problem."

"I'm the owner of Whispers, the bookshop at the other end of the pier."

"I know."

An extraordinary quality underlay the very ordinary words. Charity had the feeling that she was being summoned. Uncertainty made her pause.

When in doubt go into full executive mode, she told herself. She had been out of the intense, competitive corporate world for a year, but she could still tap the old skills when she needed them. The important thing was to take charge immediately. She cleared her throat.

"As the President of the Crazy Otis Landing Shopkeepers Association, I want to take this opportunity to welcome you to our little group," she said.

"Thank you."

Elias Winters did not sound particularly impressed. On the other hand, he did not sound unimpressed, either. There was something unnaturally calm about that dark, velvety voice. She wondered if he was tanked to the gills on tranquilizers and then decided that was highly improbable. No one who was stuffed full of sedatives could have managed to infuse so much subtle power into such softly spoken words.

She took a step closer. A floorboard creaked. The gentle lapping of the waves beneath the aging pier was clearly audible in the solemn quiet. Another step produced a ghostly moan from a protesting timber. Dust motes danced in the air.

Whenever she entered Charms & Virtues, she thought of haunted houses and old cemeteries. As she had occasionally pointed out to the previous owner, Hayden Stone, a little dusting and some decent lighting would do wonders for the place.

Elias stood, unmoving, behind the counter. He was cloaked in the false twilight created by the weak lamps and the little slits of windows located high on the walls. She could not make out his face. In fact, she could barely distinguish him from the looming bulk of the antique fortune-telling machine positioned just behind the counter.

Elias Winters had opened the doors of Charms & Virtues three days ago on Monday, the first day of August. Thus far she had caught only brief glimpses of him as he came and went down the central walkway between the pier shops. She had been left with disturbing images that intrigued her and aroused her curiosity.

For some reason she was pleased that he was not too tall, just under six feet. A rather nice height for a man, Charity reflected. He was not built like a side of beef, either. There was, however, a disturbing aura of elegant, lean strength about him. He did not walk, he paced.

Each time she had seen him he had been wearing a dark, long-sleeved pullover and a pair of jeans anchored at the waist by what appeared to be a leather thong. His nearly black hair was a little too long for a man who appeared to be in his mid-thirties.

Yesterday Charity had assigned her counter assistant, Newlin Odell, the task of foisting off Hayden Stone's obnoxious parrot, Crazy Otis, on the new owner of Charms & Virtues. The excuse she had instructed Newlin to give to the unsuspecting Winters was that Crazy Otis missed his old, familiar surroundings. It was true, as far as it went. Otis had fallen into a serious depression when Hayden had failed to return from his last trip to Seattle. It was Charity who had nursed the ungrateful bird through the trauma.

She had held her breath while Newlin ambled down the length of the pier to deliver Crazy Otis and his cage. She had fully expected that Elias would refuse to accept the responsibility. But to her unmitigated relief, Newlin had returned empty-handed.

Newlin's only comment on Elias was that he was "kinda strange." Newlin tended to be a young man of few words. Luckily he could sell books and magazines.

"I'd also like to talk to you about some business matters that concern all of us here on the Landing," Charity continued crisply.

"Would you like a cup of tea?"

"Tea?"

"I just made a pot." Elias set two round, handleless cups on the grimy counter. "A very fine grade of China keemun. The Abberwick Tea & Spice shop in Seattle imports it especially for me."

"I see." Charity did not know any men who drank tea. All the men she knew in Seattle were into espressos and lattes. Here in Whispering Waters Cove, they tended to favor plain coffee. Or at least they had until Bea Hatfield, owner of the café a few doors down on the pier, had installed the town's first espresso machine three months ago. "Yes. Thanks. I'd appreciate a cup."

"Please come back here and join me." The deep voice echoed in the cavelike surroundings.

Feeling uncomfortably like a small, very reckless fly, Charity made her way through the cluttered shop.

Elias seemed to be alone. She glanced around to be certain, but there definitely were no customers to disturb the tomb-silent atmosphere. She frowned. This was just the way things had been when Hayden Stone had run Charms & Virtues.

The curiosity shop had been closed since Hayden's death two months ago. Hayden had been away in Seattle when he had collapsed from a heart attack. A quiet funeral had been arranged by some unknown associate in the city. It had all been over before Charity or any of the other shopkeepers on the Landing had even learned of their odd landlord's demise.

There was no question but that Hayden would be missed by the Crazy Otis Landing crowd. He had been a little strange, but he had also been a sympathetic landlord.

No one had ever gotten to know him well. Hayden had lived in his own world, detached and remote from those around him, but he had never been rude or unfriendly. Everyone had accepted him as a harmless eccentric.

His death had precipitated a potential financial catastrophe for the shopkeepers of the pier, however. The threat had roused Charity's executive instincts, which had lain dormant for months. Like a butterfly emerging from a cocoon, she had shaken out her wings and allowed them to dry in the sun. She was determined to head off disaster before it overtook her newfound friends.

Her plans required that the shop owners form a united front. That meant that the new proprietor of Charms & Virtues had to be convinced to get with the program.

She went forward determinedly between the aisles formed by the sagging, disorganized counters. What little summer sunlight managed to filter into the room through the high, narrow windows was dimmed by the years of grime on the glass.

Charity wrinkled her nose at the sight of the heavy shroud of dust that covered the assortment of bizarre goods heaped on the display tables. She was dismayed to see that the new proprietor had made no effort to tidy the premises. The goods were still stacked willy-nilly on the counters. There was no organized pattern to the displays.

Odd little carvings were piled high in one corner. A jumble of brass bells and whistles overflowed a nearby packing crate. Small, colorfully dressed dolls with exotic faces painted with startlingly grim expressions tumbled from a box. Plastic masks leered down from the walls. Below was a counter laden with invisible-ink pens, little magic smoke-producing tubes, and puzzles composed of interlocking metal rings.

And so it went throughout the shop. Oddities and imports from far-off lands filled the shelves of Charms & Virtues. Handwoven straw baskets from the Philippines sat next to a hoard of mechanical toy insects manufactured in Hong Kong. Miniature plastic dinosaurs made in Southeast Asia occupied shelf space with rubber worms produced in Mexico. Cheap bracelets, music boxes, imitation military medals, and artificial flowers littered the countertops. Most of it looked as if it had been sitting in the same spot for years.

The wares sold in the dusty import shop could be described in a single word so far as Charity was concerned. And that word was *junk*. The new owner would have to apply some energy and enthusiasm if he wanted to revive his newly purchased small business. She made a mental note to present him a feather duster as a welcome gift. Perhaps he would take the hint.

Charity had never figured out just how Hayden Stone had managed to make a living from Charms & Virtues, or the pier rents, for that matter. He had lived a life of stark simplicity, but even eccentrics had to pay real estate taxes and buy food. She had finally concluded that he'd had a private income from some other source.

"I don't have any milk or sugar," Elias said.

"That's all right," Charity said hastily. "I don't take anything in my tea."

"Neither do I. Good tea should be as clear as a pool of pure water."

The comment brought back memories. "Hayden Stone used to say the same thing."

"Did he?"

"Yes. He was always muttering weird little Zenny comments about water."

"Zenny?"

"You know, Zen-like. He once told me that he was a student of some sort of ancient philosophy that had been forgotten by almost everyone. He said there was only one other person he knew who also studied it."

"Hayden was more than a student. He was a master."

"You knew him?"

"Yes."

"I see." Charity forced herself to a more confident pace. She held her clipboard in front of her as though it were a talisman and summoned up what she hoped was a bright smile. "Well, on to business. I realize that you haven't had a chance to get settled here on the Landing, but unfortunately the lease problem can't wait."

"Lease problem?"

"The shopkeepers have decided to band together as a group to deal with our new landlord, Far Seas,

Incorporated. We'd like you to join us. We'll have a great deal more negotiating power if we go in as a united front."

Elias lifted a simple brown teapot with a curiously precise but fluid motion. "What do you intend to approach Far Seas about?"

"Renewing our leases." Charity watched, fascinated, as Elias poured tea. "As you no doubt know, this pier was owned, lock, stock, and barrel, by Hayden Stone, the former proprietor of this shop."

"I'm aware of that." A muted shaft of sunshine from one of the ceiling-high windows slanted briefly across the right side of Elias's face. It revealed a bold, hawklike nose and savage cheekbones.

Charity drew a deep breath and tightened her grip on the clipboard. "From what we can gather, at the time of Hayden's death, the ownership of the Landing was transferred automatically to a company called Far Seas, Incorporated."

A low hiss interrupted Charity before she could continue. It was a familiar sound. She spared a brief glance for the large, brilliantly plumed parrot that was perched arrogantly atop a fake tree limb on a stand behind the counter.

"Hello, Otis," Charity said.

Crazy Otis shifted from one clawed foot to the other and lowered his head with a menacing movement. His beady eyes glittered with malice. "Heh, heh, heh."

Elias examined the bird with interest. "I sense some hostility here."

"He always acts like that." Charity made a face. "He knows it irritates me. And after all I've done for him, too. You'd think that bird would show some gratitude."

Otis cackled again.

"I took him in after Hayden died, you know," Charity explained. "He was extremely depressed. Moped around, let his feathers go, lost his appetite. It was terrible. He was in such bad shape I was afraid to leave him alone. During the day he sat on the coatrack in my back room office. I kept his cage in my bedroom at night."

"I'm sure he's grateful," Elias said.

"Hah." Charity glared at the bird. "That bird doesn't know the meaning of the word."

Crazy Otis sidled along the tree limb, muttering with evil glee.

"You don't know how lucky you were, Otis," Charity said. "No one else on the pier was willing to take charge of you. More than a couple of people suggested that we try to sell you to some unsuspecting tourist. And one individual, who shall go unnamed, wanted to call the pound and have you taken away. But I was too softhearted to allow that. I gave you shelter, food, free rides on Yappy's carousel. What did I get in return? Nothing but nasty complaints."

"Heh, heh, heh." Otis flapped his clipped wings.

"Take it easy, Otis." Elias reached out with one long-fingered hand and scratched the bird's head. "An obligation exists until it is repaid. You owe her."

Crazy Otis grumbled, but he stopped chortling. He half-closed his eyes and promptly sank into a contented stupor as Elias stroked his feathers.

"Amazing," Charity said. "The only other person that bird ever treated as an equal was Hayden Stone. Everyone else is just so much old newspaper beneath Crazy Otis's grubby claws."

"Otis and I had a long talk after Newlin brought him over here yesterday," Elias said. "He and I have decided that we can share this shop together."

"That's a relief. To tell you the truth, when I sent Newlin down here with that nasty beast, I expected you to refuse to take him. In all fairness, Crazy Otis isn't your responsibility. Just because you took over Charms & Virtues doesn't mean you have to take charge of him."

Elias gave her a long, considering look. "Otis wasn't your responsibility either, but you took him in and gave him a home for the past two months."

"There wasn't much else I could do. Hayden was very fond of Otis, and I liked Hayden, even if he was a little weird."

"The fact that you liked Hayden didn't mean that you had to take care of Otis."

"Unfortunately, it did." Charity sighed. "Somehow, Crazy Otis has always seemed like one of the family here on the pier. A particularly unpleasant relative, I admit, one I'd prefer to keep stashed out of sight in the attic, but, nevertheless, a relation. And you know what they say about your relations. You can't choose them. You have to take what you get."

"I understand." Elias stopped rubbing Otis's head and picked up the teapot again.

"You don't have to keep him, you know," Charity said in a burst of rash honesty. "He's not a very lovable bird."

"As you said, he's family."

"Parrots like Otis have long life spans. You'll be saddled with him for years."

"I know."

"Okay," Charity said, cheered by the fact that Elias was not going to change his mind on the subject. "Otis is settled. Now about this situation with Far Seas."

"Yes?"

"All of the rents on the pier are due to be renegotiated before the end of September. Today is the fourth of August. We've got to act quickly."

"Just what action do you plan to take?" Elias set down the teapot.

"As I said, we want to approach Far Seas as a united front." Charity realized with a start that she was staring at his hands. They were very interesting hands, powerful hands imbued with a striking, utterly masculine grace.

"A united front?" Elias watched her as she hurriedly raised her gaze from his hands to his face.

"Right. United." She noticed that his eyes were the color of the sea during a storm, a bleak, steel gray. Her fingers clenched around the clipboard. "We intend to contact Far Seas immediately. We want to lock in long-term leases at reasonable rents before the corporation realizes what's happening here in Whispering Waters Cove."

"What is happening here?" Elias's mouth curved faintly. "Aside from the impending arrival of our visitors from outer space?"

"I see you've already met some of the Voyagers?"

"It's a little hard to miss them on the street."

"True." Charity shrugged. "They're quite an embarrassment to the town council. Most of the members think the Voyagers give Whispering Waters Cove a bad image. But like the mayor says, one way or another, the cult should be gone by the middle of August."

"What happens then?"

"Haven't you heard?" Charity grinned. "Gwendolyn Pitt, the leader of the group, has told her followers that the alien spaceships will arrive at midnight on the fifteenth to take them all away on an extended tour of the galaxy. During said tour, everyone will apparently be treated to a lot of pure sex and philosophical enlightenment."

"I've been told it's difficult to mix the two."

"Yeah, well, evidently the aliens have mastered the problem. As you can imagine, the town council is hoping that when nothing happens that night, the Voyagers will figure out that the whole thing is a hoax and will leave Whispering Waters Cove bright and early on the morning of the sixteenth."

"In my experience people tend to cling to a belief even when they are confronted with clear evidence that it's false."

"Well, it won't bother me or anyone else here on the pier if some of them decide to stay in the area," Charity admitted. "Most of the Voyagers seem pleasant enough, if a little naive. A few have become good customers. I've made a killing during the past two months with paranormal and New Age titles."

The long blue and white tunics and bright headbands worn by the members of the Voyagers cult had become familiar sights in and around the small town. Gwendolyn Pitt and her followers had arrived early in July. They had parked their motley assortment of trailers, motor homes, and campers on a patch of prime-view land that had once been an old campground.

The town's mayor, Phyllis Dartmoor, had initially been as hostile toward the group as the council members, but after a short flurry of fruitless efforts to force the Voyagers out of town, she had become surprisingly sanguine about the situation. Whenever the local newspaper produced an editorial denouncing the newcomers as a blot on the landscape, she reminded everyone that the cult would likely disintegrate in the middle of August.

"The Voyagers do add some local color," Elias said as he handed Charity one of the small, handleless cups.

"Yes, but they don't enhance the new upscale image that the town is trying to create to draw tourists."

Charity took a sip of tea. The warm liquid rolled across her tongue, bright, subtle, and refreshing. She savored the feel of the brew in her mouth for a few seconds. The man did know his tea, she thought.

"Like it?" Elias watched her intently.

"Very nice," she said as she put the cup back down on the counter. "There is something very distinctive about keemun, isn't there?"

"Yes."

"Well, back to business. Actually, it's the town image thing that makes it necessary for those of us here on the pier to move quickly on the lease issue."

"Go on." Elias sipped tea.

"The mayor and town council would like to see this pier converted into a boutique art mall filled with cutesy shops and antique galleries. They want to attract high-end tenants. But in order to do that, they have to convince the owner of the landing to remove the current shopkeepers. We're not exactly trendy, you see."

Elias glanced around at his own gloom-filled store. "I get the picture. And you think Far Seas will go along with the council's plans to kick us out?"

"Of course. Far Seas is a big corporation in Seattle. Its managers will be interested only in the bottom line. If they think they can lease these shops to a lot of up-market art dealers who can afford sky-high rents, they'll jump at the chance to get rid of us. Or, they may try to sell the landing itself."

"What do you know about Far Seas?"

"Not much," Charity admitted. "Apparently it's some kind of consulting firm involved with the Pacific Rim trade. A couple of weeks ago all of us here on the pier received a letter from Hayden Stone's attorney instructing us to start paying our rents to Far Seas."

"Have you spoken to anyone at Far Seas?"

"Not yet." Charity smiled grimly. "It's a question of strategy."

"Strategy?"

"I decided it would be best to wait until the new owner of Charms & Virtues arrived before we made our move."

Elias took another meditative sip of tea. "So at this point you're operating on a lot of assumptions about Far Seas?"

The hint of criticism irritated her. "I think it's safe to assume that Far Seas will react in the same way that any large company would in this situation. As the new owner of a piece of commercial real estate, the company will naturally want to get the highest possible rate of return. Or the best offer, if it chooses to sell the pier."

"When one studies an opponent's reflection in a pool of water, one should take care to ensure that the water is very, very clear."

Charity eyed him uneasily. "That sounds like more of Hayden Stone's old sayings. Were you a very close friend of his?"

"Yes."

"I suppose that's why you got Charms & Virtues?"

"Yes." Elias's eyes were unreadable. "It was his legacy to me. I also got his cottage."

"I'm sorry to be the one to tell you this, Mr. Winters, but you won't hang on to your legacy for long if we don't get those leases renegotiated with Far Seas. We've got to move fast now that you're here. There's a strong possibility that someone on the town council or Leighton Pitt, a local realtor, will contact Far Seas directly."

"Elias."

"What? Oh, Elias." She hesitated. "Please call me Charity."

"Charity." He repeated her name the way he sipped tea, as if he were tasting it. "Unusual name these days."

"You don't meet a lot of people named Elias, either," she retorted. "Now, then, if you'll just give me a few minutes to explain our plans for dealing with Far Seas, I'm sure you'll see how important it is for you to join with us."

"Yes."

"I beg your pardon?"

Elias raised one shoulder in a lethally graceful movement. "As the new owner of Charms & Virtues, I see the importance of joining with you in your— what did you call it? Ah, yes. Your united front. I've never been part of a united front before. How does it work?"

She smiled with satisfaction. "It's quite simple, really. I'm the president of the shopkeepers association, so I'll do the actual negotiating with Far Seas."

"Have you had much experience with this kind of thing?"

"Yes, as a matter of fact, I have. I was in the corporate world before I moved here to Whispering Waters Cove."

"Charity Truitt." Recognition gleamed in the depths of Elias's eyes. "I thought the name sounded familiar. Would that be the department-store Truitts of Seattle?"

"Yes." Charity's spine stiffened in automatic reflex. "And before you say anything else, let me answer all your questions in three sentences. Yes, I'm the former president of the company. Yes, my stepbrother and stepsister are now running the business. And, yes, I intend to remain here in Whispering Waters Cove."

"I see."

"While I am no longer involved in the operation of

Truitt department stores, I haven't forgotten everything I learned during the years I ran the company. If your résumé is stronger than mine, I'll be glad to turn the job of confronting Far Seas over to you."

"I'm satisfied that you're the best person for the task," he said gently.

Chagrined, Charity set the clipboard down on the counter. "Sorry to sound so belligerent. It's just that my decision to leave Truitt last summer was, uh, complicated and difficult."

"I see."

She studied him closely, but she could not tell if he had heard the rumors of a broken engagement and a nervous breakdown. She concluded that he had not. He showed no signs of curiosity or concern. But, then, he showed no real emotion of any kind, she thought. She decided to plunge ahead.

"The pier is prime property," she said. "We're going to have to fight to keep our shops."

"Something tells me that you will be successful in renegotiating your leases."

"Thanks for the vote of confidence." Charity glanced at Crazy Otis. "If I'm not successful, we're all going to be looking for new locations. And that includes you, Otis."

"Heh, heh, heh." Otis slithered along the perch until he reached the far end. He stepped off the fake branch onto Elias's shoulder.

Charity winced, recalling the occasions when Otis had climbed onto her arm. Elias did not seem to notice the heavy claws sinking into his dark green pullover.

"Another cup of tea?" Elias asked.

"No, thanks." Charity glanced at her watch. "I'm going to call Far Seas this afternoon and see if I can get the lease negotiations started today. Wish me luck."

"I don't believe in luck." He looked thoughtful. "The stream flows inevitably into the river and then on into the sea. The water may take on different aspects at various points in its journey, but it is, nevertheless, the same water."

Newlin was right, Charity thought. Elias Winters was kind of strange. She smiled politely. "Fine. Wish me good karma or something. We're all in this together, remember. If I don't pull this off, everyone on this pier is going to be in trouble."

"You'll pull it off."

"That's the spirit." Charity turned to go. Belatedly she recalled the other item on her agenda. "I almost forgot. The shopkeepers are having a potluck here on the pier Monday night after we close for the day. You're invited, naturally."

"Thank you."

"You'll come?"

"Yes."

"Good. Hayden never came to the potlucks." Charity glanced at the notes on her clipboard. "We still need hot dishes. Can you manage an entrée?"

"As long as no one minds if it doesn't contain meat."

Charity laughed. "I was just about to tell you that a couple of us here on the pier are vegetarians. I think you're going to fit in nicely."

"That would be a novel experience," Elias said.

Charity decided not to ask him to elaborate. Something told her she would not like the answer. Her comment had only been a polite, offhand remark. She doubted that Elias made those kinds of comments. She had the feeling that everything he said was laced with several layers of cryptic meaning. She'd had the same sensation whenever she talked to Hayden Stone. It did not make for a lot of comfortable, casual conversation.

Charity experienced a surge of relief as she walked quickly out of the dark confines of Charms & Virtue into the sunlight. She hurried down the wide corridor between the shops and entered the airy, well-lit premises of Whispers.

Newlin Odell looked up from a bundle of weekly news magazines that he was placing on a rack. His thin features were pinched in the expression of someone who had just recently returned from a funeral. For Newlin, that was normal.

He was a skinny young man of twenty-four. His narrow face was partially obscured by a scruffy goatee and a pair of wire-framed glasses. Charity was almost certain that he trimmed his lanky brown hair himself. It hung in uneven hunks around his ears.

"How'd it go?" Newlin asked in his blunt, economical fashion.

Charity paused in the doorway of her small office, aware of a familiar wave of sympathy for Newlin. She had hired him a month ago when he had shown up out of nowhere to ask for a job. He had come to Whispering Waters Cove to be near his girlfriend, a young woman named Arlene Fenton, who had joined the Voyagers. He spent the time that he was not working at Whispers trying to coax Arlene away from the influence of the cult.

Having thus far failed in his mission to talk sense into Arlene, Newlin had stoically determined to wait out the situation. He hoped that on the fifteenth of August Arlene would finally understand that she had been taken in by a scam.

Charity sincerely hoped that he was right. She found his devotion to Arlene heartwarming and quixotic in an old-fashioned, heroic sense. But she secretly worried about what would happen if Arlene did not come to her senses at midnight that night. Having nursed a depressed parrot for two months, she was not eager to deal with a stricken Newlin Odell.

"You were right, Newlin," Charity said. "Elias Winters is kind of strange. He was a friend of Hayden Stone's, so I guess that explains it. But the good news is that he's willing to go along with the rest of the shopkeepers in order to negotiate the new leases."

"You gonna call Far Seas?"

"Right away. Cross your fingers."

"It's gonna take more than luck to talk Far Seas into giving you a break on the leases if Pitt or the town council has already gotten to 'em and convinced 'em that the pier is valuable real estate."

"Don't be so negative, Newlin. I'm banking on the fact that the town council doesn't yet know who owns Crazy Otis Landing. We only found out ourselves a couple of weeks ago. I told everyone on the pier to keep quiet."

"I don't think anyone's blabbed."

"I hope not." Charity pushed open the door of the back room and wound her way through stacks of boxes to her desk.

She sat down and reached for the phone. Quickly she punched in the number for Far Seas, Inc., which had been included in the letter Hayden Stone's attorney had sent to the shopkeepers.

There were some odd noises on the line, a click, and then the phone finally rang on the other end. Charity wondered if the call had been forwarded. She waited impatiently until the receiver was lifted.

A newly familiar voice answered.

"Charms & Virtues," Elias said.

Shallow water sometimes reveals shallow answers. But deep water holds deep questions.

—"On the Way of Water," from the journal of Hayden Stone

The riptide rush of fate swept through Elias a second time in less than five minutes when Charity stormed back through the front door of Charms & Virtues.

So the strange sense of anticipation that he had experienced the first time he saw her had not been a fluke.

He watched, fascinated, as she bore down on him via an aisle formed by display counters. He had deliberately subjected himself to this second experiment in order to verify the initial results. No question about it. He felt as if he were being swept out into very deep water.

Not good. Not good at all.

But oddly beguiling.

"Who are you, Elias Winters, and what kind of a game are you playing?" Charity demanded.

Elias did not look at his wrist to check the time. He hadn't worn a watch since he was sixteen. But he needed to regain some sense of control. He forced himself to look away from the red fire buried deep in the curving wings of her heavy, dark hair. The battered old cuckoo clock on the wall provided a convenient distraction.

"I'd estimate that took approximately one minute, forty-five seconds, give or take a couple of seconds. You're fast, Ms. Truitt. Very fast. Did you run the whole length of the pier?"

"You timed me?"

Crazy Otis, who was back on his perch nibbling on a large seed, chortled.

"Quiet, Otis," Elias commanded gently.

Otis subsided, but there was a cheerfully malicious gleam in his eyes. He cracked the seed that he gripped in one claw with a particularly loud crunch.

Elias noticed that there was a distinctive gleam in Charity's vivid hazel eyes, too, but it was neither cheerful nor malicious. She was simply outraged.

She was several inches shorter than he was, but she somehow managed to glare at him down the length of her very straight nose. Her full, soft mouth was compressed into an uncompromising line. There was unmistakable warmth just beneath her delicate cheekbones.

Elias felt his insides tighten. He did not understand his own reaction. Something indefinable in her drew his whole attention.

"Mr. Winters—"

"Elias."

"Mr. Winters, I want an explanation, and I want it now. You're up to something, that's obvious."

"Is it?"

"Don't you dare start answering questions with questions. That's manipulative, sneaky, and downright passive-aggressive."

"If there's one thing you can be sure of when you deal with me, Charity, it's that when I'm feeling aggressive, there's nothing passive about it."

"You know something? I believe you. That still leaves manipulative and sneaky. And I warn you, *Mr. Winters*, I know everything there is to know about manipulative and sneaky. I grew up in the corporate world."

"I appreciate the warning," Elias said softly.

He liked the way the skirts of her gauzy, white cotton dress billowed and snapped around her gently rounded calves. Only a short while ago when she had arrived to introduce herself, those same skirts had floated discreetly, even protectively about her legs. Now she was angry, and she and her skirts had both thrown discretion to the winds.

The deep sensual hunger rising within him made him uneasy. An attractive, strong-minded woman in a summer dress and strappy little sandals was always an appealing sight, but his reaction today was definitely over the top. What was wrong with him?

Perhaps he shouldn't be too hard on himself, he thought glumly. It had been a long time since he had been involved with a woman. His long-planned vengeance had become an all-consuming passion during the past few months as his grand scheme moved into its final phase. It had become so strong that it had temporarily blotted out even the desire for sex.

And then Hayden Stone had died, and everything had changed forever. Ever since Hayden's death he had felt as if he had been cut adrift on a dark, roiling sea. None of his reactions seemed quite normal. He had lost his sense of internal balance. This intense response to Charity Truitt was a good example.

She was not the sort of woman who normally aroused his interest. For years he had been drawn to the cool types found in film noir movies. Savvy, sophisticated women who wore a lot of black. Women who moved in the high-stakes world of the Pacific Rim trade, either as power brokers or as powers behind thrones. Some had been attracted to him because of the contacts and connections he could offer. Some had simply wanted the satisfaction of being seen with a man who was as powerful as themselves. Others had been intrigued by the perception of danger. Whatever the terms of the sexual bargain, Elias had always made certain that the exchange of favors had been equal.

But Charity was different. He sensed intuitively that if he pursued the relationship, there would be no simple, straightforward arrangement with her. She would be demanding and difficult in ways that he had always avoided.

"Are you or are you not connected to Far Seas?" Charity fumed.

Elias flattened his hands on the glass counter in front of him. "I am Far Seas."

"Is this a joke?"

"No." He considered briefly. "I don't think I know any jokes."

"Well? Where's the rest of the company?"

"The rest of it?"

She threw up her hands. "Secretaries, clerks, managers, and assorted flunkies."

"My secretary took another job a few months ago. I didn't bother to replace her. There are no clerks or managers, and I never could get any reliable flunkies."

"That is not funny."

"I told you, I don't do jokes."

"Assuming you're telling me the truth, why were you so secretive about the fact that you now own the pier?"

"I learned a long time ago never to initiate a business discussion. The clear spring waters of open dealing and plain-speaking are too often mistaken as evidence of weakness. I was taught to let others come to me."

Charity came to a halt in front of the counter. "You mean you prefer to hold the advantage. I get the point. But for the record, I never took any of those expensive seminars from rip-off management consultants on how to do business according to the principles of the Tao. I prefer to do business the old-fashioned way. Level with me, Winters. Do you really own Crazy Otis Landing?"

"Yes." Elias looked into her huge hazel eyes and wondered at the deep wariness he saw beneath the anger. He recalled vague gossip about the chaos that had followed a failed merger between Truitt and a company called Loftus Athletic Gear. There had been an abrupt resignation of Truitt's CEO. Rumors of a problem with said CEO's nerves. He had paid little attention because neither Truitt nor Loftus were involved in Pacific Rim trade.

"Well?"

"Hayden Stone did not leave only Charms & Virtues to me," Elias said. "He left me the whole pier."

"Plus the cottage on the bluff." She narrowed her eyes. "That's a lot of real estate. Why would he leave so much to you?"

Elias chose his words carefully. "I told you, Hayden was my friend and my teacher. He helped me establish Far Seas."

"I see. Just what kind of company is Far Seas?"

"A consulting firm."

Charity crossed her arms beneath her breasts. "What kind of consulting?"

"I provide contacts, connections, and advice for business people who deal in Rim trade." He probably should have made that past tense, he thought. He wondered if he would ever again return to his former line of work. For some reason, he doubted it. Along with everything else in his life these days, it seemed to be drifting farther and farther away from him.

"Whispering Waters Cove is not exactly a thriving outpost of Pacific Rim business."

He smiled slightly. "No, it's not."

"So what are you doing here?"

"You're a very suspicious woman, Charity."

"I think I have reason to be suspicious under the circumstances. A short while ago, I made the mistake of assuming that you were one of us here on the pier and that we would all be going up against Far Seas together."

"I warned you that when one studies an opponent's reflection in a pool of water, one should take care to ensure that the water is very, very clear."

"Yeah, yeah, I heard you the first time. Forget the double-talk. When I want philosophy, I'll go to Ted."

"Ted?"

"Ted Jenner. He has that little shop called Ted's Instant Philosophy T-Shirts next to the carousel. You must have seen it."

Elias recalled the racks of T-shirts billowing in the breeze at the end of the pier. The shirts all bore various legends and slogans that ranged from the clever to the crude. "I've noticed it."

"I should hope so. You walk by it every day. The

least you could do, by the way, is drop in and introduce yourself to your fellow shopkeepers."

"I've just met you," he pointed out.

She raised her eyes toward the ceiling in an expression of acute disgust. "Never mind. Let's get back to more pressing issues. What's your excuse for failing to tell me the truth about yourself while I was explaining the lease situation here at the pier?"

"You never asked."

She threw up her hands. "How was I supposed to know that you were Far Seas?"

"The degree of clarity of the water makes no difference if one does not ask the right questions about the image that is reflected on the surface."

She gave him a fulminating look. "Skip the mumbo-jumbo and get to the point. If you are who you say you are, then tell me the truth. What do you intend to do about the pier leases?"

"Renew them at the present rates when they come due in September."

Charity's mouth fell open, revealing neat, small white teeth. She closed it swiftly. "Why would you do that now that I've told you about the town council's plans to use Crazy Otis Landing as the centerpiece for the new, improved Whispering Waters Cove?"

"I don't know."

"I beg your pardon?"

Elias shrugged. "I don't have an answer to your question. That's one of the reasons I came here to Whispering Waters Cove. To get some answers."

To get a clear answer, a man had to ask a clear question. And he was not able to do that. Every time he looked into the water to see his own true face, he caught only glimpses of a badly distorted reflection.

Elias rolled smoothly out of the last of the series of

ancient exercises Hayden Stone had taught him. The deceptively effortless movements formed a pattern known as Tal Kek Chara. They represented the physical expression of the ancient philosophy in which Hayden had been a master. Tal Kek Chara was a state in which mind and body were balanced in a flow of energy for which water was a metaphor.

The coiled length of leather anchored to Elias's wrist represented the philosophy, and it was named for it. Tal Kek Chara was a weapon as well as a way of living.

As Elias ended the pattern, the leather thong unfurled as if it were an extension of his arm. It whipped around the branch of a nearby tree with enough force to chain the limb but not enough to snap it in two. Control was everything in Tal Kek Chara.

Elias straightened and retrieved the supple strip of leather. He took a few seconds to assess the effects of the routine he had just completed. He was breathing deeply but not hard. The light breeze off the waters of the cove was already drying the perspiration on his bare shoulders. It had been a solid workout, but he had not exhausted himself. That was as it should be. Excess in anything, including exercise, was a violation of the basic principle of Tal Kek Chara.

Automatically, he snugged the leather back into place around his waist. He wore it outside the loops of his jeans. A weapon that could not be accessed in a hurry was useless.

He turned and walked back along the cliff toward the spare little cottage that Hayden Stone had lived in during the last three years of his life. When he reached the garden gate he opened it and stepped into the serene, miniature landscape Hayden had created. The focal point of the garden was a calm reflecting pool.

Elias went up the porch steps and opened the front door of his new home. He paused, as Hayden had taught him, to allow his senses to absorb the essence of the small dwelling. All was well.

He padded barefoot across the hardwood floor. There were no chairs in Hayden Stone's house. There wasn't much else in the way of furniture, either. Two cushions, a low table, and a sisal mat completed the living room decor. A wide, clear, heavy glass dish that was partially filled with water sat in the center of the table. The walls were bare.

The only touch of color in the room was Crazy Otis. It was enough. The parrot's brilliant plumage was spectacular against the simple surroundings.

Otis, perched on top of his open cage, bobbed his head in greeting and stretched his wings.

"I'm going to take a shower, and then I'll fix us both some dinner, Otis."

"Heh, heh, heh."

Elias went into the single bedroom, which contained only a futon-style bed and a low, heavily carved wooden chest. The kitchen and bath were outfitted with the basic necessities of modern life, but basic was the operative word.

Bicoastal interior designers and architects talked effusively about minimalist design, but Hayden Stone had created the real thing here in this small, spare house. Its simple lines held layers of complexity that only one skilled in the ways of Tal Kek Chara could detect.

Elias's house in Seattle had been similar to this one. It had been located on the edge of Lake Washington. He had sold it shortly after the interview with Garrick Keyworth. He did not miss it. Tal Kek Chara had taught him not to become too attached to things. Or to people. Since his sixteenth year, Hayden had been the one exception. And now Hayden was gone.

Elias went into the bathroom, stripped off his jeans, and stepped into the stall shower. Memories of Hayden flickered in his mind. For some reason he saw a scene from his sixteenth year, a scene that had occurred several months after his father had died.

"Why do we have to sit on the floor when we eat our meals?" Elias asked as he folded his legs on the cushion in front of the low table.

"To remind us that we don't need chairs." Hayden ate soba noodles with a strange, handmade implement that was part fork, part knife. It was both a sophisticated eating utensil and an equally useful weapon. "A man who learns that he can be comfortable without a chair will learn that he can be comfortable without a lot of other things, as well."

"Did they teach you that in that monastery where you stayed after you got shot up?"

"Among other things."

Elias knew the story well. Hayden had been a mercenary until his thirty-fifth year, a man of violence who had sold his unique talents and pieces of his soul to anyone with the money to pay the price. In a world where small brushfire conflicts simmered in many regions of the globe, there was never a lack of buyers for the commodities that Hayden offered for sale.

He had been badly wounded in the course of one such campaign, a small civil war that had been waged in a forgotten corner of the Pacific. He had been left for dead by his companions.

Hayden had told Elias that he had fully expected to die there in the jungle. Not relishing the prospect of being gnawed on by some of the local wildlife while still alive, he'd readied a bullet for himself. He'd figured that he had just enough strength left to pull the trigger one last time.

But he kept making excuses for putting off the inevitable.

Hayden had told himself he would wait until nightfall or until the pain became unbearable or until the first hungry scavenger appeared. His instinct for survival had been stronger than he had expected, however. Night came, the pain got worse, and he could hear the tell-tale rustle in the bushes. But still he could not bring himself to put a bullet in his brain. Something stilled his hand.

The monks found him shortly after dawn.

"How long were you at the monastery?" Elias asked as he fiddled with his noodles. He was getting the hang of the eating tool, but he still fumbled a bit with it.

"I lived in the House of Tal Kek Chara for five years. Now the House lives inside me." Hayden deftly dipped noodles into a clear broth and transferred them to his mouth. He chewed in silence for a while. "You did well in your training this afternoon."

"It felt better. Smoother, somehow." Elias plunged noodles into his own bowl. He grimaced when broth splattered on the table. Until he had come to live with Hayden, he'd been addicted to hamburgers and pizza. Now the thought of eating meat made him queasy for some reason. "Do you think I'll ever be as good at Tal Kek Chara as you are?"

"Yes. Better, probably. You've started your training at a younger age than I did, and your body responds well to the discipline. You have a natural talent, I think. And it helps that you're not walking around with an old bullet in your gut."

Elias stared at him. Hayden made few references to

his former life as a professional mercenary. "Yeah, I guess so."

"But learning the exercises of Tal Kek Chara will not teach you what you need to know in order to be able to look into the pool and see truths."

"If this is going to be another lecture on the subject of giving up my plans to get Dad's killer, you might as well forget it, Hayden. Someday I'm going to find out who sabotaged the Cessna. And when I do, I'll make sure the bastard pays."

"A man cannot see truth clearly in water that is clouded with strong emotions. One day you will have to decide whether revenge is more important to you than owning your own soul."

"I don't see why I can't have my revenge and still own my own soul."

Hayden looked at him with ancient eyes. "I have great faith in you, Elias. You're smart, and you have power. You will eventually see clearly enough to find your true inner flow."

He had finally seen the truth about revenge, Elias thought as he toweled off and reached for a clean shirt and a pair of jeans. But he could not yet see the truth about himself.

He went into the kitchen to prepare his dinner. The routine brought back more memories of Hayden. This time he gently pushed them aside and lost himself in the creative process of cooking.

Half an hour later he sat down on a cushion in front of the table. He surveyed the bowl of steamed rice, seaweed-flavored soup, and vegetable curry and realized that, for the first time in a long while, some part of him was not plotting vengeance or business strategy. No, for the first time since the funeral, he had a new goal.

He wanted to go to bed with Charity Truitt.

"It won't be simple or easy, Otis. I have a gut feeling that Charity is one of those very expensive women Hayden used to warn me about. He said that to lure one, a man had to be prepared to pay a very high price."

"Heh, heh, heh."

He'd have to get her attention with something costly, Elias thought. A piece of himself, no doubt.

An expectant hush fell on the small crowd gathered at the end of the pier just as Charity set her herbed couscous and green lentil salad down on the picnic table. She tried without any success to squelch the tingle of anticipation that went through her. She didn't need the low, speculative mutters of those around her to know who had arrived.

If someone hadn't chanced to look in his direction, though, no one would have heard Elias approach. His low, soft, well-worn boots made no sound on the pier timber. When he moved through the shadowed areas created by the walls of the various shops, it was difficult to make out his gliding form.

Charity was intrigued by the sight of a covered bowl in his hands. His eyes met hers as if he had been waiting for her to notice him. He inclined his head a scarce fraction of an inch in greeting. Charity heard a small gasp. She was chagrined to realize that the person sucking in air in such an inelegant manner was none other than herself.

"There he is," Radiance Barker whispered in her high, sweet, breathy tones.

Radiance, who in a former life had been named Rhonda, cultivated the feathery voice. It went with the rest of her, which Charity privately thought of as neo-hippie. Much to Radiance's everlasting regret, she was too young to have been a genuine flower child of the fabled sixties. She considered herself a spiritual descendent of the era, however, and dressed accordingly. Long loops of beads decorated the flowing, multipatterned dress she wore this evening. Her waist-length hair was trimmed with a flower-studded headband.

"Something fishy about this whole thing, if you ask me," Roy Yapton, better known as Yappy, declared. "Hayden Stone was weird, but at least he played straight with us. I ain't so sure about this guy."

"He owns the whole shooting match," Bea Hatfield said, "so you'd best watch what you say, you old coot."

Roy and Bea were both on the far side of sixty. They'd been operating their respective pier enterprises for over twenty years. Their affair had been going on for as long as anyone could recall. No one knew why they had never married or why they bothered to pretend that they were just good friends.

"Wonder what he brought to eat." Ted Jenner absently scratched his stomach, which was barely concealed by an extra-extra-large T-shirt. "I'm starving."

The shirt was from his own shop, Ted's Instant Philosophy T-Shirts. Charity glanced at the slogan on the one he was modeling this afternoon. It read, *I May Be Dysfunctional, But You Are Definitely Crazy.*

"That's not exactly news." Radiance scanned Ted's portly figure with an amused expression. "You're always starving. I keep telling you that if you switched to vegetarian, you'd lose weight."

"Dropping a few pounds ain't worth havin' to eat nothin' but nuts and berries for the rest of my life," Ted said cheerfully. "Even if Charity can cook that bunny rabbit food better than anyone I ever met."

It was a long-running argument. No one paid much

attention. Everyone was too busy watching Elias, and no one seemed quite certain how to greet him. Last week he had been one of them, albeit a newcomer, Charity thought. This week he was their landlord.

The new leases had not yet been signed. Elias had nearly two months to change his mind about extending the old contracts, and everyone present knew it.

Charity decided that, as president of the shopkeepers association, it was her duty to take charge. She smiled very brightly at Elias when he reached the little group.

"You can put your dish down on that table over there," she said, deliberately infusing her voice with authority. It was an old trick, one she'd had to learn quickly when she'd faced a roomful of creditors all bent on salvaging what they could from the failing Truitt department store chain. It was her intuition that had gotten her through those early days of overwhelming responsibility. She would use it to deal with Elias. "Have you met everyone?"

Elias glanced around as he set the covered pan down next to Bea's potato salad. "No."

Charity hastily ran through the introductions. "Roy Yapton. He owns the carousel. Bea Hatfield. She owns the Whispering Waters café. Radiance Barker, owner of Nails by Radiance. Ted Jenner. He operates the T-shirt shop. And you've already met Newlin Odell. Newlin works for me."

"Hi." Newlin peered at Elias through his small, round glasses. "Otis doing okay?"

"He's fine." Elias nodded politely at the small circle of faces. Then he leaned back against the pier railing, crossed one booted foot over the other, and folded his arms.

Charity lifted her chin and prepared to pin him down. "I've explained to the other shopkeepers that you've committed to renew the leases at the old rates."

Elias nodded, as if the subject held little interest.

Yappy scowled. "That true, Winters?"

"Yes," Elias said quietly.

"Whew." Bea fanned herself with a napkin. "I don't mind telling you, it's a relief to hear you say it. Charity told us that you know all about the town council's plans to turn Whispering Waters Cove into a sort of Northwest Carmel."

Elias glanced out over the cove, his gaze thoughtful. "Somehow, I don't see that happening."

Ted frowned. "Don't be too sure about that. Phyllis Dartmoor, our illustrious mayor, says the council's already come up with a couple of possible new names for Crazy Otis Landing. They want something that sounds more up-market, she says. Indigo Landing or Sunset Landing."

Charity groaned. "They sound so generic. No character at all."

"Charity has been doing battle with Mayor Dartmoor and the council on a regular basis since the spring," Radiance told Elias. "We all go to the monthly council meetings, but we let Charity do the talking. She's good at that kind of thing."

"I see." Elias rested his gaze on Charity. "Crazy Otis Landing suits the pier. I don't see any reason to change it."

"I'm glad you agree with the rest of us," Charity said. "But I warn you, you're going to get a lot of pressure to change not only the name of the pier but everything else about it as well."

"I think I can handle it," Elias said softly.

Charity was not sure how to deal with that simple statement. She looked around at the others. "Well, what do you say we eat first and then talk business?"

"Good idea," Ted said. "What did you bring, Winters?"

"Chilled green-tea noodles with a peanut dipping sauce," Elias said. "There's some wasabi on the side for those who like it hot."

Charity stared at him in astonishment.

"Figures," Ted muttered. "Another fancy gourmet vegetarian from Seattle. May have to put a ban on you folks moving here to the cove. You're ruining our regional cuisine."

Radiance raised her brows. "You mean those old hallowed recipes such as hamburger casserole and mushroom soup gravy are in danger of going extinct? Groovy."

Bea laughed. "Better look to your laurels, Charity."

Radiance giggled. "Charity is a fantastic cook," she explained to Elias. "Ted grumbles a lot, but even he likes her food."

"Best bunny food in the Northwest," Ted agreed as he ambled over to the picnic table.

"You can say that again." Yappy crossed to the table and removed the cover from Elias's dish. He smiled with satisfaction at the sight of the green noodles. "But I think we may have some real serious competition here, folks."

Charity heard the universal relief in the good-natured laughter that followed Yappy's comment. She felt the tension seep out of the group as everyone trooped toward the buffet table.

A few minutes later she sat down on a bench, a plate of Elias's green noodle concoction in her hand. The late summer twilight settled softly over the cove. The last rays of the setting sun turned the sky to molten gold.

Elias sat down near Charity. She glanced covertly at his plate and noticed that it was laden with her couscous and lentil salad. For some obscure reason, that pleased her.

The sound of chanting voices drifted across the cove. It was accompanied by the lilting tones of a badly played flute and the throb of a drum.

"What the hell is that?" Elias asked.

"The Voyagers," Radiance answered. "They chant the sun down every evening. You probably can't hear them from your house on the bluff, but the prevailing wind sometimes carries the sound across the cove to the pier."

"Bunch of crazies," Ted said around a mouthful of green noodles.

Radiance frowned. "I think it's a lovely ancient custom."

Elias glanced at her. "Ancient custom?"

"They used to do things like that in the old days," Radiance said.

Elias paused, a forkful of Charity's salad halfway to his mouth. "Which old days?"

Charity hid a grin.

Radiance softened her voice to a level approaching reverence. "The sixties."

"Ah." Elias nodded very soberly. "Those old days."

He caught Charity's gaze and gave her a slow, deliberate wink. She almost dropped her fork.

"Be interesting to see how long the Voyagers keep up the quaint custom after winter hits," Yappy said gruffly. "They'll freeze their asses off out there on the beach if they try that in November."

"They won't be here in November," Bea reminded him. "Like the mayor says, they'll all leave when the spaceships fail to show up as promised."

Newlin Odell raised his head abruptly. His eyes glittered with anger behind the round lenses of his wire-rimmed glasses. "That chanting-down-the-sun shit is just another stupid ritual Gwendolyn Pitt created to add a little color to her scam."

"Take it easy, Newlin," Ted advised. "So far as anyone can figure out, Pitt ain't doing anything illegal. Believe me, if there was something shady going on with the Voyagers, the town council would jump on it. They'd send the police chief out there in a red-hot minute if they had grounds."

"That's true," Yappy agreed. "Council's been looking for an excuse to get rid of the Voyagers ever since they arrived. I'm surprised Leighton Pitt isn't more upset than he is. You'd think he'd be real pissed. He owns half-interest in that old campground the Voyagers are using."

Elias ate couscous with a contemplative air. "Is there a connection between Leighton Pitt, the realtor, and Gwendolyn Pitt, the cult leader? Or is the name just a coincidence?"

"No coincidence," Bea said. "Leighton is the wealthiest man in town. Gwen is his ex-wife. They both used to run Pitt Realty together. But Leighton divorced Gwen a year ago to marry a new real estate agent named Jennifer who went to work for them. It was a real nasty mess."

Elias flicked an inquiring glance at Charity. "And Pitt's ex-wife showed up this summer with the spaceship cult in tow?"

"Uh-huh." Charity swallowed another spoonful of delicious noodles. "Makes you wonder, doesn't it?"

"Gwen's up to something, all right," Yappy said thoughtfully. "Must be cash in it somewhere. That woman always knew how to make money. Pitt was an idiot to dump her. Business hasn't been near as good for him since the divorce. Jennifer can't sell real estate the way Gwen could."

"I'll tell you one thing." Newlin's fingers clenched

around his can of pop with such force that the thin aluminum crumpled. "Gwendolyn Pitt shouldn't be allowed to get away with what she's doing. She's ruining people's lives. My Arlene turned over every cent she had to that damn cult. Someone oughta take care of Gwendolyn Pitt for good."

3

The most dangerous tides are those that swirl in the shallow waters close to shore where a man believes himself to be safe.

—"On the Way of Water," from the journal of Hayden Stone

"Things are looking up, Davis. The new owner says he's going to renew the leases."

Charity scrunched the phone between her ear and her left shoulder so that she could use both hands to unpack a box of books that had just been delivered that morning. Although she had no competition as yet from other bookstores, she believed in getting the latest titles out onto the shelves as quickly as possible. Regardless of the size of a business, good service was the best way to ensure customer loyalty. She had salvaged the Truitt chain with that simple philosophy and saw no reason to alter it with Whispers.

"You got contracts yet?" Davis asked with typical pragmatism.

"No. And you don't have to tell me that nothing is for sure until the paperwork is signed in September, but this guy is a little off-beat. Definitely not your typical business mentality. I think we may be out of the woods."

"He knows about the town's plans for Crazy Otis Landing, and he still wants to renew the leases at the old rates?" Davis still sounded skeptical.

"That's what he says." Charity smiled as she discovered twenty copies of the latest Elizabeth Lowell release in the box she had just opened. She had a long waiting list of readers who were eagerly awaiting the popular author's newest title.

"What kind of an idiot did you get for a landlord, Charity? Must be a life-is-like-a-box-of-chocolates kind of guy."

"Not exactly. He's more of a noodle type."

"Noodle? As in limp?"

Charity grinned in spite of herself. "Wrong image, Davis. Try a life-is-like-water-but-if-the-water-is-muddy-you-don't-get-a-good-reflection kind of guy."

"That doesn't sound like much of an improvement."

"Actually, he's a little hard to explain." After ten days of having Elias in the vicinity, Charity found him more intriguing than ever. Her curiosity and her fascination were both growing daily. "Anyway, about the leases. As I told you, we're not in the clear yet. But you know me and my intuition. Something tells me that Winters isn't likely to change his mind next month."

"The new owner's name is Winters?" Davis asked sharply.

"That's right. Elias Winters."

"I'll be damned." Davis whistled softly. "There wouldn't be any connection to Elias Winters of Far Seas, Inc., would there?"

"Yes. You know him?"

"Not personally." Davis paused. "But I've heard about him. Very low-profile, very high-impact. Has important connections all over the Rim. Knows the right people."

"He said something about being a consultant."

"Word has it that if you need help establishing business relationships in certain quarters, he can open doors. For a price. He can also close them, if you get my drift."

"I see. How come I've never heard of him?"

"He's strictly Pacific Rim, and Truitt wasn't involved in Rim trade when you were at the helm. But lately Meredith and I have been thinking about expanding again. Winters's name came up when I started exploring certain possibilities."

"Hmm."

"Far Seas is apparently a one-man operation," Davis continued. "Winters seems to have carved out a unique niche for himself. He handles business negotiations in small, out-of-the-way places that others ignore. Speaks two or three obscure languages that no one else can be bothered to learn. His clients are usually very rich and very low-profile. The kind of big-money movers and shakers who avoid the spotlight. Are you sure you're dealing with *that* Elias Winters?"

"That's who he claims to be. What's wrong?"

"I'm not sure," Davis admitted. "But I can tell you that, from what I've heard about him, he sure as hell isn't the type to move to a small town and run a curio shop on a pier. Keep your eyes open, Charity. My guess is he knows something you don't."

"Such as?"

"Who can tell? Maybe one of his off-shore clients is preparing to move into Whispering Waters Cove."

"And Elias is here to pave the way?"

"It's about the only scenario I can think of that fits the situation. If that's the case, there's money involved. A lot of it."

"He said he inherited the pier from Hayden Stone, our former landlord."

"Maybe he did and maybe he didn't," Davis mused.

"Are you saying that Elias Winters may have bought the pier from Hayden Stone on behalf of his off-shore client?" It worried Charity that she had not thought of that possibility herself. She hoped that she hadn't been out of the corporate world for so long that she could no longer trust her instincts. "Maybe that's why Hayden was in Seattle when he had the heart attack. He was finalizing the deal. But why would Elias lie about it?"

"Use your head, Charity," Davis said. "The pier may be just the beginning. If Winters has been hired to pick up a lot of choice real estate for a foreign investor, the last thing he'll want to do is drive up property values around Whispering Waters Cove."

"True." Charity drummed her fingers on the stack of Elizabeth Lowell books. "If he's going to buy a lot of land here, he'll try to keep the purchases quiet as long as possible. Pretending that he inherited the pier and has no immediate plans for it would be one way of deflecting curiosity."

Davis chuckled. "You told me the town council wants to go boutique. But, believe me, they ain't seen nothin' yet. Not if Winters is a player. Some of his clients are into world-class resort developments. Waterfront is perfect for them."

Charity considered the situation. The town council was already salivating at the prospect of converting Crazy Otis Landing into an upscale tourist attraction. But the mayor and the council members would go wild if they believed that a wealthy off-shore investor was preparing to turn Whispering Waters Cove into a glitzy destination resort.

"Any company moving into Whispering Waters Cove will want to pick up the land it needs as cheaply as possible before word gets out and all the locals decide to try to make a killing," Davis added. "It's common to send in a good point man to buy the big parcels before anyone knows what's happening."

Crazy Otis Landing was a nice chunk of waterfront property, Charity reflected. It could easily form the heart of a major resort. "You think Elias Winters might be acting as a point man for an off-shore investor?"

"I think it's a reasonable assumption, given what I've heard about Winters."

"But why would he agree to renew the leases at the old rates if he wanted the pier for his client?" Charity was irritated by the rising note in her own voice. There was no call to get emotional about this, she thought. This was business. She had once been very good at business.

"If I'm right, you're looking at three- to five-year planning in action," Davis explained.

"In which case, renewing the leases for another year is no big deal," Charity said glumly. "Whoever is behind the operation may not intend to start construction for another couple of years."

"Exactly. Why not let the present tenants hang around for a while? Besides, it helps maintain the low profile."

"I get the picture," Charity said. "If we want secure leases here on the pier, we'd better negotiate them for at least three years, maybe five."

"Relax," Davis said cheerfully. "It's not your problem. You've got more than enough business savvy to keep your little bookstore going regardless of what happens to the pier. In fact, a major resort would probably do wonders for your bottom line. People on vacation read a lot. You'll be okay."

But Bea, Yappy, Radiance, and Ted didn't have her skills and business acumen, Charity thought. They were not what anyone in the corporate world would call players. It was true that they had improved their business methods in the past year, but their little shops were unlikely to survive a sudden, major redevelopment of the pier.

"Thanks, Davis. Say hello to Meredith."

"I will. About time you came into the city to see us, isn't it?"

"I'll get in one of these days."

"Good." Davis hesitated. "Sure you're not bored with running that little pier shop yet?"

"I'm sure."

"I have a bet with Meredith. I give you six more months before you come back to Seattle."

"You're going to lose, Davis."

"We'll see. By the way, Charity, one more thing."

"Yes?"

"A word of warning. Watch your step with Winters. Rumor has it he's not just a player, he's a winner. Every time."

"No one wins every time, Davis."

Charity said good-bye and hung up the phone. For a while she gazed blindly at the display of mystery titles that occupied a large section of one wall.

Why was she feeling such a letdown, she wondered. She knew how the players in the business world worked. Davis had only said aloud things that she, herself, should have suspected from the start.

The truth was that she did not want to believe that Elias Winters might be deliberately deceiving her. During the past ten days she had begun to hope that he was exactly what he claimed to be. A man who had come to Whispering Waters Cove to find some answers.

A man who had something in common with her.

The soft knock on the kitchen screen door came after dinner that evening. It startled Charity, who was sitting at the table, filling out yet another in the seemingly endless series of bureaucratic forms that always threatened to drown a small business. Her pen slipped on the first letter of her name just as she was about to add her signature. The *C* came out as an odd little squiggle.

Charity threw down the pen and shot to her feet. She whirled to face the door. A dark figure loomed on the step.

"Who's there?"

"Sorry, didn't mean to scare you." Elias gazed at her through the screen. His eyes gleamed in the fading twilight.

The small jolt of fear dissolved into a tingle of relief. "You didn't scare me. I just didn't hear you." Feeling like a fool for having overreacted, she rose and went to the door. "I had a little trouble here last month. Someone trashed my house one evening while I was out attending a meeting of the town council. I guess I'm still a little jumpy."

"I didn't know Whispering Waters Cove had a crime problem."

"We don't. At least, not by city standards. The police chief, Hank Tybern, suspects some summer visitors. But there's no way to prove it. I just hope they've left the area. What are you doing here? Is something wrong?"

"No. I was out for a walk. Thought I'd stop by and

see if you'd care to join me for an evening of scintillating theatrical entertainment."

"Entertainment? What entertainment?" The temptation to open the screen door was almost overwhelming.

"A musical drama known as chanting down the sun. I can arrange front-row seats for tonight's performance if you're interested."

Charity smiled in spite of herself. "It's gotten lousy reviews."

Elias shrugged. "I figure it beats trying to conduct a conversation with Crazy Otis. He wanted to go to sleep."

"So you got bored and decided to come over here?" The minute the words were out of her mouth, she wished she could recall them.

"It was just a thought." Elias held up a hand. His expression was shadowed and unreadable. "If you'd rather do paperwork . . ."

She winced. "Hang on, I'll get my key."

He contemplated her kitchen table and chairs as she turned away from the door. "Bet you didn't buy this stuff down at Seth's New & Used Furniture Mart, did you?"

Charity flicked a glance at the sleek lines of her expensive Euro-style furnishings. "Nope. Brought it with me from Seattle. Thank God the vandals contented themselves with throwing food from the refrigerator onto the floor and writing nasty words on the walls. They didn't get around to ruining my furniture."

With the key in the pocket of her jeans and the door securely locked behind her, she joined Elias in the warm summer twilight. Without a word they walked toward the old dirt path that wound along the bluffs above the beach.

Charity had made it a habit to walk several times a

week. It was part of the self-prescribed therapy she had adopted to help herself recover from burnout. She hadn't had a panic attack in months, unless one counted the brief twinge she had gotten when Rick Swinton had tried to pressure her into a date.

The storms of anxiety had eased shortly after she had moved to Whispering Waters Cove. But she had maintained the exercise ritual along with some of the other stress-reducing techniques she had learned. They had become her talismans.

She loved the feel of the cove breeze on her face. It never failed to invigorate all her senses and clarify her mind. Tonight the effect was even stronger than usual. She was keenly aware of Elias gliding along beside her. She sensed the heat and the quiet strength in him even though he had not touched her.

"I'm sorry I snapped at you a few minutes ago," she said at last. "The crack about your coming over to see me because you were bored was rude."

"Forget it."

She hesitated and then decided to take the plunge. "I had an interesting conversation with my brother today."

There was just enough light to reveal the brief, wryly amused twist of Elias's mouth. "I assume that I was the main topic of conversation."

She sighed. "To be honest, yes. Davis said he'd heard of you and Far Seas, but he'd never met you."

"I've heard of him, too. Our paths have never crossed."

"He said I should be cautious around you, that you weren't the type to run a little curio shop on a small-town pier. He said you were probably here in Whispering Waters Cove on behalf of some big off-shore client."

Elias kept his gaze on the grove of trees that

marched down to the edge of the bluff. "My reasons for being here have nothing to do with business. Your brother's assumptions are based on a faulty premise."

"In other words, he's looking through murky water?"

"Sounds like you picked up a few things from Hayden."

Charity smiled briefly. "I liked Hayden. But I never felt as if I knew him well. There was always something distant and remote about him. It was as if he existed in his own private universe."

"You're right. He did. As far as I know, I was the only one he ever allowed into that universe."

Something buried in his dark voice caught and held Charity's attention. "He was more than a friend to you, wasn't he? And more than a teacher, too."

"Yes."

She breathed out slowly. Empathy washed away several layers of common sense and caution. "It's only been two months since his death. You must miss him."

Elias was silent for a couple of heartbeats. "I was with him when he died. Made him go to the emergency room. He kept telling me it was a waste of time, that he was going to die and that no doctor could do anything about it. But he knew that he had to let me take him to the hospital because if I didn't, I would have spent the rest of my life wondering if he could have been saved. He would have preferred to die quietly in my house."

"But you took him to the emergency room, and he died there, instead?"

"Yes." Elias looked out over the cove. "He was very calm at the end. Centered. Balanced. He died as he had lived. The last thing he said to me was that he had given me the tools to free myself. It was up to me to use them."

"Free yourself from what?"

Another beat of silence. "The need for revenge."

Charity stared at him. "Against whom?"

"It's a long story."

"I don't mind listening."

Elias did not respond for several minutes. Charity began to think he had no intention of answering her question. But after a while, he finally began to talk.

"My parents were divorced when I was ten. I lived with my mother. She . . . suffered from bouts of depression. One month after I turned sixteen, she took her own life."

"Oh, God, Elias. I'm sorry."

"I went to live with my grandparents. They never recovered from their grief. I think they always blamed my father for my mother's problems. And some of that blame shifted to me after her death. I waited for my father to send for me. I never heard from him."

Charity's throat tightened. "Where was he?"

"He ran a small air-freight business based on an island named Nihili."

Charity frowned. "I've never heard of it."

"Few people have. It's out in the Pacific. After a while I talked my grandfather into paying my way out to Nihili. It wasn't hard."

"What happened to your father?"

"Dad had a rival, a man named Garrick Keyworth."

Charity said nothing when he paused again. She simply waited.

"Keyworth sabotaged Dad's only plane. My father knew it, but he took off, anyway. The plane went down out over the ocean."

Charity was stunned. Whatever she had been expecting, it wasn't a tale of murder. "If that's the truth, then it seems to me that you had every right to want revenge against this Keyworth."

"It's not as simple as it sounds. Things rarely are. Dad knew the plane had fuel line problems that day, but he chose to take the chance and fly. He had contracts to fulfill. One of the things I never wanted to admit to myself was that he made his own decision to risk his life."

A flash of intuition went through Charity. "He not only risked his own life, he risked leaving you alone, didn't he?"

"You could say that." Elias's smile contained no humor. "Hayden certainly said it a few times."

"Your father may have been guilty of poor judgment, but if you ask me, that still doesn't absolve this Garrick Keyworth. Not by a long shot."

"No, it doesn't. To make a long story short, I arrived on Nihili a couple of days after Dad had gone down. It was Hayden who met me at the airstrip. For reasons of his own, reasons I never fully understood, he accepted me as his personal responsibility. He finished the task of raising me. Helped me start my business. Taught me how to be a man. I owe him more than I can ever repay."

Charity swallowed to keep herself from bursting into tears. "I see. What about the man who sabotaged your father's plane?"

"It took me a long time to learn his identity. After I found out who he was, I spent years devising a way to bring down his empire. And then Hayden died."

"And that changed things?"

"Everything. I looked at Keyworth's reflection in a different light after I said good-bye to Hayden. One of the things I hadn't seen before was that Keyworth has paid a price for his crime. He knows that everything he has today is founded on that one act of destruction. It's eating at his soul. It's what drives him, and it will ultimately destroy him. It's already cost him more than he even knows. I decided to leave him to the prison he's built for himself."

Charity exhaled deeply. "That's a very philosophical way of looking at it. Downright metaphysical, in fact. No offense, but I find it a little hard to believe that you just walked away from that situation and left Keyworth to the great wheel of cosmic justice."

Elias's dark brows rose. "Very perceptive of you. You're right. I wasn't exactly a saint about the whole thing. I went to see Keyworth before I came here. Showed him some documents that proved beyond a doubt that I had the contacts and connections to cripple, possibly even destroy, his operations in the Pacific. *Then* I walked away."

Charity was speechless for a few seconds. "And left him to live with the knowledge that you had had him in your power and let him go?"

"I decided I owed myself that much, at least."

She drew a deep breath. "Very subtle. Perhaps too subtle. Keyworth may think you backed off simply because you were too weak to go through with your plans. Or because you lost your nerve."

"I doubt it," Elias said quietly. "I studied him for a long time before I made my move. I know him well."

"You think that the knowledge that he was vulnerable to you will add to the pressure that's building inside him?"

"Perhaps." Elias made a small, dismissing movement with his hand. "Perhaps not. It doesn't matter. Keyworth no longer concerns me."

"Yet you spent years plotting against him?"

"It takes time to set up the kind of vengeance I planned."

Charity held her breeze-tossed hair out of her eyes. "Did you have the confrontation with Keyworth shortly before you moved here?"

"Yes."

"Whew. You've been through a lot during the past couple of months, haven't you? The death of your friend Hayden, the showdown with Keyworth, a major career shift, and a move to a new location."

He glanced at her with a curious expression. "What's that supposed to mean?"

"Just that you'd score pretty high right now if you were to take one of those psych tests that measures recent stressful events in your life."

"I don't plan to take any psych tests."

"No, I don't suppose you do." For some reason the thought of Elias sitting down to a battery of psychological tests almost made her smile. "You'll probably just gaze into a nice, clear pool of water instead."

"It works for me."

She gave him a sidelong look. "Mind if I ask you a question?"

He appeared to brace himself. "No."

"Why did you tell me all this? On the first day we met I got the distinct impression that you were the strong, silent type."

He smiled. "Still suspicious of me?"

"I prefer to think of it as cautious. Suspicious has paranoid connotations, and I don't think I'm that far over the edge."

"All right. Cautious. The answer to your question is that I gave you a piece of my privacy as a gift because I want something from you in exchange."

"Damn it, I *knew* it." And he had known just how to get past her defenses, she thought furiously.

She was not hurt or even disappointed, she told herself. She had known there would be a catch to this little evening stroll. Elias wasn't the kind of man who would share intimate secrets with anyone unless he had an ulterior motive.

"Let's hear it," she snapped. "What do you want from me? If this has something to do with the lease negotiations, you're wasting your time."

"I don't care about the lease arrangements. All I want from you is the chance to get to know you."

She came to a sudden halt and swung around to face him. "I beg your pardon?"

"You heard me." As if it were the most natural thing in the world, as if they shared a regular habit of walking along the bluffs in the evening, Elias reached out and took her hand. "My turn to ask you a question."

4

The approaching storm turns the surface of the sea to steel
and silver. Only danger reflects clearly from such a mirror.
—"On the Way of Water," from the journal of Hayden Stone

Charity instinctively tensed as Elias's powerful hand
wrapped around her fingers. He was strong. Stronger
than she had realized. But she still did not sense so
much as a tiny frisson of the old claustrophobic sensation that had seized her during the days when she had
dated Brett Loftus. And certainly nothing of the
twinge of the fight-or-flight response she had felt last
month when Rick Swinton, Gwendolyn Pitt's assistant
cult manager, had attempted to sweep her off her feet
with his oily charm.

At least she now knew for certain that she was
not going to be stuck for the rest of her life with
panic attacks every time a man touched her. What
a relief.

Euphoria shot through her. *Cured at last.* She felt a ridiculous grin curve her mouth.

And then she became aware of an eerie thrill curling through her insides. The sensation was not one of sharp, terrifying anxiety, but it certainly did not have a calming effect.

It took her a moment to recognize the devastating sweep of raw desire. She stopped grinning, caught her breath, and nearly stumbled when she realized exactly what it was that was affecting her senses. So this was how real sexual attraction felt.

"Are you okay?" Elias asked as he steadied her.

"Yes." Damn. She was actually breathless. "Yes, I'm fine. Tripped over a little stone. Hard to see clearly at this time of night. It'll be full dark soon."

He gave her an odd look but said nothing.

She'd had one or two pleasant, sincere relationships over the years, no more than a couple because there had never been any time. Her life had not been her own since the day the avalanche had killed her mother and stepfather. Saving Truitt for the next generation had been her only focus. Then she had developed that stupid phobia to poor Brett.

What with one thing and another, she had never experienced anything even remotely akin to this wild, fluttering excitement.

Please don't let this be another kind of precursor to an anxiety attack, she thought. *Please. Not with this man. No more dumb phobias. This feels too good.*

What shook her was the sense of intimacy involved. It was as if Elias was allowing her to sample some of his own personal energy. She wondered if he was getting a few tingles from her. Then she wondered what it would be like to kiss him.

Different, she decided after due consideration. Very different. About as out-of-the-ordinary, say, as the arrival of a fleet of spaceships carrying aliens from outer space.

"All right, it's your turn," she said briskly. "What's your question?"

"Hayden mentioned once that when you opened your bookshop a year ago, you single-handedly revived the rest of the businesses on Crazy Otis Landing."

Charity made a face. "That's a gross exaggeration. Tourism has been gradually increasing here in the cove for a couple of years. We've been discovered in a small way, and the pier is a natural draw. All that was necessary was to provide a reason for visitors and locals to stop. A bookstore does that nicely."

"He also told me that under your influence, the other shopkeepers have become more businesslike this past year. He said they come to you for advice. He credited you with convincing Bea to install an espresso machine, for example."

"I had the advantage of having spent several years in the corporate world," she reminded him. "I wasn't cut out for it, but I certainly learned a few things. When the others come to me with questions, I try to help. But the truth is, I owe them far more than they owe me."

"How's that?"

She hesitated, just as he had earlier, searching for the right words. "When I first came to the cove, I was completely burned out." She slanted a quick glance at his profile. "You probably heard a few of the rumors?"

"A few."

She exhaled deeply. "Well, most of them were true. I did make an incredibly embarrassing scene on the night I was to become engaged to a very nice man named Brett Loftus. Had a panic attack, in fact. Right there in front of half the movers and shakers of Seattle. I felt terrible. I mean, it wasn't Brett's fault that he was too big and that I didn't . . . well, never mind."

"Too big?" Elias's voice was oddly neutral.

"Yes, you know." Charity waved a hand in a vague gesture. "Too tall. Too large. All over. For me, that is." That wasn't fair, she thought. Her therapist had explained that Brett's size hadn't been the real problem. Unfortunately, her brain had linked her fear of the relationship with his physical stature. The result had become a full-blown phobia.

"I see." Elias's tone sounded even more strange.

"Have you ever met him?"

"No. But I've seen him. I heard him speak once at a luncheon at one of my clients' business clubs."

"I'm sure that he would be just fine for another woman," she said hastily. "My stepsister, for instance. Lots of women admire, uh, size in a man."

"I've heard that."

"But every time poor Brett . . . well, you know. I just couldn't stand it. He was such a gentleman. He attributed my problems to stress. It was really very awkward."

"Sure. Awkward."

"But the bottom line was that when it came right down to it, the thought of . . . of . . ." She felt herself blush furiously and was profoundly grateful for the deepening shadows. "Doing it. On a regular basis, that is. The way one would in marriage . . . I mean, a man as big as that, well, it was just too much."

"I think I get the picture."

She cleared her throat. "At any rate, the merger I had planned for months did not go through."

"You stepped down from the helm of Truitt department stores."

"Yes. With no warning to my stepbrother and stepsister. I just abandoned them. I spent a few weeks getting therapy, realized I could never go back to the business world, and decided to move. I more or less threw a dart at a map of Washington. And here I am."

"What happened next?"

"A funny thing." Charity smiled. "I rested. Walked a lot here along the bluffs. Got back into cooking. And then one day I went looking for something to read and realized that Whispering Waters Cove had no bookshop. I went down to the pier and talked it over with Hayden. He rented space to me. Within a couple of months I started to feel reasonably normal again."

"You know," Elias said thoughtfully, "under your management, Whispers would flourish in a boutique version of Whispering Waters Cove. You have nothing to fear and everything to gain if the town council's plans work out."

"I'm doing fine as it is. I prefer slow, steady growth. Big leaps are hazardous in business. If you crash, you go down in flames. Besides, my aspirations aren't as high as they used to be. I like small business. I think it's a calling. You get to know your customers personally. There's something very satisfying about it."

"But there's no reason to tie the future of your business to that of the other businesses on the pier," Elias insisted. "Why are you doing it? Why form the shopkeepers association? Why do battle with the mayor and the town council?"

Charity frowned, puzzled by his line of inquiry. "The other shopkeepers are my friends. They welcomed me with open arms when I first came to Whispering Waters Cove. They were generous and supportive, and they've been good neighbors."

"So in order to pay them back, you've committed

yourself to helping them hang on to Crazy Otis Landing?"

"It was the least I could do. You've met them. None of them are what you'd call sophisticated businesspeople. A big corporation would roll right over them."

"True," Elias admitted.

"They all ended up on the pier because there was nowhere else for them to go. They've formed a community. They need each other. I think Hayden understood that."

Elias smiled wryly. "Hayden had no interest in going boutique, himself."

"All I want to do is give the pier shopkeepers a chance to stay where they are as the town begins to pull in more visitors and tourists."

"Do you think that Yappy and Ted and the rest can learn to compete with a bunch of art galleries?"

"If necessary." Charity shrugged. "But who knows? Maybe the upscale shops will never materialize."

"In the meanwhile, you've thrown in your lot with the pier crowd."

She studied him with a long, considering glance. "So have you. If you're telling me the truth about Far Seas' intentions, that is."

The sound of an off-key flute and loud voices rising and falling in an enthusiastic chant forestalled whatever response Elias might have made to her deliberate challenge.

"Looks like the show has started," he said as they emerged from the trees.

Charity looked around. They had reached the outskirts of the old campground. A large assortment of recreational vehicles were clustered together on the bluff overlooking the cove. Several of the vehicles had been decorated with designs that vaguely resembled ancient Egyptian motifs. Others were painted with imaginative futuristic landscapes and bizarre visions of the universe.

There was no one in sight. Gwendolyn Pitt's followers were all down on the beach.

At some point in the distant past, a long fence had been installed along the edge of the bluffs. It stretched the length of the campground. There were two openings, one in the center and one at the far end. Each provided access to a narrow path that led down to the rocky beach.

The droning chant filled the air. Charity looked over the edge of the sagging fence and saw the Voyagers gathered below at the water's edge. There were about twenty of them, she estimated. The number had grown during the past week. There was just enough light left to make out the flowing blue and white robes and the brightly beaded headbands that comprised the cult's uniform.

She saw that the small crowd had formed a circle and linked hands. They swayed to the beat of the drum and flute.

The last of the coppery twilight glow disappeared as the sun sank out of sight behind the mountains. The first star appeared. The chants grew louder. The drum beat faster.

A dynamic figure broke free of the circle and raised her arms above her head in a commanding gesture. Silence fell. The Voyagers turned to face her with murmurs of anticipation.

"That's Gwendolyn Pitt," Charity said to Elias.

"I know. She introduced herself the other day at the grocery store."

"Did she? I've talked to her a few times during the past month. She seems committed to her concept, but I can't quite bring myself to buy into her act. Something about seeing a successful, hard-nosed realtor turn into space alien guru is a little tough to swallow."

"You can say that again." Elias studied the woman on the beach with a thoughtful expression. "Looks like she shops at the same places Radiance Barker does."

He was right, Charity decided. Gwendolyn Pitt looked as if she could have stepped straight out of one of the sixties' era posters Radiance had used to decorate the nail salon.

When she raised her arms, the sleeves of Gwendolyn's gown fell back to reveal rows of wide metal bracelets. But there was still the hint of the professional real estate saleswoman about her in her short, tailored, artificially blond hair and expensive shoes. It did not take much imagination to picture Gwen Pitt in a crisp business suit with a briefcase in hand.

She was in her late forties, not especially attractive, but her features were strong and assertive. There was a certain steely quality about her. Whatever else she was, she was a driven woman. Charity could almost see the sparks.

"Five nights, my friends," Gwendolyn intoned in a loud, sonorous voice that carried up the side of the bluff. "Only five more nights until the great starships come. Midnight of the appointed day will soon be here, and *they* will arrive in all their brilliant splendor."

"Something tells me that woman knows how to close a deal," Elias said.

"Enlightenment awaits, my friends," Gwendolyn continued in rolling accents. "Unparalleled knowledge of our own true sexuality and an understanding of the philosophical laws of the universe shall be ours. Our bodies will be made perfect by advanced alien science. Our lifespans will be vastly extended in order that we may have the time to learn all that we are destined to discover."

The crowd sent up a rousing shout of agreement.

"That is one angry lady," Elias said softly.

Charity glanced at him curiously. "How do you know that?"

"It takes a lot of rage to pull together an operation the size of this scam."

Charity recalled what he had just finished telling her about his own plans to destroy an old enemy. Elias knew whereof he spoke, she thought. She would do well to bear that in mind. The sizzling sexual attraction she was feeling was certainly interesting, but that was no excuse for being stupid where this man was concerned.

"Maybe she really is simply deluded," Charity mused. "I suppose it's possible that she actually believes that the spaceships will arrive."

Elias studied the scene on the beach. "If you're prepared to buy that, I've got a nice pier I can sell you. No, she's not crazy, she's got an agenda. Be interesting to know what it is."

"Power?"

"That's probably part of it, but not the whole. If she just wanted to run a cult for the sake of exercising power, she wouldn't have announced such a close deadline for the arrival of the spaceships."

"I wondered about that myself," Charity said. "The Voyagers just got here last month, and the fifteenth of August is only five days away. She's bound to lose a lot of credibility when the ships don't show."

Elias braced a booted foot on the bottom rung of the fence. He kept his grip on Charity's hand. "There must be some significance to the deadline."

"Most people think she's in it for the money. Newlin says that his girlfriend, Arlene, and the others have turned over their life savings to her."

"That's standard procedure for this kind of thing. But why bring her followers to Whispering Waters Cove? The place has got to hold some bad memories."

"And humiliation." Charity grew thoughtful. "The new Mrs. Pitt is here, after all. Gwen and Jennifer must run into each other at the grocery store and at the post office. A little awkward, to say the least."

"How's Gwen's ex, the real estate broker, dealing with it?"

"Are you kidding?" Charity made a face. "I'm sure Leighton is thoroughly embarrassed by the situation, but he can't force her to leave. She does own half-interest in this campground, after all. He's trying to ignore her."

"And the second Mrs. Pitt? What's her response?"

"I don't really know Jennifer very well. No one does. She's from California."

Elias grinned briefly. "That explains a lot."

"From what I've seen, she's keeping her cool about the whole thing," Charity said. "I guess she figures all she has to do is wait it out until the fifteenth. But it can't be easy for her, either."

"Nothing like having the first Mrs. Pitt running a cult on the edge of town while the second Mrs. Pitt tries to establish herself as the new wife of one of the most influential men in the area."

"True."

"Were you here at the time of the divorce?"

Charity shook her head. "The scandal broke shortly before I arrived. But I know most of the juicy details, thanks to Radiance."

"What's Radiance got to do with any of this?"

Charity chuckled. "She does the second Mrs. Pitt's nails. She's actually grateful to her because Jennifer did a lot to help make fancy acrylic nails fashionable here in town. Until Jennifer showed up with her long, perfect, California red nails, everyone else just used nail clippers."

"How scandalous was the divorce?"

Charity regarded him with speculation. "You know, you don't look like the type to be interested in sordid gossip."

"I collect information," Elias said softly. "Sort of a hobby."

"Hmm, well, according to Radiance, the whole thing blew up one day early last summer when Gwendolyn showed the old Rossiter place to some clients. They all walked into the cottage, which is located in a very isolated location near the point, and found Jennifer and Leighton in bed together."

"Not a pretty picture."

"No. Radiance told me that Leighton and Jennifer had been using the Rossiter place for their rendezvous for several weeks before they were discovered."

"Rough way for Gwen to learn that her husband was cheating on her," Elias said.

"Yes. You can imagine how the gossip flared up again when Gwen and her Voyagers arrived in town last month."

Elias looked down at the beach and watched as Gwendolyn held forth on the exciting events that would take place on the fifteenth. "Something tells me that the fuel that runs Gwendolyn Pitt's engine comes from something more than old-fashioned power and greed."

Charity was suddenly acutely aware of the swift fall of night. The shadows were lengthening around the looming motor homes and campers. "What else besides power and money could motivate her to go to all this effort?"

Elias shifted his enigmatic gaze from the scene on the beach to Charity's face. "You have to ask me that after what I just told you about my plans for Garrick Keyworth?"

"Vengeance? But that doesn't make any sense. How could all this"—Charity spread her free arm out to indicate the Voyagers and their campground—"be about vengeance?"

"I don't know. I'm only saying that there are other motives in the world besides power and money."

The cove breeze shifted. It tugged at Charity's shirt-sleeves. She pushed a tendril of hair out of her eyes. "Maybe we'll get the answers on the morning after the spaceships fail to show."

"Maybe." Elias's enigmatic gaze rested on her face.

"There's one thing I'm certain of," Charity continued.

"What's that?"

She wrinkled her nose in disgust. "Gwen Pitt's motives might be obscure, but her sleazy right-hand man, Rick Swinton, is very obvious. He's in this for the money. I'd stake Whispers on it."

"I haven't run into Swinton yet."

"You haven't missed anything." Charity shuddered. "A real creep."

Elias eyed her. "That sounds personal."

"It is. He made a pass at me shortly after the Voyagers got here. The cove is not exactly a mecca for singles, but I wasn't desperate enough to go out with him. When I declined his invitation, he told me I'd be sorry."

Elias grew still. "He threatened you?"

"Not exactly. Just said I'd regret turning him down." Charity smiled. "Believe me, I didn't."

"I'll keep an eye out for him." Elias's hand tightened on hers. "In the meantime, I've got another very important question."

The dark velvet of his voice sent more little chills of excitement down her spine. "What's that?"

"I've been wondering," he said very softly, "how your mouth tastes."

She stared at him. "I beg your pardon?"

"I've been thinking about it for the past ten days." He pulled her gently, inexorably, closer.

She met his eyes, saw the controlled desire in him, and was nearly overwhelmed by the sense of inevitability that descended on her. She knew then that she had been waiting for this ever since he had knocked on her door earlier that evening.

Again she stiffened, instinctively searching for the smallest sign of the heightened anxiety that presaged a panic episode. But all she felt was the rush of sensual anticipation.

Elias was definitely the right size.

He kept one foot on the lowest rung of the fence railing as he drew her forward. A delicious shock went through her when she found herself standing in the intimate space created between his thighs.

The background murmur of the light cove surf and Gwendolyn Pitt's exhortations to her followers faded into the distance. Charity dimly realized that her senses simply could not focus on all the normal stimuli that surrounded her. They were fully engaged with the feel of Elias's hard, lean body against hers. She could feel the heat of him. It drew her with the power of a magic spell.

She reminded herself that just because Elias had confided in her didn't mean that she could trust him. She couldn't even be certain that he had told her the truth. He was a subtle, clever man. Moreover, there was no doubt but that he was a little weird.

Davis's warnings echoed in her brain. *Watch your step with Winters. Rumor has it he's not just a player, he's a winner. Every time.*

But Elias's touch did not trigger any warnings from her nervous system. On the contrary, the closer she got, the closer she wanted to be.

When he lowered his head to take her mouth, she learned in one shattering second that everything she had suspected was true. Kissing Elias was definitely a different experience. Hot, sexy, and incredibly satisfying.

A spectacular flower that had been dormant within her all of her life suddenly blossomed. Elias's muscled thigh tightened against her hip, trapping her between his legs. She put her arms around his neck and parted her lips.

Elias groaned. A shudder went through him.

Charity was enthralled by the sensations that poured through her. Elias's kiss was darker and more mysterious than the fall of night. It was full of arcane secrets and layers of unfathomable meanings. It would take a lifetime to explore this kiss. Joy and excitement soared within her as she sank into the unplumbed depths.

"Damn." Elias tore his mouth from hers with an abrupt, wrenching movement of his head. He sucked in a deep breath.

Charity gazed up at him, astonished. His eyes glittered in the shadows. His expression was grim. His breathing was harsh and ragged, as if he had just run a marathon.

"Sorry," he muttered. "This is happening too fast. I didn't intend it to be like this. Not so soon. Didn't want to rush you."

"It's okay, really." She touched the side of his cheek and felt his jaw clench in response. An invigorating sense of her own feminine power rose within her. "I don't mind in the least."

Elias looked bemused, almost dazed. He stared down at her for a long time and then, with another smothered groan, he covered her mouth once more.

He did what Charity would have sworn was impossible: He deepened the kiss. His arms tightened around her in an urgent move that settled her hips more snugly against his fierce erection. He slid one hand to her ribs and moved it slowly upward until his thumb rested just beneath the weight of one breast.

It was Charity's turn to shudder.

Somewhere in the distance, she heard the chanting resume down on the beach, but she paid no attention. The only thing that mattered in that moment was Elias. His palm moved again, closing over her breast. She could feel the heat of his hand through the fabric of her shirt.

The first muffled shouts barely registered on her awareness. She tuned them out without realizing it until Elias suddenly broke off the drugging kiss.

"What the hell?" He raised his head, listening.

Charity blinked, trying to clear her mind. She felt the sexual tension in Elias transmute into another, equally primitive kind of readiness.

Disoriented, she started to step back.

Another cry sounded.

This time Charity heard it clearly. A woman's voice, half angry, half fearful. "Get your hands off me. I'll tell her. I swear, I will!"

"It came from back there," Elias said. "On the far side of the rest rooms, I think."

He released Charity and spun around in a single, lithe movement. He moved off with an easy, ground-eating stride that took him between a row of aging campers.

Charity saw that he was heading toward a maroon and white motor home parked toward the rear of the campground.

"Let me go, damn you! I'll tell Gwendolyn."

Charity broke into a run and flew after Elias.

By the time she caught up with him, he was vaulting up the steps of the maroon and white motor home. She watched as he yanked open the metal door and exploded through it into the interior.

She heard a startled scream from inside the big vehicle. It was followed by an angry, masculine shout.

"What the hell are you doing?" a man squawked. "Take your goddamned hands off me or I'll have you arrested."

Charity came to an abrupt halt as a figure stumbled wildly through the open door of the motor home. She recognized Rick Swinton immediately.

He wasn't nearly as handsome as usual, she reflected with a sense of satisfaction. In fact, he looked quite silly standing there, flailing about on the top step.

Rick missed his footing and fell. He landed on the ground with an audible grunt.

Elias appeared in the doorway. He was as serene and unruffled as the eye of a hurricane.

Charity surveyed him anxiously. "Are you all right?"

Elias glanced at her as if surprised by the question. "Yes. This jerk was manhandling a woman inside."

"Shit." Rick spit dirt out of his mouth and heaved himself to a sitting position. He shoved curling brown hair out of his eyes and glowered furiously at Elias. "I'm going to have you arrested, you bastard. You hear me, you sonofabitch? I'm gonna sue you for this."

"Going to be a little tough to file a lawsuit and get

a judgment before the spaceships arrive on Monday." Elias came slowly down the steps. "But you're welcome to try."

A young, attractive woman came to stand in the doorway. She clutched the lapels of her Voyager robe.

"Arlene." Charity stared, astonished. "Good grief. Are you okay?"

"Yeah, I'm okay." In the dim glow of a weak campground light Arlene appeared flushed and angry. Her sandy brown hair had come free of her headband and stood out in wild disarray around her shoulders. She glared at Rick as she straightened the folds of her long hooded, white robe. "Don't you touch me again, Rick Swinton. Do you hear me? Not ever again."

"Did he hurt you?" Charity hurried toward the motor home steps.

"He's a nasty little liar, but he didn't hurt me." Arlene blinked. "What are you doing here, Charity?"

"Elias and I were just out for an evening stroll, and we heard you shouting."

Rick heaved himself to his feet and brushed the seat of his black designer chinos. His Voyager blue silk shirt, which he wore open down to the navel, was also covered with dust. The multitude of gold chains that he wore around his neck glinted in the dim light. He gave Charity a sullen glare. "Should have minded your own damn business. Not everyone has your problem with sex. Some of us are normal."

Elias glanced at Charity as he went down the steps. "You two know each other?"

"Meet Rick Swinton," Charity said. "Gwen Pitt's assistant."

Elias surveyed Rick with cold disdain. "Let's skip the handshake, Swinton, I might be tempted to break your arm."

Rick narrowed his eyes. "You'll be sorry, whoever you are."

"The name is Winters. Elias Winters. Be sure you spell it right when you file your complaint."

"S.O.B."

"This is Arlene Fenton," Charity put her arm lightly around Arlene's shoulders. "She's Newlin's friend."

Elias nodded.

"Oh, my God, Newlin." Arlene's chin came up sharply. Her eyes grew very round. "Charity, promise me you won't tell him about this. It'll only upset him something fierce. You know it will. He's already having a real bad time with the idea of me going off on the ships."

"What, exactly, happened here?" Charity asked.

"Rick told me he had some special information about what's going to happen when the ships come," Arlene whispered. "He told me that I had been chosen as one of the vanguard who would make initial contact. He said he was going to teach me the secret code we'll use to communicate with the aliens."

"Bullshit." Rick gave her a fulminating look. "She came on to me, same as every other bitch under the age of sixty in this burg. When I took her up on the offer, she suddenly turned all righteous. Little cock tease, that's all she is. Just like you, Ms. Tightass Truitt. You're both the kind that gets a man worked up and then yells rape when he tries to get a sample of what they're offering."

"One more word," Elias said softly, "and you won't be in any condition to ask for more samples from any female."

Arlene flung back her head. "You're lying, Rick Swinton. I've been preparing myself for the Journey, just like Gwendolyn told us to do. We're all supposed to be getting ready to move to a higher plane where sex will be a pure, nonphysical experience."

"Give me a break," Swinton muttered.

"And what's more," Arlene shot back, "if I was going to fool around, it wouldn't be with you. I've got me a fine boyfriend, and I'm going to make sure he comes with me when it's time to go aboard the ships. And I'll tell you something else, if Gwendolyn knew how you acted when her back was turned, she'd send you packing."

"Goddamned little bitch." Rick backed up hurriedly when Elias moved in the shadows. "Keep your hands off me, Winters."

"Oh, let him be," Arlene said with acute disgust. "I'm all right, and you can bet I won't let him get me alone again. He's perverted, if you ask me. You should see what he's got inside his motor home. And he thinks it's sexy. Well, I can tell you none of it will matter after next Monday night."

"You can say that again." Rick swung around and stalked off down a dark corridor formed by several campers and some motor homes.

Charity gave Arlene a small hug. "Are you sure you're okay?"

"I'm fine." Arlene heaved a deep sigh. "Rick's a sneaky little twerp who uses his position as Gwendolyn's assistant to try to get it on with every female Voyager in sight. First time he's ever tried anything with me, though."

Elias stirred. "You said that if Gwendolyn knew about his behavior, she'd get rid of him. If that's the case, why don't you tell her?"

"The thing is, she's got so much on her mind right now." Arlene looked uneasy. "Most of us only see her at the evening sundown chant. She spends the rest of her time in her motor home preparing for Monday night. Rick's the only one who's allowed to interrupt her when she's meditating or pursuing her studies."

"I could get her attention for you," Elias offered. "No problem."

"I don't want to cause her any trouble," Arlene said quickly. "Rick Swinton isn't important. He's such a turkey, I wouldn't be surprised if he gets left behind when the aliens come."

"Don't worry," Elias said. "Something tells me that Swinton won't be going on board any starship at midnight on the fifteenth. And neither will anyone else."

Arlene straightened her shoulders with grave dignity. "I can see that you're a nonbeliever. But you and all the others will learn the truth for yourselves. I just wish I could get Newlin to understand. I can't bear the thought of leaving him behind."

Charity patted her shoulder. "Newlin cares about you, Arlene. If things don't work out, remember that he'll be here waiting for you."

Tears glistened in Arlene's eyes. She wiped them away with the back of her hand. "But I want him to come with me to see the galaxy. If he stays behind, he'll be dead and turned to dust by the time I get back."

Elias looked at her. "Sometimes the surface of the water is so distorted by a passing storm that you can't see any truth in it."

Arlene blinked away a few more tears and stared at him uncomprehendingly. "Huh?"

Charity gave her another little hug. "Don't worry about it, Arlene. Elias can be a little obscure. It's not his fault. He was raised that way. Come on, we'll walk you back to your trailer."

"You don't have to do that. I'm okay, honest." Arlene gave Charity an anxious glance. "You won't tell Newlin about what just happened, will you?"

Charity hesitated. "If that's what you want."

"What I really want is for Newlin to come with me on the spaceship." Arlene turned and trailed off into the shadows.

"I hope she's not going to be too depressed on Monday night when nothing happens," Charity said a short while later as she and Elias walked home.

"She'll have Newlin to comfort her."

Startled by the brusque tone of his voice, Charity gave him a searching look. It was impossible to see his expression in the darkness.

"Elias?"

"Yes?"

"You're sure you're okay? Rick didn't get a punch in, did he?"

"I'm okay."

Charity relaxed slightly. "That was very kind of you to go to Arlene's assistance."

Elias did not respond. He was obviously lost in his own churning thoughts.

Charity knew a no-trespassing sign when she saw one. She stopped talking and allowed the sounds of the night and the cove to fill the tense silence.

When they reached her cottage, she took out her key and walked up the porch steps to her front door. Elias made no attempt to follow her. He stood waiting at the bottom of the steps as she fitted her key into the lock.

She looked back at him as she opened the door, wondering what he would say if she invited him inside. The porch light etched his face in sharp, contrasting planes of light and shadow. He looked very remote, very distant. Back in control. She decided that in this mood he would refuse an offer of tea or a nightcap.

"Thanks for asking me to join you on your evening

walk." Deliberately she infused her voice with as much forced brightness as possible. "It was interesting, to say the least."

"Charity?"

She froze warily in the doorway. "Yes?"

"Did I scare you?"

Of all the things she might have expected him to say at that moment, his question was one she would never have imagined. "Scare me? You mean, with the way you tackled Rick Swinton? Don't be silly. Of course you didn't scare me. I was glad you tossed him out of the motor home. He deserved to land on his rear in the dirt. Arlene's right. He's a little twerp."

"I'm not talking about Swinton."

"Oh."

"I'm talking about us," Elias said very softly.

Her mouth went dry. She knew now that he was referring to the devastating intensity of the kiss they had shared. A kiss that had left him as shaken as it had her, she thought with rising satisfaction. Not that he would ever admit it.

Suddenly she felt incredibly cheerful. Incredibly sexy. Downright flirtatious. She folded her arms beneath her breasts and propped one shoulder against the doorjamb, trying for an air of unruffled, sophisticated aplomb.

"Do I look scared?" she asked.

"No."

She smiled. "What are you up to, Elias Winters?"

"Don't you know?"

"Enlighten me."

He held her eyes with unwavering intensity. There was no humor in that gaze. None at all. For Elias this was deadly serious, Charity realized. She felt a little sorry for him.

"I'm trying to start an affair with you," Elias said.

It took a determined effort, but she managed to get her mouth closed after a few stunned seconds. "I thought you were the subtle type."

"Is that an affirmative or a negative response?"

Charity struggled to maintain a few shreds of her composure. Damn if she would let him turn her into a babbling idiot. She took refuge in her old executive style.

"It's an I'll-get-back-to-you-on-that response," she said.

He nodded, accepting her words without comment. "Good night, Charity."

"Good night." Charity stepped back into the safety of her tiny hallway and very carefully closed and locked the door. Then she sagged weakly against it.

After a moment, she recovered sufficiently to go to the window and peek through the blinds. But she was too late to see Elias leave. He had already vanished into the night.

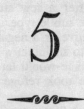

5

Volcanoes simmer beneath the deepest seas.

—"On the Way of Water," from the journal of Hayden Stone

He had not scared Charity, but he had certainly done a hell of a job scaring himself.

Two days later Elias still could not stop brooding over the kiss on the bluff.

He had just wanted to test the waters. Wade in the shallows. Check to see if the attraction was mutual. He had not expected to get caught by a riptide and swept out to sea before he knew what hit him.

Years of daily exercise, both physical and mental, designed to cultivate maximum internal balance and self-discipline, all gone in an instant. So much for playing it cool.

It had taken an hour of contemplation beside the garden pool, a cold shower, and a shot of whiskey to control the hungry need that had set his senses on edge Wednesday night. The temptation to walk back to Charity's cottage, knock on the door, and ask her to take him into her bed had nearly unhinged him.

Scary. Very scary.

But he was back in control now, he assured himself. Two days of intense Tal Kek Chara workouts had reestablished the balance of his inner flow.

Sort of.

Elias stood behind his counter with Crazy Otis stationed beside him on the fake tree limb. Together they watched as Charity moved up and down the crowded aisles of Charms & Virtues, clipboard in hand.

With a woman like this, you had to be careful what you asked for, Elias reflected. This morning he had foolishly asked for some business marketing advice.

At the time he had been pleased with the subtle maneuver. He had thought to use the request as an excuse to spend more time with her. He had envisioned giving her tea in the intimate privacy of the tiny office behind the cash register counter.

But she had taken his request far too seriously. She was attacking the job of whipping his business into shape with gusto.

If she had experienced any serious aftereffects from that out-of-control kiss two days ago, they certainly didn't show, he thought morosely. "I'll get back to you on that," she had said when he'd told her that he wanted to have an affair. It was as if she had sensed the weakness in him and knew herself to be in the driver's seat.

Dangerous. But a challenge he could not resist.

"We'll have to find Hayden's supplier files and order info." Charity paused to pick up a pen off a stack marked *Spy Pens—Write Your Secret Messages in Invisible Ink.* "I have no idea where he got most of this stuff."

"There's a big stack of order catalogs in the office," Elias offered.

He studied the graceful, vulnerable curve of the nape of her neck. He was sorely tempted to come out from behind the barricade of the sales counter and see what would happen if he touched that sexy place beneath her hair. He resisted the urge. He had the raw fire of unrequited lust tamped down now, but the force of it was undiminished. Unfortunately the flames burned all the hotter for being banked.

Control was everything in Tal Kek Chara.

"Check the business records in his old filing cabinet. There should be invoices from the companies he used on a regular basis." Charity put aside the invisible ink pen and blew dust off a collection of tiny, carved wooden boxes. "I'll have Newlin bring over one of our extra feather dusters. A clean shop has eye appeal."

"I don't know." Elias surveyed the layer of grime on top of the fortune-teller's booth. "I think the dust adds atmosphere."

"That's ridiculous." Charity brushed her hands together. "It makes the place look untended. Also, you really should do something to improve the lighting in here. It looks like the inside of a cave."

"A couple of kids wandered in yesterday afternoon. I think they liked the spooky effect."

"Anything that makes it hard for your customers to see what you have to sell doesn't help business." Charity picked up a small box and probed curiously at the latch.

"Uh, Charity, be careful with that. Those little chests are filled with—"

"Don't get me wrong. I agree that it's a good idea to maintain an air of mystery in a shop like Charms &

Virtues, but you don't want to overdo it. Maybe some old-fashioned lamps, especially in the back section, would be the—aaaah!"

A large, furry spider leaped out of the box.

"Oh-my-god!" Charity shrieked again and hurled box and spider into the air.

"Heh-heh-heh." Crazy Otis sidled along his perch, shiny eyes glittering evilly.

"I tried to tell you." Elias came around from behind the counter and started down the aisle. "Those are gag boxes. They've all got fake spiders on springs stuffed inside."

Charity recovered quickly. "I should have known better than to fool around with any of this stuff." She shoved the spider back into the box and firmly closed the lid. "As long as I live, I will never understand the appeal of this type of merchandise."

"I think it's a kid thing."

"Well, as I was saying, I recommend that you get some attractive lighting fixtures in here as soon as possible. But first things first. You've got to dust." She broke off on a delicate sneeze.

"I'll see what I can do." He watched her yank a tissue out of her skirt pocket. "Charity, would you have dinner at my place with me tonight?"

Her eyes widened above the tissue that she held to her nose. "Dinner?"

The door swung open at that moment. Irritated by the interruption, Elias glanced toward the front of the shop. The last thing he wanted right now was a customer.

A florid-faced man dressed in gentlemen's-cut slacks, a white shirt that strained at the buttons, and taupe nubuck shoes stood in the entrance. His eyes gleamed determinedly behind the lenses of over-sized aviator glasses. He carried an expensive leather briefcase in one chubby hand. The square, diamond-studded ring on his left pinky was so large that Elias could see it very clearly from where he stood in the middle of the shop.

Charity blew her nose and turned quickly. "Oh, hello, Leighton. What are you doing here? Have you met Elias Winters? Elias, this is Leighton Pitt. The owner of Pitt Realty."

Elias nodded brusquely. "Pitt."

"Winters," Leighton sang out in a jovial voice that boomed off the walls. "Pleased to meet you." He started forward, broad hand outstretched.

Elias shook hands reluctantly and as briefly as possible. As he had feared, Leighton's palm was unpleasantly damp. As soon as the ancient ritual was completed, Elias surreptitiously wiped his hand off on the side of his jeans. He caught the amused glint in Charity's eyes just as he finished.

"Charity," Leighton turned to her. "Nice to see you. Fantastic day, isn't it? Been a chilly summer. Hope we get to keep this warm weather for a while."

"Good for business," Charity murmured politely.

"That it is, that it is." Leighton swung back to Elias. "Winters, you're just the man I want to see. Can you spare a few minutes? I'd like to talk to you about a business matter that I think you'll find very interesting."

"Can it wait?" Elias asked. "Charity was just giving me some tips on running this place."

Leighton winked broadly and chuckled. "As if you need consulting advice when it comes to business."

Charity glanced at her watch with an exaggerated expression of amazement. "Heavens, will you look at the time. Elias, I've got to run. I promised Newlin he could go to lunch early today. Arlene is coming over from the Voyagers' campground to join him."

"About tonight," Elias said grimly.

She gave him a brilliant smile. "As it happens, I'm free this evening."

"Six-thirty," he said swiftly. "I'll walk over and pick you up."

"That's not necessary. I can find my own way. Your place isn't that far from mine." She glanced at Leighton. "See you later, Leighton."

He gave her a brisk nod, his attention clearly focused on whatever presentation he planned to make to Elias. "You bet. Enjoy the great weather while you can."

Elias watched wistfully as Charity disappeared out the front door. She was wearing one of her floaty little cotton dresses again today, and the sunlight outside the shop revealed the sexy silhouette of her legs.

"Well, Winters, what say we get down to business, eh?"

Elias suppressed a groan as he turned back to his visitor. "If this is about real estate, I've already got a house."

"I know, Hayden Stone's old place out on the bluff." Leighton frowned. "You know, I could find you something in much better condition with a similar view."

"Don't bother. The cottage suits me just fine."

"Sure, you bet. That's not what I wanted to talk to you about today, anyway."

"What did you want to discuss?"

Leighton glanced toward the door as if to make certain that they were still alone. Then he winked again. His teeth sparkled in a confidential, man-to-man smile. "I know who you are, Winters, and I think I can guess why you're here in town."

"What a coincidence. I know who I am, too. And

I also know why I'm here. If that's all you wanted to talk about, I've got work to do."

"Hey, hey, hey." Leighton flapped his hand. "Take it easy. No offense intended. Just wanted you to realize that you're not the only one in town who knows the real score."

"Real score?"

"Look, I'll level with you." Leighton leaned in closer. The fragrance of a recently digested breath mint wafted through the air. "I'm aware that off-shore money is planning to move into Whispering Waters Cove in the next six months. I know all about the plans for a world-class resort and spa the company wants to develop here. Going to be built along the same lines as the properties the outfit developed in Hawaii, right? Except with an emphasis on golf instead of sunbathing, of course."

Elias held his breath to avoid inhaling the odor of mint. "Is that a fact?"

"No need to play dumb."

Elias thought of the kiss on the bluff. "But I do it so well."

"Sure, sure." Another wink. "I like a man with a sense of humor."

"No one's ever accused me of having one."

"Not everyone appreciates a keen wit." Sweat glistened on Leighton's brow. "Let's put our cards on the table. I know you own a consulting company called Far Seas, and I know just what kind of consulting you do. Only one reason you'd be here in our little town."

"What reason?"

Leighton gave him a very knowing look. "You're the advance man for the off-shore resort developer who wants to move in here to Whispering Waters Cove."

"I see."

"Don't worry." Leighton held up a plump hand. The huge diamond glittered. "I won't try to pin you down. No questions asked. Man in your position has to keep a low profile. But, frankly, I wondered when you or someone like you would show up."

"Did you?"

"Of course. Your client is getting ready to move. I just want you to know that you're not the only player in this situation. I've got a piece of the action, too. Or I will have, very soon."

"Uh-huh."

The smell of breath mint grew stronger as Leighton edged closer and lowered his voice. "Can't discuss the details yet. Like you, I've got to keep things quiet for a while longer. But I'll be able to speak more freely early next week. Bottom line here is that I'm the one you'll be dealing with when the ball starts rolling. Remember that."

"Be hard to forget."

Leighton chuckled. "You can say that again. Well, I'd better be going. Got an appointment. Just wanted to put you into the big picture before everything breaks loose. Hey, enjoy the weather. Summer doesn't usually last more than a few weeks around here."

"I'll keep that in mind."

"We'll talk later." Leighton turned and strode toward the door with a purposeful air. A man with a piece of the action. A player.

Crazy Otis shuffled back and forth on his perch and hissed softly.

Elias waited until Leighton had left the shop before he picked up the phone and dialed a familiar number in Seattle.

A woman answered in low, rich tones. "Thorgood,

Green, and Esteredge." She reeled off the names of the partners in the law firm as if they had each been canonized.

"Craig Thorgood, please."

"May I tell Mr. Thorgood who's calling?"

"Elias Winters."

"Just a moment, Mr. Winters."

Craig Thorgood came on the line. "What's up, Elias?"

His voice matched his office, rich and cultivated. The sort of voice that implied Thorgood had descended from several generations of old money and had followed a venerable family tradition when he had chosen to study law. Elias was one of the few people who knew that he had actually started out life on a farm in eastern Washington.

"Got time for a small job?"

"I've always got time to squeeze in a few extra billable hours. How small is the job?"

"I want you to find out whatever you can about a woman named Gwendolyn Pitt. Until a year ago she lived in Whispering Waters Cove. She's back here now, but I'd like to know where she's been for the past twelve months."

"What kind of business is she in?"

Elias heard a faint squeak on the other end of the line and knew that Craig was leaning back in his chair. "At the moment she's running a spaceship cult. But she used to be in real estate."

"Spaceship cult, huh? You do meet some interesting people in your line of work, Winters."

"You don't know the half of it. Give me a call when you get something."

"I will. How's the curio shop business?"

"Just the way I like it. Slow."

Craig laughed. "I give you six months at the outside. You'll be back in Seattle by the first of spring."

"I don't think so, Craig."

Charity showed up on the doorstep looking like the Spirit of Summer Night in a pale, high-waisted dress made of a fabric that seemed lighter than air. Elias felt his stomach knot with anticipation. The low, rounded neckline and little cap sleeves of her dress were at once flirtatious and innocent. Her auburn hair was done up in a casual twist that allowed little wispy tendrils to flutter around her cheeks.

She carried a bottle of chilled sauvignon blanc. Feminine mischief sparkled in her eyes. Elias knew that she was feeling very much in control of the situation. What really worried him was that he was half afraid she might be right. He drew a deep breath and summoned his resolve.

"I didn't know if white wine would work with whatever's on the menu tonight," she said as she handed him the bottle.

"This is a good night for sauvignon blanc." He took the wine and opened the door wide to usher her inside. "Come in."

"Thanks." She glanced down and smiled when she saw his bare feet. Without a word she stepped out of her sandals, placed them neatly beside the door, and walked into the small front room and glanced around curiously. "What did Leighton Pitt want this afternoon?"

"He admired my sense of humor among other things." Elias inhaled the scent of her as she brushed past him. The light skirt of her gauzy dress snagged briefly on his jeans. It was going to be a very long night.

"Free advice," Charity murmured. "Don't believe everything a salesman tells you."

"I'll remember that."

Crazy Otis, ensconced on top of his cage, looked up from the wooden toy he was busily gnawing. He eyed Charity with a hard stare and then muttered a churlish greeting.

"It's easy to see why some scientists think birds are related to dinosaurs," Charity remarked. "No manners at all."

Elias put the wine on the counter. "Otis said hello, didn't he?"

"Who knows what he said? All Crazy Otis does is mutter and cackle." Charity strolled over to the cage and surveyed Otis at close range. "But I have to admit that he's settled in quite nicely with you. I'm glad you two have hit it off. I was a tad worried about him for a while."

"If you hadn't taken him in, he probably would have gone under completely."

"I didn't really know what to do for a depressed parrot. I called a vet in Seattle, but he wasn't too helpful. So I just sort of followed my instincts."

Otis tilted his head to eye her more closely. "Heh-heh-heh."

Charity made a face. "Not that you've ever shown so much as an ounce of gratitude, Otis."

"He's just too proud to admit he needed you," Elias said.

"Yeah, right. You know, Hayden once told me that Otis could talk, but I've never heard him do anything except chuckle and hiss and mutter unintelligibly."

Elias opened a drawer to find a corkscrew. "I'm sure Otis will talk if he ever has anything to say."

"I won't hold my breath." Charity turned away from Otis to examine the spare room. "I see your furniture hasn't arrived yet. You should have said something. I could loan you a couple of chairs and a table. I brought all my stuff from Seattle."

"I appreciate the offer, but I don't need any more furniture."

That wasn't strictly true, he thought as he went to work with the corkscrew. A slightly larger bed would have been nice. Making love to Charity on the narrow futon would be a challenge. Of course, he wasn't going to have to worry about it tonight. Control was everything in Tal Kek Chara.

"I suppose this, uh, minimalist style goes with the obscure water philosophy."

"Tal Kek Chara. Yes."

"Tal Kek Chara. Is that what you call it?"

"Loosely translated, it means the Way of Water. The literal translation is a lot more complicated." Elias suddenly realized that now that Hayden was dead, he was probably the only person left in the states who knew the exact translation of the ancient words. It was an eerie, lonely feeling.

"I see." Charity leaned down to touch the heavy glass bowl half-filled with water that sat on the low table. "This is a nice piece. Very nice."

Elias looked across the room to where she stood gazing down into the bowl. Something twisted inside him. "I gave it to Hayden a few years ago."

"He obviously treasured it." She ran her fingertip meditatively along the rim of the thick glass. "It's the only decorative item in the room."

Elias thought about that. "I guess he must have liked it." The tightness inside him relaxed. She was right. Hayden must have valued the bowl very highly to have kept it here in this otherwise spartan room.

Charity wandered across the small space to the kitchen area. "We were discussing Leighton. Did he compliment you on your humor in order to try to sell you some real estate today?"

"No. He informed me that he's a player."

"A player?"

"A mover-and-shaker. Wheeler-dealer. Big man here in town. A guy in the know."

"Hmm. Any particular reason why he would make a special trip down to the pier to announce that to you?"

Elias took two glasses out of the cupboard. "He seems to think that things are going to get hot here in Whispering Waters Cove."

She shrugged. "That's certainly what the town council hopes will happen."

"Pitt implied that he knows something specific. He says an off-shore developer intends to put in a golf resort and spa."

"A resort? That's specific, all right." Charity watched him fill the glasses with the cool sauvignon blanc. Her eyes were thoughtful and just a little wary. "Do you think Leighton knows what he's talking about?"

"Can't say." He handed her a glass. "But I'll lay odds that whatever he thinks is going on is tied to his ex-wife's spaceship cult."

She met his eyes. "Not to you?"

"Not to me."

"Interesting. That brings up the question of what's going to happen on Monday."

"I called a friend of mine in Seattle, a lawyer named Thorgood. Specializes in corporate law. His firm employs a whole fleet of researchers and investigators. I asked him to see if he can find out what Gwendolyn Pitt has been up to during the past few months."

"Things are getting more and more mysterious, aren't they?"

"They may be a lot simpler than they seem." Elias leaned back against the counter and took a sip of the wine. It was spicy and tantalizing on his tongue. Just like Charity. "Sounds like it may come down to money, after all."

"Guess we'll just have to wait until Monday night to see what happens." Charity's eyes gleamed over the rim of her wine glass. "Whoever said small town life wasn't exciting?"

"Not me." He looked at her and suddenly could not look away.

The air became more dense between them. The invisible currents moving through it were charged with a spectrum of possibilities. There was no rush, he reminded himself. No rush at all. He would not allow himself to be swept away by the tide.

Charity blinked first. "What's for dinner?"

"Artichoke dip with toasted pita bread. Gorgonzola and spinach ravioli, hearts of romaine salad, and some hazelnut gelati with biscotti for dessert."

Her eyes widened. "I'm impressed."

He savored her astonished wonder. "I'll admit that I was surprised to find the biscotti in the Whispering Waters Cove Grocery."

"You reaped the results of my months of negotiations with the grocery store manager. Mr. Gedding and I have a deal. He stocks the items I request, and I pay rip-off prices for them."

"Fair enough."

Laughter lit her eyes. She batted her lashes. "Have I ever told you how much I admire a man who can cook?"

"I don't believe you've mentioned it." He put his glass down on the counter and turned to the stove. "But feel free to hold forth on the subject."

"Okay. I deeply, deeply admire a man who can cook."

She was flirting again. A good sign, Elias thought. This was right where he wanted to be. The trick was to stay here in the shallows where they could both have some fun without any danger of getting in too deep.

"I'll try not to take advantage of your vulnerability to good cooks," he said as he set a large pan of water on the old stove. "How's Newlin doing?"

The mischief faded from her eyes. "I'm a little worried about him. He's afraid of what Arlene will do when the spaceships fail to show. I wish I could reassure him that everything will be all right, but the truth is, I don't know how she'll handle reality when it strikes."

"We'll keep an eye on Newlin," Elias promised. He realized as he spoke the words that he was starting to identify himself as a member of the Crazy Otis Landing gang. It was a strange sensation, but not unpleasant.

He took Charity home shortly after eleven. It was all very proper, very old-fashioned.

It was not, however, very easy.

The waves of sensual tension had grown stronger as the evening progressed. All throughout dinner she had watched him with an intriguing combination of shy anticipation and womanly knowledge in her eyes. Elias knew that she had been waiting for him to make the first move, the one that would lead to the bedroom.

It took a valiant effort to suggest that it was getting late and that it was time to return her to her own cottage. The surprise that flashed briefly across her face was almost enough to comfort the regret he knew he would feel later. Almost, but not quite.

Elias covered Otis's cage and stepped into his shoes. He paused to pick up the flashlight, but they did not need it. A partial moon and a sky full of stars provided enough illumination to see the bluff path. Across the cove the lights of the town and Crazy Otis Landing sparkled in the distance.

Charity's arm, tucked inside Elias's, was warm and supple and softly rounded. He could smell the scent of her shampoo. Something herbal, he concluded. It mingled with the balmy sea breeze and her own unique fragrance. The sum of the ingredients created a potent dish that aroused his hunger.

A balanced flow had to be restored in this relationship, he reminded himself. He had to stay centered. Hayden's words echoed in his head. *He who knows the Way of Water lets his opponent come to him.* A man and a woman hovering on the brink of an affair were adversaries whether or not they acknowledged it. Each wanted something from the other. Each had an agenda.

The good-night kiss at the door was tricky, but Elias had braced himself for it. He brushed her mouth lightly with his own. When she started to put her hands on his shoulders, he took a half step back. Her arms fell to her side.

"I'll see you in the morning," he said.

She watched him through the veil of her half-lowered lashes. "Thanks for dinner. It was wonderful. Can I return the favor on Monday night?"

Satisfaction blossomed inside him. "I'll look forward to it."

"Afterward we can walk down to the Voyagers' campground and watch the starships arrive." She grinned. "I'm sure everyone in town will be there. Fun for the whole family. Better than the county fair."

"Never a dull moment in Whispering Waters Cove."

"Tell me, Elias, if the ships do happen to show up as advertised, will you be tempted to leave with the aliens?"

"No." He looked into her eyes and felt the heat rise. "Something tells me that the answers I want are here, not somewhere out in space."

She stilled. "Are you sure of that?"

"Very sure. But I haven't finished asking all the questions yet. Good night, Charity." It was time to go. He had to get off her porch before the riptide caught him again and carried him back out to sea. He turned and went resolutely down the steps.

"Elias?"

Her soft, husky voice brought him to a halt. He looked back at her. "What is it?"

"Did you prove your point?"

"What point?"

"The one you've been trying to prove all evening." She gave him a rueful smile. "That you're back in control? That even though things got a little exciting out there on the bluff the other night, you're still Joe Cool?"

"Ah, that point." He should have known that she'd guessed what was going on. "Maybe."

"Having fun yet?"

"No, but it builds character."

She laughed and shut the door in his face.

Elias realized he was grinning like an idiot. A joke. That was definitely a joke. Maybe not a great joke, but still, what could you expect from a man who was new at this kind of thing.

He backed away from the porch, turned, and broke into an easy, loping run. With any luck, he could work off some of the excess sexual energy that was charging his senses with lightning.

In spite of the ache that desire had created in his

lower body, he felt good. Better than he had since Hayden had died. Better than he had in years. He ran faster. Below the bluff, silver moonlight played on the waters of the cove. The air was a tonic in his blood. The night stretched out forever.

He ran for a long time before he slowed to a walk, turned, and started back toward his darkened cottage.

He saw the movement at the window just as he reached the garden gate. He came to a halt and stood quietly in the dense shadow of a madrona tree. He watched with interest as a dark figure scrambled out over the sill.

The intruder grunted when he landed, panting, on the porch. As soon as he caught his balance, he started to struggle frantically with the raised window.

"Shit." The expletive was a low, muttered exclamation.

Elias recognized the voice. Rick Swinton.

Swinton finally closed the window with one last, anxious shove. He swung around and dashed down the porch steps into the garden. There was a splash as he blundered straight into the reflecting pool.

"Goddamn it." Swinton hauled himself out of the shallow pool and tore down the path, wet chinos flapping. He never saw Elias standing quietly in the thick darkness created by the madrona tree.

Elias could have reached out and touched him. Or stuck out a foot and sent Swinton sprawling. He did neither.

Instead, he followed his uninvited guest at a discreet distance. Swinton ran around to the front of the cottage and pounded down the narrow, tree-lined drive that led back to the main road.

His car was parked behind a stand of fir trees. He yanked open the door, leaped into the driver's seat, and started the engine. He did not turn on his headlights until he was a hundred yards down the road.

Elias waited at the edge of the drive for a few minutes, curious to see whether Swinton would head back toward the Voyagers' compound or into town. The headlights turned left when they reached the intersection. Toward Whispering Waters Cove.

Elias walked slowly back to the cottage. He went up the porch steps and opened the front door. He removed his shoes and went into the house.

Crazy Otis was muttering anxiously beneath his covered cage.

"It's all right, Otis. I'm here."

Otis calmed and then, true to form, turned a bit surly. "Hsss."

"My sentiments, exactly." Elias did not turn on the lights. He went to the window Swinton had used for his breaking and entering. "He either got lucky or he was watching the place all evening. When he saw me leave to take Charity home, he probably assumed I'd spend the night at her place."

"Heh-heh-heh."

"Yeah. Heh-heh-heh. Little did he know that I was using the evening as a Tal Kek Chara exercise in self-discipline and restraint." Elias gazed out into the night. "Idiot." He paused. "In case you're wondering, Otis, I was referring to myself, not Swinton."

"Heh-heh-heh."

Elias walked through the small cottage. The bare decor left few potential hiding places. It would not have taken Swinton long to go through the limited possibilities.

"I don't like guests who forget to remove their shoes, Otis."

Elias was not surprised to see that the only thing that appeared to have been disturbed was the carved chest in the bedroom. One glance inside revealed that Swinton had pawed through the contents.

The one item in the chest that Elias cared about, Hayden Stone's journal, was still safe at the bottom. He picked it up and turned it in his hands. He had not been able to bring himself to read it yet.

He replaced the journal and closed the lid of the chest slowly. It was possible that, having struck out at the house, Swinton had headed into town in order to break into Charms & Virtues. Elias hoped he wouldn't make too much of a mess.

"Everyone here in Whispering Waters Cove seems to think I'm a man of mystery, Otis." He went into the bathroom to turn on the shower. "Hope they're not too disappointed when they find out I'm just an innocent, hardworking shopkeeper with no ulterior real estate motives."

"Heh-heh-heh."

Elias emerged from the shower a few minutes later. He rolled out the futon and settled down on it. He folded his arms behind his head and contemplated the shadowy ceiling.

"So, Otis, what was it like, sleeping in Charity's bedroom?"

"Heh-heh-heh."

6

Water is deepest beneath the place where it appears the most calm on the surface.

—"On the Way of Water," from the journal of Hayden Stone

The sight of Phyllis Dartmoor striding briskly into Whispers on Saturday morning did not brighten Charity's day. The mayor of Whispering Waters Cove looked even more determined and aggressive than usual. Charity wished she could duck out of the back door, but there wasn't time.

That would have been the coward's way out, anyway, she told herself. It was just unfortunate that she'd had very little sleep, having spent the long night instead lying awake, trying to analyze Elias.

It had not been a productive task. She had replayed the final scene at her front door a thousand times, and by dawn she had been forced to conclude that she'd had a narrow escape.

Sure, she had laughed at the time, even teased Elias. But in the cold, harsh light of day, it was clear that she had been in an unfamiliar, extraordinarily reckless mood last night. Make that the whole of the last week. Playing with fire, that's what she was doing. Not like her at all. That kiss on the bluff a few days ago had done weird things to her.

Amazing what could happen to one's normal sense of caution when one realized that one no longer suffered from panic attacks in a man's embrace.

Today it was breathtakingly obvious that she could easily have been swept up into a very dangerous liaison last night. And it would have been her own fault. She had spent the whole evening flirting outrageously. She had wanted Elias to lose control again, the way he had on the bluff. She had wanted to see the passion flare in his eyes, feel his strong, sexy hands on her, know that she could turn him on.

Thank heavens Elias had been into his Zenny-mode last night. In his effort to affirm his own prodigious powers of self-control, he had given her a chance to come to her senses.

Breathing space. That was what he had inadvertently given her last night. Breathing space. This morning she was resolved to take advantage of it.

She needed time. She needed to think things through. Before she made any major moves, she needed to know a hell of a lot more about Elias Winters. She must remember Davis's advice. *Watch your step with Winters. Rumor has it he's not just a player, he's a winner. Every time.*

No two ways about it, she'd had a very close call.

Whatever was fated to happen between herself and Elias would definitely have to be postponed until they were better acquainted. Much better acquainted.

Blah, blah, blah.

She'd been giving herself the same lecture for hours. The words were a litany in her brain. She was beginning to sound like Crazy Otis.

"Good morning, Charity." The heels of Phyllis's Italian pumps clicked sharply on the shop floor.

"Hello, Phyllis." Charity stationed herself squarely behind the counter. "Something tells me you didn't come in to buy a book. Are you here on business or politics?"

"A little of both." Phyllis came to a halt and favored Charity with a cool smile that was all width and no depth. It was a practiced, charming smile that showed a lot of white, capped teeth.

It would have been easy to dislike Phyllis, Charity thought. After all, the two of them had become fierce adversaries as they did battle over the fate of Crazy Otis Landing. Their confrontations at town council meetings had already become legendary in Whispering Waters Cove. But Charity had been cursed from Day One of their association with a deeply rooted sense of sympathy for her new nemesis.

She knew her empathy was ridiculous, and she took great pains to conceal it, but she was unable to shake it. Phyllis reminded her of the person she, herself, had once been. A classic overachiever. A driven workaholic, obsessively goal-oriented. She wondered if Phyllis had ever had a panic attack.

Phyllis had a law degree from the University of Washington. She ran her own law practice in Whispering Waters Cove. She fulfilled her duties as town mayor with tireless energy. In her free time she campaigned for all the right candidates in state elections and got herself invited to the right cocktail parties in Seattle and Olympia.

She was a tall, sleek woman in her mid-thirties. Her sophistication would have caused her to stand out in

Seattle. In a small town like Whispering Waters Cove, she stood out so much she looked out of place.

Phyllis was the only woman in town who habitually wore a suit. Today's version had been crisply tailored in summer-weight linen that was already properly crumpled even though it was only five minutes after ten. The jacket was equipped with impressive shoulder pads that gave her figure a strong forties' silhouette.

Phyllis drove to Seattle every month to have her light brown hair cut in a dashing wedge. After Jennifer Pitt had given every woman in town a taste for sculpted nails, Phyllis had become a regular at Nails by Radiance. The special color Radiance had created for her was called Dartmoor Mauve.

"Are you alone?" Phyllis glanced around the obviously empty bookshop.

"At the moment. My assistant went to get himself an iced latte at Bea's place and it's a little early for weekend tourists. What can I do for you?"

"I wanted to talk to you about the new owner of Crazy Otis Landing."

"Why don't you talk to him, instead?"

"I've already tried that." Phyllis's mouth tightened. "He was civil but completely uncooperative. Kept wanting to discuss water, of all things."

"You went to see Elias?" Charity was horrified by the very unpleasant twinge that shot through her. She prayed it was not jealousy.

"Ran into him at the post office. He acted totally disinterested in what I had to say."

Charity relaxed a little. "So? What do you expect me to do?"

Phyllis lowered her voice to a gratingly confidential tone. "I understand the two of you are seeing each other."

"Every day." Charity smiled blandly. "Can't miss

each other, what with both of us running shops right here on the same pier."

"That's not what I meant, and I think you know it." A steely expression appeared in Phyllis's eyes. "The rumor is that you've started seeing him socially."

Charity was amazed. She had made no effort to keep last night's date a secret, but she certainly hadn't broadcast the news, either. Elias must have mentioned their dinner to someone, who had, in turn, spread it immediately all over the cove.

"Nothing like a small town for gossip, is there?" Charity muttered.

"Look, I'll be blunt. It's common knowledge that Winters is not just the new proprietor of that ridiculous curio shop at the other end of the pier. He's the new owner of this entire landing." Phyllis leaned closer. "And, he's also the head of a very high-stakes consulting company called Far Seas, Inc."

"So?"

"So he's a player. The question is, what game is he playing?"

Charity smiled grimly. "Whatever it is, I can guarantee that he's writing his own rules."

"That doesn't surprise me." Phyllis tapped one long, Dartmoor Mauve nail on the counter. "Winters is up to something. There's a lot of speculation going on, but the bottom line is that no one really knows what he intends to do with the Landing. That's why we need your help."

"We?"

"Those of us who care about the future of this town. You're the only one who's established any sort of relationship with him."

"Phyllis, I don't know what the rumors were like by the time they reached you, but I can assure you that it was just dinner, not an engagement party."

"Look, this isn't a joke. No one else around here can get a straight answer out of Winters."

"He doesn't exactly specialize in straight answers," Charity admitted.

"You know as well as I do that the town council has had its eye on Crazy Otis Landing for some time now. Hayden Stone was impossible. As long as he owned the pier, there was no hope of upgrading the shops. But now that he's gone, we want to convince Winters that it's in his own best interests to cooperate with the council's plans."

"There's that word 'we' again. It makes me nervous."

"The members of the council and I want you to join our team, Charity. It's time we stopped arguing about the future of this pier and worked together to make it the centerpiece of the new Whispering Waters Cove."

"I like it the way it is."

"Where's your sense of vision?" Phyllis demanded. "You were once a successful businesswoman. With the obvious exception of Elias Winters, you're the only one on this pier with a head for business. The rest of these misfits couldn't make a profit running a hotdog stand at a Fourth of July Parade."

Charity felt her temper stir. Sooner or later it always came down to this with Phyllis. "The shopkeepers of Crazy Otis Landing are not misfits. They've single-handedly kept this pier alive for the town for the past twenty years. Everyone else considered it an eyesore until recently."

"Alive?" Phyllis waved one beautifully manicured hand in an exasperated gesture. "You call this alive? You've got three shops standing empty. They've been empty for years."

"We'll get them rented sooner or later."

"No smart businessperson is going to open a store

on this pier until there's some guarantee that the image of the landing will be improved."

"You don't have to evict all of the present tenants in order to improve the landing," Charity snapped. "We're doing a good job of building business all by ourselves. Foot traffic here on the pier has tripled this summer. Bea's pulling in tourists with her espresso machine. Radiance has brought in local people with her nail parlor. Yappy's booked several birthday parties down at the carousel. Ted's T-shirt sales have skyrocketed. And I'm doing just fine with my bookstore, thank you very much."

"You can't stand in the way of progress, for God's sake."

"I can stand anywhere I like."

Phyllis drew an audible breath. "I didn't come here to argue with you."

"Really? I would never have guessed."

"Be reasonable, Charity. I came to enlist you on the side of the future. We need your help. You stand to benefit from a revitalized pier as much as anyone does. This bookshop of yours would work beautifully in an upscale version of Crazy Otis Landing. Help us convince Winters to cooperate."

Charity leaned both elbows on the counter and clasped her hands. She eyed Phyllis with a mixture of caution and growing fascination. "Let us say, for the sake of argument, that I was willing to help you accomplish your plans. How, exactly, do you expect me to convince Elias to cooperate with the council?"

Phyllis pounced on the small opening. "We need you to talk to him. Find out what he plans to do with the pier. We want to work with him."

"Work with him?"

"We're all interested in upgrading Crazy Otis Landing. If he's brokering a deal for off-shore investors, which is what Leighton Pitt implies, we need to know that."

Charity stared at her in growing amazement. "You want me to spy for you."

Phyllis scowled, then turned red beneath her makeup. "You're overdramatizing this, Charity. We're just asking you to do your civic duty."

"Hmm. Did you ever see an old Hitchcock film called *Notorious?* Forties' spy thriller with Cary Grant and Ingrid Bergman? Ingrid has to seduce and marry the bad guy in order to keep tabs on him. Everyone tells her it's her duty."

Phyllis's eyes narrowed. "I fail to see the relevance."

"I guess you're right. I really don't look much like Ingrid Bergman, do I?" She broke off when she realized that Newlin was standing in the doorway behind Phyllis.

Newlin hesitated, latte cup in hand. "Want me to wait outside, Charity?"

"It's okay, Newlin." Charity smiled at him. "The mayor and I have finished our little chat."

Phyllis frowned at Newlin. Then she turned back to Charity. "Think about what I said. This is important to all of us. The future of this town may very well depend on what you decide to do."

"Just this town? Gee, I dunno, Phyllis. Anything less than the fate of the free world seems like a waste of my talents."

"You're being extremely shortsighted." Phyllis whirled and strode out of the shop without another word.

Newlin wandered back behind the counter. "Somethin' wrong?"

"Nothing more than usual. The mayor is concerned about the pier."

"She ought to spend more time worryin' about having Hank Tybern arrest Gwendolyn Pitt."

"Gwendolyn Pitt isn't doing anything illegal," Charity pointed out gently.

"Well, it oughta be illegal." Newlin gulped down half of the iced latte. "The mayor sure worked hard enough to get rid of those Voyagers when they first moved into town. Remember how at the beginning of July she was always sendin' Tybern out to hassle 'em about health and safety violations?"

"I remember."

"Then she just backed off for some reason."

"Very wise of her. Phyllis came to the obvious conclusion that there wasn't much she could do except wait it out. With any luck, the Voyagers will disband after the spaceships fail to show."

"Maybe." Newlin's jaw tensed. "Maybe not. Folks can be real weird about stuff like that. Gwendolyn Pitt has a lot to answer for, if you ask me. Someone oughta do something about her. It ain't right. It just ain't right."

Shortly before four o'clock, Elias hung up the new feather duster Charity had given him and looked at Crazy Otis.

"I've had it with the housecleaning. I still say Charity's wrong. A little dust makes the place more interesting."

Otis mumbled a response.

"There isn't a customer in sight. I think we've had our rush for the day." Elias moved closer to the perch. "Want to go see how Yappy's doing on those repairs to the carousel?"

Otis bobbed his head and stepped onto Elias's shoulder with regal dignity.

Elias strolled out of the shop, turned right, and

headed toward the far end of the pier. He was feeling good today. The ebullient sense of anticipation that had descended on him last night still held in spite of the fact that he had been right about Rick Swinton.

Swinton had, indeed, paid a visit to the small back office of Charms & Virtues after making his late-night visit to the cottage. But other than scattering the contents of the trash can, which Swinton had apparently tripped over at some point, no damage had been done. Elias wondered what his midnight visitor had made of the mundane collection of invoices, catalogs, order forms, and sales receipts that filled the small file cabinet.

Elias made a note to call Craig Thorgood and have him look into Swinton's background, as well as Gwendolyn Pitt's.

The pier had been busy earlier in the day, but things had tapered off after four. Elias saw Newlin working at the counter of Whispers when he went past the shop. Newlin looked grim, as usual. There was no sign of Charity.

Elias strolled past the three unrented shops and paused. It would be a good idea to get tenants into the empty spaces, he thought. He'd have to see about the matter.

"How's it hangin', Winters?" Ted waved from the doorway of Ted's Instant Philosophy T-Shirts. He had a new paperback mystery novel in one hand. A bookmark bearing the Whispers logo stuck out from between the pages.

As usual, Ted wore one of his own products. The T-shirt, which did not quite cover his belly, bore the advice, *Be Good. If You Can't Be Good, Be Careful.*

"Business is a little slow right now," Elias said. "Otis and I thought we'd take a walk."

"Things'll pick up tomorrow."

"Right."

Bea nodded to Elias as she poured iced tea for a customer seated at an outside table. Radiance gave him the old sixties' peace sign through the beaded curtain of Nails by Radiance.

It occurred to Elias that even though he had been here less than two weeks, he was developing the strange feeling that he actually belonged here on the pier. For once he was not standing entirely apart from everyone else, watching them from the balanced place inside himself. He was sharing some of the same space the others shared.

It was as if the river of his life had flowed around an unexpected bend and mingled with some of the same streams that flowed through the lives of some of the others.

He was not certain how to evaluate the change that was taking place. In a way it seemed to go against his training. On the other hand, it felt right. He wished Hayden were still alive so that he could ask him about the strange sensation. There were so many questions he would have liked to ask Hayden.

Elias reached the end of the pier and discovered Yappy deep in the guts of the carousel machinery. The colorful horses were frozen in a circle around him.

"Hey there, Winters." Yappy waved a wrench in greeting.

"How's it going?" Elias stepped up onto the platform and propped one shoulder against the hindquarters of a flying horse. Otis stepped off onto the horse's tail, settled his feathers, and prepared to supervise the work in progress.

"Gettin' there," Yappy said.

Elias studied the inside drive mechanism with interest. "Find the trouble?"

"Yeah, I think so. Should have it running again in a few more minutes. Hand me a screwdriver, will you?"

Elias glanced at the array of tools lying on a small bench. "Which one?"

"Phillips head."

Elias picked up the screwdriver and slapped it into Yappy's grease-stained palm. "Going down to the beach to see the Voyagers off Monday night?"

"Wouldn't miss it." Yappy twirled the screwdriver with expert precision. "Whole town's going to be there. Or at least, a good percentage. Bea plans to set up a refreshment stand. Sell some coffee, soda. Maybe some muffins. Figure I'll give her a hand. What about you?"

"I'll be there."

Yappy paused long enough to shoot Elias a speculative look. "With Charity?"

"Yes."

"You two are getting kind of close, aren't you?"

"Is that a problem?"

"No, I guess not." Yappy sounded thoughtful. "Your business."

"That's the way I look at it."

"Just so you know," Yappy continued in a slow, deliberate drawl. "We're all real fond of Charity around here. None of us would take kindly to seeing her hurt, if you take my meaning."

"I think I know what you're trying to say. But she's not a kid. She can take care of herself."

"She's got a head on her shoulders, all right," Yappy conceded. "Knows what she's doing when it comes to running a business. She's the one who came up with the notion of renting out the carousel for catered birthday parties. Doubled my profits this summer. She gave Radiance the idea of creating a special nail color for every one of her regular customers, too. Worked like a charm."

"It's obvious that Charity has good marketing instincts."

"Damn right. Understands how to deal with the local politicos, too. Kept the town council off our backs until you showed up. But when it comes to other stuff, she's not quite so tough."

"What do you mean?"

"Bea told me that Charity went through a real nasty episode just before she came here. Broke up with some rich guy in Seattle named Loftus."

"Brett Loftus."

"Know him?"

"Saw him once." Elias recalled the business luncheon where the blond, blue-eyed, square-jawed Loftus had entertained a crowd of bankers and investors with witty stories and incisive insights into the murky world of the athletic sportswear business. Elias had thought about that luncheon a lot lately. Ever since Charity had mentioned Loftus, in fact.

"Yeah, well, she hasn't dated anyone since she hit Whispering Waters Cove. Least not that Bea and I know about."

"Until I came along."

"Uh-huh." Yappy peered at him through a maze of gears. "Until you came along."

"I appreciate your concern for her, Yappy. Tell me, is anyone equally concerned about me?"

"Figure you can take care of yourself." Yappy wiped his grimy hands on the leg of his pants. "That should do it." He stepped out of the drive house, closed the panel, and pulled a lever. "We'll give Otis a test ride."

Otis cackled with glee as the bright, gem-studded horses began to glide in a circle. He gripped the saddle of a gleaming Pegasus with his powerful claws and shook out his brilliant feathers.

"Old Otis really gets a kick out of this." Yappy shook his head. "Charity used to bring him down here after Hayden died. We all thought that bird was a goner. Real sad sight. No spirit at all. But Charity pulled him out of it."

"She thinks that Otis isn't properly appreciative, but I'm sure he's grateful."

Yappy snorted. "Yeah. Right."

Elias watched the boy from the shadows behind the counter. The kid looked to be about nine years old. He wore the universal boy uniform: a pair of jeans, sneakers, and a T-shirt.

It had been a long, lazy Sunday. Elias glanced at the cuckoo clock. It was five-twenty-five. Almost closing time. The kid had been in the shop for nearly half an hour, and thus far he had made a trip up and down every single aisle, methodically examining the entire inventory.

"Was there something special you wanted?" Elias finally asked.

The boy jumped in surprise. He turned quickly to gaze into the dark area at the rear of the shop. Elias realized the kid hadn't noticed him until that moment.

The boy shook his head quickly and took a step back. "Uh, no. I was just kinda lookin' around."

"Okay." Elias held out his arm to Crazy Otis, who stepped aboard.

The boy flinched at the movement and took another step back toward the front door.

Way to go Winters, Elias thought. Scare off the customers.

He picked up the glass of water he had poured earlier for himself and walked slowly around the edge of the counter. The boy watched uneasily. He looked as if he was about to turn and flee. Then he saw Otis. His eyes widened.

"Is he real?"

"Yes." Elias reached up to scratch Otis's head. The parrot stretched languidly.

"Wow." The boy stopped edging backward. "Does he talk?"

"When he feels like it." Elias moved closer. "Did you see the invisible-ink pens over there?"

The kid looked both fascinated and uncertain. "No."

"They really work." Elias came to a halt beside the stack of pens. "Watch." He selected one and jotted a few words on a pad of demonstration paper. "See? Nothing shows."

The kid frowned dubiously. "How do you make the writing visible?"

"You dip the paper into a glass of water that has a few drops of this stuff in it." Elias held up a small vial that contained the harmless chemical mixture.

He unscrewed the top of the tiny bottle and sprinkled a couple of drops of the contents into the glass he held. Then he put the small page of paper into the water.

The boy shifted and drew closer. "Let me see."

Elias pulled the paper out of the water with a flourish and held it out. The words *Buy this pen* were clearly visible.

"Cool." The boy looked up eagerly. "Can I try it?"

"Sure." Elias handed over the pen and the small vial.

"This is great, man." The youngster scribbled busily on the pad of paper. "I can't wait to show it to Alex."

"Alex?"

"Yeah, he's my best friend. Me and him are going

down to the beach Monday night to see if the space-ships come. My Dad's going to take us."

"I'll be there, too."

"Yeah?" The boy squinted thoughtfully. "Think the aliens will show?"

"No."

The kid sighed. "That's what my Dad says. But it would sure be neat if they did land, wouldn't it?"

"It would be interesting."

"It'd be so cool." The kid's enthusiasm lit his eyes. "If they did come, I'd go into outer space with 'em."

"Why?"

"Huh?" The boy scowled at the question. "On ac-count of they'd have such great stuff. Just think about what their computers would be like. Way ahead of ours. They'd know the answers to everything."

"No, they wouldn't."

The kid looked taken aback. "Why not?"

"Because technology, no matter how advanced, can never supply all the answers. Some things you have to learn on your own. Even the most powerful computers wouldn't change that."

"You sure?"

"Yes." Elias looked at the pen. "That'll be two-ninety-eight plus tax. No charge for the philosophical sound bite."

"What's a philosophical sound bite?"

"A personal opinion." Elias led the way back to the cash register. "That's why I'm not charging you for it."

"Oh." The boy dug into his pocket for the money. "Are you open Sundays?"

"During the summer."

"Great. I'm going to bring Alex here tomorrow."

"If you do, I'll give you a free replacement bottle of invisible ink."

"Cool." The boy grabbed the paper sack that contained his new pen and the little vial and raced toward the door.

He had to dash around Charity, who had obviously been watching the transaction. She waited until Elias's young customer had vanished, and then she walked toward the counter. Her eyes sparkled with amusement.

"You look pleased with yourself," she said.

Elias gazed thoughtfully at the empty doorway. "I think that kid is going to enjoy that pen."

"I believe you're right. I told you, it's a calling."

"What is?"

"Running a shop like this. Not everyone is cut out for it. My sister or someone like Phyllis Dartmoor, for example, wouldn't be happy operating something this small. Give either of them Charms & Virtues and neither would rest until she had turned it into a coast-to-coast chain. I would have done the same thing, myself, until last summer."

Elias smiled. "Maybe I would have, too."

"Some people," Charity said deliberately, "have to keep pushing and expanding until they've got a universe to control. They don't know how to be content with just one small, complete world."

Elias picked up a sack of bird feed and began to refill Otis's cup. "Is that a not very subtle way of asking me if I'm going to be able to settle down here in a small place like Whispering Waters Cove and find satisfaction with a shop such as Charms & Virtues?"

Charity frowned. "I thought I was being extremely subtle."

"If that's your idea of subtlety, you've forgotten everything you must have once known about the subject."

"Dang. Are you sure it wasn't subtle?"

"Afraid not." Elias refolded the bag and stashed it under the perch.

"Well, shoot. I guess this means I'm not going to be able to do my civic duty and sacrifice myself for the good of Whispering Waters Cove, after all."

Elias paused. "What sort of duty and sacrifice did you have in mind?"

"It was recently suggested to me by Her Honor, the Mayor, that I use my amazing powers of seduction to persuade you to tell me the nature of your secret plans. I have been instructed to use my womanly wiles to find out exactly what you're up to here in Whispering Waters Cove."

"In the words of my last customer: cool."

"Naturally, my first thought was of Ingrid Bergman in *Notorious.*"

"Sounds like we're on the same wavelength here."

She frowned. "Things were going great until you said I lacked subtlety. What good is an unsubtle spy?"

"Maybe you just need a little experience," Elias said. "I might be willing to let you practice on me."

"Really?"

The phone rang in the small office. Elias held up a hand. "Hold that thought. I'll be right back."

"Yeah, sure. That's what they all say. Sorry, I can't hang around. Got to go close up for the day." Charity started to turn away. "Six-thirty Monday night okay for dinner?"

"I'll bring the wine this time."

"See you." She waved as she hurried out through the front door.

Elias grinned as he scooped up the phone. He had never had much inclination to play the flirtation game in the past, but he thought he might be able to get into the spirit of the thing with Charity.

"Charms & Virtues. Winters here."

"Elias? This is Craig. Got a minute?"

"Sure." Elias leaned out of the doorway of his office and watched Charity stride past the shop window. Her long yellow cotton dress flitted with the breeze, revealing the sweet hollows at the back of her knees. "Get anything on Gwen Pitt?"

"As a matter of fact, I did. She's been a busy woman during the past year."

"Doing what?"

"What she does best, apparently. Buying and selling Northwest real estate. The interesting part is that she's been doing it very quietly in the name of a company called Voyager Properties."

"Using money she took from her Voyagers, I assume?"

"Probably. But there's nothing illegal about her firm as far as we can tell. She's the president. Only one employee on the payroll."

"Let me guess. Rick Swinton?"

"Actually, his full name is Richard Swinton. Sounds like you've made his acquaintance."

"He paid me a visit last night. Uninvited."

"I see," Craig said. "Want me to dig deeper into his background?"

"I'll probably ask for more information after I repay Swinton's visit."

"Sounds like the two of you are getting friendly."

"You know how it is in a small town. Everyone tries to be neighborly."

"Better pay your return visit before this Swinton character leaves on a spaceship," Craig said.

"I'll do that."

"By the way, I have some unrelated news that may be of interest to you."

Elias gazed at Otis through the office doorway. The

bird was sidling impatiently back and forth along his perch. It was closing time. "What news?"

"Remember Garrick Keyworth? The guy you had me do some work on?"

Elias went still. "What about him?"

"Word has it that he tried to commit suicide last night. Took a whole fistful of pills."

All of the air went out of Elias's lungs. With no warning, the river that flowed out of his own past suddenly revealed the pale form of his mother. She lay sprawled on a bed, an array of pill bottles neatly arranged on the night table beside her.

With an act of practiced will, Elias sent the image back into the darkness from which it had come.

"Did he succeed?" Elias asked.

"No. Nine-one-one was called. They got him to the hospital in time. He'll recover, but you can imagine what the news will do to the company. Once the shock wears off, Keyworth International is expected to go into a tailspin. You know how it is in an operation like that where there's no clear successor poised to take over the leadership slot. Everyone panics."

"Yes."

"Too bad Keyworth never took his son into the firm. If he had, there would be someone at the helm now to calm customers and creditors."

"Keyworth and his son are estranged," Elias said.

"So I heard. Well, I'd say this will be the end of Keyworth International."

7

A man can drown in passion as surely as he can drown
in the sea.

—"On the Way of Water," from the journal of Hayden Stone

Something was wrong.

Charity closed the new issue of *Gourmet*, which she
had been poring over for the past half hour. She could
feel the wrongness in her bones. The feeling of unease
had been growing steadily since late this afternoon
when she had seen Elias lock up his shop for the night.

He hadn't even bothered to wave good-bye to anyone, let alone see Charity to her car, as had become
his habit during the past few days. He had set off
toward the parking lot without a backward glance,
empty travel cage in one hand. Otis had perched like
a vulture on his shoulder.

For some inexplicable reason, the sight of man and
bird pacing down the pier had sent a chill through

Charity. Now, several hours later, the cold feeling was getting worse.

She tossed the glossy magazine onto the whimsically designed, frosted-glass coffee table. It landed on a bevy of cookbooks that she had brought home from Whispers. She had spent the entire evening scouring the collection for interesting recipes. Elias's tastes, like hers, were distinctive and a little eccentric. Nothing had been said aloud, but Charity sensed that a gauntlet had been thrown down. Elias had deliberately challenged her. She intended to hold her own in the next round of the Truitt-Winters cook-off.

But what she was feeling now was not a form of chef's anxiety. This restlessness was different.

She could not get the image of Elias's grim silhouette against the evening sun out of her mind.

Something was definitely wrong.

She uncurled from the curved lipstick-red sofa and walked across the small living room to open the front door. She stepped out onto the porch. It was after nine. Nearly full dark. There was a new chill in the air. Fog was gathering over the cove.

She curled her hands around the old, white-washed rail and studied the maze of trees that stretched the quarter-mile distance that separated her cottage from Elias's. She could not make out any sign of light through the thick foliage.

On impulse she straightened, locked the front door, and went down the porch steps. She paused again, listening to the sounds of the onrushing night. She thought she could hear the distant chants of the Voyagers, but it was difficult to tell for certain.

She walked out to the bluff path. Once again she gazed in the direction of Elias's cottage. From here she should be able to see lights from his windows through the trees.

Nothing. Not so much as a glimmer from his porch light. Perhaps he had gone into town for the evening.

The sense of wrongness grew stronger.

She took one step and then another along the path. She had covered several yards before she acknowledged that she was going to walk to Elias's cottage.

This was probably a mistake. Checking up on Elias could prove to be an embarrassing move in the cat-and-mouse flirtation game that the two of them seemed to be playing. He'd probably view her curiosity as a sign of eagerness or even desperation. She would lose the upper hand.

But she could not make herself turn back.

What the hell. She never had been any good at the kind of games men and women played. There had never been any time to practice.

The night closed swiftly in around her as she hurried along the top of the bluffs. When she reached Elias's madrona-shaded garden she saw that there was still no light in the windows. She walked around to the front of the cottage. Elias's Jeep was parked in the drive.

She wondered if he had gone for an evening walk farther up along the bluffs.

Charity made her way back around the cottage to the garden entrance. For a moment she stood, one hand resting on the low gate. After a moment she raised the latch and went into the garden.

She was halfway along the winding path, headed toward the unlit porch, when she sensed another presence in the garden. She stopped and turned slowly.

It took a few seconds for her to make out Elias. He sat cross-legged in front of the reflecting pool, a still, silent figure shrouded in twilight shadows. The small pond was a black mirror that revealed nothing.

"Elias?" She took a step forward and hesitated.

"Was there something you wanted?" His voice held the distant, chillingly detached quality that had unnerved her on the day they had met.

"No." She took another step toward him. "Are you all right?"

"Yes."

"Elias, for heaven's sake, what's wrong?"

"An interesting aspect of water is only revealed when there is an absence of light. The surface becomes as opaque to the eye as a wall of obsidian."

"Great, we're back to the Zen-speak." Charity walked to the edge of the pond and halted a short distance from Elias. "Enough with the cryptic comments. Tell me what's going on here."

At first she thought that he would not respond. He did not move, did not even look at her. He seemed completely focused on the dark, blank surface of the reflecting pool. An endless moment passed.

"Garrick Keyworth tried to commit suicide last night," he said at last.

The stark words hit her with the force of a wave crashing on rocks. She recalled what Elias had said about his mother's death. Suicide always held a special horror for those who had been touched by it.

"Oh, Elias."

She sank down beside him. A section of the hem of her light chambray dress settled on his knee. She followed his gaze into the darkness of the reflecting pool. He was right. There was nothing to be seen there. The night sat heavily on the garden.

Time passed. Charity did not attempt to break the silence. She simply waited. It was the only thing she could do.

"I thought that because I had decided to walk away from my revenge, the matter was finished," Elias said after a while. "But I did not truly turn aside. I went to Keyworth one last time. Showed him what I could have done to him, had I chosen to go through with it."

"You don't know that your meeting with him had anything to do with his suicide attempt."

"It had everything to do with it. I studied him for years. I should have seen the full range of possibilities when I made my last move. Maybe I did see them but refused to acknowledge them."

"Don't be so hard on yourself, Elias."

"I knew damn well that the knowledge of his own vulnerability would add to the poison brewing inside Keyworth. But I told myself that it would be only a single small drop in the mixture. Not enough to change the final results."

"You couldn't have known that it would push him over the edge. You still don't know that it did."

"It takes only a small impurity to destroy the perfection of the clearest pond."

Charity tried to think of something to say, but everything that came to mind was useless. A less self-aware, less self-disciplined man might have been comforted by her insistence that he was not responsible for Keyworth's suicide attempt. A less complicated man might have taken triumphant satisfaction from the situation. After all, some would say that had Keyworth been successful, it would have been nothing more than simple justice. But Elias was not like most men. Elias was different.

After a while Charity reached out to touch his arm. Every muscle, every tendon, every sinew beneath his skin was as taut as twisted steel. He did not move. He seemed oblivious to her fingers.

"It's getting chilly out here," she said eventually. "Come inside. I'll fix you some tea."

"I don't want any tea. Go home, Charity."

The icy remoteness in his voice made her want to

recoil. She fought the instinctive urge to leap to her feet and run. "I'm not going to leave you sitting out here. There's a fog bank moving in over the cove, in case you haven't noticed. The temperature is dropping."

"I can take care of myself. I don't need your help. Leave me alone, Charity. You shouldn't have come here tonight."

"We're neighbors, remember? Friends. I can't leave you alone."

"You have no responsibility for me."

"Listen up, Mr. Control Freak, you've got your code, and I've got mine. Mine says I can't leave you out here by yourself." She got to her feet and tugged on his arm. "Please, Elias. Let's go inside."

He looked up at her with eyes as unreadable as the surface of the reflecting pool. For a moment she thought he would refuse. Then, without a word he rose to his feet in a single, fluid movement.

She took advantage of the small victory to lead him up the steps. He did not resist, but the hard tension in him did not ease. She opened the door and urged him gently inside.

She kicked off her shoes and groped along the wall. "Where's the light switch?"

Without a word, Elias extended one hand and flipped a switch. A lamp glowed in the corner. Otis muttered a complaint from beneath the cover that encircled his cage.

For the first time Charity got a clear look at Elias's face. What she saw there made her wish she hadn't asked him to turn on the light. Some things were best left concealed in the shadows.

On the other hand, some things only got more scary if they were hidden in the dark.

"I'll put the water on," she said.

"I think you'd better leave, Charity. I'm not going to be good company tonight."

The words were an unmistakable warning. A tiny frisson of fear went through her. She shook off the sense of impending danger. "I said I'd fix you a cup of tea."

She brushed past him and crossed the barren room to the small kitchen. The kettle sat on a back burner. She discovered a pot in a cupboard. There was a cannister of Kemun beside it.

"I doubt if my tea will be up to your standards, but at least it will be hot." She ran water into the kettle.

"Charity."

She paused, kettle in hand, and glanced at him over her shoulder.

"Yes?"

He said nothing. He simply stood there, watching her with a shattering intensity that paralyzed her. She was riveted by the bleakness in his gaze. In that moment she could see straight through the wall of pride and self-discipline he had so painstakingly built around himself. An ancient loneliness crouched like some great monstrous beast in the darkness beyond the wall.

"Elias," she said very softly. Slowly she put down the kettle. "I know you think you can handle this by yourself, and you're probably right. But sometimes it's better not to try to go it alone. That stuff about the Way of Water may work just fine as a philosophical construct, but sometimes a person needs more."

"Tal Kek Chara is all I have," he said with stark simplicity.

"That's not true." She shook off the spell that had seized her and went to him.

She put her arms around him and hugged him with fierce determination. He was hard and unyielding.

Aware that she was engaged in a battle of unknown dimensions, she tightened her arms and pressed her face against his shoulder. With a sense of desperation, she willed her warmth and something more, something she was not certain she wanted to identify, into the center of his being.

A shudder went through Elias. With a low, hoarse groan, he captured her head between his hands.

"You should have gone home," he said.

And then his mouth was on hers. The beast of loneliness howled.

Charity swayed beneath the onslaught of a masculine hunger that threatened to drown her. For a moment, everything threatened to disappear.

When the mist cleared slightly, she realized that she was in Elias's arms. He had picked her up and was carrying her toward the dark opening that marked the doorway of the bedroom.

She felt herself being lowered onto a cushion of some sort. It had to be a futon, she thought. Nothing else would be this hard and uncomfortable. The man slept on a *futon*. That was taking self-discipline a little too far.

But she had no time to complain. He came down on top of her and she promptly forgot about the overly firm bedding. Elias was far more rigid than his futon.

His lean, powerful body was a sexy weight crushing her into the dense cushions. The kiss was endlessly deep, infinitely mysterious, not unlike Elias himself.

Charity wrapped her arms around his neck. His fingers went to the buttons of her loose, chambray dress. She heard him inhale sharply when he uncovered her breasts. His palm closed over one nipple, and it was her turn to gasp. She felt herself tighten at his touch. Another savage shudder went through him.

"You shouldn't have come here tonight," he muttered.

"It's all right, Elias." Her head fell back across his arm. One of his legs slid between her thighs. He pushed his knee upward, shoving aside the skirt of her dress. The denim of his jeans was rough and strangely exciting against her bare skin.

"You shouldn't be here, but I can't send you away now. God help me, I want you too much."

He pulled free of her mouth and bent his head to catch the crown of her breast between his teeth. His hand went to the rapidly dampening crotch of her panties. He squeezed gently, urgently. One strong finger eased beneath the elastic edge. He tugged off the undergarment in a single, swift movement.

A driving excitement washed over Charity, a giant wave that gathered her up and tumbled her about until she was dazed and disoriented. She had never felt so gloriously wild in her life. She yanked Elias's shirt free of his jeans and sank her fingers into his sleekly contoured back.

For some reason, it came as a shock to discover how warm he was. She sensed the muscles working smoothly, powerfully beneath his skin. The tang of his scent was electrifyingly male.

She fumbled with the pliant strip of leather that he wore outside the belt loops of his jeans. There was no buckle. She could not figure out how to unfasten the odd knot. In mounting frustration, she jerked at a trailing end.

"I'll take care of it." He levered himself away from her long enough to remove the unusual belt.

The knot that had proved so stubborn beneath her fingers, came undone at a single touch of his hand. He shifted again to toss the length of leather down beside the futon. She heard the slide of a metal zipper.

He rolled to one side, pulled off his jeans, and reached into the open chest beside the futon. Charity heard the distinctive sound of tearing foil. Elias's hands moved deftly.

A moment later he rolled back on top of her. She tensed when she felt the broad head of his sheathed erection pressing against her damp body. He was heavy and thick.

Big. Definitely big. But it was excitement she felt, not panic.

He centered himself between her legs. "Look at me."

She opened her eyes, responding instantly to the urgency in his words. There was just enough light filtering in from the front room to allow her to see the stark hunger in him. The rush of her own response made her tremble.

She drove her fingers through his hair. "I want you, Elias."

"No more games," he whispered.

"No more games."

He thrust into her in a slow, endless motion that shocked all of her senses. Everything within her froze. She could not think, could not speak, could not move. He filled her completely. Stretched her to the point of pain. Every muscle in her body was coiled spring-tight in response to the sensual invasion.

Locked deep inside her, Elias went as still as everything else in the universe. He stared down at her as if waiting for some signal to finish what had been begun.

"Are you all right?" he asked in a voice that shook a little around the edges.

Charity took a deep breath and rediscovered her own tongue. "Yes. Yes, I'm very much all right." She clenched her fingers tightly in his hair and lifted herself cautiously against him.

A husky groan vibrated deep in his chest. "I don't want to hurt you. You're so small and tight. I didn't realize—"

"I said, it's all right." She smiled up at him.

"My God, Charity." He bent his head and kissed the curve of her shoulder.

The unbearable tightness eased. The world began to revolve once more.

Elias retreated slowly, cautiously and then pushed steadily back into her. This time excitement accompanied the overwhelming sense of fullness. Charity sighed hungrily and dug her nails into his shoulders.

He responded with a swift intake of breath. One of his hands slid down her body to the point where they were joined. He found the exquisitely sensitive nub in the nest of crisp, curling hair and stroked deliberately.

Electricity shot through her. She arched and cried out.

"So good," he whispered. "So real."

She swallowed a wild urge to laugh. "Of course I'm real. What did you think I was? Just another reflection on the water?"

"I wasn't quite certain until now."

He stroked again and again and all the seething tension within her exploded in wave after wave of release. She felt his teeth on her earlobe as he drove into her one last time.

His body stiffened in climax. His hoarse, soundless cry echoed in the darkness.

Charity let the night take her.

No more games.

Elias opened his eyes and looked at the dark ceiling. The scent of spent passion mingled with the cool fog-laced air that came through the partially opened window. He was acutely aware of the warm curve of Charity's thigh pressed against his leg.

He could feel the satisfaction in every quadrant of his body. It sang in his veins and created a pleasant warmth in his belly. He stretched, languid and relaxed and content.

No more games.

It felt good.

It felt dangerous.

Control was everything in Tal Kek Chara. To lose control was to be swept away by the raging tide into the deepest part of the sea. To lose control was to be caught up in the churning rapids of a primeval river. To lose control was to go over the falls, to plummet down through the depths of an icy-cold, bottomless lake.

To lose control was to lose everything.

The following morning Charity gazed out the window at the fog that had enveloped Whispering Waters Cove during the night. "If this doesn't lift by tonight, the spaceships may not get clearance to land."

"Something tells me it won't make much difference," Elias said. "Ready for breakfast?"

"Sure." She turned away from the window. "But I hope you kept it simple. It's okay to show off at dinner, but it's not fair when it comes to breakfast. Breakfast is not a competitive sport."

Elias's brows rose as he set two bowls on the low table. "Think of it as a challenge."

She summoned what she hoped was a breezy, sophisticated smile as she sank down onto one of the cushions in front of the table. "Push me too far, and I'll throw in the towel and send out for pizza tonight."

"No, you won't. That would be the coward's way, and you're no coward." He sat down across from her and poured tea from the brown, earthenware pot. "I'm sure you'll rise to the occasion. Something tells me you always do."

"I hate to disappoint you, but I lost a lot of my competitive edge when I quit the corporate world."

The attempt at casual conversation took an extraordinary amount of effort. Charity was not in a lighthearted mood. The uncertainty that gripped her this morning came as a complete surprise. This was not how she had expected to feel after last night's intense lovemaking. It made her uncomfortable. There was no panic yet, but she could definitely hear alarm bells.

This subtle tension between herself and Elias was not right. Not the way things should be today.

Where was the sense of intimacy that ought to have enveloped both of them in a warm cocoon this morning? she wondered. Only hours ago she had felt incredibly close to Elias. Now there was a disturbing distance between them.

She was all too well aware that her experience of sex was not what anyone would call extensive, and it was several years out of date. Her responsibilities to Truitt had imprisoned her in an artificial cloister for years. This was, in fact, the first time that she had ever actually stayed the night with a man and shared breakfast with him the next morning. Nevertheless, her instincts told her that it shouldn't be like this between the two of them.

Something very special had happened between them last night. Elias had let her see a piece of his soul.

But things were all wrong today. He was back in his remote, self-contained universe. She could not touch him the way she had touched him last night.

He had said that there would be no more games, but this morning she felt as if they were both back out on the playing field.

She stifled a small sigh and looked down at the interesting concoction in her bowl. "What is this?"

"Muesli. My own recipe. Oats, rye, sesame seeds, almonds, dried fruit, yogurt, and a touch of vanilla and honey."

"So much for keeping breakfast noncompetitive." She added milk to the muesli and picked up a spoon.

"When I stay the night with you, I'll fix breakfast," he offered with suspicious generosity.

Charity coughed and nearly choked on a bite of cereal. She put down her spoon and grabbed the small teacup.

"Are you okay?" Elias asked.

She nodded quickly and swallowed tea to clear her throat. "Fine. Just fine. Sesame seed went down the wrong way."

He regarded her with a long, steady gaze. "Does the thought of me spending the night in your bed make you nervous?"

"Of course not." She gulped more hot tea. "Don't be ridiculous." With a heroic effort she summoned a confident smile. "But I'm sure neither one of us wants to rush things. We'll take our time. Let the relationship develop naturally."

His eyes narrowed faintly. "I thought we agreed last night that there would be no more games."

She felt the heat rise in her cheeks. "Letting a relationship mature and develop at its own pace is not considered game-playing. It's just common sense."

"What's wrong, Charity?"

"Nothing's wrong." She let the smile drop. "I'm just trying to sort things out, that's all."

"What's to sort out?"

Anger flared out of nowhere. "You have to ask me that?" She set the teacup down so hard that it threatened to crack. Otis grumbled at the noise. "You're the one who's been acting as if nothing out of the ordinary happened last night."

He gazed at her for a long while. "About last night."

She held up a hand. "Please. If this is the part where you tell me not to read too much into what happened between us last night, forget it. I'm trying to eat my breakfast. You can give me the lecture later."

"No."

"You want to go back to playing games, fine. Go play with yourself."

"That idea lacks a certain appeal," he said dryly. "Especially after last night."

She felt herself turn red. "You know what I mean."

"Yes. But I don't think you understand what I'm trying to say here."

"Hah. That's what you think. I understand exactly what you're trying to say." She tapped her spoon on the edge of the bowl. "You want to tell me that you weren't yourself last night, don't you? That I shouldn't assume too much because of what happened. That you're sorry we spent the night together."

He hesitated. "You've got it half right. I wasn't in a good place last night."

"Uh-huh." She stabbed her spoon into the muesli.

"I wasn't expecting you to show up. I had a lot of thinking to do."

"And I interrupted you?"

"To be blunt, yes, you did. It would have been better if you had not come into the garden when you did."

"Sorry about that." She spooned up a mouthful of muesli and chewed with a vengeance. "Won't happen again."

He frowned. "You don't get it."

"Sure, I do. I'm an ex-CEO, remember? I can boil

down even the most complicated issues into simple concepts. Problem? You wish I hadn't shown up last night. Solution? Simple. We'll just pretend it never happened."

"That's not going to be possible."

She smiled grimly. "Watch me."

"You're angry."

She thought about it. "Yeah, you could say that."

"Charity, I'm trying to get something clear between us."

"Maybe it would be better if you just ate your breakfast instead."

He ignored that. "What I'm trying to tell you is that I regret that you interrupted me while I was in the middle of a contemplation session last night. I was trying to sort out some things. I think that you might have drawn some false conclusions based on what happened after you showed up."

She halted the spoon halfway to her mouth, as realization dawned. "Wait a second. I think I'm getting a glimmer here."

"Let's just say that it would not be wise for you to assume that my actions last night indicated that I was—" He broke off, frowning.

"Weak? Normal?" She paused delicately. "Human?"

A dark flush stained his fierce cheekbones. "I don't want you to get the wrong impression, that's all."

"Elias, think of this in terms of your water philosophy. You can't stay in the shallow end of the pool all of your life, thinking you'll be safe. Sometimes you just have to take a chance and jump in at the deep end."

"That analogy is not an appropriate application of the philosophical principles of Tal Kek Chara," he said through his teeth. "The Way is a method of seeing clearly. A guide to observing reality."

"But you're not an observer. You're a participant. At least you were last night."

"You're missing the point here."

She leveled her spoon at him. "Okay, enlighten me, oh, great Master of Tal Kek Chara. Take a look into your magic reflecting pool and tell me what you see happening between us right now at this very moment."

"That's exactly what I'm trying to do," he said swiftly. "I don't want you to be under any misconceptions about me. I realize that my behavior last night may have given you the impression that I allowed Keyworth's attempt at suicide to get to me."

"Didn't it?"

"His attempt to take his own life was an unforeseen consequence of my actions." A harsh, bleak acceptance burned in Elias's eyes. "And I don't like it when unforeseen consequences occur. It means that I failed to use Tal Kek Chara correctly."

"Hey, nobody's perfect."

"That is no excuse," he shot back.

"Elias, it's not your fault that Keyworth tried to commit suicide. But if it's going to eat at you like this, I suggest you do something about it."

"Such as?"

She hesitated, thinking quickly. "You could go see him, I suppose. That would be a start. Talk to him. Make your peace with him."

"And just how the hell do you suggest that I do that, Madam Therapist? What am I supposed to say to a man who tried to kill himself because of me?"

"I don't know. I've never been in a situation like this. Maybe you need to tell him that you don't want the past to repeat itself. Does he have children?"

"A son who hates his guts."

Charity nodded. "Tell Keyworth not to do to his kid what your parents did to you."

"My parents." Elias looked thunderstruck.

"Tell Keyworth he's got no right to abandon his son. That if he really wants to atone for what happened all those years ago on Nihili, he must fulfill his responsibilities in the present."

Elias stared at her. Charity could almost see him gathering himself, searching for the center, summoning his power. She thought she caught another fleeting glimpse of the beast of loneliness prowling within him just before the barriers solidified and shut her out.

"You don't know enough about the situation to make a suggestion like that," Elias said in a voice that was more remote than the moon. "Forget about Keyworth. I'll deal with it."

"Sure."

"About us," he began deliberately. "I told you a few minutes ago that you were half right when you said that I regret that you came into my garden last night and that we spent the night together."

"I think I can guess which half I got right. You wish I hadn't seen you acting like a normal human being with your defenses down, but, what the hell, the sex was okay."

"The sex was a lot better than okay."

She managed a cool smile. "Yes, it was, wasn't it?"

He pushed his uneaten muesli aside and folded his arms on the low table. "It might have been better if we had waited to begin our relationship under more auspicious circumstances. But what's done is done."

"That's certainly a charmingly romantic view of our little night of passion."

"What I'm trying to say is that, while I wish it had

happened at a different time, I don't regret that we've moved to the next stage of our relationship."

Charity looked at her watch. "Good grief, it's nearly eight o'clock. I've got to run home, change, and get ready to open the shop at ten."

"Charity—"

"I'll see you at the pier." She leaped to her feet, scooped up her bowl and spoon, and dashed across the room to dump them into the sink.

"Damn it, Charity, wait a minute."

"Don't forget, dinner at my place this evening." She stepped into her sandals and yanked open the front door. "This is the big night for the Voyagers and their spaceships. Better bring a jacket. It'll probably be chilly out on the bluff at midnight."

She fled into the early-morning fog.

8

The currents shift without warning yet the surface of the water appears to be the same to the observer. In such a situation there is great danger.

—"On the Way of Water," from the journal of Hayden Stone

Charity pounced on the perfectly shaped red bell pepper in the grocery store vegetable bin. "Gotcha."

She slipped several more plump peppers into a plastic bag and placed her booty in the shopping cart.

Seizing the handlebar of the cart, she leaned into the task of forcing it down another aisle. It took considerable effort to keep the vehicle tracking in a reasonably straight line. One wheel kept veering off at a crazy angle.

She breathed a sigh of relief when she found the packages of dried seaweed next to the seasoned rice wine vinegar. She grabbed two envelopes full of the glistening, dark green sheets of *nori* and a bottle of the vinegar and dumped it all into the cart.

It hadn't been easy selecting a menu for tonight's dinner. Her main concern had been choosing recipes that called for ingredients she could count on finding at the Whispering Waters Cove Grocery. A year ago when she first moved into town, tonight's menu would have been an impossible dream. But her intensive efforts to cultivate the store manager had paid off.

The real problem, she decided as she did battle with the recalcitrant cart, was not locating the ingredients for tonight's dinner. The more critical issue was, why was she bothering to cook a meal for Elias Winters in the first place?

She was still simmering over their early-morning conversation. He had made it breathtakingly clear that he wanted to pretend that he had never shown her that vulnerable piece of himself last night. On the other hand, he was content to carry on with the sexual side of their relationship now that it had gotten off the ground.

Typical, Charity thought. It was just so damn typical.

No, that wasn't fair, she decided as she reached for a package of rice and some soy sauce. Nothing about Elias could be called typical.

She glanced at her list. She still needed fresh fruit for the dessert. It was getting late. She had left Newlin in charge of closing Whispers while she took off to do her grocery shopping, but she still had a number of things to do before Elias arrived on her doorstep.

She muscled the grocery cart around a corner and saw another cart blocking her path. Jennifer Pitt had the door of the frozen food case open.

"Oops, sorry, Jennifer." For some reason, Charity's cart, which until now had fought her every inch of the way, suddenly took off like a thoroughbred racehorse.

Charity dug in her heels and managed to drag it to a halt. "Didn't see you."

Jennifer smiled her cool, bored smile. "Don't worry about it. These aisles are far too narrow. When things start to boom here in the Cove, I'd like to see a major grocery chain move into town. We could certainly use a decent store here."

"This one's not so bad. Just a little small."

"You could say that about the whole damn town."

Charity started to back out of the aisle. The last thing she wanted to do was get into an extended conversation with the second Mrs. Pitt. Jennifer was not a happy woman. Of course, it had not been an easy summer for her, what with the flamboyant first Mrs. Pitt flitting around town in her outrageous Voyager costume.

In Charity's opinion, Jennifer had actually handled the whole thing with surprising grace. Perhaps the knowledge that she was the current Mrs. Pitt, not the ex, gave her the fortitude to rise above the awkward situation.

Jennifer was a tall, sleek, striking woman in her mid-thirties. Rumor had it that she had once done a short stint as a model in Los Angeles. Charity could well believe it. She had the height, and there was a certain kind of Southern California glamour about her. It whispered of hot beaches and endless summers. Everyone knew she worked out regularly on the home gym equipment Leighton had purchased for her. The results showed.

She had a sense of fashion that was alien to Whispering Waters Cove. Today she wore a silk shirt designed to imitate denim and a pair of beautifully draped trousers that flowed over the cuffs of her shoes.

Her honey-brown mane was streaked with a lot of

golden highlights, as if she lived in perpetual sunshine instead of in the cloudy Northwest. She wore her big hair in a voluminous, shoulder-length style that always managed to look just slightly windblown. The large diamond that Leighton had given her on their wedding day glittered on her left hand. She always had a pair of stylish dark glasses perched on top of her head, and her makeup was flawless.

Most folks held the view that Leighton Pitt had never stood a chance once Jennifer set her sights on him. The biggest mystery in Whispering Waters Cove was not why he had divorced Gwendolyn to marry Jennifer. The mystery was why Jennifer had ever wanted to steal him in the first place.

True, Leighton was the most prosperous man in the Cove, but most people felt that, with her looks and style, Jennifer could have done much better for herself in Seattle. After all there was *real* money in the city, everyone pointed out, what with all the high-tech companies and the Pacific Rim businesses located there.

"I suppose you'll be joining the crowd on the bluff at midnight tonight." Jennifer's long, red-tipped acrylic nails closed around a ready-made, low-fat entrée.

"Wouldn't miss it." Charity glanced curiously at the microwavable meal Jennifer had selected. It was a single-serving size. "Biggest show in town."

"Which isn't saying much, is it?" Jennifer's crimson mouth twisted with just a hint of bitterness as she closed the freezer door. "Well, at least it will all be over by tomorrow. Gwendolyn's Voyagers will finally realize that they've been had. Wonder what they'll do about it when they find out they've been ripped off?"

Charity thought about it. "I suppose some of them might sue."

Jennifer lifted one shoulder in an elegant little shrug. "I doubt if that would do any good. I'm sure

Gwendolyn and her friend, Rick Swinton, have made certain that the money is well protected."

"Maybe nothing much will change after the spaceships fail to arrive," Charity suggested. "A friend of mine says that people who want to believe in something will often go on believing in it even in the face of overwhelming proof that it doesn't exist."

"Your friend may be right." Jennifer's gaze shifted to a point just beyond Charity's right shoulder. Her eyes narrowed. "Some people who turned over their savings to a swindler might prefer to continue to believe rather than to admit they'd been conned. But others might get a little pissed when they discover the truth."

Without waiting for a response, she twirled her shopping cart around with a single-handed grip on the handlebar. The cart obeyed instantly. It never even wobbled. Under Jennifer's guidance, it maneuvered down the aisle with the pinpoint precision of a fine European sports car.

Charity watched in admiration. Some people had all the luck when it came to selecting shopping carts.

"My, my. Little Miss California seems to be in a snit today," Gwendolyn Pitt drawled behind Charity. "And you can bet she isn't feeding that low-fat frozen dinner to Leighton. Oh, no. I expect that he'll be clogging up his arteries with beer and nachos down at the Cove Tavern again tonight. Sweet Jennifer is probably hoping that he'll conveniently drop dead from a heart attack."

Charity turned reluctantly. Gwendolyn was in full Voyager regalia. Her long blue and white robes looked even more bizarre than usual against the mundane backdrop of a small-town grocery store.

The guru look was an interesting contrast to the shrewd, assessing expression in Gwendolyn's eyes. Charity was fairly certain she could still see signs of the successful real estate broker beneath the exotic attire.

"Hello, Gwendolyn. Ready for the big night?"

"Of course. All the Voyagers are ready. We have been preparing ourselves for this night for months." Gwendolyn watched Jennifer disappear around the corner of the aisle, and then she switched her sharp gaze to Charity. "I'm sure everyone in town will find it fascinating."

"You can bet we'll all be there on the bluff." Charity grabbed hold of her cart handle and prepared to escape. "Of course, if this fog doesn't lift, we might not be able to see the starships arrive."

"Don't worry," Gwendolyn murmured. "The entire town will find out soon enough that something interesting has happened."

Nothing yields so easily as water, yet nothing is so powerful. He who seeks to follow the Way must first acknowledge his own strengths and weaknesses.

Hayden Stone's advice burned in Elias's mind as he whirled through the last movement of the twisting, gliding pattern. He breathed out and allowed the leather belt to seek its target. The end of the belt struck with the speed and accuracy of a snake. It wrapped itself around the empty aluminum pop can and crushed it.

Elias drew a deep breath and bent down to pick up the crumpled can. Not good. He had used too much force. His control was not what it should have been today.

He walked to the edge of the bluff and looked out over the fog-shrouded cove.

His timing and calculation had been off during the entire practice session, and it didn't take an hour's contemplation on the Way of Water to figure out why.

Memories of last night kept getting in the way of his concentration.

Elias gazed into the gray mist as the images crashed through his head.

Charity sitting down beside him at the edge of the reflecting pool.

Charity sliding her fingers through his hair as she offered him her mouth.

Charity looking into his eyes and knowing what the news of Keyworth's suicide attempt had done to him.

Charity trembling with passion as she lay beneath him.

He'd been wrong about one thing. There had been no problem making love to Charity on the futon. He could have made love to her on the floor or the beach or anywhere else, for that matter. The thing that worried him the most at the moment was not knowing when he would be able to make love to her again.

The hot need simmered inside him. Last night had only whetted his appetite. Today, instead of satisfaction, there was only a deeper hunger.

They had agreed that there would be no more games between them. But this morning she had made it clear that she was still prepared to play them. He knew why she had shied away from a full commitment to the affair they had begun during the night. It was as Hayden Stone had warned him years ago. A woman worth wanting always demanded a great deal in return.

Elias knew that Charity wanted more than just good sex. She wanted his soul. She wanted to assure herself that she had true power over him.

He became aware of the cooling perspiration on his bare shoulders. The elaborate movements of Tal Kek Chara had done little to alleviate the tension he had been feeling all day.

He was still aware of the edgy feeling later that evening when he found himself in Charity's kitchen. Elias saw right away that they were both going to play it cool. She was no longer intense and emotional the way she had been this morning when she had left his cottage. They were back to the easy flirtation that had characterized their relationship for the past several days.

Just two friendly people involved in an affair. That was good, he assured himself. He wondered irritably why he did not feel incredibly relieved by the deliberately diminished tides of intensity.

He lounged in the doorway of Charity's kitchen and surveyed the wonderland of gleaming pans, Euro-style appliances, and high-tech gadgets. The kitchen matched the rest of the cottage, which was crammed with the sophisticated furnishings Charity had brought with her when she moved to the cove.

It was all a far cry from the stark simplicity of his own place, Elias thought. But it was oddly pleasant to watch Charity work amid her sleek, colorful surroundings.

Absently he swirled the chardonnay in his glass. "I didn't get a chance to tell you what my lawyer, Craig Thorgood, learned about Gwendolyn Pitt and her Voyagers."

Charity shot him a surprised glance over her shoulder before she resumed whisking soy sauce, ginger, lime juice, and sherry in a bowl. "Anything interesting?"

"Nothing startling. Just the guru business as usual. Gwendolyn has created a company called Voyager Investments. She's the president, and Swinton is her sole employee."

Charity paused again in her whisking and looked thoughtful. "Then the money they've taken from the cult members is out there somewhere. It might be traceable."

Elias smiled faintly. "I think it's a safe bet that it's very traceable. I'm sure Gwendolyn and Swinton have it under close surveillance."

"Maybe some of the Voyagers can get it back after the spaceships fail to show up tonight. I have a feeling Arlene Fenton, for one, is going to be in desperate straits once she realizes she's not bound for the stars. Newlin says she turned over everything in her bank account to the Voyagers organization."

"It wouldn't be easy to retrieve anyone's assets without the cooperation of Pitt or Swinton. And I doubt if either of them will be inclined to cooperate."

"They probably plan to take the money and run," Charity agreed. "Although Gwendolyn Pitt said something strange today in the grocery store."

"What was that?"

"Something about the entire town finding out soon that something interesting had happened tonight."

"I don't doubt it. The only question is, why is today's date so important to her?" Elias caught the fragrance of the ginger and inhaled appreciatively. "Are you going to tell me what's on the menu?"

"Vegetable sushi, roasted red pepper salad, and a nectarine and blueberry tart."

"I don't believe it. You talked the store manager into stocking *nori?*"

Charity smiled. "I didn't spend all those years running Truitt for nothing. I've had plenty of experience in the art of the deal."

"I can see that the competition is heating up. This could get ugly. Or maybe I should say tasty."

"I'm sure you'll think of something amusingly unpretentious yet elegant when it's your turn to cook. I can see you doing a dish of stunning simplicity that is infused with flavors that retain their integrity even as they enhance the other elements involved."

"Let me guess. You've been reading food magazines, haven't you?"

"Yep." She dropped the whisk into the sink. "I also saw the second Mrs. Pitt in the grocery store this afternoon. A touch of animosity between the first and the second. I was lucky I didn't get crushed between their shopping carts."

"Not surprising."

"No."

Elias sipped his wine. "I've got to admit, I'm getting a little curious about Gwendolyn's plans."

"Join the crowd."

"But I'm even more curious about Rick Swinton."

"Why the special interest in him?"

"Because he's interested in me."

Charity paused, cocked a brow, and gave him a look. "Funny. I wouldn't have said that you were each other's type."

"I used the word in the other sense. Apparently Swinton has some questions about me. He searched my house on Friday night."

"He *what?*" Charity whirled around, her eyes huge. "You're joking. He went through your things? How do you know?"

"I got a pretty big clue when I stood in my garden and watched him crawl out of my house through the front window."

"Good lord." Charity put down the small bowl, turned her back to the counter, and braced herself against the tiled edge. "That's incredible. I can hardly believe it."

"He seemed a little nervous, but I got the impression it wasn't the first time he'd entertained himself with an evening of B and E. After he finished at my house, he went down to Charms & Virtues and took a look around."

"That's outrageous. Absolutely outrageous. Did he take anything?"

"No."

"Did you call Chief Tybern?"

"No."

She spread her hands. "But what he did was illegal. You can't just ignore it."

"I figure Swinton and I will be even in the breaking and entering category after tonight."

"Wait a second. You don't mean that you plan to . . . to—"

"Search his motor home while everyone's watching the show down on the beach?" Elias swallowed the last of his wine. "Yes. That's exactly what I plan to do."

Charity decided that the scene on the bluff at eleven-thirty that night was a cross between a low-budget horror film and a carnival. The special effects consisted primarily of fog. The thick stuff blanketed the waters of the cove and swirled around the herd of vehicles occupied by the sightseers from town.

The Voyagers' RVs and trailers loomed in the mist. The weak lamps above the entrance to the campground rest rooms glowed bravely, but the light did not penetrate far.

From what Charity could discover, the Voyagers were all down on the beach. She could hear their hypnotic chants rising and falling above the sound of the gentle waves. The flute player was still off-key, she noticed. The drummer was trying to compensate with volume. The fog reflected an eerie glow created by flashlights and camp lanterns.

Charity glanced back over her shoulder at the array

of cars and trucks parked along the bluff. Most of the town had turned out to see the Voyagers off on their trip through the galaxy. Many adults waited inside their vehicles or visited with friends. A few men had gathered near the entrance to the primary bluff path. They were drinking beer and roaring with laughter. Dozens of small children dashed about playing tag in front of the first row of parked cars.

The teenage contingent had braved the chill and the fog to cluster near the fence that overlooked the beach. Their shouts and jokes mingled with the serious chants of the Voyagers. Several drank cans of soda that they had purchased from the tailgate refreshment stand Bea and Yappy had set up.

Radiance had joined the teenagers to hang over the railing. Ted, sporting a T-shirt that read *Beam Me Up Scotty, There's No Intelligent Life Down Here*, was keeping Bea and Yappy company. Newlin's beat-up pickup was parked on the outskirts of the gathering. He had apparently elected to stay inside the truck until midnight arrived.

"Are you sure you know what you're doing?" Charity asked for the fiftieth time.

"How hard can it be?" Elias led the way between two rows of RVs. "Breaking and entering is not what you'd call a high-tech profession. At least, not the way I plan to do it."

"What if you get caught?"

"I'll think of something."

"I don't like it."

"I told you to wait in the car."

She scowled at his sleek back. "I'm not going to let you handle this alone."

"Then stop whining."

"I'm not whining." She pulled the collar of her jacket higher around her neck and peered anxiously into the foggy darkness between two trailers. "I'm merely attempting to bring an element of common sense to this situation."

"It sure sounds like whining."

That did it. Charity set her teeth. She had used every reasonable argument she could think of to dissuade him from this reckless project. And he had the nerve to accuse her of being a whiner. She vowed she would not say another word on the subject, not even if he got himself arrested and called her to bail him out of jail.

Elias turned down a narrow, grassy aisle between two rows of campers and came to a halt with no warning. Charity stumbled against him with a muffled gasp. He reached out to steady her.

"Quiet," he whispered into her ear.

Charity shoved hair out of her eyes and leaned around him to see what had brought him to a sudden stop. She recognized Rick Swinton's maroon and white motor home parked in the last line of RVs.

"Change your mind?" she asked hopefully.

"No. Someone else got there first."

Charity stared at the darkened windows. "Are you sure?"

"Watch that rear window."

She studied the dark glass. A dim light shone briefly against the drawn curtains and then vanished. A moment later it reappeared for a few seconds. Charity swallowed.

"Flashlight?" she whispered.

"Yes."

"But it can't be Swinton. He's down on the beach with the others. We saw him join the crowd a few minutes ago."

"Right. Besides, Swinton wouldn't be using a flashlight in his own motor home."

Charity felt her mouth drop open. She closed it hurriedly. "My God. Someone else is in there doing just what you planned to do."

"It'll be interesting to see who comes out of there." Elias shifted position and pulled Charity into the small space between a trailer and a large camper.

She winced when her knee struck the trailer hitch. "Damn."

"Quiet. Whoever is in there is leaving." He eased her deeper into the shadows.

The door of the motor home squeaked as it opened. A figure in a hooded coat appeared and quickly went down the two steps to the ground. Charity tried to make out the face of the intruder, but the hood and the foggy darkness combined to make identification impossible.

The figure turned and hurried down the lane between two rows of RVs. The route would take the intruder straight past the spot where Charity and Elias stood.

Elias pressed Charity against the side of the trailer. She realized that he was using his body to shield her in case the fleeing figure glanced back into the shadows.

She stood on tiptoe to see over the barrier of Elias's arm and managed to catch another glimpse of the cloaked figure. There was something in the way the intruder moved that told her she was watching a woman flee the scene.

Elias waited a long moment before he shifted to release Charity. "Curiouser and curiouser."

"You can say that again." Charity was violently aware of her own pulse. "I wonder who she was."

"I have a feeling that Swinton has all kinds of enemies. I'd better get in and out before someone else shows up to take a look around." Elias stepped away. "Wait here."

"You're not going in there alone."

"I need you outside to keep watch."

That sounded reasonable. Charity couldn't think of a good counterargument. "Well, what should I do if I see someone?"

"Knock once on the outside wall of the motor home." Elias took one last look around the fog-shrouded scene as he removed a pencil-slim flashlight from the pocket of his jacket. "I'll be right back."

"If you don't come out of there in five minutes, I'll come in and drag you out."

Elias's teeth flashed briefly in the darkness. "Okay." He moved toward the door of the motor home.

Charity leaned around the corner to watch as he went up the steps and let himself inside.

A chilling silence descended when Elias disappeared. It seemed to Charity that the fog grew heavier. She told herself that was a good thing because it helped conceal Elias's shockingly illegal activities.

The chants from the beach intensified. The drums and flute played louder. The shouts and laughter of the watching teenagers drifted across the campground.

There was no sound from inside Swinton's motor home. No light was visible at the windows. Whatever Elias was doing, he was doing with great discretion. Charity shivered, partly from the chill and partly from increasing anxiety. The oppressive sense of impending danger thickened together with the fog.

Down below on the beach, the drummer went into a lengthy riff that carried clearly up the side of the bluff. The throbbing, pulsating chants of the excited Voyagers echoed loudly. Someone honked a horn. The teenagers' raucous laughter grew more strident. Charity heard the snap and pop of firecrackers.

After what seemed hours, the motor home door cracked open. Relief washed through Charity when she saw Elias jump lightly to the ground. He came toward her, moving with swift, silent grace.

"Come on, let's get out of here." He took her arm.

She didn't argue. "You were in there forever. Did you find anything?"

"Maybe."

She glanced at him as he hurried her through the maze of silent recreational vehicles. "What's that supposed to mean?"

"I got some bank account numbers. Ever notice how people tend to let their bank statements pile up in a desk drawer?"

"No." Charity hesitated, recalling the stack of statements she had filed in a desk drawer at home. "On second thought, maybe I have noticed. What of it? What good are the account numbers?"

"I don't know yet." Elias paused at the intersection of two lanes of campers. "But with an operation this big, you know everything is going through a bank."

"Hmm. You're right."

More firecrackers popped in the darkness. The Voyagers' chants reached a feverish pitch. The rowdy males who had gathered to drink beer near the bluff path began calling loudly down to the people on the beach. The younger set jeered and shouted.

"Things are getting exciting," Elias remarked as they moved out from behind the last row of vehicles.

"It's almost midnight." Charity glanced around. "And surprise, surprise, not a spaceship in sight. Let's go find Newlin. I want to be with him when the time comes, just in case Arlene doesn't rush into his arms."

"Right."

They made their way along the bluff to where Newlin had parked his pick-up. The battered truck was located in the outermost section of the makeshift parking lot. Nearly everyone else who had driven out to watch the spectacle had parked much closer to the campground.

The pickup was almost invisible in the fog. Charity went to the window on the driver's side and frowned when she saw that Newlin was not inside.

"He must have gone to the fence to wait for Arlene to come back from the beach," Elias said.

"Yes." The brief, sharp blast of an automobile horn made Charity jump. Someone cursed.

She turned and saw that there was one other vehicle parked a short distance away. Another truck. The passenger door was open, but there was no light inside the cab. The sound of the town's one and only rock station spilled forth into the night.

"Damn it," someone muttered from inside the truck. "I told you to be careful. You want someone to hear us?"

"The guy in the pick-up just left." There was a muffled giggle from the interior of the vehicle. "Speaking of careful, I hope you remembered the rubber. Because if you didn't, I swear to God, Kevin, you can go fly a kite tonight."

"Yeah, yeah. I've got it here, somewhere. Hang on."

Charity turned quickly back to Elias and cleared her throat. "Let's see if we can find Newlin." She grabbed his arm and started to lead him back the way they had come.

There was enough light reflecting off the fog to see Elias's amused expression, but he did not resist the forceful tug on his arm.

Charity pulled him toward the group that had gathered at the rail.

An eerie, startling hush descended on the group down on the beach. The flute and drum fell silent. The chants of the Voyagers ceased.

"Midnight," Elias said softly.

"Hey there, Charity. Winters." Yappy hailed them as they went past the tailgate refreshment stand. "We're gettin' ready to close up here. Want some hot coffee?"

"No, thanks," Elias called. "We're looking for Newlin."

"Saw him about an hour ago. Took some coffee over to his truck. Haven't seen him since."

"Everyone's gone to the fence to see the grand finale," Bea said as she packed a stack of unused paper cups back into a box. "Check over there. Sure hope Arlene comes to her senses tonight. If she doesn't, I don't know what poor Newlin's going to do with himself."

Charity turned toward the large crowd that was hovering over the fence, watching the scene on the beach. "Elias, I'm worried. I don't see Newlin anywhere."

He wrapped his hand around hers. "We'll find him."

That was going to be easier said than done, Charity thought. An air of confusion was building swiftly. Between the fog and the throng of excited, curious onlookers, things were becoming chaotic. Derisive shouts went up from the beer drinkers. The teenagers hooted as some of the Voyagers began to climb back up the beach path.

Charity and Elias moved through the clustered townsfolk, searching for Newlin. There was no sign of him anywhere.

"Hey," one of the beer drinkers yelled to the returning Voyagers, "Maybe the aliens meant Eastern Daylight Savings Time, not Pacific Daylight Savings Time."

The dispirited cult members filed past without acknowledging the taunts.

A high, shrill scream ripped through the darkness

just as Charity was about to suggest that they start looking for Arlene among the returning Voyagers.

The piercing shriek had the same impact on the crowd as a sky full of alien spaceships. Everyone, Voyagers and onlookers alike, froze.

Charity glanced around wildly, searching for the screamer. "One of the disappointed Voyagers, do you think?"

"I don't know. But it didn't come from the beach." Elias's hand tightened on hers. "It came from over there near the far end of the campground." He started forward.

A second cry reverberated through the night.

"What's going on?" Someone yelled. "Who's screaming?"

For the second time that night Charity allowed Elias to draw her into the maze of campers, motor homes, and trailers that littered the old campground. The screams were replaced by shouts for help.

"Someone call an ambulance," a man yelled. "For God's sake, hurry."

Charity and Elias emerged from between a row of camper trucks and saw that a handful of Voyagers who must have been among the first to return from the beach had gathered at the entrance to a large blue and white RV.

"That's Gwendolyn Pitt's motor home," someone said.

As she and Elias drew closer, Charity saw that light blazed from the open door of the vehicle.

Elias forged a path through the small crowd.

"It was because the ships didn't come," a woman dressed in Voyager's garb moaned. "She did it because the ships didn't come."

Charity saw Newlin and Arlene standing arm-in-arm

at the edge of the small cluster of people gathered outside the motor home. "Newlin."

He glanced at her. There was a peculiar expression of stunned shock on his face. "Charity. Mr. Winters. You aren't gonna believe what's happened."

Arlene buried her face against Newlin's shoulder. "It wasn't her fault the ships didn't come."

Elias released Charity's hand. "Wait here." He went up the steps to look inside the motor home. He came to a halt in the doorway, gazing intently at something inside.

Charity followed him up the steps and glanced past him into the interior of the motor home.

She took one look and immediately wished that she had followed Elias's orders to wait outside.

Gwendolyn Pitt was sprawled on the blue carpet. Her blue and white robes were drenched in blood. Rick Swinton was pressed back against the built-in desk, staring down at the body. He looked up and saw Elias and Charity.

"We just found her like this," he said in a shaken voice. "A few of us came back here to see why she hadn't joined us down on the beach. And we found her like this. I sent someone to call an ambulance. Not that it will do any good."

Without a word, Elias crossed the short distance and crouched beside the body. He pressed his fingers against the side of Gwendolyn's throat and shook his head.

"You're right," Elias said quietly. "It's too late."

"She must have killed herself because the space-ships didn't come," someone whispered.

Elias met Charity's eyes. "This wasn't suicide."

9

Blood in the water clouds the reflections on the surface, making it difficult to see the truth.

—"On the Way of Water," from the journal of Hayden Stone

"Murdered." Radiance leaned over Yappy's shoulder to read the article on the front page of the *Cove Herald*. "But last night everyone was saying that it was suicide."

Bea gave Charity a meaningful look as she handed her a latte. "Not everyone."

Yappy frowned as he scanned the article. "It says those who reached the scene first assumed Gwendolyn Pitt took her own life because she was despondent over the failure of the ships to arrive at midnight. But Hank Tybern states that it was obvious to him from the start that it was murder."

"It was obvious to Elias, too." Charity sipped her tea and glanced at the faces of the others who were gathered around the small table inside the Whispering Waters Café. "Besides, none of us really believed that Gwendolyn Pitt actually expected the ships to arrive. We all suspected the whole operation was a scam. So why would she kill herself because of despair and disappointment?"

"Good point. Things went just the way she had planned." Ted scratched his broad belly, which today was partially concealed behind a gray T-shirt decorated with the words *What Goes Around, Comes Around*. "She was into that cult thing for something besides a tour of the galaxy. Pretty clear she was murdered. But who would have killed her?"

"Seems to me Chief Tybern has himself a whole slew of suspects," Yappy said. "Starting with all those disappointed Voyagers who must have realized at about one minute after midnight last night that they'd been conned."

Charity and the others nodded solemnly in agreement and sipped their morning lattes.

They had congregated inside Bea's café because it was too chilly to be outdoors. The fog that had descended on the cove showed no signs of lifting. It cloaked the entire town and the shoreline for several miles.

It was nine-thirty. The pier shops wouldn't open until ten, but all of the shopkeepers had arrived early by unspoken consensus to rehash the previous night's events.

All but one, Charity thought. She glanced out the window. There was still no sign of Elias. She hadn't seen him since he had left her at her door at two o'clock that morning. He hadn't even kissed her good night. He had been back in his cryptic mode, distant, remote, self-contained.

Of course, she hadn't been in what anyone could

call a cheerful mood herself last night. Her short stretches of restless sleep had been poisoned with instant replays of the horrifying scene inside Gwendolyn's motor home. Every time she closed her eyes, she was forced to endure the image of Elias crouched beside the blood-soaked body.

She was becoming increasingly uneasy by his failure to show up early at the pier. She wished she had followed her first impulse and stopped by his cottage on her way to work. The two of them needed to talk. They had to get their stories straight.

They had both spoken to Hank Tybern, the town's chief of police, last night, but the conversation had been necessarily brief. Hank had had his hands full securing the crime scene and warning the confused, anxious Voyagers not to leave town. There hadn't been time to take complete statements. He had instructed Charity and Elias to come by the station later today so that they could give him the details of what they had seen.

When she hadn't been dreaming about blood during the night, Charity had lain awake fretting over what to tell Hank this afternoon. She had never been involved in a police investigation. She had no idea how much information she and Elias would be expected to provide concerning their activities before the murder. With luck, not much. After all, they hadn't even been the ones to discover the body. Rick Swinton and a small group of Voyagers had done that.

Nevertheless, she had seen enough crime shows on television to guess that Tybern would want to know something about what had been happening in and around the campground prior to Gwendolyn's death. And there was no getting around the fact that she and Elias had been engaged in a highly questionable activity shortly before the murder. Namely, a spot of B and E. How did one put a respectable gloss on that kind of thing, she wondered.

"Does the article say when Gwendolyn was killed?" Ted asked.

Yappy read through the remainder of the lengthy piece. "The chief is waiting for the official results of the autopsy, but the reporter says that it appears she was shot between eleven-thirty, which is when she was last seen alive, and midnight. Swinton and a few of the Voyagers found her body a few minutes after twelve."

"That's when the screaming started," Bea said.

"I'll bet the county medical examiner won't be able to nail down the time of death any closer than that," Ted said, with the ghoulish authority of a devoted aficionado of the mystery genre. "Who was the last one to see her alive?"

"I think it was that Rick Swinton character." Yappy ran his forefinger along the column and paused midway. "Yeah. Rick Swinton and a couple of Voyagers. They all saw Gwendolyn go into her motor home at eleven-thirty. She told them she needed privacy in order to focus her mind channel for the aliens. Apparently she was supposed to act as their radar control for the landing."

"Well, if you ask me," Bea said, "I'll put my money on one of those Voyagers as the murderer. A lot of those poor, misguided souls lost their entire life savings to Gwendolyn Pitt."

"At least a few of them must have been furious last night when the ships didn't show," Radiance said.

"Yeah." Yappy put down the paper and picked up his latte cup. "And just about any one of 'em could have killed her."

Ted scowled. "If it was a Voyager, he or she would have had to work fast. They were all down there on the beach until the stroke of midnight. The kids hanging around the fence saw the first ones return."

"Don't forget, there are two beach access paths," Yappy reminded him. "The old one's been blocked off for years because it's unsafe, but it's still there."

"That's right." Ted brightened. "And there was a lot of fog last night. One of those Voyagers could have climbed up the old beach path, gone straight to Gwendolyn's motor home, shot her, and then rejoined the crowd on the beach. No one would have noticed because of the fog. The killer could have returned to the campground with the main group shortly after midnight."

"This is beginning to sound complicated," Bea muttered. "When you think about it, any one of those Voyagers could have done it that way. Couldn't tell them apart in the fog what with those blue and white hooded robes they all wear."

"I sure don't envy Chief Tybern," Ted said sagely. "Hell of a job sorting out this mess."

"Especially given his lack of experience," Radiance murmured dryly. "We haven't had a murder in Whispering Waters Cove in over ten years. And the last one was easy to solve, remember?"

Ted nodded. "Right. That was the time Tom Frazier's wife finally got fed up with old Tom beatin' up on her. She conked him on the head with a tire iron. Jury called it self-defense."

"Which it most certainly was," Bea added. "That Tom was a real sonofabitch."

The door of the café slammed open. The crash riveted everyone's attention. Charity and the others turned to see Arlene Fenton, breathless, disheveled, and obviously on the thin edge of rising panic. She flew into the café and then came to a quivering halt. Her wide-eyed gaze went straight to Charity.

"Ms. Truitt, thank God," she breathed in a shaky voice. "I went to your house, but you weren't there. And you weren't at your shop. I finally realized you must be in here."

"Arlene." Charity put down her latte and got to her feet. "What is it? What's wrong?"

"You have to save him. You have to save Newlin."

"Newlin? Calm down, Arlene." Charity started toward her. "Tell me what happened."

"Chief Tybern arrested Newlin a few minutes ago."

There was a collective gasp of shock from the small group gathered in the café.

"Oh, my God," Charity whispered. "Not Newlin."

Arlene rushed toward Charity with a stricken expression. "Ms. Truitt, what are we going to do? Everyone in town knows how much Newlin hated Gwendolyn Pitt. He was always saying that someone should do something about her."

Charity put her arms around her and looked at the other shopkeepers.

No one said a word. Arlene was right. Everyone in town knew that Newlin had been enraged by Gwendolyn Pitt's scam.

"He didn't do it," Arlene wailed. "I know he didn't. Newlin's no murderer. But he's got no one to help him."

"I'll go down to the station and talk to Chief Tybern," Charity said quietly.

Not that she had any notion of what to say to the chief, Charity thought, as she walked up the steps of the small Whispering Waters Cove Police Station twenty minutes later. Newlin was her employee and her friend. She felt she had to help.

Mentally, she started to tick off an action item list. The first thing to do, obviously, was see about getting

Newlin out on bail. She had no idea how that process worked, but Hank Tybern could explain it to her. The second thing on the agenda was to get a lawyer for Newlin. A good one. The only lawyer in town was Phyllis Dartmoor. She handled estates and wills, not criminal cases. That meant contacting someone in Seattle.

Charity was concentrating so hard on the logistics of freeing Newlin that she didn't see him standing in the shadowed doorway of the police station until she nearly blundered straight into him.

"Charity." Newlin stared at her in astonishment. "What are you doing here?"

"I came to rescue you." Charity glanced around the empty interior of the small station. "Arlene said you were under arrest."

"Nah." Newlin grimaced. "At least, not yet. The Chief just asked me to come in for questioning. I guess Arlene leaped to a few conclusions."

"She was very worried about you, Newlin."

Newlin looked considerably cheered by that news. "Yeah?"

A sturdy, bald-headed man ambled out of the small office behind the station's unattended front desk. "Mornin', Charity. Bit early to be rushin' around like this, isn't it?"

Charity turned and smiled politely. She had met Hank Tybern several times during the past few months. He was middle-aged with the weather-beaten features of a man who had spent his early years on commercial fishing boats.

Tybern was the old-fashioned sort, solid family man, steady and calm in his ways. A bit of a plodder, perhaps, but thorough. Charity suspected that the slow, easygoing facade masked a savvy intelligence. Hank had lived in Whispering Waters Cove most of his life, and he enjoyed the respect of the townsfolk.

"Good morning, Hank. I heard you had arrested Newlin, but it looks like the rumors were wrong."

The lines around Hank's eyes creased slightly as he eyed Newlin. "Just wanted to talk to him. Going to have to talk to a lot of people today. Thought I'd start with young Newlin, here."

Newlin's mouth tightened. "Chief Tybern says it would sure help if I could find someone who saw me in my truck between eleven-thirty and a few minutes before midnight."

"My God." Charity glanced uneasily at Hank. "You need an alibi?"

Hank settled his bulk against the front desk. "No call to get excited, Charity. Just be helpful if we could find someone who noticed him in that truck during the half hour before twelve."

Charity thought quickly. "Elias Winters and I went to talk to him right around midnight." She broke off abruptly and gazed helplessly at Hank.

"And?" Hank prompted gently.

"I wasn't in the truck," Newlin muttered. "I told you, a couple of minutes before midnight I got out of the truck and went to join the crowd waiting at the top of the beach path. I wanted to find Arlene. And I did. She was on her way to confront Gwendolyn Pitt. I went with her. By the time we got to the motor home, Rick Swinton and a couple of the other Voyagers had already found Pitt's body."

"Unfortunately, that still leaves plenty of time unaccounted for," Hank said softly. "Like the half hour before midnight, during which time someone went into Gwendolyn's trailer and shot her."

"Wait a minute." Charity spun back to Newlin.

"You said you waited inside the truck until a couple of minutes before midnight?"

Newlin shrugged. "Figured there was no point freezin' my butt off hanging over the campground fence until the show was over. I knew Arlene wouldn't be coming back from the beach until she was convinced the spaceships weren't going to arrive."

"The people in the other pick-up," Charity said swiftly.

Hank looked at her. "What people?"

"I don't know who they were, but they were parked just behind Newlin. A young couple. Teenagers, maybe. Or a little older. College age. I didn't see them, but I heard them. They had the radio on, and the door on one side of the truck was open. Maybe one of them noticed exactly when Newlin left to find Arlene."

Hank's frown was thoughtful. "Don't suppose you happened to get a license number?"

"Of course not. I wasn't thinking about alibis at that time." Charity tried to remember every detail. "The kids were, uh, doing what you'd expect a young couple of that age to be doing in the front of a pick-up."

"Making out?" Newlin asked with honest innocence.

Charity cleared her throat. "Well, yes."

"Color of the truck?" Hank asked.

"It was midnight, remember? And foggy." Charity wracked her brain to summon an image of the truck. "It was dark. The truck, I mean. Newlin's pick-up is a light color, and I spotted it easily. I didn't even notice the other pick-up until I heard voices and the radio. The cab light inside was off. Maybe Elias will be able to give you more information."

Hank nodded. "I'll ask him when I see him this afternoon."

"Wait a second," Charity said. "I heard the girl call the guy Kevin. Does that help?"

"Kevin. Dark pick-up. College age." Hank nodded, straightened, and reached for the phone book. "That'd likely be Kevin Gadson. He's home from college for the summer, and he's seeing the Turner girl. His Dad's got a dark green pick-up."

One of the advantages of small towns, Charity thought, as she watched Hank dial the number he found in the book. The local chief of police knew everyone. And he knew their vehicles.

Ten minutes later, after a short conversation with Kevin Gadson, Hank put down the phone and grinned cheerfully at Newlin. "You're in the clear, son. Kevin says he and his girlfriend had the radio on. He recalls seeing you in the pick-up several times during the half hour before midnight. You didn't leave until right after the start of the twelve o'clock news broadcast, which begins at five minutes before the hour. There wouldn't have been time for you to run clear across the campground and shoot Gwen Pitt."

Newlin grinned with relief. "Hey. That's great." He turned to Charity. "Thanks. I owe you."

Charity exhaled deeply. "I'm glad that's settled. Let's go, Newlin."

"You bet." Newlin started toward the door.

Hank folded his arms across his broad chest. "Going to be a busy day. Got a whole hell of a lot of people to interview." He caught Charity's eye. "I'll see you and Winters later. Say, four-thirty?"

"We'll be here," Charity promised. "But I don't think there's much more we'll be able to tell you. Come on, Newlin. We've got a shop to open."

When they arrived at Crazy Otis Landing a few minutes later, Arlene came flying out of Bea's cafe. She threw herself into Newlin's arms.

Radiance, Bea, Yappy, and Ted trailed out to watch the reunion.

"Newlin, I was so scared." Arlene raised tearful eyes to search his face. "Are you sure you're okay?"

"Yeah, sure." Newlin stroked her hair with an awkward, soothing touch. "Thanks to Charity. She remembered a couple of kids in a truck parked behind my pickup. One of 'em was able to give me an alibi."

Arlene turned to Charity. "I don't know how to thank you, Ms. Truitt. I've been a fool about the Voyagers and those spaceships and everything. It's bad enough knowing all my money is gone, but if Newlin had been arrested for murder on top of that, I don't know what I would have done."

"Don't be too hard on yourself." Charity patted her on the shoulder. "Everyone's got a right to dream."

"Well, from now on, I'm keeping my dreams right here on earth." Arlene squared her shoulders. "And the first thing I've got to do is get a job. I don't have anything left in my bank account."

Newlin's jaw tightened. "I didn't murder Gwendolyn Pitt, but I sure ain't gonna weep over her grave. She stole a lot of money from a lot of people."

"Why don't you come inside and have a latte, Newlin," Bea said in a motherly tone. "Then you can go to work."

"Thanks." With one arm around Arlene's shoulders, Newlin went into the Whispering Waters Café.

Radiance looked at Charity. "Good thing you remembered seeing those people in the truck. Newlin's an outsider here in town. And everyone knows how much he detested Gwendolyn Pitt. It would have been real easy for people to assume that he killed her."

"You saved that boy a heap of trouble," Yappy agreed. "Nice going, Charity."

Ted chuckled. "Something tells me you've got a friend for life in Arlene."

Charity hardly heard him. She was looking at the *Closed* sign in the window of Charms & Virtues. It was well after ten, and there was still no sign of Elias.

"What the hell do you think you're doing?" Rick Swinton stumbled backward as Elias came through the doorway of the motor home. "Get out of here, Winters. You've got no right barging in like this. I'll have you arrested."

"Sit down, Swinton." Elias closed and locked the door. "You and I are going to have a little talk."

"Fuck off."

"Sit down." Elias moved forward.

"Damn you, if you think you can just—" Rick retreated. The back of his knees hit the edge of the built-in couch. He sat down hard. "You can't come in here like this."

"I just did." Elias smiled slightly. "Don't worry, we'll both be leaving in a few minutes. Right after we talk."

"What the hell do you want to talk about?"

"Let's start with your private bank account." Elias pulled a sheet of paper from the inside of his jacket. "The one you've been using to siphon off funds from the business account Gwendolyn Pitt set up for the Voyagers' so-called contributions."

A startled expression flashed in Rick's eyes. It was gone almost instantly, concealed behind a look of aggrieved anger. "I don't know what you're talking about."

"I'll be glad to spell it out." Elias tossed the paper down onto Rick's lap. "I used your social security number and a telephone to access the records of both accounts. The pattern is clear. You've been channeling funds from the business account into your own personal account on a regular basis. Now, since Gwendolyn Pitt is too much of a businesswoman not to have noticed, I'm betting you covered the transactions with phony receipts and contracts."

"You can't prove a damn thing."

"No, but that's the way embezzlement is usually done. Fairly routine stuff, and you don't strike me as an original thinker. An audit should be able to piece it all together."

"Bullshit."

"The good news is that it looks like most of the money Gwendolyn Pitt got from her Voyagers is still around. It's sitting in your personal account, Swinton."

"That's a lie."

"No. Among other things, it's a motive for murder."

"Murder." Rick stared at him, mouth agape. "You can't pin Gwendolyn's death on me."

"If I go to Tybern with the information I uncovered about your bank account juggling act, he'll jump to the obvious conclusion. He'll assume you killed Gwendolyn because she confronted you about the embezzlement and threatened to have you arrested."

"That's not true." Panic flared in Rick's face. "Are you crazy? I didn't kill her. Hell, I didn't even know she was dead until I came back from the beach with some of the others."

"Going to be a little tough to prove, isn't it? Everyone knows that, what with the fog and those hooded robes the Voyagers wear, anyone on the beach could have disappeared from the crowd long enough to murder Gwendolyn. But you have a solid motive, and you're new here in town. That gives you an edge on the competition, Swinton."

"I didn't kill her, I tell you. I can prove it, if it

comes to that. Plenty of people saw me on the beach during the half hour before midnight."

"Maybe. Maybe not. Lots of excitement down there on that beach last night. But I'll leave that to you and Tybern to sort out." Elias leaned back against the dinette. "In the meantime, you and I are going to work on your image problem."

"Now what are you talking about?"

Elias smiled. "We're going to prove to the Voyagers and everyone else in town what a nice, honest guy you are. We'll show them how bad you feel about the fact that the spaceships didn't arrive last night. You're going to do what you know Gwendolyn Pitt would have wanted to do in such sad circumstances."

"And just what would that be, you sonofabitch?"

"We're going down to the bank to set up a trustee account. With the bank serving as trustee, of course. Then you'll call your bank in Seattle and arrange to have all of the funds in your personal account wired into the new account."

Rick's face reddened furiously. "Like hell, I will."

"A representative of the First National Bank of Whispering Waters Cove will disperse the funds to the Voyagers. Being the competent, thorough, hardworking employee of the company that you are, I'm sure you've got a list of everyone's contributions."

"Goddamn you." Rick leaped to his feet and launched himself at Elias.

Elias stepped aside. Rick hit the dinette table and sprawled across it in an ungainly heap.

"Let me put it this way, Swinton. If you don't decide to play the good guy, I'm going to call Tybern. He'll take it from there. He shouldn't have too much trouble figuring out how to put a hold on those funds in your Seattle account while he arranges for the audit. After all, he's conducting a murder investigation. One way or another, you're going to lose that money. Might as well make the process work in your favor."

"Bastard." Rich heaved himself slowly off the table. His eyes narrowed viciously.

"My way, you come out of this looking like you tried to do the right thing. Your way, you look like a murder suspect. Take your pick."

Rick slammed the laminate tabletop again and again with his fist. "Bastard, bastard, bastard. You'll pay for this. I swear it. Nobody screws Rick Swinton and gets away with it."

"Let's go. It's ten o'clock. The bank is open."

Elias had just allowed Crazy Otis to step off his shoulder and onto the perch behind the counter when Charity rushed through the front door of Charms & Virtues.

"It's after noon." She raced toward him, skirts flying. "Where have you been? I've been worried sick."

"Heh, heh, heh," Otis said.

Charity ignored the parrot. "I was beginning to think something dreadful had happened to you."

"Such as?" Elias hit a key on the ancient cash register. The drawer shot open with a satisfying clang.

"How was I to know?" Charity reached the counter. She was breathless. "It could have been any number of things. There's a murderer on the loose, or have you forgotten?"

"No." Elias took a moment to savor the sight of her. Her cheeks were flushed, and her eyes were bright with concern. Concern for him, he thought with a stab of wonder. "I'm surprised you even missed me. I hear you've been busy saving Newlin from the gallows."

"All I did was find an alibi for him." Her brows drew together. "How did you know about that?"

"I saw Ted and Radiance on my way down the pier. They told me what you'd been up to this morning."

"Is that right?" She heaved a deep sigh. "Well, a woman's work is never done. I've been working on your alibi ever since I got Newlin out of Tybern's clutches."

"Mine?"

"Don't you think that it's going to be a little difficult to explain to Chief Tybern that you were busy searching Rick Swinton's motor home at approximately the same time that Gwendolyn was getting murdered? B and E is not exactly a great alibi."

Elias smiled slowly. "Got a better one for me?"

"I've been thinking about it." She glanced over her shoulder, apparently making certain that no one had entered the shop. Then she leaned closer to Elias and lowered her voice. "We can tell Tybern that we just decided to take a stroll while we waited to see what happened on the beach."

"A stroll?"

"Right."

"In the fog?"

"Right."

"You don't think that sounds a little weird?"

She scowled. "Dozens of people were out of their cars, milling around."

"Most of those who were out of their cars were hanging around the fence, watching the action on the beach."

Charity threw up her hands. "Who's to say some of them weren't taking a casual stroll in the fog?"

He was beginning to enjoy himself. "What about the woman we saw coming out of Swinton's motor home. Do we mention her?"

Charity nibbled on her lower lip. "Damn. That's a tricky one."

"It gets trickier. If we mention her and where we saw her, then we admit we were hanging around that section of the campground. Gwendolyn's motor home wasn't far from Swinton's."

"Maybe we shouldn't mention her. After all, we have no idea who she was. Could have been anyone."

"Lie to Chief Tybern? Charity, I'm shocked."

"This isn't a joke, Elias. Gwendolyn Pitt was murdered last night, and you and I were engaged in what most people would call an illegal activity at the time."

"What's this 'we' stuff? I was the only one inside that motor home."

"I was the lookout, remember? I'm just as involved in this as you are. We're in this together."

He smiled slowly. "I'm touched."

"I'm glad you find this amusing. I certainly don't."

"You know what your problem is, Charity?"

She eyed him with deep suspicion. "What?"

"You don't realize that the truth is most visible in a still pond."

"Meaning?"

"Meaning that we answer any question Chief Tybern asks with the truth."

"But, Elias—"

"Relax. Tybern isn't going to throw either of us in jail." Elias paused. "But for the sake of discussion, let's say he tossed me into the slammer. Would you come and visit me?"

"Are you kidding?" She gave him a sugary smile. "I'd bake you a cake with a file in it."

"I'm flattered."

"Don't be. I'd do whatever it takes to get you out because I know I'd be stuck with Crazy Otis until you were free."

Otis snorted.

Elias met Charity's eyes. "There is just one thing

we should get clear before the interview with Tybern this afternoon."

"Yes?"

"Let me do the talking when we get to the part about the B and E stuff."

She looked uneasy. "Think you can come up with a good story?"

"If I can't, I'll let you step in and save me."

10

The sea tastes as salty as blood. Life depends on both.

— *"On the Way of Water," from the journal of Hayden Stone*

Hank Tybern glanced at his notes through a pair of reading glasses that rode low on his nose. "Let me see if I've got this straight. You went to Rick Swinton's motor home shortly after eleven. Saw an unidentified woman leaving—" He broke off and looked at Elias across the desk. "You're sure you don't know who it was?"

Charity held her breath. Thus far Elias had done all the talking. She had to admit that the interview had gone very smoothly. As smooth as the surface of an untroubled pond.

"Positive," Elias said. "The hood of her jacket was pulled up to cover her head. The only reason we could tell that it was a woman was because of the way she

193

moved. Although the fact that she was coming from Swinton's trailer was also a strong hint."

Hank grimaced. "Yeah, I've heard the rumors about his womanizing. Okay, so you checked inside the motor home to see if Swinton was there, and then you went back to where the cars were parked on the bluff to find Newlin. You heard the screams and took off with the others to see what had happened. Joined the crowd in front of Gwendolyn Pitt's motor home, went inside, and saw the body. That about it?"

"That's it," Elias said easily. "Charity and I were together the entire time."

"Fine. It doesn't help me out a lot, but that's not your problem." Hank's wooden chair squeaked as he settled back into it. "Anything else about the murder scene, itself, that you noticed which you think might be helpful?"

Elias reflected briefly. "I think I told you everything. Swinton was there ahead of me. He was crouched on the floor near the body. The Voyagers who had accompanied him were standing outside together with some other people. That empty tape player in the drawer was the only thing that caught my eye."

Startled, Charity broke her silence. "What empty tape player?"

It was Tybern who answered. "Found it in a half-open drawer. Doesn't mean much because there was no tape in it. Apparently Gwendolyn Pitt routinely recorded her business meetings. We found a box of tapes, but I doubt if they'll be of much use."

Charity frowned. "I suppose it would have been too much to hope that she had taped her own murder."

"Afraid so." Tybern smiled wryly. "No one ever makes things easy for the people who have to clean up the mess. Well, that's my job. To clean it up. Meanwhile, now that we've taken care of the formalities, I'd like to say thanks on behalf of a lot of people, Winters."

"Forget it," Elias said.

Charity glanced at him. "What did you do?"

Hank raised his brows. "Don't you know? Thanks to Winters, the Voyagers are going to get back most of their money."

"What are you talking about?" Charity demanded.

Elias shrugged. "Let's just say that Rick Swinton decided to make amends."

"I don't believe that for one minute," Charity said.

"Neither does anyone else." Hank chuckled. "Everyone knows it was Winters who somehow convinced Swinton to do the right thing and put the Voyagers' funds into a trust account to be dispersed by the bank. No one's dumb enough to ask Winters just how he pulled off that neat little trick."

Charity was dumbfounded. "Swinton turned over the funds?"

"Yep." The lines around Hank's eyes crinkled. "I had a talk with Seth Broad down at the bank around noon. He says that Swinton walked in with Winters right behind him at about ten-twenty this morning and announced he wanted to see to it that the Voyagers got their money back."

"Amazing," Charity breathed.

"Swinton had a couple hundred grand wired in from a Seattle account and signed it over to the bank's trust department," Hank continued. "He also very kindly provided the bank with a list of the amounts each Voyager had contributed to the so-called cause. The trust department will take it from there."

Charity looked at Elias. He gave her his mysterious smile. His eyes warned her not to say too much.

"That's just terrific," she said brightly.

"You can say that again." Hank picked up his thick, white coffee mug and took a long, weary swallow. "Not all of those Voyagers were from out of town, you know. My cousin's daughter got involved with Gwendolyn's crowd. Turned over a thousand bucks to her. That money was supposed to help pay for this year's college expenses."

Charity grinned. "So Elias is a local hero, hmm?"

"If he decides to run for the town council, he'll be a shoo-in." Hank chuckled. "Hell, I'll vote for him myself."

"That won't be necessary. I'm not interested in politics." Elias got to his feet. "If you're finished with us, Chief, we'll be on our way."

"That should do it," Hank said. "If I have any more questions, I'll give you a call."

"Do you have any suspects yet?" Charity asked.

"Just between you and me," Hank looked at her over the rims of his reading glasses. "I'm up to my ass in suspects."

"Come on, Charity, you know he can't talk about the case." Elias took her arm in a firm grip. "Let's get out of here and let the man do his job."

She managed to keep her curiosity in check until they reached the sidewalk in front of the station. As they walked toward her car, she gave Elias a sidelong glance. "So, you just took a quick look inside Swinton's motor home to see if he was there last night?"

"He wasn't."

"You don't say. I've got to hand it to you, Elias. That was very, very smooth. You told Chief Tybern the truth without quite telling him the whole truth."

"Trust me, Tybern didn't want the whole truth. He's smart enough to know that some things are better left alone. He's satisfied with the results this morning."

"In other words, he doesn't intend to ask you to

explain the method you used to persuade Rick Swinton to turn over the Voyagers' funds to the bank."

"I didn't lay a hand on Swinton."

"Hah. You may not have touched him, but I'll bet you intimidated him something fierce."

"Some people are easier to intimidate than others." Elias reached down to open the car door. "I just mentioned to him that keeping all of the money he had siphoned out of the Voyagers' account could look like a pretty good motive for murder to some people."

Charity blinked. "Whew. You play rough."

He straightened and braced one hand on the roof of the car. His eyes met hers, searching without betraying his own thoughts. "Does it bother you?"

"What? That you bullied Swinton into returning the Voyagers' money?" Charity smiled. "You must be kidding! He deserved it. But I do have a couple of questions."

"What questions?"

"First, do you think Swinton really might be the murderer?"

"I doubt it. He might be capable of hiring someone to pull the trigger, but I don't think he could do it himself. He's an embezzler. He doesn't have the stomach for heavy violence. Too much risk."

"You sound very certain of that."

"No one can be absolutely certain about another person. But I think the odds are against Swinton being the killer. What's your other question?"

"Why did you do it?" she asked very softly. "Why confront Swinton and force him to turn over the money? You don't really know any of the Voyagers except Arlene, and you're barely acquainted with her. There was no reason for you to get involved."

There was a heartbeat of silence. And then another.

The stillness in Elias was absolute. Charity could feel him retreating into himself.

It occurred to her that he might not know the answer to her question. It also occurred to her that he didn't like the fact that he didn't know it.

"The river of justice flows through many channels," he finally said in a very neutral voice. "Some are obvious. Others must be opened by the observer."

"Forget I asked." Charity wrinkled her nose. "I know why you did it."

His gaze narrowed. "Why?"

She stood on tiptoe and touched the side of his face with her fingertips. "Because you're very sweet."

"Sweet?"

"Yes. Sweet." She patted his cheek. Then she brushed her mouth lightly across his, stepped back briefly to admire the stunned expression in his eyes, and then got quickly behind the wheel of her car.

She turned the key in the ignition and hit the gas. Something told her it would not be a good idea to hang around.

Sweet.

Elias eyed the curry paste he was in the midst of preparing. He had already taken the recipe to the outer limits, heat-wise, but he added a few more of the intensely flavored, hot red chiles, just for the hell of it.

Whatever else Charity would be able to say about tonight's dinner, she would definitely not be able to call it sweet. He had spent the entire day plotting the menu.

The meal was built around a fiery potato and garbanzo bean curry. It was accompanied by a salad laced with a pepper-flavored dressing. Dessert was a very tart lime sorbet.

"This is war, Otis."

Crazy Otis, perched on top of his cage, bobbed his head and uttered his evil chuckle.

Elias held up a plump jalapeño chile pepper. "As you are my witness, Otis. She shall never call me sweet again."

"Heh, heh, heh."

Elias still wasn't sure why the word rankled. He only knew he had been fuming quietly since the previous afternoon when Charity had patted him as if he had been an especially good dog, given him that airy little butterfly kiss, smiled, and called him sweet.

He was fairly certain that *sweet* was a word women used for babies, puppies, and brothers.

Sweet. It was an unpleasant, unsettling, uninspiring word. It was a bland, noncommittal, very dull word. And it sent a chill through him.

Charity's eyes watered at the first taste of the curry. She blinked back the moisture, put down her fork, and snatched up her glass of wine.

"I'm still experimenting with the recipe," Elias murmured.

"Tasty." She gulped another swallow of wine, hoping the alcohol would kill the fire.

"The curry paste emphasizes three different varieties of red chiles."

"I could tell."

"Not too hot?"

She smiled grimly as she set the wineglass on the low table. "Hotter than Mount St. Helens, and you know it."

Elias looked pleased. "Try the salad."

Warily she forked up a bite of salad. The dressing was almost as hot as the potato and garbanzo bean curry. She breathed deeply and swallowed the smoldering greens. "Zesty."

He frowned thoughtfully as he munched lettuce. "You don't think the dressing is just a tad on the sweet side?"

"Sweet?" Alarm bells went off in Charity's brain. Sweet? She reached for a slice of corn bread. "Not in the least."

"How about the corn bread? I don't like sweet corn bread, myself."

Charity swallowed and took another deep breath. "I don't think you have to worry about the corn bread. All the jalapeño chiles you put into it do an excellent job of masking any trace of sweetness."

His eyes gleamed. "Thank you."

She pondered his expression for a few seconds, read the challenge in him, and picked up her fork again. She was not entirely certain what was going on, but she knew she would eat every bite on her plate even if it resulted in the first fully documented case of spontaneous human combustion.

The sound of a big car in the drive came as a welcome distraction.

"You've got a visitor," Charity announced with relief. She put down her fork.

The gleam vanished from Elias's eyes. The familiar enigmatic expression returned. "I'm not expecting anyone."

A car door slammed. A moment later someone knocked loudly on the kitchen entrance.

"I'll be right back." Elias rose from the low cushion. "Go ahead and finish the curry. Wouldn't want it to get cold."

"This stuff wouldn't get cold if you froze it in a glacier for a few thousand years."

Elias's mouth tilted at one corner. He crossed the room into the kitchen and opened the back door.

"Sorry to bother you, Winters," Leighton Pitt said. "Wondered if I could talk to you for a few minutes."

"I've got company."

"This is important," Leighton muttered.

Charity looked up from her seat on the cushion. "Hello, Leighton. I'm very sorry about Gwendolyn. I know the two of you were divorced, but, still, it must have been a terrible shock."

" 'Evening, Charity." Leighton nodded distractedly as he stepped through the doorway. Behind the lenses of his aviator glasses, his eyes looked haunted. "It was a shock, all right. Look, I don't mean to intrude, but I need to talk to Winters, here, if you don't mind."

"No, of course not," Charity said.

Elias moved to shut the door behind Leighton. "Anything you want to say to me, you can say in front of Charity."

Leighton scowled. "This is business, Winters."

"The nature of water and the nature of business share certain properties," Elias said. "Neither is as simple as each appears at first glance."

Leighton stared at him. "How's that?"

"Don't pay any attention to him, Leighton." Charity waved him to a cushion. "He gets into these moods. Have a seat."

Leighton started forward and then came to a halt when he saw the two low cushions on the floor. "That's all right. I'd rather stand."

"First, take off your shoes," Elias said.

"Huh?"

"Your shoes. You can leave them at the door."

Leighton stared, obviously bemused, at Charity's bare feet, and then he noticed that Elias was also shoeless. Awkwardly, he stepped out of his tasseled taupe loafers.

Charity could not help but notice that the richest man in town had holes in his socks.

Elias glided around Leighton and went back to his cushion. He sank down onto it with an effortless movement. "What did you want to talk about, Pitt?"

Leighton glanced uncertainly at Charity and then appeared to steel himself. "Look, I'll be blunt here, Winters. I want in on whatever you're setting up for your off-shore clients. I can carry my own weight. I've got the kind of inside information you're going to need to pull off your project."

"There is no project," Elias said.

"Don't give me that bullshit," Leighton exploded. "I know you've got something brewing and that it involves that pier. The whole damn town knows it. Let me in on it. I can make it worth your while to take me on board."

"I didn't acquire Crazy Otis Landing for off-shore clients or anyone else," Elias said quietly.

"Look, I'm going to put my cards on the table." Leighton began to pace the small room. "I admit that I'm in kind of a bind, financially speaking."

Elias studied him. "A bind?"

"Gwen screwed me over but good." Leighton's mouth thinned. "She had her revenge, all right. Just as she promised at the time of the divorce. She ruined me. And I was such a fool that I never even saw it coming until it was all over."

Charity watched Leighton pull a handkerchief out of his pocket and mop his brow. "What do you mean?"

"She conned me." Leighton turned and trundled heavily back across the room. "It was a hell of a scam, and I fell for it. Just about wiped me out. I've got almost nothing left. I think Jennifer's going to leave me if I don't do something to recover from this quagmire. Things have been getting a little tense between the two of us lately, and this will tear everything apart."

"What was the scam?" Elias asked.

Leighton drew a weary breath. "A couple of months ago I got a phone call from someone who claimed to represent a California developer. The guy said that his firm wanted to acquire view property along the bluff for a golf course and spa resort. Maybe eventually put in a community of resort condos. Naturally they wanted to get the land at reasonable rates."

"Naturally," Elias said. "And they had selected you to help them pick up the first big parcels in a discreet manner."

"I realize now that the man who called me was probably Rick Swinton, although I can't prove it. At any rate, I saw my chance to pull off the deal of a lifetime. Gwen and I still owned that old campground on the bluff, you see. It was the one piece of property we didn't sell at the time of the divorce. We both knew it might be very valuable in the future, so we agreed to hang on to it together."

"I know," Elias said.

"Prime view land. Naturally the developer wanted it. I figured all I had to do was get Gwen to sell me her half-interest. Then I could turn around and sell the whole parcel to the developer."

"For a small fortune?" Charity clarified.

Leighton shot her a quick glance. "Let's just say for a very nice chunk of change. But before I could make my offer to Gwen, she showed up with those damn Voyagers. I couldn't figure out what the hell she was doing. Then I realized she had to be using the cult to milk investment funds out of people dumb enough to believe alien spaceships would come to take them away."

"Did you approach her about selling you her half-interest in the campground?" Charity asked.

"Of course." Leighton waved a hand. "Figured we could do business together, in spite of the past. Whatever else she was, Gwen was a real first-rate businesswoman."

"What happened?" Elias asked.

Leighton shook his head. "She admitted up front that she was running a con on the Voyager crowd. Said they were all getting what they deserved. I told her I wanted to buy out her half of the campground. She agreed, provided she could use the property until the fifteenth of August. She said that by the middle of August she'd have collected the money she needed to finance some investments she had in mind. We had a deal. Or so I thought."

"She agreed to let you buy out her half-interest in the campground?"

"Right." Leighton mopped his brow again. "I offered her a fair price for her share."

"You mean you offered her a price based on land values in the current Whispering Waters Cove real estate market." Elias took a sip of his wine. "Not what the land would be worth to a major resort developer."

Leighton scowled. "Business is business."

Elias shrugged. "Water is water, but no two waves are the same. Some break harmlessly against the shore. Others conceal riptides that can carry the unwary out to sea."

Leighton looked briefly baffled. "Uh-huh. Well, to make a long story short, Gwen came to see me a couple of weeks ago. Said she'd heard the rumors about the resort development. Said the fact that you were here in town, Winters, meant that something really big must be in the air. I thought she was going to renege on our deal."

Charity toyed with her fork. "But instead she just raised the price for her share of the campground, right?"

Leighton frowned. "How did you know?"

"I sort of saw it coming," Charity said gently.

"Wish I had." Leighton sighed heavily. "Gwen wanted five times what I had offered her for that land. I said it wasn't worth it. She claimed that, based on what she knew about Elias Winters, it was worth ten times as much as she was asking."

"You let her convince you that even if you paid her five times the value of her share of the campground, you would still make a fortune when you sold to the developer?" Charity asked.

"I know it sounds stupid in hindsight." Leighton's soft, plump hand bunched into a thick fist. "But it wasn't just Gwen who kept the pressure on. I was getting almost daily calls from the representative of the phony developer."

Elias watched him. "Swinton?"

"Probably. He kept increasing his offer for the land if I could just get title to the whole piece. He said his people wanted to be certain they could get that one parcel. Said the developer was willing to pay top dollar for the old campground if the deal was handled quietly so as not to drive up the values of the surrounding properties."

Charity watched him intently. "So you kept upping your offer to Gwendolyn?"

Leighton shuddered. "I told myself I had to get hold of that land, whatever it took. It was like a fever or something. I lost my sense of perspective. Then the developer's representative called again. Offered to make me a partner in the resort deal."

Elias watched him intently. "All you had to do was put up a large chunk of investment cash, right?"

Leighton closed his eyes. "I went way out on a limb."

"Let me guess what happened next," Elias said. "You turned over whatever cash you had on hand, then took out a loan to finance the rest of the cost of your partner's share."

"That's it in a nutshell," Leighton admitted. "Got in way over my head. We closed the deal on the morning of the fifteenth. The funds from my account were transferred into what I thought was the developer's business account that day. Gwen came to see me late that afternoon. To gloat."

"That's when she told you that she had just taken you to the cleaners," Elias concluded.

Leighton's head drooped. He came to a halt in front of the window and gazed despondently out into the darkened garden. "She took everything I had. I'll have to file for bankruptcy. Jennifer is furious. It's hard to believe, but I'm beginning to wonder if she married me for my money."

Charity raised her eyes to the ceiling but said nothing.

"You do realize," Elias said very softly, "that what you've just told us would constitute a motive for murder to some people's way of thinking?"

Leighton whirled around, his eyes huge behind his glasses. "I didn't kill Gwen. God knows I wanted to for a while there, but I didn't."

"Calm down," Elias said. "I'm not making any accusations. It's Chief Tybern's job to sort out the alibis. But if I were you, I'd come up with a good one."

"An alibi?" Leighton was visibly rocked. "But I wasn't anywhere near the campground the night Gwen was killed. You want to know where I was? I went out and got rip-roaring drunk at the Cove Tavern. I walked home sometime around midnight."

Elias shrugged. "Like I said, that's between you and Tybern."

Leighton took a step forward and halted. "I came here because I'm desperate. I'm begging you to give me a piece of whatever action you're putting together for your clients."

Elias got slowly to his feet. "For the last time, there is no deal. I'm sorry, Pitt. I can't help you."

Leighton shook his head in disbelief. "There's got to be something left. Jennifer will leave me, I know she will. I hate to admit it, but I . . . I think she's been seeing someone else lately."

Charity was alarmed by the dejection in Leighton's face. She glanced at Elias. "The Voyagers are going to get at least some of their money back. Maybe Leighton could put in a claim for the amount he lost, too."

Elias shook his head. "Leighton's money didn't go into the Voyagers' account or into Swinton's. I checked the recent records, remember? There were no deposits at all on the fifteenth. In fact, there's only a couple hundred thousand total in those accounts. Nothing the size of what Leighton just described."

"On the fifteenth, Gwendolyn had the escrow company transfer the money I paid for that land into her private account, not her business account," Leighton said. "It will become part of her estate. We didn't have any kids, but she's got a couple of brothers and a sister. Everything will go to them. They've all hated my guts since the divorce. You can bet they sure as hell won't give any of the money back to me."

Charity bit her lip. "It sounds like a mess, Leighton."

"I'm going to have to start over," he whispered. "At my age. I can't believe it."

He turned and walked heavily toward the door.

"Don't forget your shoes," Charity said.

"What? Oh. My shoes." Leighton got his loafers back on with an effort. Then he opened the door and plodded out into the foggy night.

Silence descended. Charity waited until she heard Leighton's big car pull slowly out of the drive. She met Elias's eyes across the low table. "What do you think?"

"I think Tybern was right when he said that he was up to his ass in suspects."

"Do you really believe that Leighton might have killed Gwendolyn?"

"He's certainly got a solid motive." Elias rose to his feet and picked up some of the dishes. "But so do a lot of people, including all those disappointed Voyagers. Ready for dessert?"

"That depends. What are you serving? Habanero chiles stuffed with wasabi ice cream?"

"Relax." Elias set the dishes in the sink and opened the freezer compartment of the old refrigerator. "Just some homemade lime sorbet."

Crazy Otis stretched his wings and gave Charity a baleful look. "Heh, heh, heh."

Charity got to her feet, collected the last of the dishes, and started toward the sink. "Okay, I'll take some sorbet. But just for the record, are you satisfied yet, Elias?"

"No."

He took the plastic container of sorbet out of the freezer, dipped a spoon in, and turned toward Charity.

"Have a bite," he said in a deep, sexy voice. "It will clear the palate."

Charity folded her arms and leaned warily back against the refrigerator door. "I'll just bet it will."

Elias teased her lower lip with the tip of the spoon. "Open wide."

The fragrance of lime was fresh and invigorating. Against her better judgment, Charity parted her lips.

Elias smiled slowly. His eyes narrowed as he slipped the spoon into her mouth.

The lime exploded on her tongue, icy fireworks that sent wildly conflicting signals to her senses. She breathed deeply and watched as he took a bite of sorbet for himself from the same spoon.

"Mind telling me what this is all about?" she asked.

"This is about not being sweet." Elias set the spoon down on the counter and turned back to her. He planted both hands on the refrigerator door on either side of her head.

Charity's pulse went into high gear. A tiny shiver of excitement lanced through her. "What isn't sweet?"

"Me. Us. What we have together. Whatever the hell else it is, it isn't sweet."

He slid one bare foot between her legs, lowered his mouth to hers, and crushed her against the hard refrigerator door.

11

⁕

The observer must be prepared for the fact that the ripples
in a disturbed pool will always crash against the rocks.

—"On the Way of Water," from the journal of Hayden Stone

Her mouth was still cool and fragrant from the effects
of the lime sorbet. Elias felt Charity's lips part beneath
his. He heard her small, muffled cry of excitement as
she responded to him. The thrill of it reached deep
into his body.

"We didn't finish dessert," she whispered.

"This is dessert. Like I said, it won't be sweet." He
took his hands off the refrigerator door and fitted
them to her waist.

He lifted her, pressed her back against the blank
white surface, used the weight of his body to pin her.
He moved his hands lower. She clutched at him, bury-
ing her fingers in his hair, and kissed him with delicate greed.

Heat from a fire hotter than that of the most exotic chile peppers surged through him. Elias cupped the rounded tops of her thighs and squeezed gently. Then he reached down to find the hem of her skirt.

He heard her draw in her breath as he shoved the folds of the fabric up to her hips. She was not wearing stockings. Her skin was supple and warm and incredibly soft beneath his hands.

"Wrap your legs around me," he whispered.

"This will never work."

"Hold on tight."

He felt her answering shiver of response and gloried in it. One firm, curved thigh slid slowly up along the length of his denim-clad leg. The exquisite caress was nearly his undoing. He fought for his self-control.

"Now the other one," he said against her throat. "You won't fall. I've got you."

"Oh, my God." She clung to him as she circled his waist with her bare legs.

The long turquoise blue skirt was a tropical pool of color around her hips. The scent of her arousal was a drug that threatened to destroy the grip he had on his own response.

"Elias." Charity clenched her thighs around him as he traced a random pattern between her legs. Her fingers dug into his shoulders. "Ohmygod."

He eased two fingers beneath the edge of the panties and stroked deeply. She was slick and wet and tight. He could feel his erection pushing hard against the front of his jeans.

Charity released his head and tore at his shirt. She got it open and immediately began sliding her warm palms across his chest. Her fingers tangled in the crisp hair. She tugged gently. He sucked in his breath.

"You feel good." Urgency hummed in her voice. "Very hard. Very strong."

"Not too big?"

She gave a choked laugh. "Just right. Perfect."

"You're the one who feels good." He cupped the plump, hot folds that shielded her secrets. "Soaking wet, in fact."

"This isn't fair. You have all the advantage. Let's go to the bedroom."

"No, right here. Unzip my jeans."

Her hand slipped to the fastening. She freed him, took him into her hand, and then hesitated.

"Front pocket of my shirt. You do it."

The feel of her palm curled around him almost sent him over the edge. He closed his eyes briefly and gathered himself.

"You planned this?" She sounded half amused, half shocked as she removed the packet from his pocket.

He opened his eyes and met hers. "Let's just say I wanted to be prepared."

"You must have been a Boy Scout."

"No." He teased her swollen clitoris. "One thing you can be sure of. I was never a Boy Scout."

"Elias." Her legs scissored around him.

He felt her fingers tremble. She was in no condition to handle the small chore. "Give it to me."

She quickly surrendered the small packet. He tore it open with his teeth and eased the condom into place with one hand. He watched her eyes widen as he lowered her slowly onto his erection.

Her nails sank into his shoulders. Her head fell back. Her whispered gasp was incredibly erotic. It took every ounce of control Elias possessed to hold himself back from the brink. The pull of her snug body was irresistible.

He went to his knees with Charity wrapped around

his waist. He eased her back onto the wooden floor and buried himself completely inside her. She closed around him with such seductive strength that he thought he would explode.

"Yes. Yes, Elias. Just like that. I want you so much."

A wild desperation seized him without warning. It severed the last remaining bonds of his control. He sank himself into her again and again until he felt her clench even more fiercely around him.

Her climax ripped through her, compelling his own. He covered her mouth in order to savor her soft shriek.

The release that tore through him was both surrender and victory. It was impossible to tell where one left off and the other took hold. The only thing he cared about in that moment was that he was as close to Charity as it was possible to get.

A long while later she stirred beneath him. "Okay, so it's not sweet."

Elias lifted his head. He cradled her face between his palms. "No."

Her smile was infinitely mysterious. "What is it, then?"

The question stunned him. He did not know the answer. He took refuge in the sanctuary that had never failed him, the place where he knew he was strong, where all the questions had answers, Tal Kek Chara.

"The transparency of water is most often described by saying what it is not, rather than what it is."

She put her fingers over his mouth. "Forget I asked."

She was still smiling, but there was a wistfulness in her eyes that worried him. Elias got to his feet, helped

Charity up, and walked with his arm around her toward the darkened bedroom. He paused beside Otis's cage to cover the bird for the night. Otis was already inside. He kept his back to Charity and Elias and muttered darkly.

"I think we embarrassed him," Charity murmured.

"He's actually a very straitlaced sort of bird," Elias said as he adjusted the cage cover. "Hayden's influence, I think."

The panic swirled out of a dream, a dream in which she could not breathe. The old claustrophobia seized her in a nightmarish grip.

Charity came awake with unnatural suddenness, every sense shrieking. She opened her mouth to scream, but the cry was blocked in her throat.

Elias's palm clamped over her mouth was her first clue that this was not just another routine panic attack. Something really was terribly wrong.

She opened her eyes and stared up at him. Fear lanced through her. He was pressed against her, holding her very still on the futon. In the darkness, she could just barely make out the shadowed profile of his face. He was looking toward the bedroom door.

Charity heard the sliding squeak. Wood on wood. An aging double-hung window made that kind of noise when it was slowly pried opened. Otis gave a soft, inquiring whistle from inside his covered cage. The sliding squeak halted for a few seconds.

Then it came again.

Elias lowered his head and put his mouth to Charity's ear. "Stay here."

She nodded quickly to let him know she understood. For some odd reason, the fact that there was a genuine focus for her fear had a steadying effect on her senses. Her body could deal with the real thing. She was painfully alert, her fingers shook, but she was not on the verge of hysteria.

Elias removed his palm from her lips and rose from the futon without a sound. As he passed in front of the window she saw something in his hand, something he had picked up as he got to his feet. It looked like the strip of leather that he habitually wore around his waist.

There was a very soft thud in the other room. Someone was sneaking into the house through the front window.

Charity stared at the shadow that was Elias. He was flattened against the wall just to the side of the partially open door. She could barely make out the curve of his naked shoulder and thigh.

She was cold. Tension gripped her from head to foot. Her palms tingled. Her stomach felt weird. But she was not going out of her mind.

The narrow beam of a small pinpoint flashlight swept past the doorway. Otis muttered again, a soft, curious hiss.

Elias waited until the ray of light had moved on, and then he slipped through the doorway.

Charity nearly screamed then. Her mouth opened. Everything inside her wanted to cry out for him to come back to the safety of the bedroom.

She bit back the useless words. There was no safety in the bedroom.

"What the fuck? Lenny, watch it. There's someone—"

"Sounds like a bird."

"It's no goddamned bird." A man's voice broke off on a sharp exclamation.

"Christ, what the hell? Get him. Get him, damn it."

Charity heard a resounding crash. She scrambled up from the futon and grabbed the shirt Elias had left draped over the carved wooden chest. The garment fell to mid-thigh on her.

"Lenny? Lenny? Where the fuck are you?"

Silence from Lenny.

Silence from Elias.

Another thud.

Charity remembered the heavy glass bowl that sat on the low table in the front room. It was the only thing she could think of at that moment that might serve as a weapon.

She took a deep breath and plunged through the bedroom door. She veered awkwardly to the right, tripped over a cushion, and sprawled painfully on the low table.

She heard a shuffling sound on the floor behind her. Just as her fingers brushed against the rim of the bowl, a man's arm locked around her throat.

"No. Let me go." Charity clawed at the imprisoning arm.

She was hauled forcibly to her feet and pinned against a sweating male body.

"Freeze, you sonofabitch," the man named Lenny shouted into the darkness. "I've got your girlfriend. Move and I'll break her neck, I swear it."

Everything went still. Charity fought for breath. Lenny was a hulking bear of a man. The panic welled up inside her.

"Okay," Elias said in an oddly calm voice. "I'm not moving."

"Turn on the light," Lenny ordered. He sounded shaken. "Do it slow."

There was a sharp click. The lights came on. Charity blinked against the glare. Lenny's arm tightened spasmodically around her.

"Let her go." Elias stood next to the door, near the

wall switch. The prone figure of a man lay on the floor, unmoving.

Charity felt an insane urge to laugh. Elias was the only one in the room who wasn't wearing clothes, but he somehow managed to make everyone else look overdressed for the occasion. The harmless-looking strip of leather that he usually wore around his waist still dangled from one wrist.

"I ain't lettin' her go." Lenny edged back a step, dragging Charity with him. "What d'you think I am? Stupid?"

"You won't get far if you try to take her with you. Let her go and make a run for it."

"I need her to keep you from following. Get away from the door," Lenny snapped. "Move."

Elias took two steps away from the door.

Lenny started to haul Charity toward the entrance. She tried to make herself a dead weight.

"Stop it, bitch." Lenny jerked his arm around her throat. He looked at Elias. "Go on. Back. Farther. I don't want you gettin' any ideas."

Elias took another step away from the door. He glanced briefly at Charity as Lenny dragged her past. She looked into his eyes and did not know whether to be reassured or completely panicked by the controlled savagery she saw there. He switched his attention back to Lenny before she could decide.

Lenny stretched out his hand and groped for the door handle.

Elias moved. The leather thong that had hung from his wrist flicked out so swiftly that Charity never even saw exactly what happened.

She felt the violent jolt that went through Lenny as the leather whipped around his extended arm. He screamed, reflexively releasing her in order to free himself.

Charity leaped to one side. Elias brushed past her to get at Lenny.

It was all over in a few stunning seconds. Charity turned in time to see Lenny fly through the air. He crashed against the kitchen counter and slid silently to the floor. He did not move again.

Charity touched her throat as she stared at the two prone figures. A baseball bat and what looked like a tire iron littered the front room.

"Are you all right?" Elias asked. His voice still sounded strangely neutral.

"What?" She turned to gaze at him. "Yes. Yes, I'm all right."

"Did he hurt you?"

"No. I'm okay. Really. Oh, Elias." With a cry, she threw herself against him.

His arm closed around her, fiercely protective. The panic receded.

After a moment, Charity raised her head and stared at the loop of leather. "What is that thing?"

"It's called Tal Kek Chara. I'll tell you about it some other time." Elias released her gently. He eyed the shirt she had loosely buttoned around herself. "Why don't you call Tybern? And then you'd better get dressed."

Crazy Otis snorted. Charity glanced at him and saw that his cage cover had come partially off during the struggle. He leered at her.

"Dirty bird." Charity shook off the dazed sensation that had settled on her. "Tybern. Right." She lunged for the phone on the kitchen wall. "By the way, I'm not the only one who should put on some clothes before the cops get here, Elias. That Tal Kek Chara thing doesn't even qualify as a thong bikini."

"I'll get dressed in a minute." Elias crouched beside one of the fallen men.

Charity hesitated, her hand hovering over the phone. "Where did you learn to fight like that?"

"Hayden and I moved around a lot out in the Pacific. Some of the places we did business were not what you'd call tropical paradises."

"I see." Charity swallowed and started to punch in the telephone number that would summon Hank Tybern.

"I don't like guests who fail to remove their shoes before they come into my house," Elias said as he began to go through the pockets of his victims.

Crazy Otis peered out through the bars of his cage. "Heh, heh, heh."

Half an hour later Charity stood with Elias and Hank Tybern in the front drive. They all watched as Jeff Collings, Hank's only officer, bundled the handcuffed intruders into the backseat of one of the town's two police cars.

"A couple of small-time thugs," Hank said. "Not what you'd call pros."

"That's Swinton's style," Elias said. "Small time. He wouldn't have the kind of contacts it takes to find heavy muscle. And even if he did, he wouldn't want to pay for it."

"Swinton?" Charity whirled around to look at him. "You think Rick Swinton was behind this?"

He shrugged. "That's my best guess."

Hank studied him with a shrewd look. "Be my guess, too. Unless you've got some other enemies you forgot to tell me about?"

"None that would go this route."

Charity scowled at him. He sounded far too philosophical on the subject for her taste. "What does that mean?"

Elias gave her a humorless smile. "It's a good policy to study the reflections of your enemies in still water.

I've always made it a habit to know mine well. This was an act of simple revenge, nothing more. Swinton, being Swinton, wouldn't want to take any personal risks, so he hired someone else to do the heavy lifting."

Hank folded his notebook and stuffed it back into his shirt pocket. "Got to admit Swinton's the most likely candidate. Probably wanted to teach you a lesson. He wasn't real happy with the Mr. Nice Guy role you convinced him to play."

"No," Elias agreed. "He wasn't happy."

Hank nodded. "I'll go out to the campground and have a talk with him."

"I'll go with you," Elias said.

"The hell you will," Hank said dryly. "You let me do my job, Winters. You've already done enough tonight. It hasn't escaped my notice that we've had more trouble around here since you hit town than we've had in the past ten years."

Charity was incensed. "You can't blame any of this on Elias. You said, yourself, he did everyone a favor when he forced Rick Swinton to pay back the money. And it's hardly Elias's fault that those two vicious men broke into his house and tried to brain him with a baseball bat and a tire iron. If you think for one minute—"

"It's all right, Charity." Elias looked amused. "I'm sure Hank was just making a casual observation."

"It sounded more like a nasty insinuation to me," she snapped.

Hank grinned briefly. "Winters is right. I wasn't implying a cause and effect connection. Just a simple observation."

Charity glared at him. "Well, it would be more accurate to observe that the real trouble in Whispering Waters Cove started after the Voyagers hit town."

Hank nodded. "Can't argue with that. Gwen Pitt and Swinton have plenty to answer for around here, and now one of 'em's dead. An interesting turn of events." He started toward his car and then paused. "Looks like I'll need you to stop by my office again, Winters. More paperwork. Say tomorrow morning?"

"I'll come in before I open the shop," Elias said.

Hank rested one hand on the top of the open car door. "Sort of peculiar, the way you were able to take on two guys in the dark. Not many folks could have managed that."

Elias shrugged. "I've had a little training."

"Would that be military training?"

"No. Hayden Stone."

Hank exchanged a long, silent glance with Elias before he nodded again. "Yeah, that figures. Old Hayden Stone was a bit peculiar, too."

Charity did not like Hank's speculative expression. "Now what are you implying, Chief?"

"Nothing. Just making another observation." Hank lifted a hand and got into the car.

Jeff Collings started the engine and drove off toward town. The lights of the car glowed in the fog. They vanished as the vehicle turned a corner in the distance.

"It's cold out here." Elias took Charity's arm. "Let's get back inside the house."

"I didn't like the way Hank implied that you might have had something to do with the trouble around here. It's just a coincidence that you were here when Gwendolyn Pitt was killed."

Elias smiled faintly. "It's Tybern's job to pay attention to coincidences. And you've got to admit that if I hadn't been around, there wouldn't have been the kind of trouble we had here tonight."

"You can hardly be blamed if Rick Swinton tried to take revenge against you."

"When one throws a pebble into a pond, the ripples travel outward for a great distance."

Charity groaned as she stalked up the steps to the kitchen door. "I warn you, Elias, I am in no mood for one of your lectures on the nature of water. We've got other problems on our hands."

"Such as?"

"Hank is reasonably discreet, but I can't say the same for Jeff. Rumors and gossip spread fast."

"True." He met her eyes as he opened the door. "I think it's safe to say that there's going to be a lot of talk about both of us tomorrow. Does that worry you?"

"Of course it worries me." She stormed through the door and into the kitchen. "Do you think I want people saying that you're connected to the murder of a cult leader and other assorted acts of violence? You're new in town, Elias. It's always easier to blame outsiders when there's trouble in a small place like this."

He seemed taken back by her words. "That's not the kind of talk I meant."

"Well?" She planted her hands on her hips and swung around to confront him. "What the heck did you mean?"

Elias closed the door slowly and leaned back against it. He folded his arms across his chest and regarded her with one of his patented enigmatic stares. "I meant that there will be talk about the fact that I was not alone here tonight when those two men broke in. It must have been clear to Collings and Tybern that you were spending the night with me."

Charity opened her mouth, closed it, and felt the heat rush into her face. "Oh, that."

"Yes, that."

"That won't be news to anyone," she said gruffly. "I told you that Phyllis Dartmoor had already guessed that we were seeing each other, uh, socially."

"It's one thing for people to suspect that we're dating on a casual basis. It's something else for the local constabulary to find you in my house at two in the morning."

His serious tone of voice was beginning to worry her. "What's the difference?"

"The first is cause for comment and curiosity in any small town. The second confirms the fact that we're having an affair."

"Does that bother you?"

"No. Does it bother you?"

She had a sudden, inexplicable urge to laugh. "Elias, are you worried about my reputation?"

"Maybe what I really want to know is your opinion on the matter. Do you think we're dating casually or are we having an affair?"

"Is this a trick question?"

Crazy Otis cackled.

"I don't know." Elias unfolded his arms and started toward Charity. "What's the answer?"

"Can I circle both A and B?"

He wrapped his powerful hands around her forearms. "Damn it, Charity, tell me if what we have is important to you or not."

"I'm amazed that you even have to ask." She put her hands up to frame his hard face. "Elias, you make me a little crazy at times, and I worry about you and that Tal Kek Chara stuff, but I promise you that our relationship is very important to me."

He pulled her tightly to him. "That's okay, then."

She waited, crushed against his chest, for him to say that what they had together was equally important to him.

"When I touch you, the water between us is so clear, it's as if it weren't even there," he muttered into her hair.

Charity stifled a small sigh and wrapped her arms around his neck. With Elias, a philosophical remark on the nature of water was probably equivalent to a declaration of undying passion from another man.

Probably.

She hoped that was true because something warned her that it might be all that she was going to get from him.

A whisper of panic flickered somewhere deep inside her as Elias bent his head to kiss her. She decided it was just leftover nerves from the night's scary events. When Elias's mouth moved on hers, the spark of claustrophobia faded back into nothingness.

But it left its fingerprints in the form of a tiny chill that did not quite vanish. Not even when Elias scooped her up in his arms and carried her back into the bedroom.

"Do you know what it did to me to see that creep's arm around your throat?" Elias said very softly.

"It's okay, Elias. You saved me."

"Tomorrow I'm going to show you a couple of things."

"Things? You mean Tal Kek Chara things?"

"Not the whole of it. Just a couple of simple moves that you can use to get out of a situation like that."

She started to tell him that she had no intention of getting into any more such situations, but she held her tongue. She sensed that he needed to teach her the martial arts moves in order to gain some peace of mind for himself.

"Okay. But nothing complicated, all right? I've never been the athletic type."

"Nothing complicated," he agreed. He lowered her gently to the futon and pulled her into his arms.

She allowed herself to relax into the warm safety of Elias's embrace.

She found Newlin hard at work when she walked through the door of Whispers.

"Morning, Newlin."

Newlin looked up from the display of the latest Suzanne Simmons title that he was arranging on a wall rack. "Hey, Charity. I heard that there was some trouble out at Elias Winters's place last night and that you were there."

"You heard about it already?"

"Something about two guys breaking in and trying to beat up Elias."

Charity wrinkled her nose as she went into the back room. "News travels fast around here."

"Saw Jeff Collings on the way to work. He told me what happened. He said Chief Tybern thinks Rick Swinton hired some out-of-town toughs to kick Elias's ass. Jeff said that it was the bad guys who got their asses kicked."

"A colorful but accurate summary of events." Charity stuffed her purse into a drawer.

"Jeff says Elias knows some kind of weird martial arts stuff that Hayden Stone taught him."

"Uh-huh. He's teaching me a couple of simple moves."

Newlin came to stand in the office doorway. "Think Elias would teach me whatever it was that he used on those guys last night?"

Charity looked up, startled. The tentative hope on Newlin's narrow face surprised her. "You want to learn that Tal Kek Chara stuff?"

"Is that what it's called?"

"I think so. Has something to do with a philosophy that uses water to make its points. Pretty murky, if you ask me. You'd have to ask Elias for the details."

"Well, that's just it, see." Newlin glanced down at the floor and then raised his eyes to meet hers. "He's kind of different. You get the feeling you shouldn't just barge in and ask him anything he doesn't want to tell you."

Charity smiled wryly. "Aloof is the word you're searching for, I believe."

"Huh?"

"Aloof, remote, self-contained." Charity frowned in thought. "Intimidating, perhaps. But just between you and me, Newlin, Elias isn't nearly as unsociable as he appears on the surface. If you want to study the Way of Water, ask him to teach you."

"You don't think he'd mind?"

"You won't know until you ask. But be warned, you're going to learn more about water than you probably ever wanted to know."

"Water, huh? Okay. Hey, Charity?"

"Hmm?"

"You and Winters." Newlin shifted awkwardly in the doorway. "Mind if I ask if you two, are like, well, you know, a couple? I mean, it's all over town that you were with him last night."

"Ah." So Elias had been right, Charity thought ruefully. Rumors of a torrid affair were no doubt being swapped at the post office at that very minute.

At least she was maintaining an unblemished record in the scandal department. For a town the size of Whispering Waters Cove, confirmation of a passionate liaison between herself and the new mystery man had to be right up there with walking out on her own engagement party last summer. It was certainly a lot more exciting so far as she was concerned.

"Jeff says you called Chief Tybern from Winters's place at two o'clock in the morning." Newlin turned a deep shade of red. "And it looked like, well, you know."

"I know," Charity said dryly.

Newlin started to back out of the doorway. "Sorry, I know it's none of my business."

Charity took pity on him. "Don't worry about it. To answer your question, Elias and I are seeing each other socially."

Newlin nodded sagely. "Socially."

"Right." Charity glanced at the order forms on her desk. "How's Arlene?"

Newlin shifted gears with enthusiasm. "Guess what? Bea hired Arlene to help out at the café. She said that business has picked up so much here on the pier that she needs someone to run the new espresso machine full-time."

"Does this mean you and Arlene plan to stick around Whispering Waters Cove for a while?"

"We're sorta getting used to the place, if you know what I mean. Besides, it's not like the two of us have anywhere else to go." Newlin hesitated. "It's okay if I keep on working here at Whispers, isn't it?"

"Sure. You're doing a great job, and if business stays brisk, I can keep you on for the winter."

Newlin's anxious look eased. "Thanks. Well, guess I'd better get back to work."

The shop bell clanged as someone slammed open the front door.

"Newlin? Newlin, where are you?" Arlene's voice sounded shrill. "Is Charity here yet? Something awful is happening down at Elias's shop."

"What in the world?" Charity stood in the doorway of the back room. "What's going on?"

Arlene, looking neat and tidy in a Whispering Wa-

ters Café apron, stared at her wide-eyed. "Ted just
came running past the café with Yappy. They said
some guy walked into Charms & Virtues and took a
swing at Elias."

"Oh, my God, not again." Charity bolted for the
front door.

12

---ↄ⌒ↄ---

He who observes a still pond closely will notice that there
is no such thing as an isolated event. Everything that
happens within the pond affects all aspects of life beneath
its surface.

— "On the Way of Water," from the journal of Hayden Stone

Crazy Otis shrieked in outrage as Elias reeled back
against the perch. The stand that supported the fake
tree limb shuddered under the impact.

Elias hit the floor.

"Take it easy, Otis." Elias levered himself up on
one elbow and gingerly touched the side of his mouth.
His fingers came away wet with his own blood. He
glanced at the streak of crimson and then looked up
at Justin Keyworth, who was standing over him with
clenched fists. "Satisfied?"

"No, you sonofabitch. I'm not satisfied." Justin's
blunt features were twisted with rage. His cheeks bore
the shadow of two day's growth of beard. His hand-
tailored, cream-colored shirt was badly creased and

stained with sweat. "It's your fault, and by God you're going to pay."

A great weariness settled on Elias. "What do you want from me, Keyworth?"

"I want to know what you said to my father that made him try to kill himself, you bastard."

"I don't have an answer for you."

"You're damn well going to come up with one," Justin said through clenched teeth. "I read Dad's suicide note. It mentioned your name and then said that the past could not be changed. What did you do to him?"

"I didn't touch him."

"Goddamn liar." Justin reached down to haul Elias to his feet. "It was your fault. I know it was."

Otis screamed and flapped his wings in agitation as Elias allowed himself to be hauled to his feet.

"This isn't going to do any good." With a sense of deep fatalism, Elias readied himself for the next blow.

"Maybe not." Justin slammed his fist into Elias's stomach. "But I'm going to enjoy it."

The punch was awkwardly delivered. It lacked the power and focus a trained fighter would have given it, but it carried the force of Justin's rage. Elias absorbed the pain as he sprawled back against the counter and slid to the floor.

"What happened between you and my father? Tell me, damn you."

Elias sucked in his breath and eased himself into a sitting position beneath the cash register. "You'll have to ask your father."

"He won't talk to anyone." Justin took a step forward. "The doctors sent him home yesterday. He just sits alone in a room, staring out at his garden. He won't see anyone. Won't even take business calls."

"I know you aren't going to believe this, but I regret the fact that your father tried to commit suicide."

"The hell you do. You did this to him." Justin started to reach for Elias again.

Crazy Otis spread his wings and screeched a warning.

Elias heard the shop door slam open. Voices called out. Feet pounded in the aisles between the display counters. From his position on the floor behind the cash register he could not see anyone, but he could hear quite clearly.

"What the devil's going on here?" Yappy shouted.

"Told you, some guy just walked into the shop and took a swing at Winters." Ted sounded out of breath as he pounded down the aisle. "Saw him myself."

"I don't get it. Everyone was saying this morning that Winters could take care of himself."

"Yeah, well, it looks like he needs a little help this time," Ted huffed. "That's why I went and got you. Personally, I'm not the physical type and neither are you. Figured it was going to take both of us to stop this dude."

"Hey, what's happenin'?" Newlin called from the far end of the shop.

"Stop him." Charity's voice rang out through the cavernous old wharf building. It carried the authority of a woman who had once commanded a CEO suite. "Stop that man. He's trying to kill Elias. Somebody do something. Call Chief Tybern."

Bemused, Elias listened to the sounds of approaching rescue. The voices and footsteps had a surreal quality, not unlike the blood on his fingers. He thought about telling everyone to go away so that Justin Keyworth could finish beating him to a pulp, but somehow he didn't think Charity would allow him that option.

"Get away from him," Charity shouted. "I'll have you arrested." She had almost reached the counter.

"Back off," Yappy growled.

Ted's breathing was labored. "You heard him, back off, whoever you are."

Justin seemed to finally become aware of the fact that he and Elias were no longer alone in the shop. He swung around to face the first rescuers as they reached the counter.

Elias looked up at the faces gathered around the cash register. Newlin, Yappy, and Ted confronted Justin with belligerent expressions. Justin glowered at them with the nothing-to-lose air of a wild animal brought to bay. He looked prepared to take on all three.

Elias roused himself from the waking dream. It was time to get control of the situation before someone besides himself got hurt.

"It's okay." He propped himself up against the counter. "It's over. Keyworth was just about to leave, weren't you, Keyworth?"

Justin said nothing. He stood, tense and grim, as if he expected to be brought down and ripped apart by the newcomers.

"Elias." Charity rounded the end of the counter. She ignored Justin to fall to her knees. Her fingers fluttered anxiously over Elias. "You're bleeding. Where else are you hurt?"

"It's all right, Charity." Elias watched Keyworth. "Like I said, it's over. Isn't that right, Keyworth?"

Justin jerked his gaze from the group facing him and looked down at Elias. "No, it's not over. Not by a long shot. But I'll finish it some other time." He started toward the door.

Yappy, Newlin, and Ted blocked his path. Justin halted.

"Let him go," Elias said quietly.

The three hesitated briefly and then reluctantly stepped aside. There was strained silence until the front door closed behind Justin Keyworth.

Charity looked at Yappy, Newlin, and Ted with deep gratitude in her eyes. "I can't thank you enough for saving him. It was very brave of you."

Elias watched as all three men blushed furiously and looked ridiculously pleased with themselves. There was nothing quite as satisfying as a woman's admiration of one's manly prowess, he thought wryly. He had a fleeting regret that he had not given a better account of himself.

Would he have acted to change the outcome of the fight if he had known Charity would be a witness? he wondered. Maybe. Then, again, maybe not. It was hard to decide because everything about the scene still felt unreal. It was as if he were walking on the bottom of the sea. Everything moved in slow motion.

"We didn't do much," Ted said modestly.

"Nonsense." Charity plucked a tissue from a box on a shelf beneath the counter and carefully dabbed at the blood that was trickling down Elias's chin. "You drove that man off before he could do any more damage. I'm sure Elias will want to thank you as soon as I've got him cleaned up. Isn't that right, Elias?"

Elias had to work to think of a response. "I'll buy 'em all a beer tonight after we close."

The three rescuers exchanged glances, and then they looked down at Elias.

"Want one of us to call Tybern and report that guy?" Ted asked.

"No. This was personal. But thanks for the help."

Yappy leaned over the counter to peer at him. "Word is, you didn't need any help last night."

Elias looked at Charity. "This was different."

"Uh-huh." She took him by the hand. "Come with me."

He followed her obediently out the door and down the pier to the small public rest rooms in the center. She pushed open a door and led him inside the door marked ladies.

He glanced around the confines of the small, functional room as Charity turned on the faucet over the sink. It occurred to him that, in spite of a life lived in some unusual places, he had never actually been inside a women's room. There was an alien quality to the experience that meshed surprisingly well with the other elements of the bizarre underwater world in which he was moving.

"Maybe we should take you to the doctor." Charity dampened a clean paper towel to sponge off his mouth.

"Hell, no. It's just a cut lip." Elias winced as she gently touched the wet towel to the small wound. "No real damage."

"You're lucky you didn't lose a tooth. I saw the way you handled those two thugs last night. I doubt if either of them laid a finger on you. So why on earth did you let that man beat on you today?"

"I wasn't stupid about it." He felt oddly defensive. "I went with the punches. I've still got all my teeth, and my nose isn't broken."

"If that was an example of rolling with the punches, I'd hate to see you do something really dumb like stand still and let him use you for a punching bag." She finished cleaning his mouth and dropped the towel in the sink. "Who was he, anyway?"

"What makes you think I know him?"

"Don't give me that." She reached into the small first-aid kit she had found beneath the counter. "You deliberately took that punishment. You didn't even try to fight back. There has to be a reason."

"Justin Keyworth. Garrick Keyworth's son."

Charity stilled, a small bottle of antiseptic in hand. She met his eyes in the mirror. "I see. He blames you for what his father tried to do?"

"Yes."

"And you blame yourself." She swung around to face him. "So you let him pound on you. Is that the kind of basic psychology taught by the Way of Water?"

"Tal Kek Chara isn't big on modern psychological theory." He grimaced as she dabbed the antiseptic on his lip. "That hurts."

"I doubt if it hurts as much as getting punched in the first place. Hold still."

"I sense I'm losing some of your feminine compassion and sympathy here."

"The problem that you've got with Garrick Keyworth isn't going to get settled this easily, Elias." She taped a Band-Aid carefully in place. When she was finished, she studied him with a soul-deep concern that somehow pierced the strange atmosphere that surrounded him.

He knew she was right, and he fought the knowledge with the old tried-and-true weapons. He stepped back into himself and drew the invisible defenses of Tal Kek Chara around him.

"None of this has anything to do with you, Charity. I don't need or want your advice. I'll handle it in my own way."

Her soft mouth tightened. "I'm sure you will." She turned back to the sink and began to repack the first-aid kit.

He was suddenly furious. "Does this mean I'm not invited to dinner tonight?"

"I'm afraid not," she said coolly. "I won't be home this evening. The regular meeting of the town council is scheduled for tonight. I plan to attend. I'm sure the mayor and the council members will have come up with yet another plan to get their hands on Crazy Otis Landing."

"They can't do a damn thing. I own the pier, remember?"

"Yes, but you're an enigmatic, mysterious, unpredictable stranger in these parts." She closed the first-aid kit and started toward the door. "No one knows what your plans are or how long you intend to hang around town. Who can predict what you'll do if the council comes up with an offer to buy the landing?"

"You know I'm not going to sell the pier."

"Do I?" She gave him a brittle smile as she paused with her hand on the door knob. "I almost forgot, you were supposed to see Hank Tybern this morning. What did he do about Rick Swinton?"

"Nothing."

"Nothing? But he should have arrested him or something."

"That would have been a little difficult under the circumstances. Swinton has disappeared."

"What? Tybern let him get away? That's inexcusable. Why didn't the chief move more quickly last night? What's so hard about finding Swinton, even if he has left town? That motor home of his should be easy to spot on the highway. It's too big to just vanish."

Her outrage gave Elias a small measure of satisfaction. "Apparently Swinton came to the same conclusion. He's gone, but his motor home is still parked out at the campground. Tybern figures he probably caught a ride back to Seattle with one of the departing Voyagers."

* * *

The after-work crowd gathered in the comfortably dingy shadows of the Cove Tavern was sparse. In addition to himself and his stalwart band of rescuers, Elias counted only a half-dozen other people. One of them, he noticed, was Leighton Pitt, who sat in a dark corner, huddled over a martini and an extra-large plate of cheese-drenched nachos. Leighton looked even worse than Elias felt.

At least he had companions, Elias thought. Newlin, Yappy, and Ted shared his table. Leighton was alone. It was the first time that day since Charity had abandoned him in the women's room that Elias had seen anything that was even remotely positive in his situation.

Newlin wrapped his hands around his bottle of beer and studied Elias with disconcerting intensity. "So, if you're some kind of martial arts expert, how come you let that guy stomp you this morning?"

"Who says I'm a martial arts expert?" Elias asked.

Newlin scowled. "Jeff Collings told me about what happened out at your place last night. Said you took on two guys and never even got a scratch on you."

"That explains it," Yappy offered. "Elias, here, was probably tuckered out after last night's fight. Didn't have any strength left for another round today."

"That right, Elias?" Ted set down his beer bottle and leaned back in his chair. His T-shirt du jour read *No Good Deed Goes Unpunished*.

"Damned if I know." Elias eyed the T-shirt. For some reason it seemed remarkably apropos.

"That guy who decked you," Newlin said. "Did you know him?"

"I know his father."

Newlin brightened. "So that's maybe why you didn't flatten him, huh? Friend of the family?"

It occurred to Elias that Newlin was very intent on

discovering an explanation for this morning's poor showing. "I don't think the family considers me a friend."

"Still, you know 'em and all." Newlin looked satisfied.

"I know them," Elias agreed. *Always study your enemy's reflection in the calmest water.* Yes, he knew the Keyworths very well. It was himself he didn't recognize today. The realization sent a cold chill through him.

Yappy eyed him thoughtfully. "Sure upset Charity to see you bleedin' all over the floor."

"You think so?" Elias took a swallow of beer.

Ted frowned. "Yeah, she was upset, all right. She's been through a lot lately. I mean, there was the murder and then that big fight at your house last night and now this."

Yappy squinted. "Heard she was with you when those two guys broke into your place last night."

There was a short, tense silence. Elias noticed that the others were watching him expectantly. Slowly he put his beer bottle back down on the table. "She was with me. What about it?"

"It's your business," Ted said. "Yours and Charity's. But none of us wants to see her get hurt."

Elias jerked a thumb at his black eye and the Band-Aid on his jaw. "In case no one has noticed, I'm the one who's been getting hurt around here lately."

"Yeah, well, that's different," Yappy said.

Ted and Newlin nodded in somber agreement.

Elias could not think of a response to that so he took another mouthful of beer. The other three followed suit.

After a while Newlin fixed Elias with a peculiar, searching look. "Did you use that Way of Water stuff on those two dudes who broke into your house last night?"

Elias glanced at him. "Who told you about the Way of Water?"

Newlin shrugged. "Charity mentioned it a couple of times. So did Yappy and Ted."

"Hayden used to talk about it a little," Yappy explained. "Always meant to ask him more about it. But I never got around to it."

Elias studied the thick glass mug in his hand. It was clouded with foam and smeared with beer and fingerprints. Everything he could see through it was blurred and fragmented. "There were some things that I never got the chance to ask him, either."

"About this water thing," Newlin said hesitantly.

Elias took a swallow of beer. "What about it?"

Newlin looked uncomfortable, as if he was trying to gather his nerve. "Well, Charity said you might be willing to teach it to me."

Elias was briefly startled out of his underwater dream world. "She said that?"

"Yeah." Newlin was ill at ease but determined. "So I was just wonderin' if you would."

He had always been the student, Elias realized. The thought of himself as an instructor struck him as marvelously strange. "I don't know if I can teach the Way."

"Well, could you, like, try?" Newlin asked.

Elias thought about it some more. Instructing Charity in a few simple self-defense moves was one thing. Teaching the whole of Tal Kek Chara was something else again. "I don't know. Maybe."

Newlin's smile completely altered his thin face. "Hey, thanks."

Elias forced himself to swim through the currents of the dream. He looked at his companions. "That reminds me. I'm supposed to thank the rest of you for coming to my rescue this morning." He saluted them with his beer mug. "So, thanks."

"No problem," Yappy said.

Ted nodded. "Forget it. If the situation was reversed, you'd have done the same."

"Yeah, we've all got to stick together down there at the pier," Newlin said.

"Which reminds me." Yappy glanced at his watch. "Council meeting's due to start in a few minutes. We'd better hustle our butts on down to town hall. Can't leave Charity, Radiance, and Bea to face that crowd of barracudas alone."

"Right." Ted heaved himself to his feet. "You coming, Elias?"

"Hadn't planned on it," Elias said.

Newlin cleared his throat. "Charity says it's kind of important. Word is, there's gonna be a resolution to use public funds to buy the pier from you."

"I'm not selling."

Yappy looked at him. "Maybe you should go to the meeting tonight and make that real clear, Winters."

Phyllis Dartmoor, dressed in a pearl gray suit styled with an aggressive pair of shoulder pads, stood at the center of the long table. She banged the gavel with her customary authority.

"This meeting will now come to order," she announced.

Charity listened to the hum of conversation fade around her. She was seated in the third row. Radiance and Bea sat next to her on the left. There was no sign yet of Yappy, Ted, or Newlin. She had kept one seat vacant beside her, but she was not really expecting Elias to put in an appearance.

"The secretary will please read the minutes of the last meeting," Phyllis ordered.

Liz Roberts, a large woman who had served on the council for longer than anyone could recall, rose at the end of the table. She began to read in a strong voice that carried clearly to the last row of seats in the small auditorium. Charity tuned her out. Everyone knew that reading the minutes was the high point of Liz's month.

While the secretary droned on through the summary of the July council session, Charity ruminated on the subject that had been plaguing her all day. She was becoming more and more concerned about Elias.

It was bad enough that Rick Swinton had apparently escaped justice. But what worried her the most was the confrontation between Elias and Justin Keyworth that morning. Elias had been in a strange mood when she had patched him up in the women's room.

"Mayor Dartmoor emphasized that the Voyagers would be gone by the fifteenth of August and suggested that no more council time or public funds be wasted on efforts to force the group to leave—" Liz broke off as a soft buzz of speculation rippled through the crowd. She glowered at the audience above the rims of her reading glasses, but no one noticed. Everyone was too busy staring at the doorway of the council chamber.

Charity felt the hair on the back of her neck stir. She turned her head and saw Yappy, Ted, and Newlin saunter into the room and take seats in the last row. Newlin gave her a cheerful wave across the heads of the onlookers.

Then she saw Elias. He didn't join the other three men in the back of the room. Instead, he came toward her down the aisle between the seats. His eyes never left hers.

"The issue of the renaming of Crazy Otis Landing was brought up again," Liz read very loudly. "A committee was established to look into the matter. Gabe Saunders put forth the idea of purchasing the pier from the new owner, whoever that proved to be. The committee assigned to investigate renaming of the pier was told to check into the possibility of an outright purchase."

Elias sank into the empty seat next to Charity and gave his full attention to the council session in progress.

Charity did not like the grimness of his expression. She frowned and leaned over to whisper in his ear.

"What are you doing here?" she demanded.

"You know me, enigmatic, mysterious, and unpredictable."

"You're still in a lousy mood, aren't you?"

"Yes."

People were beginning to stare. Charity gave up in disgust and straightened in her seat.

Liz Roberts concluded the reading of the minutes and sat down. Phyllis rose. She gave Elias an approving look.

"I'm pleased to see that we have the new owner of Crazy Otis Landing here with us tonight," she said. There was a murmur of interest from the crowd. "Given the importance of the pier to the future of this town, I think we should proceed directly to the committee report. Gabe?"

Gabe Saunders, a wiry little man who looked as if he should wear a green eyeshade and who was, in fact, a certified public accountant, got to his feet. He cleared his throat and picked up his report.

"I'll begin with the renaming issue. Your Honor, as you know, the names Sunset Landing and Indigo Landing have both been suggested for the pier. The committee selected Indigo Landing on the grounds that it had more of an upscale ring to it."

Charity leaped to her feet. "Hold on here, you can't just rename the landing by fiat. That pier is private property."

Beside her Bea and Radiance muttered angrily to themselves. The audience murmured appreciatively. Charity knew that it was preparing to be entertained with another skirmish between herself and Phyllis.

Phyllis gave Charity a frosty smile. "You can hardly object to a new name for Crazy Otis Landing."

"On behalf of the Crazy Otis Landing Shopkeepers Association, I want to make it clear that we most certainly do object," Charity said firmly. "The present name has character and a uniquely whimsical quality which we feel will appeal to tourists. We like it, and we intend to keep it."

Phyllis's eyes narrowed. "You heard the committee report. Everyone agrees that Crazy Otis Landing sounds too unsophisticated to attract the high-end tourist market."

"I don't care what the committee decided," Charity said. "You can't rename the pier without permission of the owner."

"True." Phyllis fixed Elias with a determined smile. "And since he's here tonight, I suggest we ask him what he thinks about renaming the property."

Hushed expectation smoldered in the room. Everyone looked toward Elias.

"Well?" Charity glowered down at him. "Say something."

Elias glanced at her and then looked at Phyllis and the rest of the council. "The current name suits the pier. We'll keep it."

Phyllis scowled. Another murmur went through the crowd. There was a smattering of applause.

Charity sat down with a sense of triumph. Radiance and Bea grinned at her. In the back row Newlin let out a whoop.

Gabe Saunders scowled. "The mayor's right. It doesn't sound real sophisticated, Mr. Winters."

"The pier isn't what anyone would call real sophisticated," Elias pointed out.

Laughter greeted that observation.

Phyllis banged the gavel for silence. "That brings us to the second issue before the committee. Gabe, you agreed to check out the possibility of making an offer for the pier. What did you conclude?"

Gabe shrugged. "Like I told you yesterday, Phyllis, we can afford to do it if we want, provided it's for sale and assuming Mr. Winters doesn't inflate his asking price above current market value."

Charity prodded Elias's arm. "Tell them you aren't interested in selling."

Elias gave her a laconic look. Then he turned obediently back to the council. "The pier isn't for sale."

Another ripple of conversation passed over the crowd. It was louder this time. Charity noticed Tom Lancaster, the editor of the *Cove Herald,* scribbling swiftly on a notepad.

Phyllis frowned at Elias. "Are you absolutely sure about that, Mr. Winters? The town is prepared to make a reasonable offer."

Charity shot back up to her feet. "You heard him. He just told you the pier is not for sale."

Phyllis's mouth tightened with barely restrained anger. "I was under the impression that Elias, here, actually owned the pier, not you, Charity. Would you mind very much if he spoke for himself?"

"She's doing a pretty good job of speaking for me," Elias said very politely. "Might as well let her finish."

Someone gave a snort of laughter. The crowd tittered. Charity felt herself turn crimson as she subsided into her chair.

"I believe we'll table this issue until next month." Phyllis smiled coldly and turned to another member of the council. "Clark, would you please give us the report of the Fair committee?"

Clark Rogers rose to his feet.

Elias did, too. Without a word, he turned and walked out of the council chamber. Charity watched uneasily.

An hour later at the conclusion of the council session, she joined her fellow shopkeepers on the front steps of the town hall. Everyone was jubilant.

"Hope that settles the thing once and for all," Bea said. "It'll be all over town by tomorrow morning that we told the mayor and the council to their faces that the pier was not for sale."

Ted yawned. "Sure hope it's the last time I have to sit through one of those council meetings. Damned boring."

"I don't think Crazy Otis Landing will be on the agenda again anytime soon," Radiance said. "Elias made it clear that he's not interested in renaming the pier and he's not open to offers."

"Glad he decided to attend the meeting tonight. Nothing like having the new owner of the pier make a public statement to put the rumors to rest," Yappy said.

"Right," Ted nodded. "Only way to stop the gossip—" He broke off at the sound of high heels clicking on the cement steps. "Evening, Phyllis. We were just talking about how the results of tonight's meeting should put paid to a lot of the rumors that have been goin' around lately."

"If you believe that, Ted, you're in for a surprise." Phyllis came to a halt on the steps and pinned Charity with a seething expression. "A lot of fresh gossip is just getting started. Maybe you haven't heard it yet, but I'm sure you will soon enough after what happened tonight."

Charity groaned. "What's that supposed to mean?"

"You have to ask?" Phyllis gave her a derisive smile. "I should think you'd be able to figure it out for yourself. Everyone saw Elias Winters say exactly what you told him to say tonight. And everyone knows you're having an affair with him. People are bound to assume that you're sleeping with him in order to influence his decisions concerning the pier."

Charity sucked in her breath. "That's not true."

The men gaped.

"That's an outright lie," Radiance declared.

Bea drew herself up. "How dare you imply such a thing?"

Phyllis gave her a grimly polite smile. "I'm only telling you what other people are saying. Personally, I don't believe a word of it, myself."

"I should think not," Bea muttered.

"After all," Phyllis said, "Anyone who knows anything about the Far Seas Corporation knows that Charity wouldn't stand a snowball's chance in hell of seducing the president of that company with the goal of influencing his business decisions."

"Christ, Phyllis." Ted looked pained. "That's playing it a little rough, isn't it?"

She rounded on him. "You think I'm playing rough? Well, let me tell you, Winters is the cold-blooded one. Charity may think she's in control of the situation, but my hunch is that Elias is just amusing himself with her while he bides his time waiting to close whatever deal he's brokering with his off-shore clients."

Newlin frowned. "Just what kind of deal would that be?"

Phyllis clenched her fingers around the strap of her leather shoulder bag. "I'm sure we'll all find out soon enough. But you can be certain of one thing. Elias Winters has no long-term personal interest in Charity or in Crazy Otis Landing. He's only here to make a profit."

She marched down the steps and strode off toward the parking lot. The staccato click of her heels echoed in the light fog.

Silence settled on the small crowd gathered on the steps.

Charity gazed thoughtfully after Phyllis. "Does this mean I don't get to play the Ingrid Bergman role in the Whispering Waters Cove production of *Notorious* after all?"

13

It's easy to see the reflections in the water. The difficulty lies in recognizing the truth when it appears there.

—"On the Way of Water," from the journal of Hayden Stone

Charity didn't see Elias waiting in the shadows of her front porch as she brought her car to a halt in the drive and switched off the engine.

She was fumbling with her keys, her mind on the scene on the town hall steps a short while earlier, when she realized she was not alone.

Elias glided out of the shadows into the weak glare of the porch light. If he hadn't moved, she would never have seen him at all. Her keys flew out of her hand as she started in surprise.

"Elias."

He caught the keys with a casual, precise movement. "Sorry."

"Good grief, you scared me half to death." She

snatched her keys from his fingers and stalked to her door. "What are you doing sneaking around my house?"

"Waiting for you."

"Too bad you didn't hang around the town hall steps, instead." She shoved the key into the lock. "You missed quite a scene."

"What happened?"

"Oh, just the usual—a nasty little skirmish between me and the mayor." Charity opened the door. "She won."

Elias followed her into the house. "How?"

"A one-two punch. First she accused me of sleeping with you in order to influence your decisions about the future of Crazy Otis Landing. And then she socked me with the news that my efforts at seduction were wasted. Apparently, you're just too darn clever for me to handle. According to Phyllis, you're using me."

"In what way?"

"She believes that you're amusing yourself with me while you bide your time waiting to carry out your nefarious plans for the pier." The toe of Charity's shoe brushed against an object lying on the floor. "What in the world?"

She groped for the hall switch, flipped it on, and glanced down. A medium-sized brown envelope lay on the floor.

"I'll get it." Elias scooped it up and handed it to her. "Someone must have shoved it under your door while you were out this evening."

She frowned at the sealed envelope. There was no address or name on the outside. "How long have you been waiting on my front porch?"

"About half an hour. Whoever left that for you must have come by before I got here."

"Which brings up an interesting question. Why are you here?" Charity started to unseal the envelope.

"To tell you that I've decided you're right. I've been thinking about it all day. I'm going to Seattle tomorrow to see Garrick Keyworth."

The bleak determination in his voice shocked her. Charity dropped the unopened envelope on the hall table and turned toward him. "Are you sure that's what you want to do?"

He was motionless in the open doorway, his face an unreadable mask. "I doubt if it will do either me or Keyworth any good, but I can't think of any other way to handle it."

Charity went to him, wrapped her arms around him, pressed herself against him. "Neither can I."

For a few seconds he stood, rigid and unyielding in her embrace. Then, with a wordless groan, he locked his arms around her.

"Something's happening to me, Charity. My training, my philosophy. The things I've used to keep myself centered since I was sixteen. They're all starting to fade in and out. It's like watching lousy reception on TV."

"I think you've probably been going through some of the same things Crazy Otis did after Hayden died."

Elias gave a hoarse laugh that held no trace of humor. "Maybe we should rename the pier after all. Call it Crazy Elias Landing."

"The situation with Keyworth didn't help matters, that's for sure. It was too much on top of Hayden's death. The thing with Keyworth was unresolved, and now it's come back to haunt you."

"Complete with ghosts." He tightened his hold on her. "Damn, I wish I could talk to Hayden one last time."

"What do you think he would tell you?"

Elias was silent for a long while. "To study the reflections in clear water. Water that was not distorted with images of the past."

"Do you understand what that means? Because I'm not sure I do."

"I think it means I have to see Keyworth one more time."

"I'll go with you."

"To Seattle? No. I appreciate the offer, but I have to do this alone."

"I know. But I can drive into the city with you. Davis said something about being out of town on business this week, but I'll do lunch with my sister while you're busy with Keyworth."

"I'm not going to argue." He hesitated. "I've got to tell you, Charity, lately, sometimes you're the only thing that feels real to me."

A shiver of deep uncertainty chilled her to the core. She hugged Elias with all her strength, but the warmth of his body did not banish the cold sensation his words had created within her.

If Elias was drawn to her only because the passion they generated between them was powerful enough to cut through the mists of his melancholy, what would happen when those same mists lifted? she wondered.

She could only hope that he would learn to love her once he no longer needed her. Because she suddenly understood with blinding clarity that she was in love with him.

She raised her lips to his.

Elias claimed her mouth with a sensual hunger that was powerful enough to drive out the doubt and the fear. At least for a while.

An hour later, Elias roused himself from the sweet lethargy imposed by sexual satisfaction. He shifted on the soft mattress, rolled onto his back, and looked up at the bedroom ceiling. Beside him, Charity snuggled, warm and soft and wonderfully curved.

It was amazing how things were beginning to seem more solid and real now that he had made up his mind to talk to Keyworth. He had no idea what he would say to his old nemesis, but the decision to see him was the right one. It had to be done. Elias knew that he owed Charity, not Tal Kek Chara for that insight.

He also knew he had reached a turning point of some kind. He was reluctant to explore all of the ramifications. But there was no getting around the fact that this decision to see Keyworth was a radical departure from his usual path. It was the first time since he had been a teenager that he had consciously selected a crucial course of action without consulting his philosophy and training.

It was a dangerous move. It left him feeling vulnerable.

He had known from the beginning that Charity represented a threat to his carefully structured, self-contained world, but he had recklessly pursued the relationship. Now it was too late to turn aside.

"Elias?"

"I'm here."

"Are you hungry?"

"I guess I never did get around to dinner."

"Me, either." Charity sat up amid the rumpled sheets. "I was too busy plotting ways to defend the pier against Phyllis and the council."

"I was occupied buying beers for the three musketeers who rescued me. By the way, Newlin wants me to teach him about Tal Kek Chara. I gather you put that notion into his head."

"It was his own idea. Do you mind?"

He thought about it. "No, but I don't know if I

can teach the Way to someone else. I've always been the student."

"Every teacher was once a student. I would think that teaching others would be a continuous learning process for an instructor. At least it would be for a good instructor."

"Hayden used to say that student and teacher reflect each other in the way that water reflects moving light. The images are forever shifting, never quite the same but always there."

"That sounds like Hayden. Nice and cryptic. Want a snack? No competitive cooking. Just a peanut butter sandwich or something?"

He admired the pale sheen of moonlight on the elegant slope of her breast. Lazily he stretched out a hand and touched her nipple. It hardened into a tight bud beneath his finger. "Or something." He slid his palm down to her waist and then moved it lower.

"Enough with the lechery, already." She batted at his questing hand. "Time to eat."

"Your wish is my command." He tumbled her back down on the bed and made a place for himself between her thighs.

"For heaven's sake, Elias. How can you think of this and peanut butter sandwiches at the same time?"

"A man has to get his nourishment where he can." He kissed the inside of her thigh and inhaled the intoxicating scent that flooded his senses.

She gasped and clutched at his hair. "I think this may be getting a little kinky."

"It would only qualify as kinky if we actually brought the peanut butter into bed with us."

"You're sure?"

"I'm sure." He took her delicate little clitoris between his lips. It grew firm and plump and taut. The taste of her was incredible.

"Elias."

"Better than peanut butter."

"Okay, okay, you win." She sounded suddenly breathless. "But we take a shower before we make the sandwiches."

"If you insist."

Forty-five minutes later, freshly showered and garbed in a white terry cloth robe, Charity stood at the kitchen counter and sawed through the center of a stack of peanut butter sandwiches.

"Ready in here, Elias."

"I'm on my way." His voice came from the hall.

"You know, I'm never going to look at a jar of peanut butter in quite the same way again."

"Me, either." He appeared in the kitchen doorway. He was wearing his shirt unbuttoned over his jeans. He had used his fingers to comb his shower-damp hair straight back off his high forehead. His eyes slid possessively over her. "You sure know how to whet a man's appetite."

"Sit down before you slip on your own drool."

"Good idea." He waved the brown envelope at her as he walked to the table. "Did you forget this?"

"Guess I got distracted." She carried two plates laden with sandwiches to the table near the window. "Go ahead and open it. I've got peanut butter on my fingers."

"I could lick it off for you," he offered earnestly.

She gave him an eloquent glance. "Open the envelope."

"Spoilsport." He sat down, ripped open the envelope flap, and glanced inside. "Looks like photos. Polaroids."

"Really?" Charity went back to the sink to rinse

her fingers under the faucet. "Who would put a bunch of pictures under my door? Is there a note?"

"I don't see one." Elias turned the envelope upside down and dumped the photos onto the table. "No note. Maybe someone from the pier took these and thought you'd like to see them." He paused briefly. "On second thought, cancel that theory."

Charity dried her hands on a kitchen towel. "What's wrong?"

He sat back in his chair and gestured toward the three pictures scattered on the table. "See for yourself."

Curious, she walked to the table and glanced at the shots.

They weren't very clear. The scene was blurred in the background. The color was off, and the composition was amateurish. She frowned, uncertain at first of just what she was looking at.

Then the image of a woman spread-eagled on a bed registered.

The woman's blond hair was fanned out on a pillow. Her ankles and wrists were bound to the bed with what appeared to be handcuffs. She was clad only in crotchless leather panties and a leather brassiere with holes cut out to reveal puckered nipples. A massive dildo lay between the woman's legs. An object that looked like a riding crop was positioned on the bed beside her.

"Oh, my God," Charity whispered, horrified. "It's Phyllis Dartmoor."

Fifteen minutes later Elias wolfed down the last peanut butter sandwich. He hadn't realized he was so hungry. He brushed the crumbs from his hands and looked wistfully at the empty plate. He'd eaten all but one of the sandwiches.

He realized he felt better than he had all day.

Nothing had changed. He still had Keyworth to face. But the decision to go back to Seattle to deal with the situation had made things clearer.

And sex with Charity had done wonders for his sense of reality.

Charity, however, looked very troubled. Her mood was beginning to worry him. She was still nibbling on the first half of the sandwich she had started fifteen minutes ago. Her eyes kept straying to the brown envelope on the table beside her. She had shoveled the photos of Phyllis Dartmoor back inside as soon as she had realized what she was looking at, but it was obvious her mind was still on the pictures.

Elias lounged in his chair, shoved his hands into the front pockets of his jeans, and stuck his legs straight out under the table. "What are you going to do about those photos?"

Charity sighed. "Give them to Phyllis, I suppose. I don't know what else to do with them." She met his eyes. "Who could have left them under my door? And why?"

Elias considered briefly. "There's a limited market for that sort of thing. It's no secret that you and Phyllis have been feuding for the past few months. Maybe someone wanted to give you some ammunition to use against her."

"That's sick."

"True."

"What did the person expect me to do with those awful pictures?" Charity asked.

Elias shrugged. "Try to blackmail poor Phyllis? Get her to back off her plans for Crazy Otis Landing?"

"That's outrageous. How could anyone possibly think I'd do something like that?"

"It does seem a little over the top, doesn't it?" Elias

agreed. "Whoever it was must not know you very well. But that leaves a hell of a lot of possibilities. Like most of the population of Whispering Waters Cove."

"It doesn't make sense." Charity hesitated. "Unless—"

"Unless what?"

"Unless Phyllis has a really serious enemy here in town. But I can't imagine who it would be. I mean, she can be forceful and even difficult at times, but let's face it, most people supported her position on the pier. The only ones who didn't were the Crazy Otis Landing shopkeepers, and I refuse to believe that Bea or Radiance or Yappy or Ted would do something like this."

"Doesn't seem very likely." Elias paused. "There's another possibility."

"Which is?"

"Maybe whoever took those pictures tried to blackmail Phyllis with them. Maybe she refused to pay off."

"So the blackmailer decided to punish her by leaving the photos under my door? He must have assumed that I disliked Phyllis enough to embarrass her with these pictures." Charity's mouth twisted. "Someone doesn't think much of me."

Elias raised his brows. "It's probably safe to assume that whoever left those pictures here believes that everyone else in the world operates in the same moral vacuum as himself."

"But if the photographer's goal was revenge against Phyllis, why not leave the pictures with Tom down at the newspaper?"

"Even a scandal sheet wouldn't print that kind of stuff, and the *Cove Herald* is no tabloid. It's a family newspaper."

"Good point."

"When you think about it, you were the logical

choice as far as the blackmailer was concerned," Elias said. "Because you are the one person in town who has been going toe-to-toe with Phyllis. Everyone knows that the two of you are involved in a feud over the pier."

"We were in a feud until you showed up," she reminded him tartly. "I'd hoped the matter was settled now that you've made it clear that you're not going to sell, but it looks like some people are still expecting you to pull an off-shore rabbit out of the hat. Enigmatic man of mystery that you are and all."

He watched her intently. "You believe me when I tell you that I have no plans to broker a sale of the pier to one of my clients, don't you?"

She wrinkled her nose. "Uh-huh."

"Why?"

"What do you mean, why?"

"I just wondered why you believed me, that's all. It's not like I've given you any proof of my intentions."

"Contrary to popular opinion, I don't find you to be nearly as mysterious and enigmatic as everyone else seems to think you are."

It wasn't, he realized, the answer he was looking for. But he did not know what that other, more elusive answer was, so he would have to settle for this one.

"What about the photos?" he asked.

Charity shuddered. "I wish I could burn them, but I'm afraid that wouldn't solve the problem."

"The good news is that they're color Polaroids. That means it's highly unlikely that there are any duplicates."

Charity looked up quickly. "Are you sure?"

"The photographer would have had to take the originals to a sophisticated photo lab to get them copied. And no reputable lab would handle them. That's the reason for using a Polaroid in the first place."

"Well, that's something at least. I'll take the pictures to Phyllis first thing in the morning before we leave for Seattle. Lord knows what I'll say to her, but she needs to know what's happened."

"Want me to go with you?"

"No. It would only humiliate her further if she knew you had seen them."

"You may be right. Although, judging by those pictures, she's not exactly the shy, retiring type. Who would have guessed that the mayor of Whispering Waters Cove was into whips and leather?"

"Someone knew," Charity whispered. "And he tried to use the information. I wonder what piece of slime did this to her."

"Rick Swinton." The stunned shock in Phyllis's face transmuted itself into tight-lipped rage. Her hand trembled as she stared at the photos she held. "That lousy son of a bitch. That goddamned, sleazy bastard. I told him I wouldn't pay. I was so sure he was bluffing."

"Swinton?" Charity was briefly startled. "Well, I guess that makes a certain kind of sense. He is definitely a low-life."

"The lowest form. And to think I thought he was devastatingly sexy when he first came to see me last month." Phyllis's mouth twisted. "He wanted to talk about reaching an accommodation between the community and the Voyagers, he said. Suggested we go out to dinner. Insisted we drive to another town so that we could have some privacy."

Charity sat tensely on the pale sofa in Phyllis's elegant taupe and beige living room. She tried to think of something helpful or supportive to say. Nothing much came to mind. "That's when he took the photos?"

"No. That was just the start of our affair. He didn't take the pictures until a couple of weeks ago."

"You've been seeing him ever since the Voyagers came to town?" No wonder Phyllis had taken a rather laid-back attitude toward the problem of the Voyagers' presence in Whispering Waters Cove, Charity thought. Phyllis had been laid-back in more ways than one.

"You can't know what it was like. Rick was incredible in bed. I had never met a man with enough stamina to keep up with me until I met him."

Charity swallowed. "I see."

Phyllis stared at the bowl of cream roses on the glass coffee table. "He was the only man who had ever really responded to my needs. He understood the fantasy. But I broke it off after he took the pictures. He said it was all part of the game, but it made me nervous. I had to think of my career. Then he came to me with his demands for blackmail."

"The bastard."

"I tried to get the photos back. I searched his motor home for them the night those silly Voyagers were all down on the beach waiting for the spaceships. But I couldn't find them."

So it had been Phyllis she and Elias had seen leaving Rick Swinton's motor home, Charity thought. One small mystery was solved.

"It's none of my business, but I think you did the right thing when you refused to pay blackmail," Charity said. "Obviously when you didn't meet his demands, he tried to retaliate by leaving those photos under my door. Not exactly a brilliant stroke of revenge."

"He must have believed that you'd use them against

me somehow. If nothing else, he wanted to humiliate me. Rick has a thing about getting even with people. But I thought he was just bluffing with those photos."

"A real charmer."

Phyllis dragged her eyes away from the roses and gave Charity a searching glance. "You didn't fall for his charms."

"Not my type."

"Lucky you. It irritated him, you know."

"What did?"

Phyllis shrugged. "The fact that you refused to go out with him. He mentioned it once or twice. I could tell it rankled. I'm surprised he didn't retaliate in some way."

Charity had a sudden vision of the night she had returned home to find her cottage vandalized. The damage had been done less than a week after she had turned down Swinton's demand for a date. "Maybe he did," she said softly.

Phyllis didn't seem to hear her. "You came straight to me with the pictures. You didn't even try to manipulate me."

Charity clasped her hands tightly together. "What do you think I am?"

"You've made it clear during the past couple of months that you're determined to fight me every inch of the way when it comes to the issue of Crazy Otis Landing."

"You must have a pretty low opinion of me even to suggest that I'd use photos like that to get what I want."

A dark flush appeared in Phyllis's cheeks. "Sorry. I should be down on my knees thanking you, not lashing out. I suppose I've gotten so accustomed to thinking of you as an adversary that it's hard to understand why you came here today to do me a favor."

"Is it? I think that if the situation were reversed, you would have done the same for me. We've been on opposite sides in a struggle over the pier, but we certainly don't hate each other."

Phyllis frowned. "No, of course not."

"And we both play fair."

"Yes. But sometimes it's too easy to become totally focused on a goal. Too easy to forget about the personal side of things. Law and politics do that to a person."

"Other things besides law and politics can have the same effect." Charity glanced at the envelope. "Is that all of the photos?"

"Yes, thank God. When I realized what he was doing, I came unglued. I undid the cuffs and grabbed the camera. Smashed it. But he already had those three shots." Tears glistened in her eyes. "I still can't believe I was so stupid."

Charity was stunned by the sight of the unstoppable Phyllis Dartmoor in tears. "Don't. It'll be all right." She rose quickly and crossed the short distance to put her arm around Phyllis's stiff shoulders. She recalled what Elias had said. "At least they're Polaroids. Single shots. That means it's very unlikely that there are any duplicates."

Phyllis's eyes widened. "Good God. I forgot about that possibility."

"From the looks of those photos, Swinton was obviously not a professional photographer. I think it's safe to assume he didn't have any way to duplicate them in that motor home of his, and he could hardly take them to a commercial photo lab."

"That's true." Phyllis blinked back her tears. She did not look entirely reassured, but she had regained a measure of composure. She looked up at Charity. "I'll burn these immediately."

"Good idea." Charity hugged her quickly and released her. "Hang in there, Phyllis. You've got the photos. The worst is over."

"You're right." Phyllis raised her chin. It was clear that her natural self-confidence and determination were already kicking back in. "I swear, I could kill that S.O.B., Rick Swinton."

Charity rose quietly and let herself out the front door.

She was still reflecting on the interview with Phyllis an hour later as she sat in the passenger seat of her Toyota and watched the narrow road unwind through the windshield. The fog had lifted, but it had begun to rain. The tall, stately firs on either side of the pavement dripped. Puget Sound was a leaden gray.

Elias drove her car the way he did everything else, with a control that was so complete it appeared effortless. Charity could feel him sinking deeper into the cold waters of his own thoughts.

"What did you do with Otis?" she asked to break the silence.

"Left him with Yappy."

"That's good. Otis loves the carousel. After Hayden died there were some days when a spin on a horse was the only thing that would lift his spirits enough to give him an appetite."

"You know, Charity, Otis really is very grateful for the way you looked after him during the weeks following Hayden's death. He just doesn't know how to express himself well."

"Yeah, right."

14

〜◆〜

He who would change the future course of the river must
be prepared to get his hands wet in the waters of the past.
— "On the Way of Water," from the journal of Hayden Stone

"So you managed to force your way in here, Winters." Garrick Keyworth did not turn around. He
spoke from the depths of a wingback chair that faced
the rain-drenched garden. "Disappointed that I was
unsuccessful? Never did like pills. Couldn't keep the
damn things down long enough to do the job. But
don't fret. Hell, maybe next time I'll use something
that's more effective."

"Don't do it for my sake, Keyworth." Elias walked
slowly across the terra-cotta tiles that covered the
floor of the glass-walled solarium.

The Keyworth house was a huge, aging brick relic
on the shores of Lake Washington. In another era it
had no doubt dripped with gracious elegance. But as

Elias had walked through the dark-paneled hall to the garden room, his footsteps had echoed with a bleak, hollow sound. It seemed to him that there was no soul in this house. It was as if something had died here long ago.

He had been obliged to get past an electronic gate, two rottweilers, a sullen gardener, and a determined housekeeper in order to gain access to Garrick Keyworth. Now that he was here, he wasn't sure what he was going to say.

"Bullshit," Garrick muttered. "It's the perfect vengeance. Isn't that what you wanted? Revenge?"

"The perfect revenge requires that you live. I want you to look down the river into the future and change the reflections you see there."

"What is this garbage? An updated version of the Ghost of Christmas Past? Someone told me that you practice some bizarre martial arts philosophy crap. Whatever it is, don't try to foist it off on me. I may be suicidal, but I'm not crazy."

"Your son came to see me yesterday." Elias circled the wingback chair so that he could see Garrick's face.

He was not prepared for the sight of the pale, gaunt features and lifeless eyes. It was nearly noon, but Garrick was dressed in pajamas and a bathrobe. He had a pair of slippers on his feet. The coffee on the table beside him was untouched.

"Justin went to see you?" Garrick's voice was flat, devoid of all emotion. He stared past Elias into the garden. "What the hell did he want?"

"Revenge."

Garrick scowled. "What's that supposed to mean?"

"Take a good look at me, Keyworth. Justin is responsible for this black eye."

Garrick raised his head with a surprised, jerky

movement and stared at Elias's face. "Are you trying to tell me that Justin took a swing at you?"

"Several swings. Would have flattened me if help hadn't arrived."

"Why?" Garrick looked genuinely baffled.

"Can't you guess? He blames me for your attempt at suicide. Seems to think I'm responsible. Sound familiar, Keyworth? Do you see the pattern of the ripples in the water here?"

Garrick's mouth worked. "I don't understand."

"Don't you?" Elias turned away from Garrick's haunted gaze.

He went to stand in front of the floor-to-ceiling windows that looked out over the garden and the gray surface of the lake. In the distance, the towers that marked the Seattle skyline were dark shadows in the mist. Charity was in one of those high-rise buildings at this very moment. He wished she were here, instead. She would have known how to handle this scene. He knew he was floundering badly.

"Goddamn it, say what you came to say, Winters."

"It's no secret that you and your son don't get along very well, Keyworth. But when the chips were down, Justin proved that blood is still thicker than water. He came to see me because he blamed me for what happened to you."

"That's hard to believe. Justin doesn't give a damn about me. He wants me out of the way."

Elias absently fingered his bruised face. "That's not the impression I got."

"You don't know anything about Justin."

"You're wrong." Elias turned slowly. "I know a great deal about him. I made a thorough study of him as well as everyone else connected to you and your organization before I put my plans together. I can tell you why your wife left you, and about the affair your

Pacific operations officer had with his secretary, and how your Singapore account rep got lured away by the competition."

"I believe you." Garrick rested his head against the back of his chair and closed his eyes. "Your plans were all so exquisitely detailed. You missed your calling, Winters. You should have gone into politics or worked at the Pentagon. I've never seen such a strategist."

"Are you interested in what I learned about Justin?"

"I'm more interested in why you want to tell me anything at all about him. Is this another act in your grand scheme of vengeance? If so, you can save yourself the effort. You can't do any damage to my relationship with Justin. I lost him years ago."

"You may be able to get him back."

"Stop talking about Justin." Garrick's lashes lifted to reveal the first trace of real emotion. "Leave him out of this."

"He's a part of it."

"No, he's not, by God." Rage gathered in Garrick's face. "He had nothing to do with what happened out on Nihili. He wasn't even born. Do whatever you think you must to me, you cold-blooded, manipulative bastard, but don't touch Justin. So help me, if you—"

"Justin is safe from me. But he's not safe from you."

"What are you talking about?"

"You're the one who has the power to hurt him. Hell, if you're not real careful, he could turn out just like me. He could become the kind of cold-blooded, manipulative bastard who can spend years plotting revenge. Is that what you want for him?"

"That's a stupid queston," Garrick roared.

"There's another possibility. Maybe he'll turn out

like you, instead, Keyworth. A robot of a man who can sacrifice his family and everything else important in life because he can't let himself get beyond the past."

Garrick pushed himself halfway out of the chair. His arms trembled. His eyes, which had been dead a few minutes earlier, burned with fury. "What is going on here? Why do you keep talking about my son?"

Elias steadied himself. He had known this would cost him. "If you want to save Justin, take some advice. Don't do to him what my parents did to me. Don't abandon him."

Garrick's mouth worked. It took him several attempts before he could speak. "What is that supposed to mean?"

"You've ignored your son for years because the only thing you cared about was fighting your own private demons. Both of my parents did the same thing to me. My mother committed suicide. My father was so busy wrestling with his own devils that he never had a lot of time for me. And then he got into the plane that you had sabotaged, knowing that it was in bad shape, and he never came back."

"I told you, I never meant for Austin Winters to die."

"Yeah, well, that's the way it goes. The two of you played hardball out there in the islands, and one of you died. A kid got left without his father. Someone else had to step in and finish raising him. And now you're trying to kill yourself. If you succeed, your son is going to be left without a father, too. You see anything screwy with this picture?"

"Justin doesn't need me. He despises me. Besides, he's not a kid. He's twenty-five years old."

"The young man who gave me this black eye needs you very badly. If you don't make things right between the two of you, I can guarantee that he'll turn out to be just like me or you. Hell of a legacy to leave your only son, isn't it?"

Elias did not wait for a response. He knew he had made a hash of things, but he couldn't think of anything else to say. He moved past Garrick Keyworth, went down the sad, echoing hall, and walked out into the gray mist.

A sleek, dark green Porsche pulled into the long curving drive and slammed to a halt. Justin Keyworth jumped out.

"What the hell are you doing here, Winters?"

"You got here fast." Elias opened the door of Charity's car. "Did the housekeeper call you?"

Justin's hands clenched. "I said, what are you doing here, damn it?"

"I'm not sure." Elias got behind the wheel and turned the key in the ignition. "Ever notice how difficult it is to identify the exact place in the river where the past and the future meet?"

Justin frowned, clearly baffled. "Someone told me that you were strange, Winters. I didn't believe him. But now I'm starting to wonder."

"You and me both." Elias closed the door.

He drove off down the long drive, away from the gloomy house on the lake. He needed to find Charity.

The neat, efficient-looking young man seated behind the wide desk surged to his feet in wide-eyed alarm as Charity breezed past him.

"Wait, you can't go in there. I just told you, Ms. Truitt is in conference."

"You can't fool me." Charity gave the secretary a cheerful wave as she went to the closed door of the inner office. "I know Meredith instructs her staff to say she's in conference whenever she wants to be alone for a while. Don't worry, if she gets annoyed, I'll handle her. I am not without influence around here."

"Please, you don't understand—"

Charity smiled and twisted the knob. "Hey, Meredith," she sang out as she pushed open the door. "The prodigal sister has returned. Want to do lunch?"

There was a flurry of movement near the desk. Two entwined figures attempted to disengage in a hurry.

"Sanderson, I thought I told you I didn't want to be interrupted." Meredith broke free from what had obviously been an extremely passionate kiss and glared at Charity. She had to look past the very broad shoulder of a blond Viking in order to see who had barged into her office. *"Charity."*

Charity came to an abrupt halt. She blinked at the sight of her stepsister in the arms of Brett Loftus. "Oops."

"What the hell?" Brett slowly released Meredith and turned. His handsome features were set in an annoyed frown. Then he saw Charity. A flush darkened his fair skin. He ran a hand through his sun-colored hair and adjusted his expensive silk tie. "Uh, hello, Charity. This is a surprise."

"Guess this will teach me not to ignore your secretary, Meredith." Charity started to back out of the office. "Sorry. Just happened to be in town. Thought I'd see if you'd like to grab a bite to eat."

Meredith glanced at Brett, who raised one brow and shrugged a massive shoulder. Charity was sure she saw a silent message pass between the two.

Meredith turned resolutely back to Charity. "Lunch sounds great. Let's go to my club. I've got something important to tell you."

"What can I say?" Meredith gazed at Charity across the expanse of a tablecloth that was whiter than a man's new dress shirt. "You were right last summer when you told me that if I thought Brett was so terrific, I should marry him myself. We're going to announce our engagement in a couple of weeks."

"Congratulations." Charity dipped a forkfull of plump Dungeness crab cake into a bit of hot wasabi paste. "Maybe I'm psychic."

She studied her stepsister as the wasabi cleared her sinuses. Meredith looked good, she thought. Better than good. She looked radiant. The corporate world and Brett Loftus obviously suited her.

Meredith's strawberry-blond hair was swept back and away from her dramatically attractive face. her black and tan jacket and pencil-slim skirt were exactly suited to her role as a corporate executive. Her specially blended lipstick exactly matched the color of her nails. She looked very much at home here in the confines of one of the most expensive business clubs in the city.

The only factor that marred the impression of a successful, accomplished businesswoman was the ill-concealed anxiety in Meredith's light green eyes.

It was about ten minutes after one o'clock. The velvet-lined booths that circled the dining room were filled with men and women dressed in business attire. The muted hum of muffled voices and the soft *ting* of silver against china provided privacy for the high-stakes conversations taking place.

The scene brought back memories. Charity thought of the luncheons she had once conducted in this very room. There had been a time, not so very long ago, when the maître d' had called her by name, and the headwaiter had known her tastes so well that she had not even had to look at the menu. She did not miss those days one little bit, she decided.

Meredith frowned. "Charity, I know the news about my relationship with Brett has come as a shock."

"Not really."

"I didn't want you to find out this way. I wanted to be able to tell you—" Meredith broke off, blinking. "What do you mean, not really? You knew about me and Brett? That's impossible. We've been very discreet. How could you possibly know about us?"

"I didn't say I knew about your relationship. I just said it didn't come as a shock."

Meredith watched her uneasily. "Are you sure you're all right with this? I mean, it was only a year ago that you were engaged to Brett."

"Not quite."

Meredith flushed. "Okay, you were almost engaged to him. You know what I mean. The two of you had a relationship. You were considering marriage, for God's sake."

"It would never have worked. I knew it long before the engagement party, and I think Brett did, too. I don't know why one of us didn't call it off sooner."

Meredith glanced briefly down at the grilled salmon on her plate. "Brett told me he had been growing increasingly concerned but that he wasn't sure what was wrong. He thought perhaps the two of you both needed some more time to get to know each other. He assumed the engagement would give you that time."

"Brett is obviously too much of a gentleman to tell you the entire truth," Charity said dryly. "He and I rushed the whole thing through because we were both reacting to the business factors involved in the situation."

"I know everyone saw both the marriage and the merger as a good move for both firms."

"Truitt and Loftus are a natural match. And Brett and I both felt the pressure to do what was best for our families and our companies. We liked each other, but neither of us wanted to admit that business was the motivating force behind our decision to get engaged."

"Thank goodness you came to your senses at the last minute."

Charity raised her brows. "You mean, thank goodness I had my little breakdown? Let's be honest. I didn't just come to my senses. I went bonkers."

"You didn't have a breakdown." Meredith glowered. "You just needed to get out from under all the pressure. Something inside you made the decision for you."

"Call it whatever you want." Charity sighed. "I suddenly realized that night that I couldn't go through with it. I panicked."

"You had every right to panic. Davis and I had several long talks after you left for Whispering Waters Cove."

"You did?"

"We realize now what it must have been like for you, trying to hold the company together after Mom and Dad were killed. Things were in such chaos. You had so many people depending on you. Relatives, employees, suppliers, customers. And you never even liked the business in the first place. You only went into it to please Dad."

"It was my own fault that I got into that situation with Brett. I should have turned things over to you and Davis much sooner."

"We weren't ready to run the company until about a year ago," Meredith said simply. "We needed experience. You bought us the time to finish college and learn our jobs. But looking back, do you know what I appreciate the most?"

"About what?"

"You."

Charity was startled. "Me?"

"Yes, you." Meredith smiled. "You never once made Davis or me feel that we had a duty or an obligation to take over the reins of Truitt. You gave us the freedom to choose. We both realize now that you felt you never had that choice."

Charity blushed, embarrassed by the admiration she saw in her stepsister's eyes. "Forget it. It's not like I sacrificed my whole life or anything. I just turned thirty, remember? Lots of time left."

"I know." Meredith's eyes narrowed. "Are you really happy living in that little burg, though?"

"Yes."

"Charity, it's been a year. You've had a chance to get yourself back together. Don't you miss good restaurants? The theater? Shopping? And that bookstore of yours is so small. What sort of challenge could it be after Truitt? How can you stand it? Aren't you bored to tears?"

"It's amazing how much can happen in a little place like Whispering Waters Cove. And I never did like the corporate world. I was born for small business. As I told Elias, it's a calling."

Meredith's gaze sharpened. "Elias?"

"Elias Winters."

"Of Far Seas, Incorporated?"

"Yes."

Meredith frowned. "Davis mentioned that Winters had a deal going with the pier."

"Not really. He runs one of the shops on it, but other than that, there's nothing special happening."

"Davis implied that Far Seas had something cooking up there in the cove."

Charity smiled. "How did you know that Elias likes to cook?"

"I'm serious."

"It may interest you to know that Elias Winters and Far Seas have recently gone through a few changes, too. Elias has decided to settle in Whispering Waters Cove."

"Charity, let's get real here. You may have opted to leave the corporate world, but it's unlikely that Winters has done the same thing. He's brokered some very big deals."

"Yes, I know. But he's not going to sell Crazy Otis Landing to any of his clients."

Meredith leaned forward. "Davis tells me that he's a little, uh, different."

"He is."

"It sounds as if you and Winters have become well acquainted."

"Actually, we're having a torrid affair."

Meredith stared at her. "Is that supposed to be a joke?"

"Nope."

"An affair with Winters? You can't be serious."

"Why not?"

"Because he's Elias Winters." Meredith was clearly both exasperated and appalled. "Far Seas, Incorporated. If he's started an affair with you, it can only be because he's planning to use you somehow in whatever plans he's got for a deal in Whispering Waters Cove."

"Thanks a lot." Charity grimaced. "Why is it everyone assumes that Elias is using me as a pawn in some nefarious scheme?"

"Because everyone who knows anything about Winters knows what he's like. Davis did some investigating when you first mentioned him. He says the guy is sort of—"

"Strange? I know."

"How about some specifics?" Meredith broke off abruptly as a large shadow fell over the table. "Oh, hello, Brett."

"Thought I'd join you for coffee." Brett slid onto the banquette beside Meredith. He gave Charity a rueful smile. "To be honest, the suspense was killing me. Everything okay here?"

"Just fine," Charity said. "We're almost finished."

"Meredith wasn't sure how to tell you about us. I advised her to just lay it out, but she was concerned that you might be hurt."

Charity smiled. "I'm glad for both of you. You're a perfect couple."

Brett grinned. "I agree."

Meredith frowned. "Charity tells me that her relationship with Elias Winters has become personal."

Brett whistled silently and leaned back in his seat. "Winters, huh? I don't know a whole lot about him. Don't think anyone does. But that alone is a good reason to be careful. He swims in some very deep waters, Charity."

"Funny you should put it that way." Charity smiled. "But for the record, he's changed career paths recently. He's become a small business proprietor."

Brett made a face. "Like hell."

"It's all right, I know what I'm doing," Charity said quietly.

Brett lifted a hand. "I get the point. I'll back off. But speaking as a future member of the family, be careful, okay?"

"Don't worry."

Meredith looked far from reassured. "I don't like this, Charity."

Brett's gaze went to the front door of the dining room. "Speak of the devil."

Charity turned halfway around in her seat and saw

Elias walking toward them. In his faded jeans and black pullover, he should have looked completely out of place in a room full of suits. Instead he subtly dominated the setting. Every eye in the place went to him and then slid away.

Elias seemed oblivious of the discreet, assessing glances. He held Charity's gaze as he came toward her. A pang of disappointment went through her when she saw his shuttered, enigmatic expression. She knew at once that things had not gone well in the interview with Garrick Keyworth. She wondered if she had been wrong to urge him to pay the visit to his old nemesis.

"Is that Winters?" Meredith asked in a low voice.

"Yes." Brett slowly, politely got to his feet as Elias approached. "Someone pointed him out to me once at a business luncheon."

"He looks as if he's been in a fight," Meredith said, in a low, shocked voice.

"Usually he wins," Charity assured her.

"Winters." Brett stuck out his hand when Elias arrived at the table. "Brett Loftus."

Elias shook hands briefly.

Charity summoned up a bright smile. "Elias, I'd like you to meet my sister, Meredith."

"How do you do," Meredith said very coolly.

Elias took her elegantly manicured hand. "Your secretary told me where to find you and Charity."

"We were just finishing lunch," Charity said quickly. "Do you want something to eat?"

Elias looked at her. "I went to the Pike Place Market before I came looking for you. Had something to eat there. I also did some shopping."

"I hope you stocked up on soba noodles and balsamic vinegar."

"Among other things." Elias remained on his feet.

"Join us for coffee?" Brett asked blandly.

"No, thanks."

No question about it, Elias wanted to leave, Charity thought. "We'd better be on our way." She grabbed her purse and got to her feet. "Long drive ahead, you know. Good-bye, Meredith. Brett. And congratulations."

"Drive carefully," Brett said casually.

"Good-bye, Charity." Meredith smiled, but her eyes rested thoughtfully on Elias. "Maybe Brett and I will get a chance to drive up to Whispering Waters Cove in a couple of weeks."

"That would be wonderful." Charity leaned down to give her a quick hug. Then she straightened and looked at Elias. "I'm ready."

He took her arm and led her away from the table.

Charity was almost through the French doors at the far end of the dining room when she caught the low-voiced comments from a nearby table.

"That's Winters, all right. Wonder what he's up to these days."

"Heard he had a major deal going down somewhere up north."

"Must be something involving Charity Truitt."

"Can't imagine what it would be. She flamed out a year ago. Stressed to the max, they said. Walked away from everything."

Charity knew Elias had overheard the remarks, but he said nothing. She waited until they were alone in the elevator.

"You see?" she murmured. "Big city or little town. The gossip factor remains the same."

"Yes." He said nothing more as the elevator cab started to descend.

"Well? How did it go with Garrick Keyworth?"

"We didn't exactly get closure, if that's what you mean."

"No need to be sarcastic. I just asked."

Elias exhaled slowly. "Sorry. It was my decision to see him. I shouldn't have snapped at you just because it didn't go well."

"It may take a while to see the results of your visit. How do you feel about it?"

He looked at her, his eyes intense. "I don't know."

She took his arm. "It's okay, Elias. You did what you could. Now you have to let it go."

The elevator fell another five floors.

"Cozy little family scene back there in the dining room," Elias said.

"Mmm."

"Was it hard?"

"Was what hard?"

"Seeing Loftus and your sister together? Looks like they're a couple."

"Yes, they are now." She was surprised by his insight. "And, no, it wasn't hard to see them together. I think they belong together."

"Did Loftus mean a lot to you?"

"I walked out on our engagement party, remember?"

"Yes, but the two of you were lovers, and knowing you, that had to mean something."

"Oh, for heaven's sake, Brett and I were never lovers. Whatever gave you that idea?"

Elias blinked the way Otis often did, an enigmatic gesture that betrayed no hint of emotion. "You were almost engaged."

"I told you, he was too big. You saw him. He's six and a half feet tall if he's an inch and at least a yard wide across the shoulders. He's a mountain. I got a severe attack of claustrophobia every time he kissed me."

"Claustrophobia?"

She shuddered delicately. "I couldn't imagine getting into bed with him. Poor Brett. I think he assumed I was just too stressed out to be interested in sex. I could hardly tell him that I felt smothered every time he put his arm around me."

"That's what you meant when you said he was too big? That he was too tall?"

"Too tall, too wide, too heavy. What did you think I meant?" Charity widened her eyes as understanding dawned. "Oh, my God, you didn't think I meant that he was, uh, too well endowed?" She broke off as a fit of giggles overtook her.

"It seemed a reasonable conclusion under the circumstances," Elias said dryly.

"Reasonable?" More laughter swept through her. She put her hand over her mouth in a vain effort to choke it back. "This is incredible. Reminds me of an old joke."

"What joke?"

"You know, the one about the guy who's six feet, six inches," Charity gasped. She was laughing so hard now, she could barely stand. "The lady says, forget about the six feet, tell me about the six inches."

"Very funny."

"Sorry. I never could tell a joke."

Very deliberately Elias moved to cage her against the wall of the elevator. He planted both hands beside her head and leaned over her. "I'm glad you're finding this amusing."

"Are you kidding? This is hilarious. I can't believe you thought I meant that Brett's . . . that his . . . that his—"

"Family jewels?" Elias offered helpfully. "Manly root? Cock?"

Charity gasped for breath. "Thingy? I can't believe

you thought that was what was so big about him. Good grief, I've never even seen it."

"Don't worry, you can look at mine any time. On one condition."

She fluttered her lashes outrageously. "What condition?"

"That you never, ever call it a thingy."

15

——◦∾◦——

A woman's love is a relentless flood that threatens any
dam in its path.

—"On the Way of Water," from the journal of Hayden Stone

The journey down to the lobby in the elevator had
been a trip through the looking glass. Elias considered
the magic of it all as he drove north with Charity. No
doubt about it. He had stepped into the cab on the
thirtieth floor feeling grim and morose. By the time
he had reached the lobby, his mood had undergone a
sea change. Charity's laughter had had a reviving effect on his spirits. And other parts of his anatomy
as well.

None of his problems had disappeared during the
thirty-floor trip, he reminded himself. If anything he
actually had a few more of them now than he'd had
earlier in the day.

The newest one on the horizon was the obvious

fact that Meredith Truitt did not approve of Charity's relationship with him. He had seen the deep suspicion in her eyes. Her sentiments were undoubtedly echoed by her brother, Davis. Elias wondered how much Charity would be influenced by her step-siblings' attitude. She had not seemed worried about the opinion of the movers and shakers of Whispering Waters Cove, but family was a different matter.

It had also made him uneasy to witness Brett Loftus's comfortable relationship with the Truitt women. It was not sexual jealousy that bothered him. He was satisfied that Charity felt no lingering attraction there. But the intimacy of a long-term friendship was evident. Elias was not certain how to compete with that kind of familiarity. He had spent a good portion of his life learning to keep others at a distance.

And, of course, he had still not found a way to float on past the whirlpool in the river that was his relationship with Garrick Keyworth.

But all of those problems seemed more manageable now than they had before he had stepped into the elevator.

"What else did you buy at the Market besides noodles and balsamic vinegar?" Charity asked.

"Some good capers, fresh basil, extra-virgin olive oil, bread, wine. The basics."

"Wonderful. I do believe it's your turn to cook."

"Going to be tough to beat your peanut butter sandwiches."

"I'm sure you'll come up with something."

Elias let that slide. "Your sister doesn't approve of me. I doubt if your brother does, either. Loftus looked worried, too."

"It's your reputation as a man of mystery that concerns them. They don't really know you. Don't worry about it, Elias. It's not as if we're getting married."

Elias's good mood went south in a single heartbeat. He gazed straight ahead at the road that was taking them back to Whispering Waters Cove. "What if we were?"

Charity turned her head to look at him. The wariness in her was sudden and profound. "I don't understand."

"I just asked a simple question."

"It's not so simple, and you know it."

It had seemed simple enough to him, but he did not want to get into an argument about it. He could sense the riptide waiting in the shallows. "Will you answer it?"

She was silent for a few seconds. "All right, if we were planning to get married, which we're not, I wouldn't let Meredith's or Davis's opinion influence me. There. Satisfied?"

"Yes," he lied. He was far from content with her answer. But he knew that was his own fault. He hadn't asked the right question. Water flows in the channel that is provided for it. The wrong question created the wrong channel.

Crazy Otis was perched on a slow-moving carousel horse, preening his feathers, when Elias arrived to fetch him late that afternoon. The parrot squawked in greeting and stretched his wings.

"Ready to go home, Otis?" Elias stepped onto the revolving carousel and held out his wrist. "Our turn to cook tonight."

"Heh, heh, heh." Otis ambled onto Elias's arm and climbed up to sit on his shoulder. He nibbled playfully on a few strands of hair.

"Sure am glad to see you," Yappy said as he shut down the carousel. "Gettin' tired of running this thing for that bird. He's been riding all day for free."

"Thanks, Yappy." Elias stepped down onto the pier planking. "I know Otis is very appreciative."

"Uh-huh." Yappy scowled at some parrot droppings that had landed on a golden horsetail. He jerked a handkerchief out of the pocket of his overalls and wiped up the evidence of Otis's recent presence. "It's Charity's fault. If she hadn't hit on the idea of using my carousel to cheer Otis up, he'd never have developed a taste for riding it."

Elias reached up to scratch Otis's head. "Guess there's a bit of the thrill-seeker in Otis. Charity discovered it."

"Well, I can't complain too much." Yappy wadded up the soiled handkerchief and tossed it into a sack. "The kids go crazy when they see Otis sittin' on one of the horses. Always do a lot of business when that bird is here."

"If you're thinking of a long-term contract, I'm sure Otis would be willing to negotiate a reasonable rate for his time."

"What are you? His manager? I ain't payin' that bird no fee. He gets free rides, and that's it. Take it or leave it."

"When you put it like that, how can he refuse?"

Otis uttered his dark chuckle again.

Yappy shrugged. "Deal."

"Any local news? Has Tybern made an arrest?"

"No. If you ask me, it was one of those Voyagers that killed Gwen Pitt. Most of 'em have left town. All had alibis, Tybern says, but who can be sure where everyone was that night? Seems logical to me that one or two of 'em could easily have lied for some of the others."

"If you want my opinion," Ted said as he came up behind Elias, "I think Swinton did Gwen Pitt. Probably pissed because she wouldn't give him what he considered a fair share of the profits."

Yappy shrugged again. "Possible. Real possible. Bea thinks Swinton did it, too. So do most folks in town."

"I don't know," Elias rubbed Otis's head. "Swinton is the type who sends other people to do his dirty work."

"So maybe he hired someone to kill her," Ted suggested. He walked forward and lounged against a carousel horse. The slogan on his T-shirt of the day read *Tectonics Happen.*

"Maybe," Elias said. "But I don't think so."

"Why not?" Ted asked.

"It's not as easy to find a hit man as films and mysteries make it appear. It costs, for one thing. A lot more than I think Swinton would have been willing to pay. And there are risks. The hit man is the first one to talk if he's picked up."

Yappy squinted. "You sound like you've had some personal experience along those lines."

"I had a client a few years back," Elias said. "He decided to renege on a contract, but he didn't want to leave any witnesses. I was a witness."

Ted stared. "Was the client from Seattle?"

"No. It all happened in a place where business is done a little differently than it is in Seattle. Any sign of Swinton?"

"No," Yappy said. "His motor home is still parked out there on the campground. Wouldn't think he could afford to just up and walk away from an expensive RV like that."

"The motor home is too conspicuous," Elias said. "Swinton must have decided to cut his losses when he left town."

"Tybern says if no one shows up to claim it by the end of the week, he'll have it towed away as an abandoned vehicle." Ted absently scratched his belly. "So, how did things go in the big city today? Meet Charity's stepbrother and stepsister?"

"I met Meredith." Elias stroked Otis's neck. "And the ex-fiancé."

"That'd be Loftus," Yappy muttered. "He as big as Charity says?"

"Only about six-three," Elias said.

"Guess that looks big enough when you're five-foot-four like Charity," Yappy said.

"He's about to get engaged to Charity's stepsister," Elias added.

Yappy looked thoughtful. "That a fact?"

"Charity said something once about Meredith and Loftus being a good match," Ted muttered.

"She didn't seem to mind that Loftus and her stepsister were going to get engaged," Elias said carefully.

Yappy beetled his brows. "Hard to tell with women."

"Yeah," Ted nodded sagely. "Real hard to tell with women."

When it came to philosophies that a man could live by, that one was as good as any, Elias thought.

"That was great, as usual. You do incredible things with noodles, Elias." Charity dried the last dish and stacked it neatly on the shelf above the sink. "It's getting late, and we've had a long day. I should be on my way home."

Elias stilled in the act of crouching to place the vegetable steamer inside a cupboard. "You're going home?"

"It's nearly nine o'clock. I've got some bills to pay. I should do a wash, too. I've been so busy lately that I'm getting behind on my routine maintenance."

Elias straightened slowly. "Is that a polite way of

saying that you think we're spending too much time together?"

"No." She saw the chill, remote quality gather in his eyes and sighed inwardly. She took two steps forward, moving to stand directly in front of him. She put her arms around his neck and kissed him lightly on the mouth. "It's a polite way of saying that I've been so busy, I'm getting behind on things at home. Simple. Straightforward. No hidden meanings."

He rested his hands on her hips, his fingers warm and strong on the curve of her waist. "I've got a simple, straightforward solution."

"What's that?"

"Move in with me."

It was Charity's turn to go very still. Suddenly, it was hard to breathe. The old sense of panic welled up out of nowhere, threatening to swamp her. Elias had said nothing about love. She could not be sure the word was even in his vocabulary. Another man who did not love her was asking for a commitment from her. And she could not, dared not give it.

"I don't think that would be a good idea," she whispered.

Elias's jaw could have been hewn from stone. "Why not?"

"We're still getting to know each other." She struggled desperately for logical reasons, reasons she could use to convince him. There was no way to tell him the real truth. He would not understand. "We're two very independent people. We shouldn't rush into anything. What if it doesn't work out? It would be awkward to try to go back to the way things are now."

"You're making excuses. What's the real reason you won't move in with me?"

"I'm telling you the real reasons." Her palms tingled. Her skin got hot and then very cold. She could feel her heart pounding as the panic swirled within her.

"It's because I haven't turned out to be one of your more successful projects, isn't it?" Elias's hands tightened around her waist. "You're not content with the results you're getting."

"Elias, that's not how it is."

"You'll never turn me into another Brett Loftus."

"I don't want another Brett Loftus." Her voice was starting to rise. She could hear the anxiety in it, a thin, edgy, discordant note.

"What do you want from me, damn it?"

Anger came to her rescue, diluting some of the hysteria. "The real question is, what do you want from me?"

"I told you, I want you to move in with me."

"Why?" The single word came out as a small shriek.

"Why?" Elias's eyes were brilliant with an emotion that could not be clearly identified. The only thing certain about it was that it was very, very intense. "You have to ask me that?"

"I don't think it's too much to expect a reasonable answer. Is it because we're good together in bed?"

He looked startled, although whether from her question or her tone of voice, Charity did not know.

"That's only one reason." Elias suddenly sounded cautious. "There are others."

"We both like to cook?"

"An interest in good cooking is something we have in common, isn't it? I thought women liked that in a relationship."

"Are you implying that our relationship is based on sex and food?"

"There's a lot more to it than sex and food."

"Such as?" she challenged.

"We both came to Whispering Waters Cove to reinvent ourselves. We both own small businesses on Crazy Otis Landing." A hunted look appeared in his eyes. "Hell, what's wrong with sex and food, anyway?"

How could he be so blind, she wondered. Didn't he see what they really had between them? Didn't it matter? She smiled grimly. "Nothing is wrong with sex and food. But I was looking for a relationship with something more than just the basics in it. When you buy a car, you don't buy the stripped-down model. You usually get one with a few nice accessories. Leather upholstery, maybe. Or tinted windows."

His eyes narrowed. "You're upset."

"You noticed, did you?"

"Is it because I asked you to move in with me?"

"No, because you asked me for all the wrong reasons." She tried to step back out of his arms. She had to get free before she made a bigger mess of this situation than she already had.

His hands clamped more fiercely around her, imprisoning her. "What the hell are the right reasons?"

The panic exploded. "Love is the little accessory that I had in mind."

Otis, perched on top of his cage, responded to her high, shrill words with a loud squawk of alarm. Out of the corner of her eye Charity saw him stretch his wings and fan the air. He lengthened his neck and lowered his head as if preparing for an attack.

Elias's reaction was just as startling. He looked dumbfounded.

"Love?" He sounded as if a bone had gotten caught in his throat. The single word came out hoarse, ragged, chewed to pieces.

"Yes. Love." Charity took a deep breath. The panic seeped away as quickly as it had come. The claustrophobia vanished. Bringing the truth out into the open had cleansed the wound, but now it ached.

A terrible silence descended.

Elias stared at her as if she had metamorphosed into an alien creature from Saturn. Too bad the spaceships had never come to Whispering Waters Cove, Charity thought. At that moment there was nothing she would have welcomed more than a nice little getaway tour of the galaxy.

She tried to shake off the misty despair that seemed intent on creeping in on the heels of the recently departed panic.

It was over. She had gone too far, too fast. Elias was not ready for love. He might never be ready. The shield of Tal Kek Chara had become his prison.

"Sorry." Charity steadied herself. "I got a little carried away there. Like I said, it's been a long day. I really should go home now."

Elias released her slowly. "I'll get your jacket."

He turned his back to her, walked across the room, and plucked her green jacket from a wall hook. Without a word he held it out to her.

Charity was horrified to see that her fingers shook a little when she took the jacket from his hand. She pulled it on quickly, fumbling with the buttons. Then she hurried to the door, opened it, and stepped into her shoes.

Elias eased a still-tensed Otis into his cage. The bird glowered accusingly at Charity.

Elias shut the cage door. He crossed the room, put on his shoes, and picked up the flashlight that he kept in the hall. He followed Charity out onto the porch.

Silently they went down the steps, through the shadowed garden, and out the gate.

Charity huddled into her jacket, keenly aware of

the chill wind off the cove waters. A storm was headed toward shore. It would strike before morning.

"It's certainly been cold for August." Charity winced at the inanity, but she could not seem to help herself. It was as if some primitive communication instinct automatically generated a conversation about the weather when it became clear that there was nothing else to talk about. "Looks like we've had our summer for this year."

She sounded just like one of the clerks at the checkout counter in the Whispering Waters Grocery, she thought.

Elias did not respond. He walked beside her, but he might as well have been in another world. He had retreated all the way back behind the facade of complete control that his philosophy provided.

Charity's spirits sank lower. She'd ruined everything, she told herself. Then again, perhaps there had been nothing of importance to destroy. Just an illusion of a growing love between herself and Elias. In the end, all illusions crumbled.

The last of the late-summer evening twilight was nearly gone. The cove was an endless, restless sheet of gray steel that would soon turn black as night descended. Charity looked down at the beach. There was just enough light left to see the object that had been deposited on the rock-strewn shore by the incoming tide.

She came to a halt.

"What's wrong?" Elias asked as he stopped beside her.

"There's something down there." She held her blowing hair out of her eyes with one hand and studied what appeared to be a tangle of seaweed and old clothes. "I hope it's not a dead seal. We get one washed ashore every once in a while."

Elias glanced disinterestedly over the edge of the bluff. "Probably something lost overboard from a boat." His attention suddenly sharpened. "Damn. Not another one."

"What do you mean?" Charity stared harder at the dark shape on the beach. A queasy sensation stirred in her stomach. "Oh, no. You don't think that it's . . . a person, do you? It can't be. We would have heard if some tourist had been lost or washed overboard or . . . or—"

"Wait here. I'll take a look." Elias flicked on the flashlight. He walked along the edge of the bluff until he found the path that led to the beach. He went down it with a reckless ease.

Ignoring his terse instructions, Charity followed at a more cautious pace. By the time she reached the beach, Elias was already crouching beside the object that had washed ashore. He aimed the flashlight at one end of what appeared to be a twisted bundle of rags.

Charity stopped several feet away when she realized that her worst fears had been realized. It was not a dead seal that lay there. "Oh, my God."

"Looks like we just found out where Rick Swinton went when he disappeared," Elias said.

Elias stood near Hank Tybern and watched as Rick Swinton's body was loaded into the town's one ambulance. Not that there was anything useful that could be done for Swinton in a hospital, he thought. Swinton was headed for the morgue.

"Have to wait until the county medical examiner does the autopsy," Hank said. "But I've seen enough people pulled out of the water to estimate that Swinton was in the cove for no more than a day or so. And he sure didn't drown."

"No," Elias remembered the large hole in Swinton's chest. "He didn't drown."

"What do you want to bet that we'll discover he was shot with the same twenty-eight-caliber that was used on Gwen Pitt?"

"No bets." Elias glanced at Charity. He was worried about her. In the harsh glare of the ambulance lights he could see the sick, stark tension in her face. A body pulled out of the water was not an easy thing to look at. Then again, no dead body was easy to look at, and Charity had seen two of them recently.

"So much for my little theory that Swinton murdered Gwen Pitt," Hank muttered. "Too bad. I was gettin' real fond of that one."

Elias thought about it. "You don't have to rule it out. You don't have the autopsy results yet. Could be two different guns. Swinton could have killed Gwen Pitt and then gotten himself killed by someone else. He must have made a few enemies in his time."

"Can't argue with that. Not a real nice guy." Hank exhaled slowly. "But I'd stake my job on the hunch that it was probably the same killer using the same gun. Be stretching things a bit to believe that we have us two murderers running around Whispering Waters Cove this summer."

Elias considered the situation from that logical angle. "Could be the same motive, too. A disgruntled Voyager might have concluded that Swinton was just as guilty of fraud as Gwen Pitt."

"And said Voyager would be right." Hank looked at him. "But I don't think it was one of those cult members. I talked to all of them. Double-checked their alibis. They were all clear. And besides, they're getting most of their money back, so why would one of them risk another murder?"

"That leaves you with the possibility that Pitt and

Swinton were killed by someone from Whispering Waters Cove," Elias said. "Either a local resident or a tourist who's staying in the area."

"Yeah." Hank planted his weathered hands on his hips and watched the medics close the ambulance doors. "You know, when you get right down to it, there is one curious similarity between the two murders which strikes me as more than a little interesting."

Elias winced. "I know."

Charity stirred slightly. "What's the similarity, Hank?"

"Just the little fact that in both cases Winters, here, was one of the first folks on the scene."

Charity started as if she'd touched a live electrical wire. Elias watched with a sense of relief as the vibrancy returned to her face. Her eyes widened in anger. Her chin came up swiftly. She glowered at Hank.

"Just what are you implying?" Charity demanded.

"Nothing." Hank spread his hands in an gesture of complete innocence. "Only making an observation."

"Well, it's a really stupid observation," Charity snapped. "You had better not be suggesting that Elias had anything to do with these murders. Just because he's a newcomer in this town is no excuse for you not to do your job properly."

"Take it easy, Charity." Elias knew that his voice lacked conviction. A part of him did not want to halt her tirade. "Hank was making a legitimate observation."

"Really?" She gave him a disgusted look. "It sounded more like an accusation to me."

Hank waved that off. "Now, Charity, I was only commenting on the situation."

Elias watched in admiration as Charity drew herself

up to her full five feet, four inches. She was suddenly the dominant presence on the beach. Everyone else, including Hank and Jeff and the ambulance medics faded into insignificance as she rallied to Elias's defense.

It was suddenly very easy to see how Charity had once run a successful corporation, he thought. When she shifted into this particular gear, she was an Amazon.

"If you make any more such comments, Chief Tybern, I will have a whole team of lawyers from Seattle here before noon tomorrow," Charity said with icy disdain. "Truitt, Inc. has some of the best attorneys on the West Coast on retainer. I'm sure they'll have a few things to say about your observations. And when they've finished saying them, I'll see to it that they sue you and your police department."

"For crying out loud, Charity," Hank muttered.

"How do you think the people of Whispering Waters Cove will react when they discover that you, personally, have been responsible for bankrupting the entire town with a lawsuit?"

Hank appealed to Elias. "Tell her to calm down, will you? She's overreacting."

"I am not overreacting," Charity said through her teeth. "I am telling you what will happen if you make any more of your not-so-veiled accusations. If you think I'm bluffing, guess again."

"I don't think you're bluffing," Hank said quickly. He threw Elias another desperate, pleading look.

Elias gave him a helpless, what-do-you-expect-me-to-do shrug. But inside he could feel a singing relief. The exuberant sensation flooded his veins, driving out the chill.

Charity did care, after all. She had to care. After that fight in his house he hadn't known what to believe. But no woman would leap to a man's defense with such determination if she did not care for him.

"For the record, Chief Tybern," Charity continued, "I will remind you that on the occasion of Gwendolyn Pitt's murder, Elias was with me for the entire time period during which you said the murder occurred."

"I know, I know," Hank said soothingly.

"Furthermore, he has been with me almost continuously for the past several days. I would like to point out that you, even with all the resources available to you, were unable to locate Rick Swinton after he disappeared."

"You don't have to remind me," Hank growled.

"I can assure you that Elias certainly has had neither time nor opportunity to track him down and kill him. I would have known if he had done any such thing."

"I believe you," Hank said.

"I should hope so."

Maybe she was not satisfied with what they had together, Elias thought. Maybe what they had together wasn't enough for her. Maybe her strange mood this evening was a result of having seen Brett Loftus and her sister together earlier today.

There were a lot of maybes in this situation, but he knew one thing for certain, and he seized that knowledge with both hands. Charity definitely cared.

She cared enough to spring to his defense. She cared enough to threaten Hank and the entire town of Whispering Waters Cove, the new community that she called home, with her family's company lawyers.

Yes, she cared, Elias thought. They were bound together by something more than sex and food. He could work with that.

"By the way," Hank said. "What with all the excitement, I forgot to tell you that I did learn something of interest from those two punks who broke into your place, Elias."

"What was that?" Charity asked.

"They admitted that Swinton had hired them to vandalize your cottage last month, Charity." Hank gave her a considering look. "Mind if I ask what you did to piss off Rick Swinton?"

Elias sensed rather than saw the small shiver that went through Charity.

"I declined his invitation to dinner." She rubbed her arms. "I'm told he liked to get even with people who crossed him."

Hank shook his head. "Should have kicked the whole damn lot of 'em out of town last month. Now look at the mess I've got on my hands."

"Why didn't you run them out of the cove?" Elias asked.

"It's not as easy to get rid of a bunch like that as you'd think," Hank said. "Besides, the mayor pretty well tied my hands when she decided to let things ride until the fifteenth. Thanks to Her Honor, I've got two murders to deal with now."

16

⟞⟐⟝

When one cannot stop the rushing river, go with the flow.

—"On the Way of Water," from the journal of Hayden Stone

Charity parked her car two doors down from Phyllis
Dartmoor's law office shortly after nine the next
morning. She got out and started walking toward the
town's one drugstore. She had some errands she
wanted to complete before she opened Whispers at
ten.

The items on her list included a new bottle of shampoo, some soap, and toilet paper. She also needed a
roll of stamps. Life went on, even when one made
a hobby of getting seduced by an enigmatic male or
happening upon murder victims, she thought glumly.

It was going to be a long day, and she was definitely
not in top form. Lack of sleep was part of the problem. Her dreams had been filled with images of Rick

Swinton's body floating on an endless ink-black sea.
She had awakened several times during the night, each
time instinctively reaching out for the comfort of Elias's warm, strong frame. But he had not been there.

It was her own fault, she told herself. She had been
the one who had insisted she would be just fine on
her own last night. At the time, she had meant it.
When Elias had left her at her front door, she had
still been fuming about Hank Tybern's comments.
Anger had given her strength. It was only later, in
bed, that the grisly images had invaded her head.

Her only consolation was that Elias's parting words
had been an invitation to dinner tonight. When she
had tentatively pointed out that it was her turn to
cook, he had shrugged the issue aside, saying he owed
her a meal as payment for the way she had defended
him to Tybern.

Charity had not argued. She sensed that, in his own
way, he was trying to repair the rift that had opened
between them when she'd gone bananas earlier in
the evening.

If a sexy friendship was all he could offer now, she
would accept it. It was a foundation, she told herself.
She could build on it.

She eyed the small cluster of people gathered at the
end of the block in front of the post office and had
second thoughts about buying stamps. It was a safe
bet that the chief topic of conversation this morning
was the latest murder. She had no desire to answer a
lot of questions.

The glass door with the words *Phyllis Dartmoor,
Attorney at Law* painted on it opened just as Charity
was about to walk past. Phyllis looked out at her with
exhausted, desperate eyes.

"Charity, I've got to talk to you."

She did not need this, Charity thought. She definitely did not need an extended conversation with Phyllis. But she could think of no civil way to avoid it. Reluctantly she came to a halt.

"I suppose you've heard about Rick Swinton," Charity began cautiously.

"Yes. And so has everyone else in town." Phyllis glanced up and down the street as if afraid of being seen with Charity. Apparently satisfied that no one was watching, she motioned quickly. "Come in. Please. This is terribly important."

Charity sighed and walked slowly into the office. "I can't tell you very much. All I know is that he was shot. Tybern thinks that the same kind of gun was used, but other than that, I don't know anything."

"Yes, you do." Phyllis sat down behind an elegant, exquisitely polished nineteenth-century heirloom desk and folded her hands on top of it. "You know that I have a reasonably good motive for murder."

Charity was stunned. Very slowly she sank down into one of the brown cordovan leather chairs. "Are you talking about those photos that Swinton tried to use to blackmail you?"

"Yes." The sturdy shoulder pads of her ivory-colored linen suit jacket could not conceal the tension in Phyllis's neck and back. "A lot of people would be willing to kill someone who threatened blackmail. I won't deny that I was very relieved when I first heard that Swinton was dead."

"I don't blame you."

"But then I remembered that you had seen the photos. You're aware that Swinton tried to blackmail me. You know I had a reason to kill him. Charity, I need to know if you intend to tell Tybern about those pictures."

"No, I certainly do not intend to tell him about them. Phyllis, I swear, I never once thought you had murdered Swinton. And even if I had, I wouldn't go out of my way to tell Tybern about the pictures."

A glimmer of relief appeared in Phyllis's eyes. "Thank you."

"Rick was a nasty little weasel. Hank says that Swinton was the one who arranged to have a couple of young toughs vandalize my house a month ago. Just because I wasn't turned on by his obnoxious seduction routine. Can you believe it?"

Phyllis sighed. "Yes."

"Rick said I'd regret it, but I didn't think he'd go that far."

"I told you, he claimed that he always got even, one way or another. Nobody got away with screwing him over, he said."

"Looks like someone did this time."

"Yes." Phyllis rubbed her forehead as if she was trying to get rid of a headache. "Damn it, I don't know what I ever saw in him. No, that's not true. I know what drew me to him. It was raw sex, pure and simple."

Charity winced. "Pretty basic stuff. Did he like to cook?"

"No." Phyllis frowned. "What makes you ask?"

"Never mind. Look, don't be too hard on yourself, Phyllis. You weren't the only woman who found him attractive."

"I know." Phyllis's mouth twisted in a self-mocking smile. "I think he took both of us to the same little love nest, too."

"Both of you?"

"There were at least two of us. Maybe more, for all I know. It's a wonder we weren't tripping over each other coming and going from the old Rossiter place. I used to find tissues in the bathroom that someone else had used to blot her lipstick. Once I discovered a pair of ripped pantyhose under the bed. Really disgusting when you think about it. But at the time I was only interested in the hot sex. I ignored the hot sheets."

"Swinton may have taken some of the Voyagers there." Charity recalled what Arlene had said about Rick Swinton's sexual habits. "I was told he entertained himself by seducing some of the younger women in the group."

"That wouldn't surprise me. He was really a creep, wasn't he?"

Charity looked at her. "Do you think he might have been blackmailing someone else besides you? One of the Voyagers, perhaps?"

"Who knows what that vicious little worm would have done?" Phyllis hesitated. "Wait a second. Are you implying that one of his other victims might have killed him?"

"I don't know." Charity got to her feet. "It's Hank Tybern's job to look into things like that, isn't it?" So long as Tybern did not try to implicate Elias, she was willing to stay out of his way. "Look, I've got to run. Don't worry, I won't say anything about the pictures. I assume you've destroyed them?"

"Are you kidding? I burned them all right after you left my house."

"Good." Charity went to the door and raised one hand in a half-mocking salute. "I'll see you at the next town meeting, councilor."

"Wait. Please. One more thing."

Charity turned to look at her over her shoulder. "What is it?"

"What makes you so certain that I didn't kill Swinton?"

Charity smiled ruefully. "You're not going to believe this, but you and I have some things in common."

Phyllis raised one brow. "You're into bondage fantasies? Tsk, tsk."

"Uh, no. I'd probably go straight off the deep end if someone tied me up and tickled me. I tend to be a tad claustrophobic in, uh, certain interpersonal situations."

"Don't knock it until you've tried it."

Charity took a breath. "What I meant was, if someone tried to blackmail me, I'd have done exactly what you did."

"Call his bluff?"

"Right. And if that hadn't worked, I'd have gone to the cops."

Phyllis straightened her crisply padded shoulders. "Yes. I wasn't looking forward to it, but if I'd received more threats, I'd have contacted Tybern or hired a private detective to deal with the situation."

"Exactly." Charity shrugged. "Rick Swinton would not have been worth the risk of a murder conviction to either of us. But even if one of us had decided to take such a drastic step, we would not have been dumb enough to leave the body on our own doorstep."

Phyllis frowned. "I doubt that the killer intended for Swinton to be found. I heard that he was washed ashore by the tide. That means someone tried to ditch him in the cove. Probably threw the body off the bluff thinking it would be carried out into the Sound."

"Everyone who has lived around here for more than a few months knows that things that get dumped off the bluff tend to wash up in the cove."

Phyllis's well-defined brows came together in a sharp, considering expression. "You're right."

Charity pursued her new line of thought. "Which

means that the murderer either didn't care if Swinton was found or else he actually wanted the body to show up."

"Not likely. Why would anyone want it to be found? There's too much potential evidence on a dead body. More likely the killer was not a local person. Didn't know about the peculiarities of our tides."

"Someone who just assumed that Swinton's body would be carried out to deep water and disappear forever?"

"Yes." Phyllis toyed with a plump fountain pen. "I suppose that points back to one of the Voyagers, doesn't it? They were the outsiders in town. They wouldn't know about tides and such, and they had motive. Maybe the same Voyager who murdered Gwendolyn Pitt killed Swinton, too. For similar reasons. After all, both Pitt and Swinton conspired to fleece the members of the cult."

"True. But Tybern says all of the Voyagers have good alibis. Which means he's looking for someone local," Charity added.

"Someone who would have known about the cove tide and who didn't care if the body was found?"

"Or someone who was so distraught that he was not thinking clearly when he pulled the trigger."

With that, Charity went out the door and closed it behind her.

Food and Sex.

He liked the idea of rebuilding on such strong, solid basics, Elias decided. Food and sex were about as fundamental as things got between a man and a woman. And both were very, very good when he and Charity shared them.

It was just after nine. He was doing his shopping early in the day before he opened Charms & Virtues because he wanted to get first crack at the vegetables. He had discovered that if he waited until later in the afternoon, the best were frequently gone.

He stood, pondering, in front of the produce counter. The broccoli was a rich dark green with a hint of purple. Just right. He examined several bunches, searching for perfection.

Tonight's meal was a critical event. It would establish that his relationship with Charity was still intact. He wanted to make her understand that what they had together was solid and real and substantial. A lot more solid, real, and substantial than what she'd had with Brett Loftus. Or anyone else, for that matter.

He had planned an earthy, rustic menu. Twisty fusilli pasta tossed with an olive and caper mixture. Fresh broccoli. Some of the dense, chewy, Euro-style bread he had brought back from Seattle. It could be dipped in olive oil and sprinkled with salt. He had already chosen the wine, a deep, rich cabernet.

After dinner, they would have solid, real, substantial sex. The kind of earthy sex that would make Charity want to stay for the entire night. The kind that would make her see that moving in with him was a logical thing to do.

Back to basics.

He put the broccoli into a plastic bag and headed toward the checkout counter. He would stop by the house, leave the vegetables in the refrigerator, collect Otis, and then drive to the pier.

He saw Charity as he walked toward the Jeep a few minutes later. She was exiting the drugstore with a paper bag in one hand. The expression on her face sent a stab of unease through him. She looked troubled. He wondered how well she had slept last night.

Elias changed course so that his path would intersect with hers. She was concentrating so hard on her private musings that he almost had to tap her on the shoulder to get her attention. She finally noticed him when she came within a hairsbreadth of colliding with him.

"Good morning," he said.

She halted abruptly, blinked, frowned, and focused. "Oh. Good morning."

"Think the fog will burn off by noon?" he asked pleasantly.

"Is that supposed to be funny?"

"Just trying to make conversation. Figured the weather was a safe topic."

She blushed furiously. He knew she was recalling her own comments on the weather during the walk along the bluff last night. Two could play the casual game, Elias thought.

"What have you got in the sack?" she asked gruffly.

"Dinner. Or at least the part of it that I didn't pick up in Seattle yesterday. By the way, thanks for getting Tybern off my back last night. Nice of you to leap to my defense. I was impressed."

She scowled. "Hank had no business implying that you were somehow involved in the murders."

"He just made a couple of professional observations. In his shoes, I'd have made the same ones."

"He could have made similar observations about me, but he didn't."

"You're not as new in town as I am. Besides, you don't look like a murderer."

"Neither do you. Furthermore, you don't have a motive, either."

"Thanks. Some people might not agree with you, though. Me being such an enigmatic, mysterious type and all. Who can say what dark motives I might have?"

She gazed at him with wide, considering eyes for

what seemed like forever. "I know you didn't kill
Gwen Pitt because I was with you that night. And
even though I wasn't with you every minute on the
day Tybern thinks Swinton died, I know that you
didn't kill him, either."

He was warmed by the grave certainty in her voice.
"You don't think I'm capable of murder?"

"I didn't say that. I think you would be capable of
killing under certain circumstances. But these aren't
the circumstances. And if you did kill someone, I don't
think you'd use a gun."

"No?"

"No." Her gaze did not waver. "For you, something
so primitive and violent would be a very personal act.
You'd use your bare hands."

Elias stared at her. He could not think of anything
to say for the space of several heartbeats. She was
right, but it did not seem like the sort of observation
a man should casually confirm while standing in the
middle of a sidewalk.

"Nice to know I have your unqualified support," he
finally said.

"Don't you dare get sarcastic. I am not in a great
mood today."

"Sorry." A door opened halfway down the block.
Elias watched as Phyllis Dartmoor left her office,
turned, and walked away in the opposite direction.
"You know, speaking of motives, there goes someone
who has a damned good one."

Charity glanced down the block at the departing
Phyllis. "She's worried that Tybern might think so,
too. Fifteen minutes ago she called me into her office
and asked if I intended to tell Hank about those
dreadful photos."

"And you said no, naturally."

"Of course I said no. She very wisely burned the

pictures, so the evidence is gone, anyway. But I seriously doubt that she killed him. And she certainly had no motive to murder Gwen Pitt."

"No motive that we know of," Elias corrected absently. He glanced past Charity and saw Hank Tybern's car pull into a parking space in the middle of the block.

"I refuse to believe that Phyllis Dartmoor is a murderer," Charity insisted. "She's just not the type."

"How many murderers have you met?"

"That is not a relevant question. You know, Phyllis said something that got me thinking. She said a couple of things, in fact."

"What things?" Elias watched Hank climb out of the patrol car.

Tybern had a grim expression on his broad face. When he reached the sidewalk he turned to the right and walked stolidly past Phyllis's office.

"She said that Rick Swinton once told her that he always got even," Charity said. "That no one ever got away with screwing him over. We've got a lot of evidence that she's right. The vandalism of my kitchen and the two thugs he sent to beat you up, for example."

"What about Arlene Fenton? She told him to get lost."

"He was more angry at you for interrupting him the night he tried to force himself on her," Charity said. "In any event, he probably figured he'd already gotten even with Arlene because he and Gwen had stolen her money."

"Good point." Elias thought about it. "And he was the one who left the blackmail pictures under your door hoping you'd use them against Phyllis."

"Right. He definitely had a policy of getting even. The other thing Phyllis said that interested me was that Swinton took someone else besides her to the old Rossiter place."

"The Rossiter place?" Elias watched as Hank stopped in front of Pitt Realty. "Didn't you once tell me that was where Jennifer and Leighton Pitt used to meet before the Pitt divorce?"

Hank Tybern hesitated briefly and then appeared to gather himself, as if anticipating something unpleasant. He opened the door and went inside.

"Yes," Charity said. "The old, rundown cottage on the bluff. Anyhow, as I was saying, it got me thinking. If Tybern's right in assuming that we've only got one murderer around here, then he's looking for a killer with some connection to both Gwen Pitt and Rick Swinton. Someone who would have had cause to hate both of them. When you think about it, that narrows the list."

Elias saw the door of Pitt Realty open again. "You can save yourself the effort of drawing up a list. I think Tybern has just arrested the number-one suspect."

"What?" Charity suddenly seemed to realize that his attention was on something going on behind her. She spun around. "Oh, my God. Leighton Pitt. Hank is arresting Leighton Pitt."

Elias watched as Hank put the dejected-looking Pitt into the car. The handcuffs on Leighton's wrists glinted briefly just before the door closed.

"Looks that way," Elias said. "You've got to admit, it's logical. Pitt had plenty of reason to be angry with both his ex-wife and Rick Swinton. Together they ruined him."

"Yes." Charity watched Hank get behind the wheel of the patrol car.

"Well, that's that." Elias felt a twinge of deep regret. "I suppose this means that I won't get to watch you go into your Amazon routine in order to defend me from Hank Tybern anymore."

"I'm not so sure you're in the clear, yet, Elias." She sounded serious.

"Why not?"

"Because I don't think that Leighton Pitt killed his ex-wife or Swinton."

Shortly before eight o'clock that night, Elias sat cross-legged on the cushion in front of the low table and watched Charity polish off the last of his carefully prepared pasta. She had eaten every bite, he noticed, but she had not made a single comment on the food. Her attention was riveted on the subject of Leighton Pitt's arrest.

So much for getting back to basics. Elias was feeling morose and irritable. Things were not going according to plan tonight.

"Ted told me this afternoon that Tybern found Leighton Pitt's gun in the trunk of his car. It's a twenty-eight-caliber. The same kind that was used to kill both Gwen and Rick Swinton." Charity put down her fork and regarded Elias with an expectant look. "Well?"

"Well, what?"

"Well, don't you think it's a little odd that Leighton kept the murder weapon in the trunk of his car? I mean, it doesn't make sense."

"Murder rarely makes sense. People who kill are not usually thinking clearly."

"Yes, I know, but Leighton's not stupid. He must have known that he was a possible suspect. Why would he keep the gun?"

"Maybe he had plans to use it again."

Charity looked horrified for a split second. "I hadn't thought of that." Her expression switched instantly to a thoughtful frown. "No, that wouldn't make sense, either. Gwen and Swinton were the only ones he could logically blame for the bankruptcy."

"You're wasting your time trying to figure this out, Charity. It's Tybern's job to make the case."

"Know what I think?"

He groaned. "No, but I have a hunch you're about to tell me."

She leaned forward over the low table and fixed him with a steely-eyed look. "I think someone set Leighton up to take the fall."

He considered that briefly. "Not likely, but possible."

"Very possible, if you ask me. Leighton Pitt was not in a murderous mood. He was looking to find a way to salvage his financial situation, not plotting revenge."

"You could tell?" Elias asked dryly.

"Call it a hunch."

"That's about all you can call it. Charity, what are you leading up to here?"

She straightened her shoulders. "You are still vulnerable. And it makes me nervous."

"I beg your pardon?"

"If it turns out that Leighton has been framed, the finger of blame is going to be pointed right back at you again. I don't like it."

"It's not my favorite finger, either," he conceded, "but I doubt that it will be pointed in my direction."

"You're not in the clear, yet, Elias. I've been thinking about this all day. I've come to the conclusion that we should take proactive measures to make sure that no one tries to implicate you in this mess."

Elias was suddenly very wary. "Proactive measures?"

"Right." She got to her feet and scooped the dishes

off the table in a single move. "We need to look into the facts ourselves. See if we can turn up a few clues."

"Clues?" Wariness turned to outright alarm. "Are you nuts? This thing is over. Tybern's a good cop. He wouldn't have arrested Pitt unless he had solid grounds."

She turned in the kitchen and looked at him over the top of the counter. Her eyes were shadowed with concern. "I don't care what kind of evidence they found in the trunk of Leighton's car. I don't think he killed Gwen and Rick. That means that there's still a killer running around loose. And as long as that's true, you're at risk. Because if Leighton Pitt can prove his innocence, you're the next most likely suspect."

"The hell I am."

"It's true, Elias. We have to do something to protect you. We need more information. If Swinton was black-mailing Phyllis, he may have been blackmailing others. It's a reasonable assumption, isn't it?"

She was doing this for him, Elias reminded himself. He took consolation from that knowledge.

"Just where do you suggest we start?" he asked cautiously.

"The old Rossiter place." She dumped the dishes in the sink. "I would feel better if we could find some-one else who was involved with Swinton. Someone who may have had something to hide. It will be dark soon. I want to take a quick look around Rick Swinton's little love nest."

The old Rossiter house was more than a quarter mile from the main road. It was hunkered down in the heavy shadows of a thick stand of fir. The rising slope of a hillside loomed over it, concealing the dilap-idated structure from casual view.

It was a miserable-looking little cabin, Elias

thought. Even at night it was plain that no one had done any repairs in years. The eaves drooped precariously over a back porch that looked as though it was on the verge of total collapse.

"So much for worrying about someone seeing our flashlights," Charity said cheerfully as she walked around the hood of the Jeep to stand beside Elias. "You see? I told you this would be a piece of cake."

He looked at her. She was dressed in a pair of jeans and a dark sweater. Her hair was tied in a ponytail. There was an air of anticipation and enthusiasm about her that made him distinctly uneasy. "For the record, I want to go down as saying that, while I appreciate your motives here, I'm not real happy with this plan of yours."

"Did I carp and complain when you searched Swinton's motor home?"

"Yes, you did. Endlessly."

"Well, that was different. That night we had half the town parked nearby. Here we're all alone."

"Charity, this is not necessary. The odds of finding anything here are slim to nothing."

"You never know. It's a place to start. Come on, let's go inside." She walked determinedly toward the sloping back porch.

Elias thought wistfully of his original plans for the evening. Food and sex. Nice, basic, elemental things. By now he and Charity should have been in bed. But he could tell that there was no dissuading her from her goal.

Reluctantly, he followed her to the porch steps. Charity was already at a window. She trained the flashlight at the bottom of the sill.

"Do you know how to pry open a window?" she asked, fiddling with the latch.

"Why don't you try the door, first?" Elias crossed

the porch to the back door. "I doubt if anyone would bother to lock this place."

He gripped the knob and twisted firmly. The door opened with a loud groan.

"Good thinking," Charity said.

"Thank you. A man likes to feel useful around the place." Elias led the way into the small cottage.

Charity followed quickly. The scent of mildew was strong.

"Whew." Charity made a half-choking sound. "It smells terrible in here. Not exactly a perfumed love bower, is it?"

"No." There was a feeling of unending dampness inside the house, as if it had not been aired out for years. "Maybe Rick's partners liked the sleazy ambience."

The flashlights picked up grimy gray covers draped over heavy furniture that was probably rotting quietly into the floor. The inside of the brick fireplace was blackened, but there was no sign that anyone had used it recently.

"Must have been a little chilly for Rick and his friends," Elias said.

"I suppose they generated their own heat." The floorboards groaned as Charity walked to a doorway and peered around the corner. "One small bedroom and a bath. That's it."

"What are you looking for?"

"I don't know. Let's start with the bedroom. I gather that's where most of the action took place."

Without waiting for a response, she disappeared around the corner. A couple of seconds later Elias heard a startled gasp.

"What's wrong?" He went to stand in the doorway. He took in the scene revealed by his flashlight and grinned in spite of his mood.

Charity was in the bedroom, her light aimed at the sagging carcass of an ancient iron bedstead. A bare, badly stained mattress sat on the drooping springs. A pair of padded leather handcuffs dangled from one post.

"I can't imagine ever wanting to be chained to a bedpost," Charity whispered.

"Those handcuffs aren't real. They're the quick-release gag type. Twist them a certain way, and you're free."

"How do you know?"

"A good shopkeeper knows his merchandise," Elias said. "I've got some just like those for sale in Charms & Virtues."

"Amazing." She glanced at him and scowled. "Don't just stand there. Help me look around."

"Right. Clues. We need clues to save my hide in case Tybern comes gunning for me." Elias started to stroll around the tiny bedroom. "What about the handcuffs? Think they might be a useful clue?"

"You're not taking this very seriously, are you?" She was on her knees, bent low to look under the bed. "I'm telling you, Elias, you're in a tricky position here."

He aimed the beam of his flashlight at the enticing curve of her buttocks. Her jeans were stretched taut across her derriere. "You don't have to tell me that. I'm well aware of it."

"Go check out the bathroom."

"To hear is to obey." With a small sigh of regret, he turned away from the engaging sight of her up-thrust bottom. "But I have to tell you, I still don't like this one damn bit. We're not going to find anything useful, and even if we do, we won't need it because Tybern has his suspect in custody."

"Just in case," Charity said. "I'll feel a whole lot

better if we can find something, anything, that points to someone else who might have had a reason to kill Swinton."

"That still leaves the problem of finding someone other than Pitt who had a motive to murder Gwen."

"There must be some other suspect. After all, Pitt himself told us about his financial problems after Gwen's death. Why would he have done that? It was tantamount to telling us that he had a motive. A guilty man would never have done such a thing."

"An interesting point," Elias conceded. He wandered into the seedy-looking bathroom and flashed the light around the cracked and chipped porcelain fixtures. "Charity, there's something I'd like to ask you."

"What's that?" Her voice was muffled.

"Are you doing this because I've become one of your salvage projects?"

"Salvage projects?"

"Like pulling Otis out of his depression or saving the landing."

"I can't hear you," she called from the other room.

He went to the door of the bath. "I said, are you going to all this trouble because you've decided that you have some kind of responsibility toward me? Because, if that's the case, I'd like to make it clear, I'm not just another pier shopkeeper or a depressed parrot who needs saving."

"Elias, look at this."

He walked out into the short hall and saw her standing in the bedroom doorway. He aimed the flashlight first at her excited face and then he switched the beam to the tiny object she held between her thumb and forefinger.

"What is it?" he asked.

"I can't be sure, but I think it's a piece of a chipped acrylic nail."

"So? A lot of women wear those claws."

"Yes," Charity said with great satisfaction. "And if you're from Whispering Waters Cove, chances are good that you have them done at Nails by Radiance."

"I won't argue with that conclusion. But it doesn't tell you much."

"We'll see." Charity removed a tissue from her pocket and carefully wrapped the nail fragment in it. "The only thing I can tell for certain is that it's not Phyllis's special color, Dartmoor Mauve. I'll talk to Radiance in the morning. She should be able to identify it."

"Fine. Talk to Radiance. In the meantime, would you mind answering my question?"

She looked up innocently. "What was it?"

He was beginning to get irritated. "I want to know why you're doing this."

"Isn't it obvious? I'm doing it because you're my friend."

"You're sure that's the only reason?"

"What other reason could there be?" she asked.

"Who the hell knows?" he muttered, exasperated. "I just thought that there might be a more personal reason for your great interest in my welfare."

"What could be more personal than our friendship?" she asked politely as she brushed past him in the hall.

Without any warning, his frustrated anger briefly swamped his self-control and common sense. He whirled around and trained the flashlight on her.

"Has it occurred to you that the reason you're so damned worried about me is because you're wildly, madly, passionately in love with me?" he asked with a fierceness that startled him.

"That, too," she agreed.

17

Water never disappears forever. It flows back into the
sea, becomes rain, forms a river, fills a pond, or cascades
down a mountain. In one way or another, it always returns.
—"On the Way of Water," from the journal of Hayden Stone

Big mistake, Charity thought. She had not meant to
say the words aloud. Not after last night's debacle.
They had just sort of slipped out. An accident waiting
to happen. Now here she was standing at the scene of
the train wreck.

"Elias?"

He did not respond. He loomed in the deep shadow
behind the glare of his flashlight, his face unreadable.
But she did not need to see his expression. She could
feel the impact her words had made. Elias was
stunned. Shaken to the core, no doubt.

She felt a little sorry for him. His fancy philosophy
was good at developing inner strength and self-control,
but it did not handle deep emotions well. Charity

knew of no philosophical framework that did. Human emotions were too mushy for such rigid constructs.

She should have kept her mouth shut, she thought. She knew he was not ready to deal with this. She aimed the beam of her own flashlight squarely in his face. He did not flinch or blink. He was frozen.

"Well, don't just stand there like a deer caught in the headlights." She knew her voice was laced with a distinctly waspish note, but there was nothing she could do about it. "It's your own fault. You had to go and get sarcastic about the whole thing. You know how that irritates me. And in case you haven't noticed, I'm under a lot of stress at the moment. I sometimes act impulsively when I get under stress. I've explained that to you."

He did not move or speak. With a sigh, Charity lowered her flashlight. The beam pooled on the floor at her feet while she studied Elias's dark silhouette. The silence that gripped the old cabin was eerie. She could feel her pulse.

After a moment or two she began to get really worried.

"Are you okay, Elias? We can't stand here staring into the dark all night. We've hung around long enough. We should be on our way."

He finally moved. A single step toward her. "You can't just leave it like that." The words sounded strained and awkward, as if he had trouble stringing them together in a logical sentence.

"Why not?"

"Damn it, you know why not." He took another step forward, moving with a stiff, jerky motion that was completely unlike his normal, gliding stride. "This is important. A lot more important than what we came out here to do."

"I disagree," she said crisply. "If you get arrested,

we're going to have a bigger problem on our hands than sorting out the interpersonal dynamics of our relationship."

"Don't," he said, "make a joke of it."

"Sorry."

"Are you sure?"

"Sure that I'm sorry?"

"No." He came to a halt directly in front of her. His hand was clenched around the flashlight. The light poured down on the floorboards, flowing into the white pool created by her flashlight. "Are you sure about what you said a minute ago?"

"About being wildly, madly, passionately in love with you?" There did not seem to be much point in denying it. Charity resigned herself to the inevitable.

They had managed to sidestep the issue last night thanks to the timely distraction created by the discovery of Rick Swinton's body. But she could hardly count on another, equally diverting event this evening. Not that she wanted one. Two murdered bodies were enough for one summer. She was certainly pushing the limits of her stress threshold.

"Yes." Elias's voice sounded disembodied, as though he spoke from a great distance. "Are you sure about being in love with me?"

"Very sure." She raised her chin. She was vaguely surprised to realize that she did not feel even a tremor of anxiety now. It was certainty, not panic, that welled up inside her. "I'm sorry if that upsets your delicate philosophical balance, but you'll just have to deal with it, Winters."

"Last night." He broke off, apparently searching for words. "Last night you said you wouldn't move in with me because there was no love between us."

"No, I didn't say that. You weren't listening, were you? I meant that I wanted us to be in love before we took that step. I once made the mistake of almost marrying a man for reasons based on friendship and business and feelings of family responsibility. I do not intend to repeat the error. I don't think my medical insurance will cover another round of therapy."

"Our relationship isn't like that."

"Technically speaking, you may be right. You've asked me to move in with you, not marry you. And I'll admit that moving in with a man for reasons based on friendship with good sex is a distinct improvement over my relationship with Brett. The good sex was lacking last time. But it's still not enough."

"I want more than friendship, too."

She stilled. "How much more?"

"I want you," he whispered.

The aching hunger in his voice was getting to her. She knew she was weakening. She had to be careful, she warned herself. There was so much at risk.

"What are you prepared to give in return?" she asked softly.

"Whatever I can. Take whatever you want. Please."

The stark *please* was her undoing. She could not refuse him a second time. She loved him, and he said that he was prepared to give her as much of himself as he could. Coming from Elias, that meant a lot. She wondered if he understood that he was as good as promising her that he would try to learn to open himself to love.

She smiled. "I guess I can work with that. All right, Elias. If you really want me to move in with you, I will. But I warn you, my furniture is coming with me. I'm not going to spend every evening sitting on the floor when I can kick back in my own Italian easy chair."

"You've got a deal." He reached for her.

"Uh, maybe we should get out of here before—"

Elias pulled her into his arms with such force that she dropped her flashlight in surprise. It rolled across the floorboards and fetched up against a wall.

She was crushed against his chest. She could hardly breath. Elias's mouth was ravenous. His body was hard with his surging arousal. It was as if all of the intense emotions that he could not show in any other way were channeled into this one singular form of human communication.

"Elias, wait." Charity managed to free her mouth from his, but she could not get his attention.

Denied her lips, he quested in another direction. She made a soft, half-strangled sound when she felt his teeth come together around her earlobe. A blazing excitement shot through her. Then his mouth moved lower to the curve of her throat. The handle of the flashlight pressed into her back. Elias's free hand pushed through her hair, freeing it from the ponytail clip.

"No, hold on." She caught his face between her palms. Gave him a small, determined shake to make him focus. "Stop."

"What's wrong?"

"I absolutely refuse to have a significant sexual encounter here in this sleazy cabin that appears to have been used by everyone in town who wanted to conduct a clandestine affair."

For a few seconds he did not seem to comprehend. Then she felt him relax very slightly. There was just enough light bouncing off the wall from the fallen flashlight to reveal the slow, sexy grin that transformed his face.

"But someone left a perfectly good set of handcuffs in the bedroom," he said. "Why waste them?"

"Get a grip, Winters." She scooped up the fallen flashlight. "We're outa here. Right now."

"And here I'd started to think of you as a thrill-seeker." He picked her up and whisked her outside.

He stuffed her into the Jeep, got behind the wheel, and drove back to the cottage with a complete lack of regard for the local speed limits.

Charity did not say a word as he pulled into the drive and switched off the engine. There was just enough light to see her sexy smile.

He groaned and reached for her, intending only to kiss her once more before they got out of the Jeep. But passion exploded on contact.

"Elias. Oh, my God."

He fumbled with the Jeep's door with his left hand. He got the door open, but he could not get out of the vehicle. Charity was kissing him with a sweet, frantic desire that sent need swirling through his veins.

"Here," he whispered. "Now."

"Now?"

"Right now. I won't last until we get into the house."

He struggled with her jeans. She did not argue. Instead, she kissed his throat. Her hands fluttered around his waist. He groaned when she carefully lowered his zipper. He was rigid. He knew he was thrusting through the opening in his briefs, through the opening in his pants.

He started to struggle with her jeans.

"No, wait," she whispered.

"Now, what? Don't worry, this isn't like the old Rossiter place. I swear, no one has ever had sex in this Jeep."

She did not answer. Instead, she cradled him in one soft palm.

And then she lowered her head and very delicately, a little awkwardly, as if she had never attempted anything quite like it before but was determined to experiment, she gently stroked the length of him with her wet, warm tongue.

Elias closed his eyes. He could have sworn that he saw the spaceships finally land in Whispering Waters Cove.

"It's called Tal Kek Chara. The same name as the exercises and the philosophy." Elias sat cross-legged on the mat that he had placed next to the small garden pool. He looked at his new student, who was seated on a similar mat across from him. The leather weapon lay stretched out on a towel between them. "Literally translated, it means, the tool that carves a new channel through which water may flow."

Newlin picked up Tal Kek Chara and twisted it tentatively around his wrist, the way Elias had demonstrated a few minutes earlier. "I thought it was a belt or something."

"The best weapon is that which does not appear to be a weapon," Elias said. Newlin's deep curiosity about the strip of leather reminded him of his own first youthful encounter with it.

In fact, he thought with an odd sense of deja vu, this whole session brought back his own early lessons with Hayden Stone. Newlin asked the same questions he had once asked, and the intrigued expression on his face reflected the feelings Elias knew that he had had back at the beginning.

Water never disappears forever. It may return in some new form, but it always returns.

"What language is Tal Kek Chara?" Newlin shifted a little on the mat.

Elias realized that his new pupil was probably getting stiff. Newlin had been sitting in the unfamiliar position for nearly thirty minutes, and it was chilly out here in the garden. The morning sun had not managed to burn through the fog yet.

Last night he had dug out Hayden's journal and for the first time read a few passages. He had been looking for inspiration for his first session as an instructor of Tal Kek Chara. As if fate had guided his hand, he had stumbled across something Hayden had written early on in the journal.

A good teacher must sense the natural rhythms of learning in his students and respond accordingly. The act of teaching is discipline for the teacher as well as the student.

He must end this first session soon, Elias thought, even though Newlin seemed quite willing to continue.

"The language no longer exists," Elias said. "The people that once spoke it were assimilated into a dozen different cultures over the centuries. The last place where the pure language and the knowledge that accompanied it were kept alive was in an ancient island monastery. It was a place that was cut off from the world for a thousand years. Now that monastery is empty."

"What happened to the monks who lived there?" Newlin pushed his small round glasses higher on his nose. "Were they killed in a guerilla war or something?"

"No. The monastery was well hidden. It was never discovered by the outside world. But the monks were all very old when Hayden met them. They eventually died and left only the temple stream to guard the monastery grounds."

"How do you know?"

"Because Hayden took me to see the monastery a few years ago. We hiked for three weeks through a jungle to find it. When we arrived, there was nothing left except the ancient stone temple and the stream that flowed through it."

Images of that day returned to Elias in crystal-clear forms. The journey to the monastery with Hayden had been one of the most important events of his life. But he did not have the words to describe to Newlin what he had experienced as he had stood with Hayden beside the temple stream. He only knew that he still drew strength from the memories of that time.

"Must have been kinda weird, huh?" Newlin watched him closely.

"Yes. but I'll tell you what was even more weird."

"What was that?"

"It was realizing after Hayden died that I was probably the only man in the world who knew exactly what Tal Kek Chara meant, let alone how to use the tool."

"Geez." Newlin considered that for a long moment. "I see what you mean. Kind of a lonely feeling, huh?"

"Yes." Newlin was going to make a good student, Elias decided. "But that's changed now."

"How's that?"

"Now you know what Tal Kek Chara means, too." Elias took the strip of leather and knotted it around his waist.

Newlin stared at him, astonished. And then a slow flush of pleasure rose in his thin face. "Hey, that's right. You're no longer the only guy in the world who knows the meaning of the words. I understand them, too."

"Next time, I'll start teaching you how to use Tal Kek Chara." Elias rose from the mat. "There are a lot of things to learn. It's not just a weapon and a lost language. It's a philosophy. A way of looking at the world."

Newlin scrambled to his feet. "It has to do with that stuff about water, right?"

"It all goes together." Elias went up the porch steps. "But that's enough instruction for now. Time to open the shops. I'll get Otis and his travel cage. We'll give you a lift to the pier."

"Yeah. Sure. Thanks." Newlin hesitated. "Hey, Elias?"

Elias paused at the door. "Yes?"

"Me and Arlene are going to get married in a couple of weeks. I was, like, wondering if you'll come to the wedding. It's not going to be a big deal or anything. But Charity and Bea and Radiance are going to have a party on the pier afterward."

Elias took his hand from the doorknob and turned to gaze thoughtfully at Newlin. "You and Arlene are going to get married?"

"Well, you know how it is." Newlin gave him a bashful grin. "We love each other, and we've both got jobs, and Arlene's through with that silly Voyager stuff, so we figured there was no reason not to get married."

"No," Elias said. "There's no reason not to get married. I'll be at your wedding."

Newlin looked pleased. "Okay. That's great."

Elias went on into the house to collect Otis and the travel cage.

No reason not to get married. The words had the ring of a mantra. He tried them out on Otis to hear how they sounded when he said them aloud.

"No reason not to get married, Otis."

Otis snorted as he stepped onto Elias's arm and allowed himself to be settled on the travel cage perch.

"Not you and me, Otis." Elias closed the door of the cage. "I was talking about Charity and me. But what if she doesn't go along with the idea? It wasn't easy talking her into moving in here. Something tells me she'll panic if I ask her to marry me."

"Heh, heh, heh."

"She's not sure of me, you see," Elias explained as he carried Otis's cage to the door. "And I don't know how to make her sure. Hell, the last thing I want to do is find myself in the kind of mess Loftus found himself in last year. Something tells me I wouldn't handle it nearly as well as he did."

Charity pushed aside the beaded curtain that hung in the doorway of Nails by Radiance and stepped into the small shop. She came face to face with Jim Morrison and the Doors. The scowling members of the band brooded darkly down from a glossy six-foot poster that hung on the wall.

The remaining walls of the shop were hung with tie-dyed draperies and Day-Glo art. The scent of incense wafted through the air.

"Radiance?"

"Hi, Charity. Be with you in a second." Radiance, garbed in a loose patchwork gown, did not look up from her work. She was seated in a swivel chair in front of the narrow manicure table watching her client's nails dry beneath a special lamp.

"No rush." Charity recognized the woman whose hands were receiving Radiance's full attention. "Good morning, Irene. By the way, that new self-help book that you ordered has arrived."

"*Why Self Help Books Can't Help?* Good. I've been waiting for it." Irene Hennessey, a pleasant woman in her early fifties, looked up and smiled. "I'll stop by and pick it up after I finish here."

"Be careful when you do." Radiance frowned. "Even though I'm baking these nails, you know I don't want anyone using their hands very much for at least a half hour after I've finished."

"Don't worry," Charity said smoothly. "Newlin or

I will make sure Irene doesn't ruin her new nails when she picks up the book." She walked closer to the work table and looked down at Irene's long, gleaming nails. "Nice color."

"I call it Irene's Amethyst," Radiance said. "It's perfect on her, don't you think?"

"It's great." Charity admired the way the unusual shade highlighted Irene's delicate coloring. "And I love those little pink squiggly designs."

"My signature touch," Irene said proudly. "No one else in town has them."

"Of course not. You know my motto." Radiance sat back in her chair. "Every client gets a unique design or color. I don't mass-produce my art. Okay, Irene, they should be dry. But be careful."

"I will." Irene examined her nails with a look of pleasure as she rose to her feet. "I think I'll have a latte at Bea's and then pick up my new book. I might drop into Charms & Virtues, too. My nephew has a birthday coming up next week. He and his friends love the sort of things Winters carries in his shop."

It seemed to take forever until Irene, who moved in slow motion for fear of marring her freshly done nails, finally exited. But eventually she pushed through the beaded curtain and disappeared.

"What was it you wanted, Charity?" Radiance asked as she straightened her work surface with brisk professionalism.

Charity reached into the pocket of her skirt and pulled out the twist of paper in which she had stored the clue she had found. "This is going to sound a little wild, but I want to know if you can identify the color of the polish on this chipped nail."

Radiance gave her a quizzical look. "The color?"

"I really like it." That sounded lame. Charity decided she'd better jazz it up. "I came across it when

I was cleaning up the shop the other day, and it occurred to me that if I ever do decide to get my nails done, this is a color I could go for. I assume that it's one of your special blends."

"Let me see it." Radiance set a bottle of polish neatly into a long rack. Then she turned in her chair and held out her hand.

Charity dumped the chip into Radiance's palm. The sliver of blood red acrylic glinted in the light of the work table lamp.

"Hmm." Radiance examined it intently. "I wonder why she didn't come in to see me the instant she chipped it. She's usually so particular about her nails."

Charity held her breath. "Who is so particular?"

Radiance glanced up. "Jennifer Pitt, of course. This chip is painted with Crimson Jennifer. It's Mrs. Pitt's special color."

"I see." Charity retrieved the chip. Her mind began to spin with the implications. She had to talk to Elias immediately. "Thanks, Radiance. She probably didn't come in because of all the stress she's under at the moment."

"It must be terrible for her." Radiance sighed. "Just think of what that poor woman's been through lately. She hasn't been happy in her marriage for months, and now she finds out Leighton's killed two people."

"We don't know for certain that Leighton killed anyone."

"Hank Tybern would never have arrested him if he hadn't been sure. You know Hank. He's real cautious."

"That's true."

"It's obvious when you think about it. Leighton lost everything because of his ex-wife and Rick Swinton. He had the perfect motive. It's probably all been just too much for Jennifer. No wonder she's decided to leave town."

Charity froze halfway to the beaded curtain. "Jennifer's leaving Whispering Waters Cove?"

"That's what Irene just told me. She said she saw her packing her car this morning when she drove past the Pitt house. Who can blame Jennifer for wanting to get away from this place? The town never really accepted her, you know. Most people blamed her for the breakup of Leighton's first marriage. But if you ask me, Leighton was just as guilty as Jennifer. He didn't have to start fooling around with her, did he?"

"No," Charity said. "He did not."

It occurred to her as she pushed her way back through the beaded curtain that she would never have to worry about Elias sneaking around with another woman. There was a solid, unshakable core in him that she might sometimes find maddening but that she could count on until the end.

It was a good feeling. Another part of the sturdy foundation on which she intended to build her future with Elias. A man who could be faithful could learn to love.

But first she had to make certain he did not get hauled off to jail for the murder of Rick Swinton. Resolutely, she turned and strode off down the pier toward Charms & Virtues.

Elias stood in the darkest corner of Charms & Virtues and contemplated a counter heaped high with plastic hamburgers, fake ice cubes with bugs imbedded inside, and magic relighting candles. There was something different about this section of the shop. He couldn't put his finger on it, but he knew that the mountain of wares he was studying had altered in some indefinable manner.

He decided he needed the flashlight that he kept under the cash register counter. Maybe Charity was right after all about the poor illumination in the shop, especially this section here at the rear. Ambience was one thing, but when it got to the point where a customer had to strain to read the labels on the packages, the atmosphere thing was a little too thick. He'd have to see about getting some lamps for this counter.

In the meantime, he wondered why it seemed different back here. He leaned closer and prodded a stack of small boxes containing miniature wind-up insects.

"Elias? Elias, where are you?"

He turned at the sound of Charity's excited voice. For a moment he did not respond. He just stood there in the shadows and savored the sight of her hurrying toward him between two long aisles. Memories of the night flooded through him. Just the thought of her hot, wet mouth on him was enough to give him an erection.

The good news was that he would no longer have to waste a lot of time every day working on ways to ensure that she spent every night with him, he thought.

"Good morning, Otis." Charity came to a halt at the counter. "Where's Elias?"

"Heh, heh, heh."

"Helpful, as always, I see." She glanced around. "Elias?"

"Back here, Charity. In the imitation food and insect section."

She turned quickly and peered into the hazy rear portion of the shop. "Oh, there you are. You'll never guess what I just found out down at Radiance's place."

"Did she identify that nail chip for you?" He strolled toward the counter.

"She did." Her face glowed with triumph. "It's Crimson Jennifer."

"Translate, please."

"It's the color of red nail polish that Radiance blended especially for Jennifer Pitt. Do you see what this means?"

"Jennifer Pitt was fooling around out there at the old Rossiter place?" Elias reached the cash register counter and crouched down behind it to find the flashlight he had stored there. "We already knew that. She used to meet Leighton there, remember? She could have chipped that nail during one of those little trysts."

"Know what I think? I think she met Rick Swinton there, too. It makes sense that she might have chipped a nail while playing Swinton's rough games."

"So? Judging from what we've learned about Swinton, any number of the fine, upstanding ladies of Whispering Waters Cove may have played cops and robbers with Swinton and his handcuffs out there. And we already know that the second Pitt marriage was on the rocks. Leighton told us he thought she was seeing someone, remember?"

"Elias, you're missing the point here. That nail chip may tie Jennifer to Rick Swinton."

"It indicates they may have been lovers, but that's about it." Elias found the flashlight, retrieved it, and got to his feet. "Phyllis Dartmoor can also be tied to Rick Swinton that way. So can some of the female Voyagers. And God knows how many other women may have slept with him. But Leighton Pitt is the only person who had a motive to kill both Swinton and Gwen Pitt."

"The bankruptcy, you mean."

"It usually comes down to money in the end." Elias pressed the switch on the flashlight. Nothing happened. "Needs batteries. I think I've got a bunch stashed around here someplace. Saw them the other day."

Charity crossed her arms under her breasts. Her brows came together in challenge. "What would you say if I were to inform you that Jennifer Pitt was seen packing her car this very morning. She appears to be on her way out of town."

Elias unscrewed the flashlight base. "Maybe she's decided that what with the pending bankruptcy and Leighton's arrest there's nothing left for her here."

Charity smiled cheerfully as she slipped the receipt into a paper sack together with a new novel by Stella Cameron. "You're going to enjoy that one, Mrs. Fisher. I just finished reading it myself."

"She writes such exciting stories, doesn't she?" Mrs. Fisher said with enthusiasm. "Real page-turners."

"That they are," Charity agreed.

Mrs. Fisher hurried off with her package.

"Almost time to close," Newlin said as he walked out of the back room with an armload of books.

Charity raised her brows. "You seem anxious to get out of here today. Got something planned?"

"Arlene wants to go out to Delter's Nursery to see about ordering some nice flowers for the wedding."

"Great. How did things go during your first session with Elias this morning?"

Newlin's face lit up. "Really interesting, y'know? He told me the name of that special belt he wears. He says he and I are probably the only two people left in the whole world who know exactly what Tal Kek Chara means. Weird, huh?"

"I thought it meant the Way of Water or something."

"Not quite. It's a lot more complicated."

"Well? What exactly does it mean?

Newlin opened his mouth and then closed it. "Uh, no offense, but I'm not sure I'm supposed to tell you. Maybe you better ask Elias, yourself."

"Ah, it's one of those secret guy things."

"It's not that. At least I don't think—" Newlin broke off in relief when Yappy skidded to a halt in the doorway. "Hey, Yap. What's up?"

"Trouble," Yappy said loudly.

Charity glanced at him. "What's wrong?"

"It's Winters." Yappy drew a deep breath and prepared to rush off down the pier. "Looks like he's got another problem on his hands. Some dude in a suit just drove up in a Jaguar, got out, and demanded to know where Elias Winters's shop was. Bea pointed it out, and the guy went charging over to Charms & Virtues. Bea said it looked like he was gonna clobber Elias."

"Not again." Charity locked the register with a twist of her key and scurried around the edge of the counter. "How on earth did Elias collect so many enemies? This sort of thing has simply got to stop."

18

<hr />

To understand the waterfall, one must view the world from behind it.

—"On the Way of Water," from the journal of Hayden Stone

Elias studied the tall, grim-faced man who had planted himself on the opposite side of the sales counter. Davis Truitt's expensive, summer-weight silk-and-linen sport coat looked as if it had been made for him, which was probably the case. The same was true of the pale gray shirt and the slacks he wore with it. He had the height and the patrician features that characterized his sister, Meredith. He looked ready to do serious damage.

"If you're thinking about taking a swing at me, you might want to reconsider," Elias said mildly. "Charity tends to get upset when people assault me, and we both know she's supposed to avoid stressful situations."

"Damn it, Winters, don't give me lectures on my stepsister's health." Davis narrowed his eyes. "I know a lot more about the subject than you do. What the hell are you up to?"

"I was just about to straighten out that counter back there." Elias gestured briefly toward the table piled high with plastic burgers, fake ice cubes, and other assorted items. "Something about it doesn't look quite right."

"This whole damn situation doesn't look right. I know about you, Winters. I've done some research. It wasn't easy digging up the information. I couldn't get all the details I wanted."

Elias nodded. "I'm glad to hear that."

"But I got enough to be certain that whatever you've got in the works here in Whispering Waters Cove, it probably involves a lot of cash and an offshore client."

"I hate to tell you this, Truitt, but your information is out of date. Take my advice and don't rely too heavily on it."

Davis jerked at his dark gray silk tie, loosening it. "Don't try to bullshit me. According to Meredith, you've seduced Charity. I want to know what you're doing here on this pier, and I want to know why you've dragged my stepsister into it."

Otis stalked back and forth on his perch and hissed softly.

Elias absently stretched out a hand to scratch the bird's head. "It's not complicated, Truitt. I inherited the pier and this shop. I retired from the active pursuit of my former career and came here to learn the fine art of running a small business."

"You don't do anything small, from what I can tell. Not unless it's part of a much bigger scheme." Davis scowled. "Look, we're both businessmen. I don't give a damn what you've got going on here in the cove. But I don't want you using Charity to accomplish your goals. Is that clear?"

"My relationship with Charity has nothing to do with business."

"You think I believe that?" Davis took a menacing step closer to the counter. "You've got a reputation, Winters. And nothing in that reputation makes me think that you'd chuck everything you've built up as the owner of Far Seas to come up here to run a junky little curio shop."

Otis grumbled loudly.

"Better not call it a junky little shop," Elias advised. "Otis tends to take that kind of remark personally."

"Who the hell is Otis?"

"This is Otis." Elias stroked the bird. "And he's temperamental. Just ask Charity. She's the one who nursed him through a fit of depression. He's over it now, but he's still inclined to be surly when he's irritated."

"Forget the damn bird." Davis shoved aside the wings of his coat, spread his legs aggressively, and planted his fists on his hips. "I want answers. And I want them now."

"Davis." Charity raced through the door of the shop. Newlin, Yappy, and Ted followed close on her heels.

Elias surveyed the rescue team with satisfaction. "What took you so long?"

Charity ignored him. "Davis, what on earth are you doing here? Don't you dare hit Elias. Do you hear me? I swear I'll never forgive you if you so much as touch him."

Elias smiled faintly. "See what I mean? She's very protective."

Davis scowled furiously and turned to confront Charity. "I'm not going to hit him. At least, not yet. I'm here to find out what he's up to."

"He's not up to anything." Charity halted, breathless, in front of Davis. "At least not in the way you imply. If you wanted answers, you should have called me before you barged in here and confronted poor Elias."

"Poor Elias?" Davis shot Elias a derisive glance. "That's not the way I heard it."

Elias tried to look harmless.

Newlin scowled at Elias through his small glasses. "You need any help here?"

"No." Elias nodded at Newlin, Yappy, and Ted. "Everything's under control this time. I don't think Charity will let her brother break my nose. But thanks, anyway. You might as well close up your shops and take off."

"Okay." Newlin hesitated. "If you're sure."

"I'm sure."

Ted gave him a level man-to-man look. "Holler if you change your mind."

"I will," Elias said.

Yappy shrugged and turned to lead the other two out of the shop. He lifted a hand in farewell. "See ya."

Davis ignored the three departing men. He glared at Charity. "Meredith talked to me after she had lunch with you. She says you're involved with Winters."

Charity raised her chin in the imperious style that Elias had learned to recognize. "Yes, I am. What about it?"

Davis shoved his fingers through his hair. "Hell, Charity, I told you when you called me about him that the guy was definitely a player. I warned you to be careful. He's got something going out here. Lord only knows what it is, but one thing's for certain."

"And just what is that one thing?" Charity demanded.

"When it's over, Winters and his client, whoever that is, will be the only ones who come out on top. I don't want you to be used."

"I can take care of myself," Charity said.

"A year ago, I would have agreed with you." Davis stopped abruptly and shot an annoyed look at Elias. Then he lowered his voice. "But after what happened, Meredith and I are concerned. You know you're not supposed to put yourself into highly stressful situations."

The outrage faded from Charity's eyes. A tremulous smile tugged at her mouth. "Davis, you came all the way out here to protect me, didn't you?"

Davis flushed. "You're family."

"This is so sweet," Charity said softly.

Elias groaned. "Don't you hate it when she does that?"

Davis frowned. "Does what?"

"When she calls you sweet." Elias smiled cheerfully. "Irritates the hell out of me. But, then, I guess it's different when you're her brother."

Davis began to look confused. He turned back to Charity. "What's he talking about?"

"It's complicated," Charity said. "Don't worry about it. The important thing is, I am really touched by your concern, Davis. I can't tell you how much it means to me."

"It's a little more than just concern," Davis muttered. "Meredith and I are damn worried."

"I'm okay." Charity patted his arm reassuringly. "I've been handling stress very well lately. Look, I have an idea."

"Brace yourself, Truitt," Elias murmured.

Davis pointedly kept his back to Elias. He fixed his attention on Charity. "What sort of idea?"

"I think the two of you need to get to know each other better," she said briskly. "What's missing here is basic communication."

"We're communicating better than you think, Charity," Elias said. "Your stepbrother wants to smash my face, and I would rather he didn't. Real simple and straightforward stuff."

She glanced at her watch. "It's after five-thirty. Elias, why don't you lock up Charms & Virtues and take Davis to the coffee shop in town. Neutral territory, so to speak. The two of you can sit down together and have a cup of tea."

Elias exchanged glances with Davis, who looked distinctly wary now. Elias didn't blame him. He wasn't feeling terribly enthused about the idea, either.

"Tea?" he repeated cautiously.

Charity gave him an approving smile. "You need to sit down together and communicate. I'm sure everything can be cleared up between the two of you. Run along. I'll look after Otis."

Otis muttered under his breath at the mention of his name.

Davis began to look genuinely alarmed. "Charity, I didn't come here to have tea with Winters. I'm here to make sure he doesn't drag you into one of his Machiavellian schemes."

Charity widened her eyes. "It would mean a lot to me if you and Elias made an effort to get to know each other, Davis."

Elias almost felt sorry for Davis. He decided it was time to take charge of the situation. He came out from behind the counter and slapped the other man on the shoulder. "Give it up, Truitt. You can't win this one. Come on, let's go communicate."

Davis's expression turned mutinous. "I'm not in the mood for a cup of tea, damn it."

"Neither am I," Elias said. "I've got a better idea. Let's walk down to the Cove Tavern. I'll buy you a beer."

Davis hesitated, bemused. "I don't—"

Elias paused in front of Charity and leaned down to brush his mouth lightly, proprietarily across hers. Then he took the steel key ring out of his pocket and handed it to her. "Here. You can lock up."

"Fine." Charity beamed. "Thanks, Elias. I really appreciate the effort you're making."

"Don't," he warned, "call me sweet."

She blinked. "Don't you think you're a little overly sensitive on that point?"

"That's me. A real sensitive kind of guy." Elias gave Davis a small push toward the front door. With a last, frowning look at Charity, Davis reluctantly started down the nearest aisle.

"I'll see you at home," Charity called after them.

Elias glanced back over his shoulder. "Don't forget Otis when you close up."

She wrinkled her nose. "As if I could."

"Heh, heh, heh," Otis said.

There was no point rushing home, Charity told herself. Elias and Davis were going to be gone a while. She leaned on the pier rail to watch the two walk along the beach toward town. They were soon lost in the gathering fog.

Elias and Davis would have a lot to talk about, she assured herself. With any luck, a couple of beers would facilitate their communication. She hoped she had been right to push them together like this.

Slowly she straightened from the rail and started back toward the door of Charms & Virtues to fetch

Otis. She knew he would likely become anxious if he found himself alone in the shop at the close of day. His old fears of being abandoned might return. Otis was not a lovable bird on his good days. When he got stressed, he was downright insufferable.

Charity's footsteps echoed on the pier timbers. It was nearly six. The Crazy Otis Landing shops had emptied for the day. The last of the customers and browsers had departed. The carousel was silent and still. The parking lot was empty except for Davis's Jaguar, Elias's Jeep, and her own small Toyota.

She paused to listen to the water lapping at the pier pilings. The incoming tide created a murmuring sound. At times like this when she was alone on the landing it seemed to her that she could actually hear the waves whispering, just as the old legend claimed.

It was so important that Elias and Davis become friends.

Charity became aware of the tension in her shoulders. Deliberately she stretched to release it. She took several deep abdominal breaths and felt the stress level sink. She continued on her way to Charms & Virtues.

"Don't worry, Otis, I'm still here," she called out as she pushed open the front door of the shop. "You haven't been abandoned."

Otis grumbled from his perch.

"You're going to come back to my shop with me for a while. You can sit on the coatrack just like you used to do before Elias arrived."

"Heh, heh, heh."

Charity went behind the counter and found the old towel she had used in the past to protect her skin from Otis's claws. She wrapped the towel around her arm and then held out her wrist. "Hop aboard. I'll bring your food dish."

Otis muttered but stepped smartly onto her arm. Charity braced herself. The bird was heavy. "Nothing personal, Otis, but I think you may be putting on weight."

He glared at her.

She picked up his feeding dish and walked back toward the front door of the shop. "We'll pick up your travel cage when we leave."

"Level with me, Winters. What are you doing out here in the sticks? This isn't your style." Davis took a swallow of beer and settled back in the booth. "I don't give a damn if you sell the entire town of Whispering Waters Cove to one of your mysterious off-shore clients, but I don't want Charity hurt."

"Off-shore clients aren't what they used to be." Elias mused. "There was a time when you could do almost any kind of deal with them so long as it involved the magic words *waterfront property,* but those days are gone."

He wrapped one hand around his beer glass and idly surveyed the moderate crowd that had gathered in the Cove Tavern. It was six-thirty, and the handful of local business people and shop clerks who had drifted in after work had already gone home to dinner. Local folks with families dined early in Whispering Waters Cove.

The early evening crowd, which consisted of a couple of truckers, a handful of tourists, and the town's few singles, most of whom were single for a good reason, had begun to settle in for the evening.

"I want an answer, Winters. I'm not leaving until I get it. Charity's been through a lot."

"I know."

"Has she told you all of it? How she took over

Truitt Department Stores and single-handedly pulled it out of the quicksand in which my father had managed to sink it?"

Elias wrapped his hand around the wet beer glass. "I'm aware of the fact that she was the guiding force behind its comeback. Everyone in the Northwest business community knows the story."

"Yeah, well, you may not be aware of the fact that she had to work night and day to hold the company together. Meredith and I were still in college. We were too young and inexperienced to be of much help back in those days."

"I know."

"It was Charity who took over the full responsibility of day-to-day operations. She revolutionized the way Truitt did business from top to bottom. She had incredible instincts for marketing and for managing."

Elias smiled. "Did she issue every clerk a feather duster? She's very big on dusting the goods."

"This isn't a joke, damn it. This is my sister we're talking about."

"Yes."

"She was obsessed with saving Truitt because she felt she had a responsibility to the family. The stores belonged to Meredith and me, she said. It was our heritage. She saved it for us."

"That sounds like Charity."

Davis frowned. "Hell, I don't think she even liked the department store business. She once told me that being responsible for so many people and their jobs kept her awake at nights. If it hadn't been for her sense of duty, I think she would have sold Truitt after Dad died."

"Yes."

"Meredith and I, on the other hand, took to the business right away," Davis mused. "We went to work for Truitt full-time right out of college. But Charity was still running things, naturally. The company needed her. Things were booming. And then Brett Loftus approached her with his idea for a merger."

"I know the rest of the story."

"Meredith and I thought the two of them were perfect for each other. Hell, everyone thought they were an ideal couple."

"Loftus was too big for her."

Davis scowled. "What?"

"Never mind."

"Things seemed to be going along just fine until the night of the engagement party. That was a year ago." Davis slanted him a quick, searching glance. "I suppose you heard about that?"

"Yes."

Davis winced. "You had to know Charity well to understand what a bizarre scene that was. So unlike her. Completely out of character. She just sort of came unglued. Right there in front of everyone. The rest of us couldn't believe it."

"She said she went bonkers."

"She had an anxiety attack of some kind." Davis sighed. "I hate to say it, but that evening was the first time that Meredith and I fully understood what the pressure of running Truitt had done to Charity."

"You can stop worrying about her, Truitt. She's okay now. She's happy running her bookstore. She says being a small-businessperson is a calling."

"Well, it's definitely not your calling." Davis narrowed his eyes. "So why are you pretending to operate that stupid little curio shop?"

"What you don't seem to grasp here, Truitt, is that I'm not pretending." Elias exhaled slowly. "There's something else you should know."

"What's that?"

"I'm going to marry Charity. If she'll have me."

Shortly after seven-thirty, Charity abandoned any pretense of trying to concentrate on the order forms that she had intended to complete. With a groan, she threw down her pen and sagged against the back of her chair. She used her feet to push the seat around in a half circle so that she faced Otis.

"I keep thinking about that chipped acrylic nail, Otis. Crimson Jennifer."

Otis, who had been dozing atop the coatrack, opened one eye and gave her a baleful look.

"I'll bet you any amount of sunflower seeds that Jennifer was having an affair with Rick Swinton."

Apparently realizing that he was not going to be allowed to nap, Otis opened his other eye and stretched his wings.

"Everyone keeps saying that Leighton Pitt had the perfect motive to murder both Gwen and Swinton. He lost everything because of them. He even lost his trophy wife. But when you think about it, Jennifer lost everything, too."

"Heh, heh, heh." Otis made his way from the branch of the coatrack on which he had been perching to the one where Charity had hung his feeding dish.

"Everyone seems to agree that Jennifer married Leighton for his money. Even Leighton has come to that conclusion. And then Leighton's ex-wife hits town with a plan to ruin him. Said plan, carried out with the able assistance of Rick Swinton, works. Result? Leighton Pitt is ruined. When Jennifer files for divorce, she'll get nothing."

Otis thoughtfully cracked a seed with his powerful beak.

Charity leaned forward and folded her arms on her

knees. "If you want to compare motives, Jennifer's are just as good as Leighton's. When he lost everything, so did she. I'll bet no one has checked her alibis for either murder."

Otis finished munching and hiked back to his original coatrack perch. He half-closed his eyes.

"You know, Otis, I'm getting a weird feeling." Charity rose and began to pace the room. "Look at the facts. Everyone who deprived Jennifer of whatever she hoped to get out of Leighton Pitt is either dead or in jail. It makes you wonder, doesn't it?"

Otis did not respond.

"Don't go to sleep on me. We need to work this out. If Leighton Pitt manages to prove his innocence, we're going to have a problem on our hands. I just know that Tybern will start casting suspicious glances at Elias again."

Otis, apparently unconcerned by that possibility, started to close his eyes.

"The more I think about this, the less I like it." Charity came to a halt in front of the coatrack. "That does it, I need to talk to Hank Tybern. I want him at least to look into Jennifer's alibis for the times of the murders. It's a perfectly reasonable request from a concerned citizen."

Charity picked up the worn towel and wrapped it around her forearm. "Come on, Otis, there's no telling how long Elias and Davis are going to talk. Let's you and me go find Hank."

Otis muttered under his breath, but he stepped onto her towel-wrapped arm.

Charity grimaced. "You're really going to have to start watching the seed intake, Otis. Middle-age spread in a parrot is not an attractive sight."

With the bird on her arm, Charity turned off the lights and locked the doors. The fog had thickened considerably since she had brought Otis back to Whispers. The last light of dusk had been drowned by the heavy mist that had moved in to blanket the cove during the past couple of hours.

The pier was isolated in an unnatural gloom. It was impossible to see beyond the nearest rail, but down below, the waters whispered darkly. To Charity it seemed as if she and Otis moved through a nightmarish landscape.

"Hang tight, Otis." It was not really cold, but there was a chill in the damp air. She held her jacket over Otis to protect him as she hurried toward the door of Charms & Virtues. "We'll get you inside your cage and put a nice warm blanket around you. And then we'll pop you into the car and turn on the heater. You'll be fine."

Otis muttered. He sounded disgusted. Charity had the distinct impression that he was telling her he was no wimp and that a little fog didn't bother him.

"Typical male." Charity came to a halt in front of the door of Elias's shop and fished out the key ring he had given her. "Always trying to prove how macho you are."

She got the door open and stepped inside. The interior of Charms & Virtues, never bright even at high noon and with all the lights turned on, was shrouded in deep shadow tonight.

Charity groped for the old light switch near the door. "If I've told Elias once, I've told him a dozen times to install better lighting."

"Heh, heh, heh."

"You always take his side." She found the switch and flipped it. The few lamps above the long rows of display tables glowed weakly. They cast sullen yellow pools of light that did not reach beyond the edge of the cluttered counters.

The effect was certainly atmospheric. Too much so for her taste. Charity shuddered as she carried Otis toward the far end of the shop. She could hardly make out the cash register counter.

She caught a whiff of an acrid odor. "Otis, do you smell gasoline?"

The strange chill of uneasiness that had gone through her a few minutes earlier when she had stepped out into the fog returned in a jolt just as she reached the counter. Another shiver went through her. Otis must have felt it. He stiffened on her arm.

"Oh, damn." Charity recognized the feeling with a sense of deep dismay. "Please don't let this be the start of an anxiety attack. *Please.* I've been doing so well lately."

"I'm glad someone has." Jennifer Pitt walked out of the darkened office. Light glinted evilly on the barrel of the gun in her hand. "Because I sure as hell haven't been doing well at all."

Charity froze. So did Otis. They both had to look up to see Jennifer's eyes.

Tall, with a figure that had been honed to perfection on her home gym, Jennifer looked as out of place as she always did here in Whispering Waters Cove. Her voluminous streaked hair was a mass of California-style blown-dry curls around her perfectly made-up face. She wore a snug red suede vest over a white silk shirt and silver-studded jeans. A pair of sunglasses perched on top of her head.

The only thing that was different about her today was the raw fury in her eyes.

"It's all so goddamned unfair," Jennifer whispered. "I worked so hard to make things come out right. I was going to leave this town with half a million dollars in my pocket. Half a million dollars. And they ruined everything. All my plans. Everything."

Charity had to swallow several times before she could speak. "Jennifer, it's okay. Take it easy."

"That bitch Gwen wanted revenge, you see?" Jennifer's eyes had a feverish glint. "Leighton kept telling me about the big deal he was going to pull off. I decided to stick around until he had the money. There would be so much of it, he said. The biggest deal of his life. I planned to leave him as soon as I knew I could count on the cash."

"Put the gun down. It's over now, Jennifer."

"But Rick told me the truth toward the end. He warned me that Gwen had other plans. She had set a trap, lured Leighton into it, so that she could have her revenge."

"You confronted her the night the spaceships were supposed to arrive, didn't you?" Charity asked softly. "You found her in her motor home and shot her."

"I didn't intend to kill her. But she laughed at me. Called me a fool. Told me that I would never get a single dime out of Leighton. Then she slapped me. The gun went off."

"An accident," Charity said quickly. "Not murder."

"I just wanted to scare her. Make her give me some of the money she had taken from Leighton. It was my money, you know. I sacrificed a year of my life to get it. You don't know what it was like having to put up with his grubby hands on me. I hated it. I hated every minute of it, but I had to pretend to like it."

"Was Rick Swinton any better?"

"Rick? That sleazy scumbag?" Jennifer bared her teeth in a feral smile. "I only went to bed with him because I had to find out what Gwen was doing here in Whispering Waters Cove. I knew when she arrived in town last month that she was up to something. Rick finally told me about the scam."

"But by then it was too late to stop her."

"Too late." Jennifer raised the barrel of the gun. "It's always too late in this damned town. All I wanted was to escape, but I was trapped."

"I understand," Charity said gently. "I understand, Jennifer." The arm on which she supported Otis was trembling. She could not tell whether it was she or the parrot who was shivering so violently. Maybe both of them were having anxiety attacks. It seemed reasonable, given the circumstances.

"After she was dead, that prick, Swinton, tried to blackmail me."

"Blackmail? With what?" Something clicked in Charity's memory. "Oh, God. The missing tape."

"Yes, the damned tape. That bitch, Gwen, had it running that night when I confronted her. I didn't know it at the time. Everything is recorded on that tape. Anyone who listens to it will know that I shot her."

"And Rick found it when he found her body?"

"He knew where to look. He grabbed it during the initial confusion. He knew she always taped everything that happened in that damn motor home." Jennifer's eyes narrowed. "At first he tried to make me think the demand for a payoff had come from Winters."

Charity stared. "From Elias?"

"He said Winters must have found the tape when he checked to see if Gwen was still alive. After all, he was right there beside the body for several minutes. He had plenty of time to notice the tape player and slip the tape into his pocket."

"The only thing Elias noticed was that the tape player was empty. He mentioned it later."

"As soon as I got the blackmail threat, I realized that it had come from Rick. I knew Winters was not involved."

Charity cleared her throat. "I'm sure Elias would be flattered by your faith in his integrity."

"Not *his* integrity, you stupid woman. Yours."

"Mine?" Charity's voice rose. "What does my integrity have to do with this?"

"You're having an affair with him. Everyone knows it. I realized that if you were willing to sleep with him, he couldn't be the type to steal evidence and then blackmail someone with it."

Charity's mouth opened and closed twice before she managed to say, "I see."

"On the other hand," Jennifer continued, "blackmail was right up Rick Swinton's alley. Just his style. He was a fool to think I wouldn't know that he was the one behind the demand."

"So you killed him."

"I left the blackmail payment on the back porch of the old Rossiter cabin, just as I was instructed. I drove off, but I hid the car and doubled back to wait for Rick to show up. Which he did."

"You confronted him?"

Jennifer gave her a twisted smile. "He kept screaming at me that I'd be sorry, that he had taken measures to avenge himself if anything happened to him, but I didn't believe him."

"You shot him and pushed his body over the bluff into the water."

"I knew it would wash up in the cove, of course. That made it easy to frame Leighton for both deaths. But this morning I found out that Rick had meant it when he said that he had taken precautions. I got a sealed letter expressed from his lawyer in Seattle. In it Rick told me just what he had done. That bastard."

Another shock of fear swept through Charity. "What do you mean? What kind of measures could Rick have taken?"

A frantic expression passed over Jennifer's face. "He hid that damn tape somewhere here in Charms & Virtues. Said it was the perfect hiding place. He knew that if it was found, Winters would appear guilty of blackmail."

"This has gone too far," Charity whispered. "Jennifer, listen to me."

"I came here tonight to search for the tape." Jennifer glanced desperately around at the gloomy, cluttered interior of Charms & Virtues. "But I see now that it will be impossible to find it in this mess."

"That's right. Impossible. Run, Jennifer. Run while you still can. Don't wait."

"No. Everything's under control." Jennifer locked both hands around the gun. "I came prepared. I have a can of gasoline with me. I'm going to burn this damned shop to the ground and the whole pier with it. No one will ever find that tape."

The terrible panic threatened to swamp Charity. Otis's claws were clenched so tightly around her arm that they threatened to puncture straight through the towel. She summoned her most authoritative CEO voice.

"Jennifer, pay attention. If you leave now, you can escape. If you take time to set a fire, you'll never make it out of town."

"Shut up. You have to die, you know. I really can't leave any witnesses, now can I?" Jennifer's hand tightened around the gun. Her eyes narrowed.

Charity prepared to hurl herself to the side. She knew it was highly unlikely that she could dodge the shot, but it was the only option left for her.

And then Otis screamed.

It was a loud, terrible, piercing cry designed to be heard for vast distances in the jungles where his ancestors had lived.

For the first time since Charity had known him, he uttered a clear, recognizable sentence.

"It's payback time," Otis screeched in a voice that was chillingly reminiscent of Hayden Stone's.

He launched himself from Charity's arm. Wings flapping wildly, fierce beak opened wide, he hurtled straight at Jennifer's horrified face.

19

~~~

A clear reflection on the surface of the water holds a deep truth.

—"On the Way of Water," from the journal of Hayden Stone

Charity watched Jennifer do what any reasonable person would have done in the face of a ferocious attack by an animal possessed of a large beak and big claws. She yelled in panic, dropped the gun, and covered her eyes to protect her face. Twisting wildly, she reeled aside in an effort to avoid the bird.

Otis's clipped wings prevented him from altering course to follow her. He went into a long glide that carried him straight past Jennifer. With grand majesty, he sailed on through the office doorway.

Charity heard an ominous crash from inside the small room, but there was no time to check on Otis. She leaped for the fallen gun, which had hit the floor behind the counter.

"No. No, damn you." Jennifer uncovered her face. She saw the gun and rushed madly forward to recover it.

Charity realized that Jennifer was the one who was closest to the weapon. There was no time to make a dash for the door. She had to get to the gun before Jennifer did.

Instead of circling the end of the counter, Charity planted both hands on top of it and propelled herself over in a mad dive.

She crashed into Jennifer. They fell to the floor and rolled. Jennifer landed on top and immediately attempted to get her long-nailed fingers around Charity's throat.

She succeeded.

Charity gasped for air and struggled desperately to pry Jennifer's fingers away from her throat. She was hopelessly outclassed. Jennifer had the advantage of height, weight, and a longer reach.

For an instant, everything went gray as panic welled up inside Charity. She could feel Jennifer's fingers tightening and knew a terrible sense of impending doom.

And then, as if he were standing beside her, giving instructions in a calm, dark voice that pierced the blinding fear, Charity recalled the simple self-defense moves Elias had begun to teach her.

Do not seek to block the onrushing tide. Instead, create another path for the water.

Charity stopped trying to pit her strength against Jennifer's. Going against her own instincts, she released her opponent's wrists. She shoved her hands straight up between her attacker's arms, aiming for Jennifer's eyes.

Jennifer cried out and leaned back to avoid Charity's stabbing fingers.

Charity gulped air as Jennifer's fingers loosened. Out of the corner of her eye she saw the flashlight that Elias had left on the shelf below the counter. She reached out, grabbed it, and slashed wildly at Jennifer's head.

Jennifer yelled and tried to duck the blow. The flashlight caught her on the cheek and sent her spinning away.

Charity swung the flashlight again and connected with Jennifer's skull. Jennifer lurched to the side. Charity rolled free and started to scramble to her feet. She was on her knees when she heard footsteps pounding toward her.

"What the hell is going on back there?" Davis yelled.

"Let me go, damn you." Jennifer's cry was a keening wail. "Let me go."

Charity blinked, trying to make sense of what was happening.

"Are you all right?" Elias asked. Holding Jennifer with one hand, he looked down at Charity. His face was cold and savage.

"Yes. Yes, I think so." Charity rose cautiously. She was shaking so badly that she had to steady herself with one hand on the counter.

Elias released Jennifer and reached for Charity.

Jennifer collapsed, limp and defeated. She clutched her head and burst into great shuddering sobs.

Charity stared at Elias. "I heard footsteps. Thought it was Davis."

"I'm right here." Davis rounded the end of the counter. "Elias moves a little faster than I do." He touched Charity's face. "Jesus. I don't believe this. Are you okay?"

She nodded and gave him a weak smile. "Thanks

to Otis and Elias. Oh, my God, that reminds me. Better check on Otis."

There was a disgruntled squawk from the vicinity of the office doorway. Everyone except Jennifer turned to look.

Otis swaggered out of the shadows. His feathers were ruffled, but he was obviously unhurt. He came to a halt and waited imperiously for someone to offer him a lift up to his perch.

Charity gazed at him with admiration. "It was the most incredible thing. Otis hurled himself straight at Jennifer. She was going to shoot me. He distracted her. Made her drop the gun. He gave me the chance I needed. Gentlemen, that bird saved my life."

Elias woke shortly before dawn. He lay quietly for a moment, intensely aware of the empty place beside him on the futon. Charity had gone home to her own cottage with Davis after Tybern had finished asking his endless questions. Elias had been obliged to go home alone with only Otis for companionship.

At one time he would have been able to convince himself that Otis was all the company he needed. But this morning, as he watched the sky lighten to pale gray, he realized that was no longer true.

A dam had broken somewhere inside him. The river of loneliness flowed freely. The surging current bore memories that he did not want to examine. He'd had the experience before. He knew how to stem the raging tide.

But this time he did not go through the disciplined mental exercises designed to send the images downstream. Instead, he made himself look more closely at the reflections on the water.

He saw his mother's white, lifeless face just before the ambulance attendants covered her. His grieving grandparents floated past next. The figures were so consumed by their own sense of loss that they had little energy to spare for their grandson. He saw himself waiting for the letter that never came, the one that would tell him that his father wanted him to join him on the island of Nihili.

He watched himself coax the money for the long flight to Nihili from his disinterested, angry grandfather. Saw himself as he got off the small plane on the island and eagerly search the tiny crowd for the face of his father. Then he saw the quiet man with the ancient eyes who walked toward him. Hayden Stone had been the one who had told him that his father was dead.

Elias let the memories drift past. He watched until they were lost once more in the endless darkness. Then he rose from the futon and pulled on a pair of jeans and a shirt.

He reached into the carved chest and picked up Hayden's journal.

Otis mumbled behind the cage cover as Elias padded barefoot across the small front room.

"Go back to sleep," Elias said softly. "You had a hard night."

Otis fell silent.

Elias went out onto the porch, picked up a mat, and walked down the steps into the garden. The sky had grown markedly brighter, he noticed. No fog this morning.

He settled down beside the reflecting pool and opened the journal to the last few pages.

This morning I caught a glimpse of the final lesson that I must somehow convey to Elias. I do not know if I will have time to teach it. I felt the pain in my chest again during the night. Soon the river of my life will rejoin the sea.

But Elias is young and strong, and unlike me, his soul has not yet been chilled by the icy cold of the deepest waters. He still has the capacity to hunger for life.

When he has seen the folly of his desire for vengeance, he will be free. And when he is free, I hope he will be fortunate enough to find a woman who can help him learn this last and most important lesson. I want him to discover that his true self needs more than what the discipline of Tal Kek Chara can give him. I have taught him to be strong, but if he is ever to know real happiness, he must go beyond the Way of Water. He must learn to open himself to love.

Elias closed the journal and looked down into the reflecting pond. The surface of the little pool was an opaque gray, mirroring the dawn sky. He contemplated the featureless water for a long time.

The muffled whispers of the incoming tide down in the cove and the calls of the seabirds masked the sound of her footsteps, but Elias knew the precise moment when Charity arrived at the garden gate.

He could feel the warmth of her presence, just as he had that first day when she had walked into Charms & Virtues with her clipboard and an invitation to form a united front with the shopkeepers of Crazy Otis Landing.

He watched as she opened the gate and walked along the narrow path toward the front steps. In spite of the ordeal she had been through last night, she looked fresh and bright and clear as the sparkling waters of a tropical sea. He did not try to fight the hunger and the need that she triggered within him. There was no reason to struggle against his true self.

"I'm over here, Charity."

She turned at the sound of his voice and frowned when she saw him sitting at the edge of the pool. "The sun isn't even up yet. It's a little early to be meditating on wet grass, isn't it?"

"It felt like the right time. What are you doing up so early?"

She made a face as she walked toward him along the path. "I didn't sleep very well. Thought I'd come over here and see how you and Otis were doing."

"We're both fine. Otis is still asleep."

"So is Davis. I left him a note telling him that I was coming over here for breakfast." She halted beside him. "What are you contemplating this morning? Trying to figure out how many Tal Kek Chara masters it takes to screw in a lightbulb?"

"No."

"We've really got to work on your sense of humor, Elias."

"Some other time, maybe."

"Okay," she agreed. 'So what were you contemplating?'

"How to go about asking you to marry me."

Her eyes widened. "Oh."

"There is no instruction on the subject in Tal Kek Chara."

"I told you that water philosophy of yours had a few leaks." Charity's smile was tremulous. "Why don't you just try asking me?"

Elias got slowly to his feet. He could feel the rising tide within him. If she rejected him, he would be carried out to the deepest waters of the coldest seas. He would never find his way back to shore.

"I love you," Elias said. "Marry me. Please."

Her eyes glowed. "Yes." She threw herself into his arms. "Yes, of course I'll marry you. I love you, Elias."

And then she started to laugh. It was a laugh as frothy as waves on a beach, as cheerful as a rushing brook, as sparkling as a waterfall.

He put his arms around her and buried his face in her hair. "What's so funny?"

"I think we just got officially engaged, and guess what? I'm not having a panic attack."

"Does this means that I'm the right size?" Elias said. "Perfect. Just perfect."

Elias glanced down into the reflecting pool. The first rays of sunlight had struck the surface of the water. The little pond was no longer an opaque gray. It reflected the clear, vibrant image of Charity in his arms.

Shortly before ten that morning, Elias aimed the beam of the flashlight at the heavily laden counter that had aroused his interest the previous day. "There's something about this stuff that doesn't look quite right."

"It would look a whole lot better if you got some decent lighting in here," Charity said briskly.

He glanced at her over his shoulder. She was sitting on top of the sales counter, a cup of tea in her hand. One leg swung impatiently beneath the hem of her long cotton skirt. Her eyes were brilliant with laughter and love. Davis lounged beside her, a latte from Bea's café in his hand.

The other shopkeepers, together with Newlin and Arlene, were clustered around the cash register stand. They all held latte cups, too. Otis was perched on his artificial tree, munching a piece of fruit.

"You still don't seem to grasp the importance of atmosphere in a shop like Charms & Virtues," Elias said to Charity. He started to poke at the stacks of plastic hamburgers.

"You're just making excuses," Charity said. "You know that if you ever do get around to upgrading the lighting in here, you'll also have to start dusting regularly."

"The dim light does hide a lot of the dust," Newlin offered helpfully.

"Thank you, Newlin," Elias said. "I'm glad that some-one here has the genius to understand my marketing plan."

"Some marketing plan," Davis muttered. "I still can't believe what I'm seeing here, Winters. No one in Seattle is going to believe it. The head of Far Seas, Inc., running a curio shop on a pier in Whispering Waters Cove."

"It's a calling," Elias said.

"Forget the plan." Ted patted his stomach, which today was encased in a T-shirt embossed with the slogan *I'm Having an Out-of-Body Experience. Back in Five Minutes.* "Is that the whole story? Jennifer Pitt mur-dered Gwen during an argument and then killed Swinton because he tried to blackmail her with a tape of the murder?"

"That's it," Charity said. "Then she set up Leighton by hiding the gun she had used in the trunk of his car. But the Pitts were a two-gun household. She used the second one last night."

Yappy swallowed the last of his latte. "Heard Leigh-ton Pitt was released this morning. Bet he's one relieved realtor. Bankruptcy's going to look like a piece of cake compared to a murder charge."

Radiance shook her head mournfully. "I hate to say it, but I'm going to miss Jennifer. She really helped me get my business off the ground. If it hadn't been for her, I don't know how long it would have taken to get the women of Whispering Waters Cove into fine nails."

"Speaking of Jennifer Pitt," Hank Tybern said from

the front door. "I've got some information which might interest the members of this little gossip clutch."

Charity looked down her nose at him as he ambled toward them. "You are interrupting a meeting of the Crazy Otis Landing Shopkeepers Association, Chief Tybern."

"Is that a fact?" Hank grinned broadly as he came to a halt near the sales counter. "Sure looked like a gossip session to me. Want me to leave and come back some other time?"

"As long as you're here," Bea said swiftly, "you might as well say what you came to say."

"Figured you'd see it that way," Hank said complacently.

Elias did not look up from his work. "What did you find out about Jennifer Pitt?"

"For starters, her name isn't Jennifer," Hank said.

Elias heard the gasp that went through the crowd gathered around the register. He smiled slightly and went on with his project.

"So, what was her real name?" Arlene asked.

"Janice Miller, AKA Jenny Martin, AKA Jessica Reed," Hank said. "She's wanted down in California in connection with fraud charges. Seems she's been identified as the lady who fleeced a couple of middle-aged fools there out of a total of about a hundred grand."

Yappy whistled. "So she comes up here, tries to pull off another con with Leighton Pitt, and gets bamboozled, herself. No wonder she was pissed when she found out what Gwen had done."

Charity looked at Hank. "Did you charge her with murder?"

"Not yet." Hank said. "Right now, I'm holding her on assault charges and a few other miscellaneous goodies. The murder charge may be a little more difficult."

"But she told me herself that she killed both of them," Charity said indignantly.

"Well, she isn't saying a damn thing now," Hank replied. "Clammed up but good. Waiting for her lawyer, she says. In the meantime, I'm going to have another look-see around the sites of the two murders. With any luck I may be able to turn up some useful evidence."

"Hold on a minute, Hank." Elias dug deeper beneath a mound of fake french fries. "I may be able to give you a jump start on that investigation." The beam of the flashlight fell on a small, bulging envelope. "Ah-hah. I knew something was wrong back here."

Charity looked at him expectantly. "What did you find?"

"Rick Swinton's final attempt to prove that no one screws him over and gets away with it." Elias tossed the envelope toward Hank. "I think this belongs to you."

Hank plucked the envelope out of midair. His brows rose as he felt the size and shape of the object inside. Without a word he tore open the small packet and pulled out the tape. "Well, I'll be damned."

Charity's eyes widened. "Do you think that's the tape of Gwen Pitt's murder?"

"Swinton told Jennifer that he had hidden it here in Charms & Virtues," Elias reminded her.

"Yes, but how in the world did you know where to look?" Charity asked.

Elias grinned. "I noticed yesterday that the dust on that pile of plastic food wasn't as thick and even as it had been a few days ago. It had been disturbed."

"How the hell could you notice that amid all this clutter?" Davis demanded with a derisive glance at the interior of the shop.

"A good shopkeeper knows his stock," Elias said virtuously.

"Very observant," Hank said with genuine admiration.

"Yeah," Newlin agreed. "Real sharp of you, Elias."

"Thanks." Elias carried the flashlight back to the counter.

"Don't get the idea," Charity warned, "that this incident will provide you with an excuse not to dust in the future, Elias. I still say a clean and tidy shop is the hallmark of a well-run business."

Davis grinned. "Better listen to her, Winters. When it comes to running a business, Charity's an expert."

"I've always admired professional expertise," Elias said.

"Heh, heh, heh," Crazy Otis cackled.

20

❧❧❧

It is true that the waters of the past and the future are forever joined. But those who are wise and determined can alter the course of the river.

—"On the Way of Water," from the journal of Hayden Stone

In the end, the Crazy Otis Landing Shopkeepers Association voted unanimously not to close the pier to the public in order to hold the second wedding reception of the year. Instead, they invited the whole town to the festivities.

To everyone's astonishment, virtually the entire population of Whispering Waters Cove showed up to take part. The pier was thronged. Crisp October sunshine warmed the milling crowd and danced on the waters of the cove.

Elias was amazed at the turnout. "We've got a bigger crowd than the one that turned out for the spaceships back in August."

"What the hell did you expect, Winters?" Hank Tybern swallowed the last of a large sugar cookie decorated with mauve icing and surveyed the crowd gathered on the landing with evident amusement. "The town's decided that you're here to stay. The improvements you're making to the pier are starting to show. Weekend tourist traffic is still strong even though we're well into October. And you and your lovely bride solved the crime of the century here in the cove this summer. You're celebrities."

"It was an exciting summer," Charity agreed complacently.

"What was that about spaceships?" Meredith asked as she wandered over to join the group in front of Charms & Virtues.

"Long story," Hank told her. "And best forgotten."

"Bottom line is that your sister and Elias here are local heroes." Phyllis Dartmoor came to a halt and saluted Elias and Charity with a glass of punch. "By the way, I see that the shops are starting to fill up." She nodded toward the three new signs that hung over nearby doors.

Elias followed her gaze. In addition to the new card shop that Newlin and Arlene had opened with the aid of a small-business loan from Far Seas, Inc., there was also a bakery and an aromatherapy shop. He wasn't certain how well the aromatherapy operation would work, but you could never tell on Crazy Otis Landing.

"Now that Leighton isn't fighting with us anymore about Crazy Otis Landing, it didn't take him long to find these two new tenants." Charity said.

"It's the least he could have done. He certainly owed you big time." Phyllis downed a glass of punch and made a face at the taste. "If it hadn't been for you and Elias, he'd be getting ready to stand trial for murder. Personally, I think he's going to make a comeback. The man knows real estate."

Charity laughed. "You'll never turn Crazy Otis Landing into a collection of boutiques and art galleries, but I think we can make the pier work. Right, Otis?"

Otis, ensconced on his perch, which Elias had moved to the doorway of the shop, cackled malevolently. He sidled along the fake tree limb, beady eyes intent on Charity's crystal-encrusted sleeve.

"Oh, no, you don't." Charity stepped back quickly when she realized that Otis was preparing to pluck a glittering bead from her wedding gown. "Don't you dare. This dress cost a fortune, even if I did get a deal because I got it through Truitt. I'm not going to let you ruin it."

Otis contrived to look hurt and offended.

Charity wrinkled her nose at him.

Elias hid a quick grin as he watched the pair. He could not remember a day when he had been happier or more content with life. Charity was breathtaking in the glorious, full-skirted wedding gown. He had been unable to take his eyes off her for more than a few seconds at a time since she had walked down the aisle on her brother's arm two hours earlier.

She was sunlight on a silvery sea, he thought. Moonlight on a lake. Everything he had ever wanted or needed. He wondered again at the twists and turns in the river of his life that had finally led him to this woman who had changed everything.

Phyllis heaved a sigh and looked wistfully at Elias. "I suppose this means that all the summer rumors about a rich off-shore client building a world-class resort here in the cove were just pipe dreams?"

"All I can tell you for sure," Elias said, "is that none of my old clients is planning a resort here. At least not as far as I know. But, then, I'm out of the consulting business these days. I'm too busy with Crazy Otis Landing to worry about off-shore investors."

Yappy appeared at Elias's shoulder. "Well, you might want to worry about that guy coming toward us. Ted spotted him a minute ago. It's the same dude that tried to beat you once before."

Charity whirled around. "Not Justin Keyworth? Good grief, it's him, Elias. What's he doing here?"

Elias watched as Justin walked slowly through the crowd. "I'll go find out." He set his punch glass down on the nearest bench.

Yappy squinted. "Want some backup?"

"I think I can handle him this time," Elias said. "If I need help, I'll let you know."

Ted and Newlin materialized at Elias's elbow.

"We'll be right here if you need us," Ted said.

"Thanks." Elias started forward to intercept Justin.

Charity grabbed fistfuls of her voluminous skirts and hurried after him. "I'm coming with you, Elias."

He did not argue. If Justin was here to tell him that Garrick Keyworth had finally succeeded in killing himself, it would be good to have Charity at his side.

He reached out to take her hand. She gave him a reassuring smile that said more than words. It said he was no longer alone.

Justin stopped when he saw Elias and Charity coming toward him. He glanced from one to the other, frowning slightly.

"What's going on here?" Justin studied Charity's gown. "You two just get married?"

"Yes." Elias brought himself and Charity to a halt. "What do you want, Keyworth?"

Justin looked uneasy. "This is sort of private, Winters. Can we go someplace and talk? I won't keep you long."

Charity scowled. "No, you cannot go someplace alone. For all I know, you've come here to beat up Elias again, and I won't have it. Not on our wedding day."

Justin flushed a dull red. "I didn't come here to beat up anyone. I just want to talk to Winters."

"This is about your father, isn't it?" Elias said quietly.

"Yes."

"It's all right," Elias said. He felt Charity give his hand a small squeeze. "Whatever you have to say, you can say in front of Charity."

Justin took one last look at Charity's stubborn expression and apparently accepted the obvious fact that she was not going to quietly disappear. "I came to tell you that Dad's . . . getting better. He's in therapy. Taking medication. Starting to ask questions about the business."

Relief swept through Elias. He drew a deep breath. "I'm glad to hear it."

"He and I have done a lot of talking since you went to see him that day in Seattle." Justin met Elias's eyes with a steady, determined expression. "He told me everything. About your father. The crash. Everything."

Elias nodded. "I see."

"Now I know why you did what you did." Justin hesitated. "There's just one thing I don't understand."

"What's that?" Elias asked.

"You had everything in place. Dad says you could have ruined the company's entire Pacific operation. But you pulled the plug at the last minute. And then, later, after I told you that he'd tried to commit suicide, you went to see him. He said you gave him a lecture.

Something about not doing to me what your father had done to you."

"I didn't think he was paying attention," Elias said.

"He listened." Justin glanced out across the sunlit cove and then he looked back at Elias. "He wants to merge my new firm and Keyworth International. I'd be CEO. He'd be president."

"Sounds like a solid executive team," Elias said. "Going for it?"

"I'm thinking about it. Yeah. Probably. The old man knows the international freight business. He can be an S.O.B., but he's savvy as hell. I could learn some things from him. He seems to want to teach me. After all these years, he says he'd like to show me the ropes."

"Better late than never," Elias said.

"We'll see." Justin shoved his hands into his pockets and fixed Elias with another steady look. "But I still want to know why you backed off your plans to cripple his company. And why bother to go see Dad after he tried to commit suicide?"

It was Charity who answered. "Nobody likes to swim in polluted water. Elias decided to do what he could to clean up the river."

Justin frowned. "What the hell does river pollution have to do with this?"

"It's a water thing," Charity said solemnly. "It takes years of training and self-discipline to comprehend the higher levels of consciousness and how they relate to the nature of water. However, if you want to take a short-cut to enlightenment, you can buy a really neat T-shirt from Ted's Instant Philosophy T-Shirt Company. Right over there on the other side of the pier."

Justin turned back to Elias, clearly bewildered.

Elias grinned. "Don't mind her, Keyworth. When she gets into her cryptic philosophical mode, you can't understand a word she says. Come with me to the buffet table. I'll get you a slice of wedding cake and some of the worst-tasting punch you've ever had in your life."

"I could use a beer," Justin said slowly.

"You're in luck. We've got some of that, too."

The waters of the cove were black and silver beneath a moon that was nearly full. Elias stood on the bluff, his arm around Charity, and listened to the whispers.

"What are you thinking about?" Charity asked.

"About the first time I kissed you. We were watching the Voyagers from the railing at the old campground. Remember?"

"I certainly do. Knocked your socks off, didn't I?" she chuckled. "Thought you were going to freak out on me."

"I recovered swiftly."

"You did," she agreed. "It took a while, but you definitely recovered." She turned and put her arms around his neck. "Things are going great down at the pier, aren't they?"

"I think we'll all make it through to next summer." He wrapped his hands around her waist, enjoying the feel of her warm, feminine curves.

"Town council's off our backs, at last. Shops are renting up quickly, thanks to the improvements you've made. Business is tripled over last year."

"You're about to tell me that you've got a new project in mind, aren't you?"

She smiled her brilliant smile. "How did you guess?"

"You can take the CEO out of the executive suite, but you can't take the executive suite out of the CEO. What's the project this time?"

"I was thinking that it's about time we started working on having a baby."

He stared at her, as disoriented as he had felt the first time he had taken her into his arms. "A baby?"

"Any objections? You'd make a terrific father, and Otis could baby-sit."

Dazed with a profound sense of wonder, Elias was speechless for a moment. "No objections," he finally managed to whisper.

She smiled.

He pulled her very close and gazed out over the cove.

The silvery moonlight reflected on the surface of the ceaselessly moving water. In that moment he could have sworn that he caught a fleeting glimpse of that rarest of all reflections, an image of the future. It glowed.

He saw the way the waters of the past flowed seamlessly into the future and he knew that Hayden Stone had been right.

"What are you thinking about?" Charity asked.

"About something Hayden wrote in his journal."

"What was that?"

"To know real happiness, a man must learn to open himself to love."

"I think you finally got that lesson right."

"Some things a man has to learn the hard way." Elias bent his head to kiss her.

Pocket Books
Proudly Presents

Eye of the Beholder

Jayne Ann Krentz

**Available in Paperback
from
Pocket Books**

The following is a preview of
Eye of the Beholder. . . .

Avalon, Arizona
Twelve years earlier

He swept into the house out of the hot desert night, an avenging warlock from the dark canyons carrying thunder and lightning in his fists.

Alexa froze at the top of the stairs when she heard his voice in the hall. Her sudden stillness was instinctive, the immediate, elemental reaction of any creature to the presence of a potential predator.

"I don't know whether it was you or Guthrie who killed my father, Kenyon," he said. "Hell, for all I know, the two of you planned it together."

The night was warm but Alexa shivered in the shadows above the hall. John Laird Trask was young, somewhere in his early twenties, but the taut control he exerted over his icy rage would have done credit to a man twice his age.

"You listen to me, son, and you listen good." Lloyd Kenyon spoke with a calm authority that reverberated with an underlying sympathy. "No one murdered your father. Once you've had a chance to cool down and think about it you'll accept the facts. It was a tragic accident."

"Bullshit. Dad was a good driver and he knew that road. He didn't go off Avalon Point by accident. One of you forced him over the edge."

Alexa felt suddenly light-headed. A strange, unfamiliar panic left her fighting for breath. *Trask was threatening Lloyd.* He was not only a much younger man, he was even bigger than Lloyd, who still had plenty of bulk and muscle left over from the days when he had run construction crews.

Her anxiety for Lloyd's safety took her by surprise. Until tonight she would have sworn that she had no strong, personal attachment to him. She and her mother had moved in with him eighteen months ago following her parents' divorce. She had been careful to keep a cool distance between herself and this very large, unexciting, rock-steady businessman

Vivien had married; careful to make sure Lloyd understood that he could never take the place of the charismatic hero who had been her real father.

It had been a year since Crawford Chambers had been killed by a sniper's bullet. He had been halfway around the world at the time, photographing the latest in the long list of small, brutal civil wars that had made him a legend in journalism circles.

Crawford had been everything that Lloyd was not, a rakish, dashing, larger-than-life figure who lived life on the edge.

Her father would have been able to deal with Trask, Alexa thought. But staid, steady, unflappable Lloyd probably didn't stand a chance.

Trask's accusations were nothing but crazy talk, Alexa thought. Lloyd would never harm anyone.

She had to get to the phone.

The nearest extension was at the foot of the stairs. With an enormous effort of will, she fought through the temporary paralysis. She went silently, cautiously, down the stairs.

"It was raining that night." Lloyd's voice was calm, infused with reason. "This is what we call our monsoon season. Downpours are common. That stretch of the road is treacherous. Everyone around here knows that. I've always said that portion of Cliff Drive should be closed during a storm."

"The rain had passed by the time Dad got into the car," Trask said. "I checked with the cops."

"The roads were still wet. Even the best driver can make a mistake."

"This was no mistake," Trask said. "I know all about the partnership between the three of you. And I know about the offer from that hotel chain. Dad was murdered because someone wanted him out of the way."

Alexa realized he believed every word he said. She knew that he was wrong, at least about Lloyd. But Trask was clearly convinced that his father had been murdered.

She sensed her mother's presence on the steps behind her. She glanced over her shoulder. Vivien's fine-boned, ascetic face was taut with anxiety as she listened to the two men quarrel.

"You think I was involved in some kind of bizarre conspiracy to kill your father?" Lloyd's voice rose in disbelief. "That's outrageous."

"I looked through some of Dad's papers this afternoon. I heard about the quarrel at the country club the night he died. It didn't take me long to put it together."

"Business partners sometimes disagree. It's a fact of life, son."

"That argument was more than a disagreement. I talked to the bartender at the club. He said the three of you nearly came to blows."

"Guthrie gets a little hot-headed when he drinks," Lloyd admitted. "But I restrained him. There was no physical stuff."

"Maybe not then. But you and Guthrie knew that Dad would never agree to sell the Avalon Mansion property to that chain. So one of you found a way to get rid of him."

"Damn it, I've had enough." Lloyd's voice hardened. "I'm trying to be patient. I know you've had a hellish few days and I know you've got a lot of responsibility to shoulder. But you're going too far here."

"Believe me, Kenyon, I haven't even started."

"You're going to have to get your priorities straight, Trask. You've got your brother to think about. He's only seventeen and you're all the family that boy has left in the world."

"Thanks to you or Guthrie."

"That's a damn lie. When you come to your senses and calm down, you'll see that. Meanwhile, you'd better start thinking about the future. You've got your work cut out."

"Don't talk to me about my *work*, you sonofabitch."

"Someone better talk to you about it. You're going to have to get through the fallout from your father's bankruptcy and take care of your brother at the same time. That's a man-sized job. You need to get focused and stay that way. You can't afford to waste your energy chasing a wild conspiracy fantasy."

"I don't need you to tell me what I have to do, Kenyon. I'll take care of Nathan and I'll take care of myself. But one day I'll find out what really happened at Avalon Point the night Dad died."

Alexa reached the bottom of the stairs. Neither man noticed her. They were intent only on each other. Lloyd had his back to her as he confronted Trask.

This was the first time she had seen John Laird Trask in person. She knew from what Lloyd had said that his family came from Seattle. It was Harry Trask's plan to restore the old Avalon Mansion and turn it into a destination resort that had brought him to Arizona on a frequent and regular basis during the past year. His two sons had remained in Seattle.

Alexa paid little attention to Lloyd's business affairs even though he managed the inheritance he had received from her grandmother. As a result, she knew almost nothing about Harry Trask and even less about his sons.

But after tonight she knew that she would never forget John Laird Trask.

From where she stood she could see him looming in the hall, taking up far too much space. The warm glow of the overhead fixture did nothing to soften the sinister angles of his face and jaw. She could feel the energy waves of his fury.

She was only a step away from the phone now. She took a deep breath, stretched out her hand and picked up the receiver.

"If you don't go away right now, Mr. Trask, I'm going to call the police," she said with a fierceness that startled her as much as it did everyone else.

Both men swung around to stare at her, but it was Trask's relentless green-gold gaze that riveted her. For an instant she could not move. Her hand clenched around the phone.

"It's all right, Alexa." Lloyd's face gentled as he looked at her standing there with the phone clutched in her hand. "Everything is under control. Trask is leaving now. Isn't that right, Trask?"

Trask continued to watch Alexa for another

second or two, as if assessing both her and her threat. Abruptly he turned away, dismissing her with a cold disdain that sent another chill through her.

"Yeah, I'm going now, Kenyon," he said. "But one day I'll come back for the truth. And when I do, someone will pay. Count on it."

Without another word, he walked out into the night.

Twelve Years Later

She saw the Jeep first. A layer of desert grit dulled the dark green paint, evidence of a long drive. The vehicle was parked on the side of the road above Avalon Point. The sight of it brought her to a halt on the path.

It was not unusual to see a tourist stopped here at the Point. The sun was about to set and the view of the stark, red-rock landscape with its towers and canyons was magnificent at this time of day.

Alexa glanced around, searching for the Jeep's driver.

It took her a moment to find him. He stood deep in the long shadow cast by a stone out-cropping.

The first thing that struck her was that he

was on the wrong side of the waist-high metal rail that had been erected a few years ago to protect sightseers. Alarm shot through her. He was much too close to the edge of the Point.

He seemed oblivious to the vibrant beauty of the spectacular terrain set afire by the dying light. As Alexa watched he gazed broodingly down into the brush-choked canyon. There was a dark intensity about him, as though he was engaged in reading omens and portents.

Sometimes an overly ambitious amateur photographer took one too many risks in an attempt to get the perfect sunset shot.

"Excuse me," she said loudly. "That guardrail is there for a good reason. It's dangerous to stand on the wrong side."

The man in the shadows turned unhurriedly to look at her.

Her first thought was that he could have stepped straight out of a Tamara de Lempicka painting.

The artist who had become known as the quintessential Art Deco portraitist would have loved him, Alexa thought. De Lempicka had excelled at creating a dark, sinister, edgy energy around her subjects. She had been able to endow them with a highly charged sensuality and an icy, enigmatic aura.

But in this man's case, Alexa thought, de Lempicka would not have had to invent the ominous illusion. The painter's only task would have been to capture the unsettling reality of it.

The jolt of recognition hit Alexa with such force she froze in mid-step.

Trask.

Twelve years older, harder, more dangerous, but unmistakably Trask. He looked even bigger than he had the last time she saw him. Lean and broad-shouldered, he still took up a lot of space. It was a wonder light did not bend to get around him.

He contemplated her for a moment.

"Thanks for the warning," he said.

He made no move to get back behind the guardrail. It figured, Alexa thought. This man was accustomed to standing on the edge of cliffs. She could tell that just by looking at him.

She realized she was holding her breath, waiting for him to recognize her. But he gave no indication that he remembered her from that long-ago scene in Lloyd's hall. She told herself she should be enormously relieved.

She released the breath she had been holding.

A gust of wind broke the peculiar little trance that had gripped her. She managed to keep her polite-to-the-tourist smile firmly fixed in place.

"You really should move back to the right side of that railing." She was horrified by the slightly breathless quality she heard in her own words. Get a grip, Alexa. "Didn't you see the sign?"

"Yeah, I saw it."

His voice was low and resonant. The voice of a man who did not have to speak loudly in order to get the attention of others. The voice of a man who was accustomed to giving orders and having them obeyed.

She had pushed her luck far enough. Time to make her exit before he recalled her face. No sense taking chances. She searched for a suitable exit line.

"Are you lost? Can I give you directions?" she asked.

He looked amused. "I know where I am."

"Well, in that case," she said briskly, "I'll be on my way. It's getting late."

He watched the breeze tangle her hair. "Can I give you a lift?"

"What? *No.*" Startled, she took a hasty step back, although he had made no move toward her. "I mean, thanks, but I live near here. I use this path for exercise." Lord, now she was babbling.

His brows rose. "It's all right. I'm not a serial killer."

She kept smiling. "Yeah, sure, that's what they all say."

"I take it you're the type who doesn't take lifts from strangers?"

"No intelligent person accepts rides from strangers in this day and age."

"Maybe I'd better introduce myself. My name is Trask. My company owns the new resort here in Avalon."

Stay cool, Alexa. "Nice to meet you, Mr. Trask."

"Just Trask."

"Yes, well, best of luck with the new resort." She retreated another step. "Everyone in town is very excited about it."

"Is that so?"

"Yes, it is."

"I'm glad to hear that."

She did not trust the cool amusement she saw in his eyes. She dropped her own polite smile.

"Welcome to Avalon, Trask."

She turned quickly and walked swiftly away from him.

"Better hurry," he said much too softly behind her. "I hear that night falls fast in the desert. It'll be dark soon."

She resisted the sudden urge to break into a run. With grim determination she kept moving, listening intently for the sound of the Jeep's engine.

She finally heard it come to life with a low, throaty growl. She did not look back but neither did she take a deep breath until the sound receded into the distance.

Then and only then did she allow herself to quicken her step.

Adrenaline rushed through her, creating a tingling in her hands and feet. She was both hot and cold. It was the sort of feeling one got after having had a very close call.

The other shoe had finally dropped. Trask was back in Avalon.

Visit the
Simon & Schuster Web site:
www.SimonSays.com

and sign up for our
mystery e-mail updates!

Keep up on the latest
new releases, author appearances,
news, chats, special offers, and more!
We'll deliver the information
right to your inbox — if it's new,
you'll know about it.

SIMON & SCHUSTER
A VIACOM COMPANY
www.SimonSays.com

POCKET BOOKS

POCKET STAR BOOKS